DESTINY

THE LUNA SERIES
BOOK 6

LETTY FRAME

FOXY KNIGHTS PUBLISHING

Cover Design: Damn Good Designs

DESTINY

One last chance to save her pack. One final sacrifice to make.

Lottie and her men are in for their biggest challenge yet, with higher stakes and catastrophic consequences for them and their pack if they fail. After months of enduring danger and threats to her life, Lottie finally discovers the identity of her stalker. However, the revelation comes with a shocking twist that shakes Lottie's beliefs to the core.

To bring down their enemy, Lottie and her mates must navigate dangerous alliances and bitter rivalries. As they race against time to stop the stalker's deadly plan, Lottie must also confront the dark secrets that come with the power of the original wolf. Will Lottie and her pack emerge victorious, or will they pay the ultimate price for their love and loyalty?

In this gripping conclusion to the Luna series, Lottie will face her greatest fears and make the ultimate sacrifice to protect everything she holds dear. Will she be able to conquer destiny, or will it conquer her?

This book is dedicated to all of you. It's been a labour of love, finalising my debut series, and my career wouldn't be where it is without you all for taking a chance on me.

So, readers, this one is for you.

Fᴀᴛᴇ ʟᴇᴀᴅs ᴛʜᴇ ᴡɪʟʟɪɴɢ, ᴀɴᴅ ᴅʀᴀɢs ᴀʟᴏɴɢ ᴛʜᴇ ʀᴇʟᴜᴄᴛᴀɴᴛ.

— SENECA, LETTERS FROM A STOIC

PROLOGUE
UNKNOWN POV

"*A* Guardian, a hybrid, and an otherworldly tainted being all tied to one measly wolf," I hiss, my lips curling in disdain as I shake my head. I hear footsteps enter the room, the swagger easily able to be identified. It's one of the most annoying attributes from Cain, the vampire I *persuaded* to join my cause.

"They will all need to be destroyed," I continue, dangling those words like a carrot in front of the eager fool.

I keep my gaze forward, ignoring him, and letting my feigned indifference hang in the air.

The man before me, eager for my approval, barely contains his excitement as he rushes forward those few more steps, to get into my line of vision.

"Who do you need me to get rid of, sire?" Cain asks, almost too eagerly. He's been moping around for the last few days, begging for an assignment, because he can't stand being on the sidelines any longer.

He's been a thorn in my side, but his use has finally come to fruition.

I was correct listening to my wolf when he warned me against killing the vampire. *I can't be killing all of my men, not when we're on the brink of battle.*

"The imposter has too many mates," I say, and his eyes light up. This is what he's wanted—face to face time with the fake Luna, with the liar who has stole my power. "Let's cripple the weak cunt by taking some of them out."

"Do you have a preference?" Cain's voice quivers with anticipation.

"The plan for tomorrow is to kill *one* of the men she's entrapped. I don't care which." I check my watch, making a show of not caring too much about the particulars, but I know he heard me when he came into the room.

"Will there be a reward for completing your task?" Cain dares to ask, his arrogance at being chosen once again proving why he is nothing more than a pawn.

The neglected child of Alaric Viotto has been so easy to twist to my cause. He's been desperate to be *worthy* in some way, to show that he's not just the unexceptional middle child in a very exceptional family.

It's a shame I never intended on delivering any of my promises.

Finally, I pivot, glaring down at him, my eyes boring into his soul as I snarl, "You require a reward to do your duty? Why do I waste my time on you when you're this incompetent?"

"No, sire, no," Cain says, dropping down to his knees as he bares his throat to me. The coward doesn't dare to lift his head again, and talks at my feet like the snivelling fool that he is. "I will ensure your plans are carried out, and that our future is no longer in her hands."

"That's more like it. The hybrid, the Guardian, and the vampire tainted by the otherworld are our primary targets. Weakening her greatest power sources will be her downfall."

"That's the problem with women," Cain sneers, and I kindly allow him to finish. "They're frail, weak, and allow their cunts to lead them."

"Quite right, Cain," I say, reaching out to stroke the back of his head. He eases, but I seize his hair, digging my nails into his scalp until blood oozes and I viciously yank his head back. "If you can reach the Guardian, it will be more than satisfactory."

"What about the others?"

"Hurt them if you can, but they're nothing special, so don't waste your time on them."

"Understood."

She claims that she has nine mates—though only three of them are of any value.

The Guardian.

The Hybrid.

The Otherworldly Vampire.

My first official act as King will be to kill the imposter self-appointed Queen. But as the future leader of these people, I pronounce these *fake* wolves, nothing better than dead. They're powerful men that have been ruined by her cunt and are now useless.

Their days are numbered, and my people will take them out, ready for me to deliver with the grand finale.

Watch out, Charlotte, because we're coming for you.

CHAPTER 1

The scent of blood fills the air.

The sound of howls, teeth clashing, and footsteps racing merge together so I can't differentiate what is coming from where.

The eight bonds nestled within my chest pulse with tension, their weight a heavy burden on my soul as their emotions entwine with mine.

It's understandable when I take in the current state of our pack. The sight in front of me is *terrifying*. So many wolves I don't recognise have infiltrated and are attacking my pack. They're not just in it to disarm us and take over—they're here to end as many as possible.

We're on the outskirts of the pack right now, close to the point they breached from where we dealt with James Hewitt.

I've felt numerous bonds breaking, the tie between me and them dying as their souls escape the Earth. Pack mates are being lost to a fight that never should've been theirs. Enemies dying, but still taking a tiny part of my power with them.

But it's barely a dent in the ocean-sized reservoir I have to pull from. I can feel my new power racing through me. My body is supercharged, with a mystical, old power source and it's leaking out of my pores in an attempt to help my people.

I'm not just Luna to Rose Moon, heir to Golden Eclipse.

I'm Charlotte Montgomery, the new vessel of the mystical powers belonging to the original wolf.

I wasn't returned to the creepy house Cain took me to. I was brought here, to the centre of the fight, just in time to see Noah, my Alpha mate, attack a wolf right in front of me. He's in his own shifted form, his sandy blond fur coated with dried blood, causing my nose to wrinkle. I don't even blink as he fights, my heart racing as the brown wolf tries to fight back. When he puts down the enemy, it doesn't even phase me.

This is a fight for their lives.

Noah doesn't pause before charging forward. I'm not even sure if he can see me here, because he doesn't even look my way in his pursuits. He launches onto the back of another wolf, the yelp from the enemy ringing through my mind.

I look around the area, spotting each of my men fighting, protecting our people. Warren's too far away for me to see, and Elijah's moving around too fast to keep track of. My other two Alphas are too far for my eyes to detect, and I know that one of them is in a lot of pain. But Theo's gorgeous white wolf is easily traceable through this crowd, and Dillon is sticking right by him.

Even River, the man I no longer have a bond with, is fighting for the pack. My heart is just as heavy watching him, even without the soul bond together, and it's a confusing feeling.

But my people are not fighting alone, which is the most important thing.

My dad has sent help, although I can't see him here. I can feel the slightly different bond I have with his wolves—my birth pack mates —which helps me tell them apart from my pack. They're no less important, and they're fighting just as hard to protect my lands. In a time like this, it's wolves recognising their kin, fighting and protecting their own, instead of pack loyalties.

It does help that they're going to be my people one day soon.

But the thing that's missing? The thing that's making the rage inside burn hotter than it ever has? The vampire reinforcements I called in aren't here. There's not a single vampire, outside of the two I'm mated to, and the few we have that live here, on pack grounds.

Abel isn't here.

His people aren't here.

Freya isn't here.

The first time we call in the vow we made, and he's not honoured his end. The vampires should've been here in *minutes*.

So why the fuck aren't they?

I'm fucking seething.

"Your pack is in danger," Alpha says, coming up to my side. My eyes widen, and I turn to look at my grandfather. He's wearing those weird white clothes, and he's got a beard now, which is strange. How can a dead person grow facial hair? It only adds to the mystery of the Ancestral Realm.

I thought I was sent back. I closed my eyes, and fucking willed to go home.

But somehow, I'm still here.

Alpha isn't looking at me though, his focus on the fight. It's brutal, and it makes sense now why the sounds are all dulled, why there's no breeze or smell of death. My bonds with them are the only vibrant parts of this.

I sigh when Loukas comes up to my other side, my wolf and I not happy with being trapped here. For assholes who kept me out of this place for as long as they did, it's a bit fucking rude to then trap me here.

Especially when my wolves are fighting a battle that they might lose.

"You're going to have a choice very soon, Charlotte," Loukas says. His tone is calm, his aura peaceful, but fuck, his words incite mass panic within me. "We've warned you of this before."

"So, the choice isn't about letting Cain run free?"

"No," Alpha says, his tone just as detached. He turns to me with a cheeky grin that annoys me. "That wouldn't be much of a choice now, would it?"

"It's one I'd be happy with the outcome of," I hiss. "What's the choice?"

"So hostile, granddaughter," Loukas murmurs. "You need to—"

And then the fuckers blink out of existence. I snarl, letting out a loud howl, as the battle disappears from in front of me. Now, we're back in the annoying as fuck forest. The pink and purple leaves, the bright violet floor. It's not serene any longer.

No.

Now, it's just aggravating.

"What the fuck is wrong with you?" I shout, my words echoing through the trees, but I'm met with a stony silence. "If you have nothing to say, then let me leave!" I howl once more, my aggravation being backed by my wolf. We're not impressed.

Not even a little bit.

"Luna," a voice says in my head. I dart around, my wolf and I searching, before realising it's not my grandmother. It's not even my mother. It's that weird fucking voice, that just speaks to me.

"Calm down," she says.

"Calm down," I say, with a tone dripping with honey. "I'm extremely calm. Now tell me whatever you need to share, so that I can get back to my people."

"I admire your spirit, Luna, but battles are won with more than bites and claws." I open my mouth to bite her head off, not willing to play the games of these lands. Riddles and hidden advice aren't going to cut it. *"Your wisdom will be what gets you out of this fight."*

"I'm not feeling very wise right now." I sigh, plopping down on my ass. If I'm talking to a random voice in my head, I may as well be comfortable whilst I do it.

"You're in danger."

"I know."

"You don't know the half of it."

"Oh, it's almost like I was given access to the future through a vision you or yours gave to me... and then robbed just to be assholes."

And in a bright flash, there's a wolf standing before me. She's truly captivating, giving off a serene aura. Her power is unmatched, and even just being in her vicinity is scary.

It's almost like she's emerged from the trees themselves, her fur a mesmerising mirage of pinks and purples, both giving her the ability to blend in and stand out with our surroundings.

The shades of pink in her coat intermingle with hues of lavender, and her whiskers are a deep purple. As she steps forward, the light seems to adjust to continue shining on her. It casts a pretty glow over her soft and velvety fur. I refuse to believe that that's possible, but in this place... anything is.

And why wouldn't the weird voice I hear completely embody the magical essence of the lands she calls home?

"Your time is running out." She takes a step forward and looks me properly in the eyes. Without my permission, I shift into my own wolf. Her glow is even brighter now, her beauty that much more potent with my stronger eyesight.

Her eyes are a sharp contrast to her beautiful coat—they're black, darker and deeper than anything I've ever seen. If I look into them for too long, I feel I may drown in the darkness, never once emerging.

But somehow, they seem to hold an untamed spirit within.

"You're the guardian of this place," I say, cocking my head.

The wolf nods. *"Yes. But I'm not the Guardian of this place, young Luna. I am the Guardian of all. You see... I made the deal with young Conri. With all of the young men who wished to be more than what they were."*

"You did that?"

The wolf nods once more. *"But that's not the important thing right now. I don't have long to talk to you without anyone noticing I'm gone."*

"Um, right." I have no idea what's happening right now. *"What advice do you have for me?"*

"Your grandparents were trying to warn you about your choice. I'm not. There's only one choice that you can make, Lottie—your mates come first. Always."

"Of course they do." I whine, scratching at the ground, trying to rid myself of the antsy energy.

"Trust in your Guardian. He's tried too hard to be mindful of the mate bonds, he has ignored how valuable his own bond to you is. Utilise your bond, and remind him of his place."

"And how do I do that?"

"You're a wolf, Charlotte. Use your teeth."

My sharp inhale makes it look like I'm grinning, but honestly, it's not far off considering how excited my wolf is about putting Theo in his place.

"Last time we met, you were going to warn us about something." I'm cautious bringing this up, but her aura alters ever so slightly, showing her pride at my prodding.

"I was going to warn you to be careful of the vampires. But I was taken home before I could affect the timeline."

I scoff. *"With how helpful you've been here, I can only imagine the damage you'd do."*

"You're carrying the next generation of your line, yes?" She doesn't argue, which is a little annoying. Lena, my grandmother and the wolf that's often here with me during these visits, is far more fun to spar with.

I frown, my nose scrunching up in wolf form. *"No. We think maybe, but it's not been confirmed."*

"Right. But let's say you were, and you've just taken on the power of the original wolf, that's going to impact the children inside of you. That needs checked—immediately."

"Okay." Just what I want to hear.

"Go home, little Luna. Save your pack, and prepare yourself. The battle hasn't even begun."

And I can't tell who disappears first, but I land in the battlefield, right where that vision was taking place.

The difference is, now I'm truly here, and I'm not going to stand by and let anything happen to my people. Not when I can help. Three different men shout my name, the bonds we share illuminating with our proximity. A fourth name isn't in worry—it's in fear.

I bring my fingers to my lips and blow, whistling loud and clear, drawing a lot of eyes my way. It's not enough, so I supercharge the sound, packing it with a punch of pure power.

My wolf is ready.

She knows what to do, and I follow her cues.

I reach out for the bond between me and every single wolf on my lands. It doesn't take long to differentiate between friend and foe, and I tug on those we're opposing. I see them stop fighting, and my people pause, the ones in view anyway, and turn to look my way. Some shift, but most stay as wolves, ready for retaliation.

But it won't come. I'm squeezing the bonds tighter, cutting off their fight. It's weird, doing this mentally, but somehow affecting them physically.

I let out a loud howl, and my wolves rush forward. Our enemies cower, unable to move, unable to fight against me.

As one? They're strong, sure.

But individually? They're weak and ripe for the picking.

"How long can you hold them?" Theo asks, and I flinch, not having heard him approach. I turn to face my Guardian, expecting anger in his gaze. There's nothing but pure understanding.

"As long as I need to."

He nods, reaching in to kiss my cheek. "You're holding them across the pack."

I grin at him but shake my head. "No, Theo, I'm not. I'm holding every single one that came to attack—whether they're on our lands or not."

"What?" Noah asks, shifting into his human form. The wolves in the crowd move so he can approach me. "How many more are out there?"

"About 150," I say, assessing the bonds. "They're not super close by."

Noah's jaw clenches, and like Theo, he leans in to kiss my cheek.

"Can you hold them and come with me?" Noah asks, and I nod. "Good. Caden's hurt. Rhett and Elijah are keeping him safe, but there was no—"

"Enough," Theo murmurs, he rubs circles into the small of my back. "Go with Noah. We'll handle this."

"Theo?" I ask, not moving even though Noah tugs my hand.

"Yes, little wolf?"

"Kill them all."

And then I turn and follow directly after Noah.

Caden's hurt, but he's not going to be the only casualty today.

Once we've executed these wolves.

We're then heading to Hearthstone to wipe the crown off Abel's head.

There was a man walking around claiming to be the King of the Wolves.

Well, in taking his power, it looks like my people have found themselves a new Queen.

CHAPTER 2

$\mathcal{M}$y eyes water as I crouch down next to Caden, and I smooth his sandy blond hair out of his face, pressing a soft kiss to his forehead. He's pale and clammy, and Rhett says that he's been drifting in and out of consciousness for the last ten minutes.

They were going to move him over to the clinic, but then they felt me and knew I'd be over.

"Is he—" Noah starts, but he falls silent. I don't turn to see why.

I don't need the contact to heal Caden, especially not now, but I can't help myself. I press our lips together, breathing life back into him. I take it slow, rather than just flooding his system with pure power. His blood loss has been extreme, but the moment he's awake, his baby blue eyes jolt to mine. I sit back on my heels, no longer kissing him, but still healing him.

"I'm okay, baby," he murmurs, reaching up to brush my tears away. I didn't even realise I was crying. He smiles, giving my hand a soft squeeze. I don't know if it's because that's just as hard as he can squeeze, but it's not as reassuring as he would've intended.

"No dying."

"No dying," he repeats, before frowning at me. "What have you done?"

"You're looking at the new Conri," I say, keeping my words quiet. I pull back even further once he's fully healed, and he gently sits up with help from Noah. I'm nervous, my heart beating wildly as I wait for his acknowledgement.

He rakes over me, a tiny 'v' between his brows before he loses the tension and grins. I can feel his pride radiating through the bond, and it's so overwhelming.

"That's fucking amazing," he says, and I nod, grinning right back at him. "Thank you, baby."

I roll my eyes but take Noah's offered hands and let him pull me to my feet. I turn around and raise an eyebrow at Rhett, my Alpha mate, who seems wary.

"What's the problem?" I ask when he breaks eye contact with me.

"There's no problem. I'm just getting a shit ton of reports," he says, tapping at his temple. Noah nods, so he must be the same. Caden's frown shows he hasn't been getting these updates.

"Can I help?" I ask, looking around the clearing. Considering me and the three Alphas are over here, I'm surprised that a lot of the pack members are gone. The wolves that I'm holding in place are still there, which is another problem in itself.

But whilst we're here, who is handling the pack?

"Wyatt's working to clear the area," Noah says, causing me to frown. "What?"

"Did you hear my silent question?" I'm not having another mate hearing my fucking thoughts.

"No," Noah says with a laugh. I relax, and they all grin. "Wyatt was just letting me know he's taking command until one of us is there to help."

Which is unsurprising. Wyatt is very effective and good at his job. Clearly, he's so good that he's even keeping the Alphas informed.

If only my Gammas were that intuitive.

Between Lionel who I still don't really *like*, and River who may be perfectly capable, but our relationship is strained, I don't have the easy relationship with my people that my Alpha mates do. It makes me a tad bit envious.

Then again I have Lexie, a perfect fucking life manager and an even better best friend.

"Theo's just not sure how to proceed," Rhett says, and I tune back into the conversation. "So we need to—"

I frown, and Rhett falls silent, giving me a look of pure frustration. "I made it very clear what you need to do. Kill them."

"We're not killing them," Noah says, with a sigh. I cross my arms in front of my chest, once again in opposition of my three mates. It's not a good feeling. "We need to know who—"

"Cain."

Identical frowns appear on all three of their faces, and I flinch when Warren, River and Elijah appear in front of us. They're covered in blood, Warren and Elijah more so than River since they don't shift, and my wolf twists angrily inside at the thought of them draining the dead wolves.

They should drink our blood—only.

Then again, Warren can only keep my blood down, so I doubt he did.

"Update," Noah barks. His anger is misplaced, and Warren just rolls his eyes. Elijah's unfazed, but River immediately jumps to attention.

"Dillon and Wyatt are with Theo, Luna, clearing the area and making sure that those who are hurt are being moved to the clinic," River says, and I nod my thanks. My Alphas are silently chatting to themselves, and both Elijah and Warren are aware something deeper is going on. "Lionel is in the main part of town, keeping everyone calm. I think Lexie's at Town Hall, fielding calls. She's tried to reach out to both Lionel and me, but neither of us could contact you until now."

I nod, giving him a small smile. Maybe I was too harsh in my thoughts about River's position as Beta. Or maybe... maybe it's just me who is still struggling with our work.

He wants to court me. He wants to be my boyfriend.

And yet he's so fucking professional it physically hurts.

"Katie, Dr Patterson and Golden Eclipse's Doctor are waiting for the casualties," River continues. "Dillon's slowly moving them over there, and if there's anything severe we can get you over there."

"No need," I murmur, shaking my head when he frowns. I reach for the bonds I share with my pack, and I don't know if this is because of the powers I now have or if it's something I could've done all along, but I heal every single wolf that's connected to me via the pack link who is hurt.

I'm nowhere near as drained as I was the night after Charles's coronation when I healed the council, and I know that for sure is because of the new power I hold.

Conri was a powerful man.

Which means I'm now a very *very* powerful woman.

It's the generation for women to take the ultimate power. I'm the wolf host, Freya's the vampire—or she will be when the curse has finished transferring—which leaves us with some unknowns as far as the other immortals are concerned.

"Done," I say, flicking my hair over my shoulder. River's eyes widen, and I wink at him. "Now—"

"What happened to you?" Elijah demands, shaking Warren off. "Nobody could find you."

"Lottie claims Cain is the one who orchestrated all of this," Rhett says, breaking from his mind link with Caden and Noah, to give the vampire a look.

"What do you mean that Cain was the one to do this?" Warren asks, cracking his knuckles. River tenses, but he doesn't react the way I'd expect.

"Cain? As in Cain Viotto? Prince of the Hearthstone clan?" Elijah asks. My vampire mate looks very *very* attractive right now, the dried blood of our enemies coated to his skin, his shirt ripped showing off some tanned skin. His brown curly hair is messy, and his bright green eyes are wild.

"Yes."

"Are you sure?" Elijah asks, stepping forward. The expression on his face is very serious, but it's the doubt in his tone that pisses me off. "That's a very—"

"The fucker took me, strapped me to a chair, placed a pathetic amulet around my neck to cut off my connection to my wolf, babbling away about his great plans to take all of my power," I say, giving the vampire a pointed look.

Elijah frowns. "I can't believe he'd do something like that."

"I can," Warren says with a shrug when both Elijah and I look at him. Me in awe, his brother in disbelief. "What? I don't trust many, and he was never on my friendly list. Our mate was attacked by a crazy fucking fool, and after all the torment we've been facing, he's going to want to hope someone else finds him before I do."

"What will you do?" I ask, grinning at him.

"Let's just say, there won't be a piece of him left once I'm through." Warren grins. "Or a place in the Ancestral Realm for him."

"Where is he now?" Noah demands, coming closer to me. "Did you let him get away?"

"I don't appreciate the insinuation that any of this is my fault," I warn, and Noah looks repentant. I don't give him the chance to speak, just launching into my recounted tale of what has happened since Espen came to talk with us. They're horrified at how pathetic Cain was, and even more unhappy about the fact that he wasn't working alone.

They're intrigued once more by the visits I have with our ancestors—well, mine in this instance—and confused about the weird Guardian of All. Warren's got a bond with that place, and has never heard of her, but he's promised to look into it more.

I wonder if Theo or Dillon, my resident experts on research, may have a clue.

"Well fuck," Caden mutters, shaking his head. Rhett grabs me from the ground, giving me a tight cuddle, and I try my best to soothe him. "Seems we had it easy, fighting off his fucking army."

"Is it really an army when they're here specifically to buy him time?" Noah asks, and I shrug as Rhett places me down on the ground. He doesn't move too far away, still keeping a hold on me.

"Just to make it very clear," Caden says, his words serious. I freeze, but he winks at me. "You can tell Theo this shit. I'm not being the messenger."

I snort, and lean forward to pinch his side. He smirks, as Rhett presses a soft kiss to my temple.

"What about your side of things?" I ask, still revelling in the warmth of my Alpha. "What's happened with Espen and the fight?"

Noah outlines how the moment I was taken they all gave chase, until they realised we were under attack and had to pause to organise a very rapid plan of attack. Every time one of them tried to get to me, there was someone or something in the way.

"Well, then. A lot has gone down." I rub my temples, a headache beginning to form. "This is just the beginning, isn't it?"

"It is," Noah says, with a sigh.

"What's the plan now?"

"We're tackling things with the pack," Rhett says, stepping away from me. "And then we'll need to let the Council know we've got a bunch of new prisoners."

"I want to kill them," I say, with a frown.

"You're not normally this... violent," Rhett says, making eye contact with me. "Why are you so desperate for us to kill them, love?"

"Because they're not good wolves? I can feel their souls. They're toxic."

Caden nods slowly. "Maybe so, but that doesn't mean that we're executioners, baby. There are protocols—"

"Fuck the protocols!" I snarl, glaring at them. "Nobody else has stuck to them."

"What do you mean?" Rhett asks, firmly.

"I called in reinforcements before I went off with Conri," I say, with a heavy sigh. "I made sure Abel knew exactly what was going down. I made it abundantly clear that I was calling him on the oath he willingly made, and yet he didn't come."

All of my men frown, even Elijah who wasn't truly in belief that Cain could do this to us.

"Freya's not here either," I add, dropping my head so that I'm looking down at the floor. I feel pathetic, but Freya's one of my best friends, and if the roles were reversed—*when* the roles are reversed—I'd be there for her.

We saved Marielle together, and we've got plans to do this with many more babies, boosting their numbers and giving their women things they never should have lost. Abel offered his people up, should me or mine need it because of the things I could do for his kind.

I never helped Marielle for that perk, but it was still a perk I was granted. I'm not a fool that would turn down another aid for my pack.

But then Abel didn't come. He didn't follow his part of the bargain.

He broke our vow.

He left my people for dead.

After his brother was the one to orchestrate all of this.

"Then let's divide and conquer," Noah says, firmly. I'm surprised he's the one taking charge, but grateful for it all the same. "Lottie, you can head over to the clan. Take Caden with you, and find out what's going on."

"And me," Elijah says.

I flinch, and shake my head, and he gives me a hurt look. "Look, Eli, you immediately doubted me. If we're going to confront the most cowardly—"

"I'll go with you too," Warren says, cutting me off with a delicate look.

"I'd prefer Dillon," Noah says, with a sigh. "If we can't even count on Lottie to be polite right now, then we need someone who can. Regardless of what has gone down, they're still a very powerful clan and not one we want as an enemy when everything has already gone to shit."

"Aren't they already our enemy?" Rhett asks, tilting his head. I give him a soft smile, which he returns.

"I think that's an avenue we need to explore," Noah says. He looks at me. "Can you handle that? I'm not saying you can't go in and fuck them up, but you need to be smart."

" I am smart," I say, pushing my angry wolf back a little. "What do the people staying back need to do?"

"Call the Council and alert them to the attack, round up the prisoners, reassure the pack, and inform all of our official allies."

"Then you're going to need Theo, for the Council. Mallon's so fucking obsessed—" Noah's delicate cough causes me to stop, and brush my hair out of my face as I let out an angry huff. "You're right. Sorry. You'll need to be there for the pack, Noah. Rhett and Wyatt can handle the prisoners, leaving Elijah and..." I trail off looking at River. He's my new Dillon, and he's been pretty good at it so far. "Dillon to sort out our allies."

"Sounds good to me," Caden says, cuddling me in closer. "You, Warren and I can head over to the Clan." River's face remains stoic, but I know if there were a bond between us, I'd have felt his hurt.

"And River," I add, to nobody's surprise. "Lionel's here handling the pack, so he can come with."

"Perfect," Warren says, with a nod. "Before we go, shift."

"I really shouldn't." I bite my lip, shaking my head.

"Why?" Rhett asks, rubbing my shoulder gently.

"Because my wolf is out for blood."

Warren tilts his head, before sighing. "You've got ten minutes."

Caden beams, shifting into Marshmallow. He bounds over to me, nudging my stomach with his head, and I grin.

"Trust in your Alphas, love," Rhett murmurs, bending down to kiss my neck. "Shift, and trust that we'll guide you."

I nod, and move forward, letting the call of the wild overtake me. Two feet become four, and I howl up at the sky. I charge forward, and I've got Marshmallow at my left, and the beautiful grey and white wolf on my right that is Rhett. I can hear Noah charging after us, and as one we howl.

I can hear others; my pack; my dad's pack joining in, rejoicing in the win. I charge through the forest, my men keeping me in a straight trajectory, rather than letting me go hunt out the blood I want. Every so often one of them will howl, enticing me and our people to join in, and when we finally approach the three vampires —one vampire, and two sort-of vampires—I shift back into human form.

"Good run?" Elijah asks, and I nod. He takes my hands, tugging me into his embrace. After a quick and tight hug that does little to soothe my ire, he gives me a very passionate kiss. *Fucker. As if my vagina is so powerful, it's going to rid me of my anger just because he turns me on.* "I'm sorry, I'm a fucking idiot."

"You are an idiot," I murmur against his lips, loving the way his hands roam across my body. I step back, and he pouts at me with those rosy red lips. "I get it. You've known him for a very long time."

"That doesn't mean I trust him more—"

"That's not what she means," Warren says, rolling his eyes as he throws an arm around my shoulder. "Right, princess?"

"Right. I just meant you've known him since you were kids. It's hard to see under all the layers."

Elijah nods, pushing his hair out of his face. "Won't stop me tearing him apart layer by layer though." Warren hollers, reaching over to fist bump his brother, and I roll my eyes, despite smiling.

"Since you're on the outs with the teleporter—" Caden starts, and I ignore the pang of hurt that fills me.

"Really?" Warren hisses, glaring at the Alpha wolf.

I appreciate the sentiment, but Caden's not wrong. Freya didn't turn up for me today. She's one of my closest friends—she could probably battle it out with Katie to be my best friend. We share a bond that nobody else can understand, and it hurts that she's not been here.

Abel's never been my biggest fan, but his actions do still surprise me. He's the heir to the HearthstoneViotto Clan, and if nothing else, he takes the responsibility to his people seriously. His dad's going to be handing over a big mantle, and Abel's determined to do his best.

But Freya? She's nothing like that. Her goal in life is not to be Alaric Viotto. It's genuinely hurtful that she's sided with her brother.

But maybe that's my ignorance.

"Do I have time to say goodbye to Theo? To check in on Wyatt and Dillon?" I'm more subdued and they've all noticed it. Rhett and Noah exchange nervous glances, and I try to fake a smile. "You've got the pack, we've got this alliance."

"I know you do," Noah says, dropping a kiss to my lips. "We'll see you once you're back. Don't worry about us."

"Hard not to," I mutter, and he grins.

"Right back at you, baby."

"We'll see the others once we're back," Caden says, as Warren steals me. Caden sighs but doesn't protest. Warren lifts me into his arms and winks at River. "Race you."

"Tuck your head in," Warren murmurs and before I can even move, we're off. I do exactly as he says, tucking my head into his neck as he runs. The sound of whistling races through my ears, the air freeing my fingertips, but I can also feel the warmth from him—the safety of being in his arms.

"And... we lost," Warren mutters, as we come to a sudden stop. I tentatively pull my head out of Warren's neck, and he gently lowers me to the ground. I frown, not recognising where we are.

"We're not on clan grounds," River says, noticing my confusion.

"Why?"

"Because we've not been invited," Warren replies, rubbing my back softly. "But we can approach the—"

"Luna Mason?" a man asks, and the four of us whirl around. I don't recognise the short man, and his freckly features are unique enough I'd have known if we' met previously. He's a vampire, and not a weak one either. But I have no idea of anything beyond that.

"Garrett?" River asks, stepping up to my side. "You've upgraded to border patrol?"

"Upgraded?" the man asks, before laughing and shaking his head. "Punishment."

"For what?" Warren asks.

"I may or may not have broke Cain's legs in a spar the other day," Garrett says, with a smirk. There's some laughs from my mates, but to me, it just seems off. Is that a coincidence, or is this some kind of set-up? "But then he went crying to Daddy."

"And Alaric punished you this way?" I ask, tilting my head in confusion, whilst also ignoring the joy from my wolf. She's very impressed with this vampire. Garrett shakes his head, only confusing me further.

"No, Primus Viotto was impressed I got the drop on his son. But that doesn't mean the young Prince didn't cause up enough of a fuss that I was sent here for a week to soothe his ruffled feathers."

Warren lets out a huff, but smiles. "Any chance we can go in?"

"You and River are on the permanently approved list, as is Luna Mason, but—"

"Montgomery," I murmur, and Garrett frowns. "Sorry, but, my name isn't Mason."

"Understood. Luna Montgomery is permitted access whenever she'd like, but this wolf..." He gestures to Caden, with a frown.

"Caden Jameson, Alpha of Rose Moon." To his credit, my mate is polite about it, but I can feel his frustration across our bond.

"Is not permitted," Garrett finishes, and Caden sighs.

"I can just wait here, and let the three of you handle it," Caden offers, narrowing his eyes.

I groan, before shaking my head. The anger that's been simmering, the hurt that's been pushed back, the fucking fury that's been threatening to burst out of me, all comes to a head. Fuck the bureaucracy.

Fuck it all.

"I really fucking tried," I mutter, as Garrett goes on guard. I roll my eyes, before I barge into my friend's mind, not caring in the slightest about the barriers she's got up.

"Freya."

"Lottie. Can we—"

"No." I feel her surprise, maybe at my brusque tone. But that makes no sense. She should expect my annoyance. *"Where are you?"*

"Um, technically we're in Canada."

"Technically?" I smile, before remembering I'm pissed at her and school my features. *"I need you at your clan. Now."*

There's a brief pause, and she disconnects from the mind link. Hopefully she's coming here, or I'll have to be the one to traipse down to fucking hell, and find a demon to teleport me.

"Can we have our Luna go onto clan lands with one of us?" River asks, turning to Garrett.

"Of course. Like I said—"

And then he falls silent, because the true powerhouse of the Hearthstone Clan appears in front of me, dressed ready for fucking battle. Her black hair is in a braid, wrapped around her head, and her boots are to fucking die for.

Literally. I've seen her fondness for those spikes when it comes to eyes... *and dicks.*

Roman's to her left, a similar look on his face, and... Hudson—*I think*—is on her right.

She takes us in, her eyes flashing red. "What the fuck is going on?"

CHAPTER 3

"What the fuck is going on?" Freya demands once more, as she takes in the state of our clothes, our attire, and even our attitudes. It's weird, being in her presence now, compared to before I took the power.

Conri mentioned how he could sense her energy within me, and even Alaric told us how he knew that Conri was there the day he came onto pack lands. I wasn't sure how much I believed of it at the time, but feeling this connection to Freya, has erased any doubt I had.

It's like she's my kin, but not at the same time. It's almost like the feeling of recognition and warmth I felt the day I met Everett and Grace—my biological parents—but it goes deeper than just a connection to me and my wolf.

This is a soul deep, profound connection.

Which only makes the betrayal that much fucking worse.

"Seriously, what the fuck is going on?"

"Your brother... brothers," I reply, with a grim smile. She freezes, before looking up at Roman and Hudson. Both men shake their heads, their expressions identical. I know that they can read our minds, but I'm not sure if they've delved deeper. "Can we do this in Clan lands? I think it's better than doing it out here."

Although the concern has always been about my safety in regards to my stalker—to *Cain*—and he's made it clear he doesn't want to harm Freya.

She nods, turning to Garett. Hudson rolls his eyes, and Caden laughs quietly. "Lottie is more than welcome to come onto pack lands."

"Understood, Princess. The issue isn't with Luna Ma— Montgomery. It's with the Alpha."

"Ah," Freya says, with a shake of her head. "He's fine too. I'll take personal responsibility for him." Garrett nods, and Freya reaches for me, and then we're at her place. She's moved far faster than either of my vampires could do, and she stops once we're at her parents house.

I'm not impressed about going inside, not when I can hear three heartbeats—Cassie, Alaric and one of the Viotto men. I'm praying it's Blade, because Abel might get a punch, and Cain wouldn't survive.

I feel a connection to Alaric, and it's weird. Strong. But very weird.

Freya opens the door, and there's a cheerful hello from Cassie, before a confused hello to me. Neither Freya nor I respond to her, and I think they're put off by our attitude because as we move further into the house, nobody speaks.

Cassie and Alaric are sitting on the long sofa together, both with glasses of blood, and Blade's sprawled out on the armchair. There's a movie playing on TV, and if I wasn't bursting with fury, it would be amusing that he's spending his Thursday night accompanying his parents on their date night.

Alas, right now we've got much bigger concerns.

"What's going on?" she demands, crossing her arms in front of her chest. "Which brother has done something to you? All of them?"

"Evan would never," I say, softly, and she nods. "But—"

"Lottie?" Alaric says, rising to his feet, cutting me off from speaking. "What is the meaning of this? You're—"

Roman and Hudson appear in the room with my mates and River in tow, and none of them seem impressed. Hudson steps past the coffee table, and without even realising she's doing it, Freya adjusts her position so she's closer to him.

"I think we all need to sit down," Roman says, his smooth voice radiating through the air with a firmness. Alaric and Cassie exchange nervous glances, and Blade has sat up properly with a small *v* forming between his brows. It's annoying me even further than none of them seem to know what's gone down.

"I'm good, thanks," Freya and I say at the same time. She shoots me a smile, before frowning when I don't return it. Caden, River and Warren move to take a seat on my side of the room.

"Little muse, it might be helpful for you to call Jeremy over here."

"If Jeremy comes, then Hunter will want to come," Freya says, not breaking eye contact with me. She's trying to plead with me to open up, hating the barriers between us both. "And we can't leave Ambrose with... him."

"I'll get my brother to knock him out," Hudson says, gently. "Give me two seconds." He disappears from the room.

"Why do I need my entire mating circle here?" Freya demands, imploring me to tell her the truth.

"My pack was attacked today," I say, and her eyes widen. Both Alaric and Cassie gasp, and I can feel the genuine concern from the elder female vampire. Freya shakes her head, an apology forming on her lips. "And it was because of my stalker."

"We need to find that bastard," Freya snarls.

"He's not a literal bastard," Caden says, with a smirk. Freya frowns.

"I've found my stalker," I say, and there's a pause as everyone waits for me to reveal the name of the man who has been responsible for tormenting me, but also for hurting everyone in this room. "Cain."

She frowns, before letting out the most vicious snarl. Movement happens very quickly as Roman contains his mate, and Hudson reappears with Jeremy, Ambrose and Hunter in tow. The wolf immediately locks eyes with me, dipping his head in respect, but the vampire and two angels do not.

Their concern is their mate, and they all reach for her, despite her being safely with Roman.

I open my mouth to speak, and so does Freya, each of us smiling ever so slightly at their overprotectiveness. I can feel her rage, it's paramount to my own, and somehow that soothes me. She didn't know.

I don't know how, but Abel didn't tell her.

That fucking asshole.

Alaric takes the mantle of talking first, standing once more. He regards me properly, a tense expression on his face, tight wrinkles around his eyes, a firm and straight hold on his lips. He's seemed to age a decade or five since Freya and I got here, and I'm only sorry that the shocks aren't over yet.

"You've taken his life," Alaric says, calmly. We're closer now, the bond between us settling in a strange sense of relief. It's not very strong compared to the one I have with Freya, but I can feel the... kinship that Conri talked of. "You're the new original wolf?"

Freya's mood settles, as if she can finally place the connection between us, but both Blade and Cassie go on alert.

In their defence we've shown up out of the blue, covered in blood, and are not in a good mood.

Still, they should know that I'm not going to kill them.

"Well, I'm not the original, but yes, I have his powers. They were given all too freely, as you know," I say, before turning back to Freya. Alaric's been dismissed, and he knows it. "Where is Abel?"

"What has he done?" Freya asks, from where she's trapped in Roman's arms. The mind reader's eyes are trained on me, and it's clear that I'm the biggest threat in this room.

"Why did you take the power now?" Roman asks, and Freya pauses.

"I had no choice."

He sighs, pressing a soft kiss to Freya's head, before letting go of her. He doesn't move far, still within arm's reach, but that helps settle her ever so slightly. I take a small step towards her, and glance at my mates for reassurance. Caden nods, and Warren gives me a soft smile. I don't look at River, not really sure what I'd find.

"We've had an eventful day. We had James Hewitt, the man finally labelled as the abusive prick we knew him to be from the Council, come and attack us. His plan was to take over our pack, in an Alpha challenge."

"Fucking idiot," Caden, Jeremy and Ambrose say at once. I'm not surprised by Jeremy's contribution, but I am from the vampire.

"And then... well, my stalker showed up and stole me, just as our pack was attacked," I say, and she flinches. I can feel her fury, but I give her a soft smile. "Cain is an idiot, and I'm more than willing to show my memories of it, but... he's a little too pathetic. I broke away, knocked him out, and was going to go help my pack when Conri showed up."

"Taking his powers was the only way to save your pack." Alaric's words are soft, but no less true.

I nod. "I called for help, knowing that we'd need people there, since I wasn't sure how long this transfer would take." Freya flinches, and I can see the betrayal across her face. "I would've called you, but I needed your Clan..."

"So you went to Abel," Freya says furiously. She's not the only one. Alaric's anger is simmering under the surface of his skin, an icy feeling that makes my skin crawl. I'm the least affected—well, me, Caden, Freya and Cassie—but the men in the room are all reacting to it. Fidgety movements, subdued nature, and even their own anger.

"I reached out a good...?" I trail off, not actually sure of the time.

"Maybe an hour ago?" Caden says, tilting his head. "Roughly, with the travel and such."

"Fifty eight minutes ago you were taken from in front of us," River says.

"So about forty-five minutes ago," I say, nodding my thanks. "It took us three to get here. So Abel had plenty of time to arrive, even alone... and he didn't."

"Fuck," Freya whispers, just as Roman groans, clutching at his head. His knees give in, and he falls to the ground. Warren's immediately at my back, just in case. *In case of what, I don't know.*

Freya moves to his side, and Ambrose tosses a tube of something through the air. Freya's hand moves faster than I can track; grabbing it and opening it. She's so tender as she rubs the cream in, and the groans stop. He's still not back with us, but the pain seems to have gone.

"He's fine," Hudson says, stepping towards me with a hesitant look on his face. "But you're not."

"I am?" I query, stepping closer to my men and away from him. Caden stands, but River doesn't move from the sofa. With Warren at my back, Caden turns and gives the angel a dirty look.

"What do you mean she's not okay?"

"He's seeing the future, Hud," Freya says, tirelessly, not bothering to look over at what's happening with us. Roman's still kneeling, but no longer clutching his head. His eyes are unfocused, a pearly lavender colour, and he sort of seems peaceful.

But based on the level of fear coming off the twins, who can see what Roman is seeing as he sees it, I'm not feeling reassured.

"Yeah, I know that," Hudson says. "But she's struggling now." He pauses and shakes his head. "Or they are, at the very least."

"They?" Warren demands, gripping onto me tightly.

Hudson frowns, looking over at his brother. I know the angel twins can both read minds, he looks at my stomach, before looking at me properly. "You're pregnant, right?"

"I mean, it's to be confirmed, but we're pretty sure the answer is yes."

"There's no 'pretty sure'," Hunter says, stepping forward. "And you need to be ready."

"Ready for what?" Caden demands.

"Ready for the hell your children are going to unleash on your mate's body, if you don't find a way to filter out the power racing through her... and them."

"What do you mean?" River asks, finally rising to his feet.

"If the babies inside Lottie don't find a way to filter out their power," Roman says, rising to his feet. "The world as we know it will be over."

"I don't..." I trail off, not even sure what I'm meant to say right now.

"Your wolves will become pariahs," Roman says, taking a step towards me. "Every other supernatural creature will be at war... and it all comes to down to you, and your children."

CHAPTER 4

"I'm going to go and get Abel," Blade says, breaking the silence from Roman's declaration. My brain is whirling, and my mates seem just as out of it. Nobody else knows what to say.

Because what can they say that would help?

"I'll come with you," Hudson says, causing some frowns to appear from Freya's other mates and her family. I don't care about their dynamics, but I do like the sound of Abel being brought here. "What? Am I not trusted to walk around?"

Freya rolls her eyes, a weary expression on her face. "He's not here, Hud. Let Blade go on his hunt, which is really just an excuse to leave."

"What do you mean he's not here?" Cassie asks, peering at her daughter with furrowed brows. "He's been working over at the office all day."

"Where he conveniently ignored my call for help," I helpfully add. Alaric flinches, but I'm not pulling any punches.

Freya shrugs. "Sorry, mum, but the coward ran away like a little —"

"Freya," Alaric warns, raising a finger in warning.

"He's not on Clan lands," Freya says, instead of insulting her brother. "Roman could go bring him home, but I think it's best to let him get this out of his system and pounce on his return."

"And what exactly do you mean when you refer to *this*, Princess Viotto?" Warren asks, smoothly. My eyebrows raise, but he's not looking at me.

"The cowardly run as he tries to defend our brother," Freya says, giving him a sweet smile that's almost as sweet as her words.

"And once he returns?" Warren asks.

"Once he returns I'll offer his head to Lottie, before taking it myself," Freya says viciously, causing her parents to frown deeply. She turns to them and with a deep snarl, she hisses, "He broke his oath, and as such, he's endangered our Clan with his fuckup. If Lottie wanted, she could take more than just his head. Be very fucking grateful that you'll only lose one of your heirs."

I eye Caden nervously, and my Alpha mate squeezes my hand soothingly. Sure, I'm pissed at the elder Viotto heir, but killing him?

The more rational part of me just wanted him to be beat up a little, and an apology given.

Sure, my wolf would love his head on a platter, and his heart spiced up so we can eat it... but that's not normal.

"Abel didn't make a personal oath," Caden says, directing his words to me. "He put his whole Clan in your aid for the saviour of the vampire kind. You can call on them for whatever you need and they must provide it. However, the first time you did, he didn't fulfil his side of the bargain. Allowances would've been made if they were in peril, or unable to help but that's not the case. His life is forfeit, but with a fuck-up of this magnitude? His people are not going to be happy."

"I see," I say, turning to face them all. "I knew that if I went off with Conri, you'd be there. There wasn't an inch of doubt about me reaching out to Abel. It was my last act before willingly taking these powers. I didn't know how long the ritual would take, or what condition I'd be in afterwards."

"Charlotte—" Alaric starts.

"Do not say my name in that tone. I am not being unreasonable here," I snap, and he clenches his jaw, but nods. Alaric and I have never been opponents, and it's an uncomfortable feeling to now be this way. "I relied on you, and your son was acting in your stead. You failed me, Alaric, and you failed my people. I'm not going to sit here and make you feel better when it's me and my people who have been fucked over."

I toss my hair over my shoulder, and give him a cool look. "At the end of the day, I'm one half of the person needed to save your kind. I'm now the most powerful wolf known to mankind, and I'm not going to be sitting back and letting that just fester."

"You're not just going to let it fester in what way?" Alaric demands, and I can feel his vampire pushing forward, his power pulsing out. But it barely even touches me. It's like an annoying little buzz, but I can bat it away without even struggling.

"Wouldn't you like to know. You were an ally, Alaric, one of my very first. But you're no longer in the trusted circle."

"This wasn't all of us," Freya says, quietly. "I wasn't informed, Lottie, and it seems my parents weren't either. We never meant to fail you."

"I don't blame you," I say, giving her a tight smile. It's true, and I've moved past my hurt and upset with her. I shouldn't have doubted Freya, and I really shouldn't have gone with the fucking outlined protocol. "But your father is still the leader of this clan and should've known what was going on."

Alaric and Cassie shake their heads in sadness, the weight of my words weighing heavy on their souls, but they can't argue. The

Primus sighs, and I can see the lines of worry in his face. "Tomorrow morning, young Luna, we'll meet. You can go through your demands, and we'll right this wrong."

"You can't give the wolves who lost their lives those back though, can you?" Caden says, his words harsh, but not harsher than mine would've been.

"Reparations are pointless until we find out how Abel's going to handle this," Freya adds, glaring at her parents. "I'm going to get Lottie and her men home, because they've got a lot to handle tonight, but then we'll form a plan to deal with the idiot."

Alaric pinches the bridge of his nose, but Cassie just nods.

"I'm sorry, Charlotte. From Luna to Luna... I'm sorry we failed you."

I nod, turning away from her. I don't trust myself to say anything nice, and realistically, it's not her fault. That doesn't make things easier at all though. Freya reaches over, bypassing the snarling Alpha to squeeze my hand.

"I know it's hard to trust right now, but please try. I'd never have let you or your people suffer. Wolves... wolves are slowly becoming my thing, and Jeremy's one of yours," her voice is soft and timid, even mentally, and so unlike herself. *"Not that that's the only reason I'd help."*

Roman snorts, and kisses her head, and I nod. My anger has fizzled away, and I'm not mad at Freya. I believe everything she's saying, and she's proven that she understands my position by choosing me over her family.

But with Freya comes the future telling incubus, who has lit every single cell within me alight with fear. The panic goes bone deep, a horrible chill overtaking me, and I hate it. It's horrifying, to know that the children—

"Wait," I say, turning to Roman as my mind finally reveals a big important thing from his speech. He lazily raises an eyebrow, but his eyes flash a pale red colour. *I don't know what that means.* "You said *babies*. You kept referring to them as *children*."

"Yes."

"As in *plural*."

35

"Yes."

I close my eyes, count to five, and then turn into Warren for comfort. My sort-of vampire mate seems to understand, and cuddles me in close, kissing the top of my head, sharing soothing thoughts across our mental connection.

It doesn't help that I can feel his shock just as much as Caden's.

We barely had time to prepare for the idea of one child—them less than me, at that—and now there's multiples. This likely means one of the twins is the dad, and they've condemned my poor uterus into pushing out two babies.

"How many?" Caden demands.

"I think maybe—" Roman starts.

"Just a couple," Hunter says, cutting off the incubus with a smirk. "Good thing there's ten of you, huh? That's a lot of shitty nappies to change."

Roman rolls his eyes. "You'll be fine, once you figure out how to handle it."

"Take me home," I say, with a deep sigh. I glance at Alaric and Cassie, trying not to let my wolf's growl come through my lips. "We'll arrange a meeting for the moment that Abel has returned, and figure out where we stand."

"We're owed a pound of flesh," Caden adds, rubbing soothing circles into the small of my back. "Let's hope he convinces me to not make that literal."

"Everyone hold hands," Hunter says, with a smile in his words that matches the big grin on his face. I roll my eyes, taking Freya's hand, and then we're gone. Roman has teleported me, Freya, Caden and Warren directly to our house. We land in the living room, just behind the sofas.

The twins reappear as one with Ambrose, Jeremy and River, so I'm not sure who brought who out of that group. River doesn't seem okay, but it upsets my wolf even thinking about approaching him and offering to help.

"I need a fucking drink," Warren mutters, charging through to the kitchen.

"Holy shit," Lexie says, flinching when she realises that we're all here. She's sitting in the armchair, with her phone at her ear, and papers are spread across the coffee table. She's got a laptop open, but it's Dillon's. I listen out for him, but don't hear him here.

"Um, no, sorry Alpha Duncan, I was just... yes, I understand completely." Her voice goes from apologetic to timid, and she hunches in on herself. My wolf rears her angry head, ready to channel her frustration on Alpha fucking Duncan.

I tilt my head, listening to him spew more bullshit down the line, and storm across the room, gently taking the phone from her. She shouldn't need to listen to this shit, and honestly, I'm in the mood for a fight.

"Alpha Duncan was it?" I say, sweetly. His words cut off, his breathing sharp, and I so fucking wish he could've felt my power down the phone.

"Yes. Who am I speaking to?"

"This is Charlotte Montgomery, Luna to Rose Moon. I'll kindly inform you that it's absolutely *none* of your business about who was here today, or why they decided to attack. You are not an Alpha we have an alliance with, you're not an Alpha on our potential list, and you're a fucking coward who screams down at women who were just put in a traumatic position."

"You listen here—"

"I don't think I will. In fact, I think that when we're in your neck of the woods in a few weeks, I'll pay a personal visit to you, and see how many of your pack are happy that you're the Alpha. I've not—" I stop when he hangs up the phone, and shrug when everyone looks at me. "What? He was an asshole."

And arguing with that pathetic excuse of a man distracts me from the uneasy feeling inside, even just for a moment. My children—*children*—are at risk.

And I'm not sure what to do about it.

"Where's everyone else?" Caden asks Lexie. The unsaid *why are you here* is ringing through his mind, but he doesn't voice it. Warren comes into the room, tossing River a bottle of my blood.

Warren hasn't budged on River drinking directly from me, and I refuse to make him uncomfortable. But River's adamant he needs my blood, so I've been filling bottles with it. This is only the third one he's needed, and I get the feeling that from the next batch, he'll be able to go even longer between feeds.

Or maybe he'll just take less in. I don't really know how it'll affect him, but the scientist within me is intrigued.

"Dillon's just left to grab something from the office," Lexie says, with a tense smile. Her hair had been tied up into a ponytail, but she's loosened it so much, that it's now a kind of slop on the top of her head. She's exhausted, and mentally drained, but still doing her part. I fucking admire her for that. "Theo and Noah are dealing with the Council, and I'm not sure it's going well. Elijah is with Lionel and Scottie, offering support to the pack. Katie is at the clinic, helping those—"

"I helped everyone before I left," I say, with a frown.

Lexie shrugs. "I'm not sure, Luna. I just know that's where she is."

"I'll go assist with Lionel," River offers, glancing at me for permission. "We've lost some lives, and I can help with that."

"How many?" Freya demands. Lexie tenses, but when Caden nods, she's relieved to be able to answer. Freya's our friend, but Lexie's priorities are with me and the Alphas, and our pack first.

"Eleven," Lexie says, with a sad look. My wolf howls inside my mind, and I fucking hate that we're in this position.

Eleven lives lost to a madman on a hunt for power that has never been his.

"Show me what happened to you," Freya says, turning to me. I nod, and Roman appears behind me, pressing his fingertips to my temples. I don't bother trying to help, knowing he's more than efficient at rifling through memories. Freya's jaw tenses, and she lets out a vicious snarl when I knock out her brother in the vision that's playing in my mind, but telegraphed to those in the room. She's furious.

For me.

"He's dead," Freya says calmly. "He's genuinely a dead man

walking. He's a disgrace to the Viotto name, and I so fucking wish he had tried for my power. What the fuck did he think he'd do with yours?"

"He's not the only one who owes me some fucking answers. Conri, the sneaky asshole that he is, is going to get a hell of a call tonight," I say, and Freya nods. "Have you ever met that stupid voice?"

Freya shakes her head. "No. My realm is nowhere near as annoying as yours though. They'd literally bend over and put a plug up their ass if I asked them to."

"Typical."

"But we'll go hunt down Cain," Freya says. "Fuck this waiting around. He will die by my hands."

"He can't be killed yet," Caden says, shaking his head when both Freya and I growl, turning to him in an identical move of frustration. "We need answers from him before he can be executed." He reaches over, tracing his knuckles down my cheek. "I love that you have finally accepted the need for bloodshed, but this isn't the time to be reckless."

"It's not reckless when it's the right move."

"Cain's served his purpose to whoever he's working with," Freya says. "If we don't kill him, they will, and honestly? I'm a selfish girl who wants that honour for myself."

"Cain Viotto has betrayed the Hearthstone Clan," Roman adds. "He's a Prince no more."

"But you don't have that ability. Primus Viotto or Abel need to declare that," Warren warns, and Freya nods.

"And they will, if they know what's good for them," Freya reassures me.

"You can hunt him," Caden says, looking at Roman and not Freya. "And she can take his head—but you take his memories."

Roman's eyes flash gold, and I hold my breath as I feel his inner incubus revolt at the order. The demon doesn't want to take commands from my mate, but Roman just breathes through his nose slowly, and pushes his demon back down.

The control he has is impressive.

"Understood."

"With that situation being handled, I'm not impressed with your other brother. I'm not saying having him here would've saved those lives, but we also don't know that it wouldn't have. He offered this protection shit up freely, and then failed on the very first instance to provide." I blow out a breath of air, shaking my head. "I'm so fucking angry. My wolf is screaming for his blood, but I know I can't do that."

"We know," Caden says. "We'll sit down with your dad and grandfather and go over a list that we'll be demanding from the Hearthstone Clan, and we'll figure it out, baby." He shoots Freya an apologetic look, but she just shrugs.

"You could rightfully demand eleven dead from our Clan, along with the death of my entire family," Freya says, and my wolf howls once more. She's out for blood, and I'm struggling to contain her.

Murder is wrong.

But is it wrong when it's righting the scales of justice?

"I think we're doing more harm than good right now, little muse," Roman says, and Freya flinches when he tugs her into his embrace. "Let's head back over to the Clan, and see what your parents have to say, and then we'll go hunt down the missing men."

"Missing cowards," Hudson mutters, and Hunter and Jeremy laugh. Ambrose doesn't react.

"Do you need me here Luna?" Jeremy asks. His tone is steady, but I can feel that his wolf is reluctant to part from his mate.

"No," Caden says, shaking his head. "Your parents would kill me if you died, so..."

"We're not at risk of being attacked tonight," Warren says, rolling his eyes. He licks the rim of that bottle, not willing to leave even a single droplet of my blood behind. It's strangely sexy. "Go with your mate, Jeremy. We'll be fine."

"And call your mother," Caden adds. Jeremy rolls his eyes, as the angel twins snicker.

"Yeah, baby wolf, call your mummy," Ambrose adds.

"At least my mum—" Jeremy starts before sighing when there's more than one snarl. "Yeah, yeah. Let's just go."

With a flurry of activity and some promises of talking later, they're gone, leaving me with my mates, River and Lexie. Lexie looks down at her phone which starts to buzz again, and I reach over to answer it for her.

"Lexie, I've been trying to get hold of one of your Alphas, and I know you're probably fielding a shit ton of calls, but, can you get me in touch with one of them?" The comforting voice of my favourite Alpha who I'm not mated to or related to rings through the phone, and I can't help but smile.

"Charles?" I say in surprise.

"Lottie. Hi. I need to talk to you."

"Why?" I ask, confused. "What's wrong?"

"We've had Abel and Cain here. You're... Evan kicked them out. Abel asked if we'd hide Cain with us because apparently you and yours are on the hunt for him."

"Are you fucking kidding me?" I roar, and Caden darts over to grab Lexie's phone from me. "Cain is my stalker, Charles. Cain is the one who attacked your pack, causing your people to die. That fucking spineless coward."

"I'm on my way over," Charles says, with a hiss.

"Don't," Caden says. "You can't leave your pack vulnerable. We need to reconvene as a group, but then we'll loop you in."

Charles huffs. "Fine. An hour."

"Give us two, max," Caden says, with a sigh.

"We've had a lot dumped in our laps, and we're on twenty-seven different pages," I say, when Charles's breathing betrays his anger. "But thanks for letting us know."

"Always." The phone clicks off, and I sigh, handing Lexie her phone back.

"You seem a little... off," Caden says, looking at me with a soft look. It's a shame his words are so idiotic though.

"I was attacked by my friend's fucking brother, who has been stalking me for months for some pathetic reason. He's working with some random unknown group who launched an attack on our pack, causing eleven of my wolves to die. When calling for help his older brother didn't bother to bring anyone to help. My children are somehow prophesied to end the world, I've got a big choice to make, and everything is falling a-fucking-part. So don't—"

"Breathe," he murmurs.

"Breathe?" I snarl, glaring at him. "The fuck you think I'm doing? Standing here holding my breath? *I'm already fucking breathing.*"

But then the front door opens, and the scent of cedar fills the air.

"Lottie," Dillon calls, relief filling his tone, and I turn, seeing him standing there. His glasses are perched on the edge of his nose, a crack through the left lens. I pray that's sweat that's causing his hair to glob together like that, and not blood, but I doubt I'm that fortunate.

His shirt is ripped, showing off his toned stomach, but none of that matches up to the gorgeous dimples on his face as he beams at the sight of me.

Seeing him here is like coming home, and I don't hesitate in rushing to his side. He lifts me in the air, snuggling me in close, breathing in my scent. He squeezes me tight, kissing my temple. "Do me a favour?"

I nod, mouthing the word anything, although I don't think he can hear me.

"Don't kill Caden. We need him." Warren and River snort.

"What for?" Caden demands.

"Well, nothing in particular," Dillon says after a minute, and now I'm the one to laugh. Dillon's chest vibrates with his own laughter, and he kisses the top of my head once more, before releasing me. That bone-deep chill overtakes my body once more. "Theo and Wyatt are losing their shit. Want to go visit them?"

"I'm more than wanting to go visit," I say, steeling my shoulders back. "It's time for me to tell the Council what I did."

"And if they come for you like they did Conri?" Dillon asks nervously. Lexie inhales sharply, her fear filling the air, but she doesn't say anything.

"Then I show them again why they shouldn't underestimate me. They failed to intimidate me before I became the most powerful wolf."

"I love your ego," Caden says with a smirk. At least someone does. "But they're also missing something else that's new about you."

"What's that?" Dillon and I ask at the same time.

"Your newfound love for all things bloody," River says, smirking at me.

Warren grins. "Let's fucking do this. You're not the only one with new powers around here, and I'm done hiding them."

I eye River, but he stays silent, and I decide not to push.

"Let's go over to the Town Hall then," Caden says. "Lexie, do you need a hand here?"

"Um, probably. Most are not impressed they're dealing with me," she says, with a tense smile. Her hands are moving the papers around on the coffee table, a way for her to manage her anxiety without losing herself to a full-blown panic attack.

"Then don't answer them," I reply. "Turn the work phone off, and fuck them all off. We were attacked tonight, and we've got a pack who need us. Tomorrow, we'll deal with those people." I frown. "Tomorrow was meant to be the party."

"Fuck," Caden groans, reaching up to rub his temples. "I forgot all about that."

Warren gives me a grim smile. "I think that's going to need to be cancelled, princess."

"Yeah, no shit." I shake my head. "I'm not expecting the pack to celebrate me when I brought this shit to them."

"You're not to blame for the psychos of the world," Lexie says, gently. "Nobody will blame you for this."

"Maybe not. But I definitely blame myself."

5

CHAPTER 5

"$\mathcal{W}$e need to do a meeting with the pack once we've handled the Council," I continue, and Lexie nods, making a note of it on her list. We're walking over to the Town Hall to meet up with the others, and it's pretty quiet around here. There are no pack members wandering around, outside the enforcers, and I don't see the wolves that attacked us, even though I'm still holding onto their core to stop them escaping.

No idea what's happened to them. Dillon's not been the most forthcoming. That's unfair. Nobody has really kept him in the loop, and he didn't ask.

A sharp contrast from when he used to be my Gamma.

"Lottie, baby, enough," Caden pleads, tugging on his hair as he comes to a stop in the street. I can see the Town Hall just a few feet away, but clearly my Alpha mate has hit his limit. "You've barely taken a breath since we've left the house. We get it. There's a lot to do, and a lot to cover. But your anxiety is making my wolf frustrated, and we really can't be dealing with eight—*nine*—overprotective men because their pregnant mate is up a height."

Lexie gasps, her eyebrows raising, as her eyes light up. "You're... pregnant?"

I nod slowly, as a prideful smile fills my face. My hands rise to my flat stomach which won't stay this way for long. "Yes. Roman's vision confirmed it earlier tonight."

"That's amazing," Lexie squeals, reaching over to squeeze me in a tight hug as her hand presses against my stomach. I raise my eyes at her reaction, because I can feel the genuine joy from her wolf at this and it's a bigger reaction than just a friend being happy for me. Unsurprisingly, it's Dillon who answers me.

"Your fertility is a big source of pride for the pack," Dillon says, as an instantaneous blush fills my cheeks. "It's showing our pack will continue past our generation, and that it will be strong and prosperous far past us being gone. The children of the Alphas are truly loved and protected, and to know you've blessed them with a child this soon? It's exciting, considering all this turmoil."

"And it's also a sign that we're not *too* concerned about what's happening right now," Caden adds, and I furrow my brows, not liking the sound of that. "It shows the pack that we've considered the threats we're facing, but we have the utmost faith that we can persevere through them and protect our children. We're showing them that we can protect *them*."

"But that's not the case. I didn't get myself pregnant as a fucking political move. I just didn't get my fucking birth control shot done in time. I don't want them thinking we're not taking this seriously or that we're so sure of a win that we're procreating. We're going through such a dangerous thing right now, and it affects us *all*."

"We know," Lexie says, stepping back with a big grin still on her face. See, it's hard to trust she knows the depth of the fucking panic, when her wolf is so overjoyed. "We know that there's danger, Luna.

But to our wolves, this is such a big moment. We're proud of you as our Luna, and we're excited for the next generation." Her expression dims ever so slightly, as her tone loses the excited edge. "But as humans? We understand the fear. Nobody is undermining the threats and the danger, but we are *happy* for you and our Alphas."

I nod, and try to stop grimacing. Of course, my people are going to be happy and excited that the next heir might be born. I'm just finding it hard to be on the same wavelength, when they've been prophesied to end the world as we know it.

"We'll maybe announce it at the pack meeting tonight, if you're comfortable with that?" Caden asks, tilting his head. His expression is blank, and I can't figure out how he's feeling about that. "It might give our people some hope."

I frown, weighing the pros and the cons, and ultimately shake my head. "Let's wait until my scent changes. Roman's status isn't something many know and with this threat hanging over our heads... I want to wait."

I want to wait until we can't anymore.

I want to wait until there's a plan in place to protect my children.

"Then we wait," Dillon says, squeezing my hand with a smile on his face. It doesn't show his dimples, so it isn't a true smile, but I ignore that doubt. "Now, you and Lexie may have a plan to conquer the world, but..."

"Can you find some space for us in it?" Warren finishes, giving me an exasperated look. "I'm useful, you know. Cool powers, the better-looking Ellis brother—"

"Good thing you just said Ellis," River cuts off with a smirk.

"I don't need to flaunt my beauty in front of you, brother," Warren says, grinning at River. "I just need to flaunt my mate bond."

I groan, giving Warren a dirty look, and River rolls his eyes. Caden snorts, like the dick that he is, and Dillon winces, giving him a sad look. It's awkward, and Lexie's head drops to her feet so that she doesn't need to partake.

"Well, you know..." I murmur, trailing off when I don't actually know what to say. River's been sort of amazing since our... break-up?

He's kept his word at attempting to rebuild our relationship, trying to court me properly, but when my wolf can't even stand hearing his name, how can we have a future? "Let's just keep moving."

"Good idea," Caden says, holding in his amusement. "Theo's been harassing me since we got back, and I'm not sure he's going to appreciate us just dropping in."

"He's an uptight fucker tonight," Dillon says, with a shake of his head. "We only left the Town Hall in the first place because he was snarking and snapping at everyone."

I nod, knowing I can handle that. If Theo's being an asshole then he needs a smackdown.

We head inside the building, and it's eerie how silent it is. Nobody is on the front desk, and Lexie makes her excuses to go straight to her office. River promises to grab her when we start actually doing work. Mate bond or not, he still understands me and is determined to do his job as Gamma.

I open the door to the meeting room I can feel Theo in, and he's standing hunched over, his hands resting on the table, showing off a very delectable view of his ass. Noah is at this side, sitting down, thankfully, but I can feel the anger from him just as strongly.

As soon as the voice on the other end of the phone reaches my ears, I know that Theo's interference is going to have to wait. We're putting on a united front, right now.

"—you're missing fifty percent of your leadership then?" the Elder Patriarch drawls, as if this is the most exciting information he's heard all day.

I will be crushing this bastard one day.

And it's coming so much sooner than he expects.

"I'm not sure what you count as missing leadership," I say, stepping into the room in a dramatic entrance that neither of my mates seemed to expect. Theo whirls to face me, his eyes lit up in anger, the black an enticing pit that could hold me captive if that was his desire. His jaw is tense, the sharp lines only making his face that much more gorgeous.

And fuck does he look hot all rumpled.

Noah on the other hand is perfectly controlled, the anger burning within him, but not visible. He's not even close to unleashing the fury-filled volcano, but god it'll be an exciting moment when he does. Noah's not like the other two Alphas who burn hot but cool down just as fast. No, he's far more level-headed that when he snaps... it's glorious.

Well, unless I'm the target of his anger, but we've moved past that.

"Considering both me and Caden Jameson are both sitting here alongside Noah Jameson. Rhett Simmons, the final member of the leaders for Rose Moon, is handling the rogue wolves who handled us. Surely, Elder Patriarch, you can understand the need for that?"

"Charlotte?"

"Luna Montgomery would be the only title appropriate right now."

He coughs, and I can just imagine the look on his face right now. It's probably the exact same one that Theo is wearing. Angry, disappointed, and oh so fucking fearful.

"I see," he says, trying to gain control of his shaky voice. "We're not here on a polite visit?"

"Is it a polite visit when someone calls you to let them know their pack was attacked by over five hundred rogues?" I ask, stepping between Theo and Noah so I'm closer to the phone. If anyone gets to hang up on this prick, it will be me. "Because I personally don't think it is. I think when there's a threat to a life, you should intervene where possible, but when there's a threat on this large of a scale, you really should be offering support."

"Your pack isn't that large, Luna Montgomery, and your life really isn't worth saving."

There are five large growls, and one weird hiss from Warren. It's no longer the same sound as a vampire would make, but it's not quite the deep growl that comes from the wolves. It's a strange, unique mix, but it affects me no less.

My wolf is wagging her tail, pride racing through her at having such strong men back me, and I grin.

"Well, Elder Patriarch, it's nice to know where you officially stand. Give my love to Razor, and tell Amy to choke on your son's—"

Noah ends the call, giving me a look of utter contempt. I grimace, before grinning at him.

"We handled our end. Sort of," I rush out before he can lecture me.

"And so you decided to sabotage my side?" he asks, tugging me forward by my hips. I look up into his blue eyes, unable to hide my happiness. It feels right to be home, surrounded by my people. Things are uncertain, but we're having a baby.

Two of them.

"Two of them?" Theo demands, grabbing my arm. River's loud snarl has us all freezing, and I don't dare turn to look at him. I can't bear thinking about what I'll see.

"Don't grab her," River says. His voice is a plea, and it tears my wolf up inside. She's howling in my mind, confusion rampant, and it fucking hurts. I whine, and Noah's hold on my hips tightens as Theo lets go of my arm.

My heart aches, hating this entire situation. It's fucking shit, and none of us are finding it easy. I can feel the anger from Warren's vampire and Caden's wolf at the implication that River, a random man without a bond to me, is trying to weigh in on our life.

Noah's wolf isn't bothered since I'm in his arms, but the man is agitated.

Theo's anger has shifted from Mallon, to River, and I can empathise. His wolf could *never* harm me, and the man would never and could never physically harm me. So for River to imply otherwise?

And River, well, I can't tell how he's feeling, but it's probably not good.

It's once again that we're in a weird situation.

"Look we clearly need to talk this shit out again," I mutter, stepping out of Noah's embrace. I ignore the cold feeling and the disapproving looks from too many men. If today is the day I let the opinions of a man dictate my behaviour, I may as well have let Cain just take over and make me his bitch. "But for now, we've got a bunch of fires to put out. I want a pack meeting before bed. We need to get our shit sorted out so that we can give them *something*."

Theo and Noah nod, but it's my Alpha who continues speaking. "So, since you have all been gone, Rhett and Wyatt have been knocking those who attacked unconscious. The plan was to wait for word from the Council on how to handle them, but they weren't the most helpful."

"Mallon might not have been, but I've got contacts with both Elder Linus and Elder Green," I say, with a shrug. "Let's give one of them a call, and find out what they want us to do." Theo sighs, and I round on him. "Problem?"

He shakes his head, still very agitated, and I shrug.

"That's a shame," I say, pulling on my power. "Because I have a problem with you." I push the power his way, forcing him to submit. Me, alone, he can withstand. But the power of the original wolf?

Not even my Guardian can fight that.

He drops to his knees, bowing his head, as a thin sheen of sweat appears on his forehead. He's trying to fight against it, but his wolf is pretty content being on his knees.

If only the man was.

"We're not here to belittle and upset our people who are already tense and anxious," I say, frowning at him. "It's our job as leaders to protect them from that, to *shield them*. During the months you were all... indisposed, I made sure the pack was safe and protected. That is our job." I step closer to him, gently running my fingers through his hair. It soothes the wolf even further, but the man is not impressed. "This isn't your failure, Theo."

I withdraw the power, and he lurches to his feet, towering over me, with an intense look in his brown eyes.

"Yes it is," he snarls, and I ignore the small commotion happening behind me. "This was my fucking fault. I should've known, I should've protected you." He shakes his head. "It's my one fucking purpose, Charlotte."

I roll my eyes, and step into his space. He doesn't take the hint, so I reach up and cup his cheeks, lowering his head down to mine. His arms are trembling, and his eyes are hard, but there's a desperation clinging to him that doesn't suit my Guardian.

"I love you," I murmur. "You did not fail me, Theo, and you have not failed as my Guardian. But, we're about to go and upset some people, so you can be there to protect me from the fallout if it'll make you feel better."

He sighs and nods, dropping a kiss to my forehead. "If that's what you need, little wolf."

I grin at him, and he shakes his head, stepping back.

"Now, let's give Elder Green a call and get this handled," I say, turning to the rest of the room. "Because I want a pack meeting, sleep, and then some battle strategies tomorrow."

"Sleep is good," Theo says, hesitantly. "But maybe—"

"Sleep," I say, cutting him off. "I'm so fucking exhausted with all the late nights and the extra twelve hours isn't going to accomplish anything."

The men trade looks, but I don't back down. We've done this in the past, where we've strategised all night, and I was often the perpetrating force behind it. But this time, I'm carrying twins, and they need me to rest.

"Add in a conversation with your dad, and I'm in," Caden says. I squeeze his hand and he nods. "Now, whilst you call Elder Green, I'll inform the others about Charles's warning."

"Sounds good," I say, reaching up to kiss his jaw. I take a seat at the table, commandeering the room as they slowly trickle out. River hovers in the doorway once they're all gone, and I sigh as I look up at him. "We knew it would be awkward."

"I made the choice," he says, with a tense smile. He takes a step forward. "I know I'm not meant to start until Monday—"

"You've done a pretty good job so far." My tone is teasing, an attempt to put him at ease. He grins. "I appreciate all of your help, River. Really."

"Thank you. May I sit in on this call?"

I nod. "As long as you understand that I'm not the Alphas. Whatever relationship you had with them, is going to be different to the working one that we share. For this call, I want you to keep track of what's said, provide me any extra insight I might miss, but ultimately, I'll be leading."

"That's pretty similar to what happens with the Alphas," he says, gently. "I want to be here, Luna. I want to be of value to this pack, to you. I don't want it handed to me because of the bond we used to share. I want to *earn* it."

I smile. "Then welcome to the team. You can fight with Lionel over who is the most efficient, whilst Lexie embarrasses you both."

He grins, pulls a notebook from the stand on the corner and sits opposite me. I dial Elder Green, and hope like hell he's useful.

)) ● ((

"We're safe," I reiterate, and there are some nods, but nowhere near enough to reassure me. "By morning, every single one of the wolves will be gone."

"Dead or with the Council who betrays us?" a voice asks, carrying through the crowd.

I bite my lip, the sting combined with the scent of blood, causing me to let go of my lip. Warren squeezes my hand, as Noah answers that question. He promises them that this is the best way forward, that we're following the official channels in an effort to look after ourselves better.

A political move that guarantees us allies.

I don't necessarily agree with that, considering Mallon pretty much said he wanted me dead, but I'm happy for that to be the line that's shared amongst our pack right now. I frown when I feel a disturbance in the air, and something begins to move through the forest a few miles away. I can hear the small rustles, feel the energy, but I don't recognise it.

Meaning it's a vampire.

I tug on Theo's bond, silently sharing with him, and we ready ourselves. I continue listening, feeling the malevolent creature advancing towards us, and as I guessed, it's a vampire.

The man has bright red curly hair, and is quite thin, and pale. His sunken cheeks are covered in freckles, and he's got a pretty crooked nose. His lips are stained red, and I can smell the blood that's coating his shirt. Human.

The jacket he's wearing seems expensive, and old, whereas the pants are just a dark brown that don't stand out. He's old, despite only looking around thirty, and I know for a fact he's one of Cain's people.

I can just feel the echo of it.

"Charlotte Mason," he calls, and everyone falls silent. There's a distinct accent to his words, Irish, although I can't distinguish it further. "You have been marked for death, and it is I, who calls for your soul."

I roll my eyes as there are some shrieks and gasps from the crowd. Theo's snarl is impressive, and he shifts into his wolf, charging towards the man. I'm faster, overtaking him immediately, as I dart up the middle of the audience. He waits, a weird look on his face, as I advance.

I ignore the anger and shouts from my mates as I reach him, but the little fucker is too fast to let me harm him. He slashes his own throat out, and collapses to the floor, clutching a note. I shift back, not even bothering to attempt to heal him.

He's dead either way, so I may as well save myself the energy loss.

I crouch down to grab the note, but a hand reaches out, stopping me. I frown up at the man in question, but he doesn't even look my way. He blocks me from moving, holding up a hand in front of me to stop me moving.

"No," River says, firmly. My wolf cocks her head, looking up at the familiar man with the unfamiliar energy. There's a dangerous edge to the hybrid, his essence powerful and commanding, and so beautifully balanced. "Warren?"

"I've got it," Caden snarls, and to River's credit he just nods, and doesn't move from where he's standing. My wolf sits back in my mind, and watches Caden walk towards the man. He's dead now, but that was clearly done by design.

He was sent to deliver a note, and it's not going to be ignored.

Caden reads it, paling ever so slightly as he looks behind me at the rest of the mates. Theo jogs over, and Caden hands it over to him. Caden starts snarling lightly under his breath, eyeing me up warily, before glaring at the dead man. I can feel his wolf pushing to the surface, begging to be let out so that he can shift and cause some damage.

My Alpha mate isn't happy with whatever he just read.

And neither is Theo. One by one my men struggle to control theirselves, and the curiosity is burning at me. Once Warren's read it, he sighs, and hands it to me.

My eyes glaze over the words, and a resolve fills me.

Cain will die.

But so will his mysterious leader.

I turn to the pack, seeing their nerves, and hold in my annoyance. "Go home, rest, and know we are going to guarantee your safety. We're at war, Rose Moon, but we're going to do our best to make sure that future casualties are only on their side."

Lionel and River take over at evicting the crowd, as I enact a barrier around my mates, the dead body and I.

"So," I murmur, looking at the note once more. Words like "King Lobo" and "Your death is destined" glare out at me. I shake it at my men, giving them a weary look. "What the fuck do we do about this?"

CHAPTER 6

"Drop him at the clan," I say, not even bothering to direct it to one of my mates. "See what they can tell us."

"If anything," Theo murmurs, shaking his head. "The only thing they'll do is confirm he's not loyal to the monarchy."

"Well, then it'll be another nail in their son's proverbial coffin," I mutter, wiping my hands. They still feel grimy after touching that note.

Warren nods, lifting the body, and then disappears from view. The note that the fucker brought with him is still in Rhett's hand, and it's a good thing the body is gone. Rhett was one step away from tearing into him, not caring that he'd not feel it at all.

"Breathe," I murmur, squeezing his forearm. "It'll be fine. We'll handle it."

His eyes are black when they meet mine, and he shakes his head. "No, Lottie, we won't. The moment I find that fucker—"

"Breathe," I repeat, this time infusing my tone with some dominance.

Rhett waves the note in front of me, and I sigh, snatching the disgusting letter from him. I'm not sure how mentally stable this asshole is, because his letter doesn't give me much hope, but I do know that he's dangerous.

I'm not a fool, and all the warnings we've had over the last few months absolutely build up to this.

Time and time again I've been warned to handle the Council so that I can face the bigger threat head on.

Well, I think we've found it.

I read through the note again, ignoring the seething from my wolf. She's furious at the idea that there's someone out there who thinks he's better than us, more worthy than we are.

Dear Charlotte,

Allow me to introduce myself, although I'm certain you won't find pleasure in this encounter. Your name may be pretty, but your face and demeanour are nothing more than poison. You're a waste of a wolf, a waste of power. You may call me King Lobo, as I am the true King of the Wolves.

Your actions have sealed your fate, Charlotte, the consequences of your own making. Are you ready to bear the weight of your sins?

Your misguided delusions of being a leader among the wolves are nothing but a pathetic attempt to disrupt the order that has stood for generations. You are not the person to illicit change, Charlotte. Not when your blood is as impure as your virtue.

Your audacity to claim a false destiny and challenge the established ways will not go unpunished. You are an unwelcome intruder in our world, a world I tried to rid you of. If it weren't for meddlesome fools, you'd never have seen your first birthday.

Death is calling for you, Charlotte, and it is I who has marked your soul. You'll die before those bastards of yours can be born. Your tainted branch of our bloodline will end with you.

As for the weak vampire that betrayed you, his end draws near. He has

57

outlived his usefulness. I wonder if you'll waste your time trying to save him... that weak saviour trait of yours is as pathetic as the lies you surround yourself with.

The power you currently hold is not rightfully yours, Charlotte. You're a disgrace to the original line, a taint on our power, a disgusting abomination that should've stayed gone. You are worthless, and I will take great pleasure in destroying you.

Upon your death, the true reign of a King will be restored—my reign.

Your days are numbered, by me,

King Lobo

King Lobo, or King of the Wolves, as he wants to be called, is fucking psychotic. Between the dirty blood comments, the mention of my virtue—which, is actually really rude since I *lost my virtue to my mate*, as if that's any of his business—and the constant comments about my appearance, it's very easily seen that he's a sexist elitist.

But the lines that have me peering more closely are the ones that hint towards him being more deserving than me of this power. Where does he get off on making those claims?

The only person I know who can answer those questions, is Conri, a dead man who owes me so many fucking answers. I add this to the tally, hoping he's ready when I come calling.

"Theo," I murmur, and my Guardian comes to where I'm standing. "Can you keep this somewhere safe? I'm not sure if it's going to be the last, or what, but we might want to have a more in-depth look once we're not unable to control ourselves."

"The fact that I've not yet let my wolf take over and rip out some hearts, love, shows I can control myself," Rhett snaps, glaring at me. I raise an eyebrow, not even bothering to force him to submit. He grunts, and turns away from me, the shame pouring off my Alpha mate.

He's cute, albeit wrong.

"So, where do we go from here?" Dillon asks, looking around at us all.

"We lock the pack down," Caden says, taking charge. "We secure the area, we make sure patrols are running. We set someone up on phones in case there are any important calls, and then we go to fucking sleep. Tomorrow is going to be a big day, and we've had a long enough one today."

I nod, leaning into Theo. My Guardian wraps his arms around my shoulder, tugging me into his hard chest. He presses a kiss on the top of my head, and some of the tension I was carrying fades.

"I'm going to call my dad too," I say, with a wince.

"No fucking wonder my phone has been blowing up," Caden mutters, shaking his head. "Go home, and call him. *Now.*"

"Aw, is little Caden scared of Daddy Everett?" Rhett taunts. Wyatt elbows my Alpha in the stomach, but it doesn't faze him, as he chuckles away at the face Caden's pulling.

"I'd much rather be scared of him than call him Daddy," Caden says, rolling his eyes.

"Even I don't do that," I say, raising a hand.

Caden snorts, and Rhett frowns now that the joke is on him.

"Yeah, well," Rhett says. "Fuck you all."

"Also, he's text me a good fifteen times too," Warren says, pulling his phone out. "Maybe he's chosen me over you now Caden."

"I've got... eleven," Caden says, frowning.

"Three," Dillon says, and Caden's frown deepens, his eyes darting to Noah. Noah rolls his eyes but checks his own phone and apparently, my dad has text him fourteen times.

Fuck.

I turn my head into Theo's chest, trying to smother my laughter, as my mate calls my dad.

"Caden? Hello? What's going on!"

"Why did you message Noah more than me," Caden demands.

"I didn't even message Noah," Everett says. "Now tell me about Lottie."

"I'm here Dad," I say, taking the phone from Caden who is spluttering. It's not important at all. I turn and start walking from the clearing. Elijah falls into step with me, and I take his hand in mine with the one that's not holding the phone. "How are you doing?"

"Do not be cute with me, young lady."

I giggle, and Eli squeezes my hand. "I'm okay. Stressed. Anxious. Terrified. Furious. But okay."

"Hurt?"

"No."

He lets out a slow breath. "Thank fuck."

"Can you come down tomorrow?" I ask, quietly.

"I came down tonight, but I was turned away by the barriers," he says, gently. "I can come down tonight."

"No, thank you," I say, shaking my head. "We're not doing anything tonight. Tomorrow we'll go over a game plan."

"What's happened?"

I sigh, and fill him in very briefly. Even the slightest annoyance pisses him off, and his wolf starts snarling down the line. I love my dad, but he's the most overprotective, over-the-top parent, and I can't handle that right now.

Even if my wolf and I preen under the behaviour.

"Tomorrow morning, I'll be there," he says, and I smile. "How are you feeling after taking the powers?"

Elijah drops my hand to open the front door, and he holds it open for me. I kick my shoes off, as I talk to my dad about the ritual and how I'm feeling. He gives the right reaction for what I share, and I love that more than anything else.

Just like my mates, there was a time I wasn't sure my dad would ever be himself again. But he just needed his time to grieve.

"I'll call you in the morning," I murmur once all my mates are home. My dad sighs, but lets me hang up the phone. "Are we all sorted?"

"All sorted," Rhett reassures me. "Now, get yourself up to bed. It's late, and we'll have an early start tomorrow."

I nod, and give him a kiss, before heading up to my bedroom. Nobody is there, so I go straight through to shower away the day.

It's really fucking needed.

"**C**ome cuddle," Wyatt demands, and I grin at him. He's sprawled out in my bed, topless, and so tempting. The brand on his chest marking him as one of my wolves, as part of my pack, is so fucking sexy. Not as sexy as the mark on his skin that I put there, however.

He's gorgeous, toned and fit, and all mine.

"Coming," I murmur, walking over to the bed. I slowly undo button after button on the stolen shirt, and a salacious smile appears on his face as I let it drop soundlessly to the floor. On silent steps, I pad over to the bed, and tug the duvet back.

He's just wearing a pair of tight-fitting boxers, that show off his excitement, and I lick my lips seeing the little wet spots on the white cotton. I crawl over to him, and gently tug them down with my teeth, causing him to groan. There's no denying what I want.

I don't bother taking them off fully, instead, the moment he's free, I drop my head to take him into my mouth. I swirl my tongue around the head, loving the way he tastes, getting off on the noises he makes. He moans when it feels good, and hisses when it feels *too* good.

He grabs a tight grip on my hair, gently thrusting further into my mouth, and I relax my throat letting him take over completely. He senses the moment I submit, and his wolf turns feral. It's most definitely an ego boost.

My Beta mate uses my hair as his guide as he fucks in and out of my mouth, using me for his pleasure. My eyes water, but I don't gag, as he fully bottoms out, his balls resting on my chin.

He hovers all the way in for a second before gently pulling out, giving me the chance to breathe before doing it again and again. Drool is dripping everywhere, mixing with pre-cum, and I fucking love the way it feels.

I can feel myself dripping on the bed, desperate for my own release, but my wolf won't demand it until we've satisfied our Beta.

"I'm going to cum, love," Wyatt groans, his words a tortured plea, and I nod with my eyes since I can't move my head. His moan is full of love, before he erupts down my throat. A tear drips down my cheek at the sheer intensity of this moment, and I'm gutted I didn't get to taste him.

But seeing him completely lose it, is everything.

He pulls out the moment he's done, but I don't let him get too far. I continue suckling ever so gently, coaxing out the last few droplets, lowering him from the high.

"Well fuck," he mutters, rubbing my head ever so gently. "What did I do to deserve that?"

I look up at him with a smile. "You're mine."

He returns my grin, and moves so fast my breath catches in my throat. He lays me on my back, hovering over me with a dark look in his eyes. The pure lust radiating from him has my core clenching in anticipation, and based on the smirk on his face, he knows it.

"Well, if that's all it took to be rewarded so beautifully," he murmurs, dropping down to lick over my bond mark from him. I moan, pleasure building within me so powerfully, the desire to fuck him overtakes my senses.

But he takes it even further. He licks over the bond marks created by my other men—even the faded bond with River. I can feel their annoyance, their jealousy... *their desire.* It only fuels me that much further.

Wyatt kisses down my sternum, past my belly button, and circles my clit with his tongue. Teasing me the way I did him, he plays me like a fiddle, making me melt into a puddle of pure desire. Over and over he teases and taunts, not once letting me fly off the edge.

My nerves are on fire, and my throat is hoarse from my whining and begging.

I just want to cum.

"Please," I beg, and he pulls away to smirk at me. His face is glistening with my juices, his eyes bright with hunger, and it takes my breath away. "Please."

"Ride my face then, love," he demands. "Take your pleasure from me."

He lays on his back, and I hesitantly crawl up his body. His dick is at attention, ready for round two, but neither of us pay it any mind.

How can we when my pussy is leaving a snail trail as I move up his body?

I hover over his face, nerves filling me, but Wyatt just grabs my thighs, tugs me to his face, and eats me like a starving man at a buffet. Following his cues, I grind against his face, chasing the high of the orgasm he's denied me.

And when it comes, it fucking flows, dragging me under its abyss, firing up every single nerve ending. My scream can probably be heard through the soundproof walls, but Wyatt's tongue never stops moving.

"Holy fuck," I gasp, throwing myself down beside him on the bed. My legs are trembling, my pussy quivering, my core contracting. This orgasm is still fucking going, small tiny waves of pleasure. My eyes roll back in my head when Wyatt's chuckles send another round of vibrations through my body.

"Good?" he huskily whispers, dropping a kiss to my neck. I whimper, and he laughs properly now. "You're good for my ego, love."

"You're good for your own ego," I mutter, breathlessly. As the waves of what I thought were endless pleasure stop, I turn to face him, laying on my side. I gently move his hands between my legs and he grins.

Round three knocks me unconscious, my mind lost to the sea of ecstasy.

Probably for the best, since it means nobody can pull me into the Ancestral Realm.

Orgasms beat dead relatives.
Always.

CHAPTER 7

"We're not playing this game any longer," I say, sitting back in my seat. My hand gently rests on my stomach, an innate desire to constantly be touching the tiny pups growing inside. We're all gathered in the Town Hall—me, my mating circle, River, my dad, and Malcolm. We're sitting around the large table in one of the big meeting rooms, with what Dillon's donned the Murder Board of Madness at the head of it.

Charles is on the other end of the phone, along with Landon and Evan. They tried to reach back out to Abel last night, but couldn't get a hold of him, and they didn't get much support from Alaric on how to handle the situation. Evan was so apologetic on behalf of his parents and former Clan, as if it's his apology to make.

Hell, even Landon reassured me that this wasn't my fault. The same man who still barely tolerates me, was furious on my behalf. The trio—and Charles's parents—are not impressed with Abel's actions. I do love that they're on my side, even if it does give Abel more ammunition in his argument that I'm on a crusade of his brother's demise.

The support from our allies, from the people closest to this after me, shows that I'm not just making a big deal out of nothing. Abel fucked up, and Cain's clearly had them all fooled.

Can we really blame Abel for falling for it when we did too?

Maybe not... but we can blame him for not sending the support he offered.

"I'm so sick of following this protocol that I barely even understand. I became a wolf, and was thrown into the deep end because fate had her twisted games and I became her chess piece. I've really fucking tried to adapt to this world," I continue. My rant is being backed up by a lot of angry feelings from my men, but that doesn't change the wary look in their eyes. "But I'm done. I'm done obeying a Council who are going to let a man be free after he abused and raped his pack members, and condoned those same actions from his high-ranking men. They left a pack to struggle after we were bombed, and—"

"We know all of this, little wolf," Theo says, with a firm nod. "The Council are no longer acting in our best interests."

"No, they are not," I reply, eyeing him warily. "Is that going to be a problem for you?"

His little friend betrayed us in the worst way possible, and because of her, we've got a man who needs rescued. A man who put his life on the line for me and mine, and has been in service of Conri for years. Razor is a good man, and I have no fucking idea what fate we left him to when we saved ourselves.

Theo shakes his head, tugging on our bond, smoothing out some of my more anxious edges all whilst pushing his love at me. I beam at him. My wolf is just as elated as I am that he's *finally* put us first over Amy and Alec.

Fuck the pink and purple threads—we're stronger without them.

"Then one of the steps on this agenda of ours is to finally take over that cesspool of vultures." My words are heavy, and probably a true sign of treason.

Do I care? No.

Does my wolf? Well, if the howling inside my mind and the rush of adrenaline that I'm feeling is anything to go on, no, she also doesn't care.

My dad's green eyes are wide, an excited energy pouring out of him. His sandy-coloured hair is short and fluffy, and since my mum has passed, he's had some stubble across his face. It looks good on him. He's wearing a dark blue suit that complements his tanned skin, and he winks at me when I smile. He's totally on board with whatever we're planning.

"I agree. It's not going to be easy, but if anyone can do it, it's going to be someone like you who doesn't understand all the delicacies of this world," Charles says, his voice is a little crackly through the phone but is full of determination. "What can we do to help?"

"Protect your pack," Rhett says. He's pacing the room, the uneasy feeling from him is prominent through the bond, and he's trying to maintain control of himself. It's not often that he's the loose cannon, but things have really changed since the bomb that Cain so helpfully organised. "We're going to..."

"We've got two choices." Noah takes over, and Rhett shoots him a grateful look. My blonde Alpha mate looks around the table, assessing our positions. My wolf perks up when he gives us a grin, and I have to soothe the raging hormones within me. "We can either travel the country and meet our allies, solidifying the bonds there, before showing up at the Council... or we fortify things here. We'll hold court with each pack here, host the Council on our lands, and wait for *King Lobos* to attack again."

"Option one is far more dangerous, but I like the idea of being on the offensive instead of the defensive," Caden says, eyeing me up. I can feel his wolf's excitement. My Alpha mate isn't an Alpha because he likes to play things safe. He's a good man, a good leader, and will do what is needed for his pack regardless of the personal cost.

"Especially since we owe it to the other packs," I say. There's some nods, and some scrunching of noses from those who don't care. "And it'll be easier to take the power away in the home of said power, versus making them come here and needing a second showdown."

"Another fair point," Caden says, with a nod. "If we went with the travel option, who would go?"

"This would be an entire mating circle event. We can't split up and be at full strength," Noah replies. He's tense, his shoulders rigid, but his tone remains calm. More evidence that he's grown with everything that's happened to us. We've all grown as a mating circle. I'd have preferred not to thank Cain for anything, but he has taught us how much stronger we are together. At least now he'll pay the price.

"And what about the pack?" I ask, quietly. I don't want to be the buzzkill, considering my mates are already getting excited at the prospect of violence —Warren and River more than the others, although the former Beta is a lot calmer than he would've been — but this is something we need to consider.

Of course my wolf is excited at the adventure, at the idea of taking what is rightfully ours in name, as well as power. But the Luna in me is worried about leaving my pack at such a troublesome time. They need us, they need our support, our strength

Hell, I'm currently acting as the Luna for Golden Eclipse too. It's not just those who are mine in name that I need to be here for. If we leave, I'd need to set up so much to make sure things are organised, and nothing slips through the cracks.

"We're here," my dad says reaching over the table to squeeze my hand. The excitement has faded from his face, and he's no longer enjoying the idea of a fight. Now that he and his wolf know that the battle isn't one he can manage for me... It's no longer as exciting. "Your grandparents and I can watch over the packs and make sure everyone is safe."

Rhett's face twists, his jaw clenching. I wait for him to voice his upset, but he doesn't.

"And if we're hopping around the country, we can request a few people from each pack we secure an alliance with to come back and monitor our pack," Theo says, sitting forward. Theodore Lykaois the Guardian is out to play, and he's very keyed up in the politics of our world. Another source of pride for my wolf. *As if she needs the ego boost.* "The Hearthstone Clan owe us, and *will* provide people to ensure the safety. That is non-negotiable, and not even part of the reparations that they owe."

"We can protect the pack *and* secure alliances," Caden says, with a nod. Rhett relaxes ever so slightly, but he's still not very happy with this. Is it with me going? With none of us being here for the pack? Or is it because my dad is going to be in charge? "As well as pissing the Council off, since they've refused to send us aid."

"That's probably for the best," Elijah mutters. "They're not the most helpful."

"And pissing them off is just a bonus," Warren says, rubbing his hands together. I eye the purple sparks that shoot off his hands, but nobody else seems to notice. The purple-eyed man winks at me, before nudging Elijah at his side.

The elder Ellis brother doesn't seem happy, but I know his concerns will be similar to my own. How can he gallivant around the country when he has pack members relying on him for support?

"But how do we go about tracking down Cain and his... people?" Caden asks. There's a violent edge to his words, and when he meets my eyes, they're pure black.

"We don't," I say, shaking my head when his full lips drop into an adorable pout. My wolf whines, wanting the blood, and wanting to let our mate have it. "Leave that to Freya."

"You trust her?" Dillon asks, almost hesitantly.

I nod. "With my life." Caden and River both nod too.

"Good," Evan says through the line. They've been a little more on the silent side, but they're not really much help. They need to know what we're planning so they can fortify themselves since after my dad's pack, they're the closest to us, but they don't have much to add in this new developmental stage. "Freya's loyal. She's reckless, spoiled, and a little over-demanding, but she's the most loyal person you could ever have in your corner. If she had known, she'd have been there no matter what Abel said."

"Don't forget a very powerful ally," I tease, and he laughs. He sounds exhausted, and my heart goes out to him. I've been soothing my wolves a lot whilst sitting here, but vampires just aren't my thing without Freya there to help navigate them. "I tried to follow the rules, and contact Abel since he was the one who made that stupid vow, and it backfired. Next time, I'll fuck off protocol, and contact your sister. She's powerful enough on her own, but with her mating circle, she's worth more than any Clan."

Warren snorts. "Maybe don't say that to Primus Viotto *or* Abel." I shrug, and he grins at me.

"Probably for the best," Evan murmurs, but then his tone hardens. "Although I can't imagine Abel will ever make a fuck up of this calibre again. That is, if he's even still in the running to be Primus."

"Wait what?" I ask, sitting forward so that I'm closer to the phone. "Why wouldn't he be in the running? I'm not going to take his life for this. Too many people have already died for Cain's fuck ups."

"Which is something that people will either brandish you as very foolish for," Charles says through the phone. "Or very cunning."

"Stupid," Caden says, with a sigh. "People don't value life when it comes to power. They value flashy shows of power. Letting Abel live when you could take his head? The Council will be furious. We're not at war with vampires and haven't been in centuries, but they're still not *friends*."

"No, we're not," Elijah adds. "To the wolves, killing the top vampire and his family, would solidify your Alphas as some of the most powerful of their generation."

"Lovely." I cross my arms in front of my chest, shaking my head.

"Not everyone will think that way," Noah says, gently. "But to those threatened by true power, they will."

"I didn't miss how you said *my Alphas* would be the most powerful. As if it's not me doing it." I roll my eyes when they exchange nervous looks. "I get it. My vagina takes me out of the running for being powerful. Instead, I'm just *pretty*."

"Pretty is good," Rhett starts, and Wyatt must kick him under the table. "Or not."

I smirk.

"So, since he's not losing his life, Alaric may propose that Abel lose his heir status as a result of his actions," my dad says, giving me a soft smile. Panic fills me, imagining the hate that Abel must be feeling for me. He's already in doubt that I'm trustworthy, and in his mind—even if it's inaccurate—I'm on a witch hunt for one of his brothers.

Now he's going to come home and find out that not only have I kicked up a fuss and tarnished the name of his brother, but I've potentially stripped him of his position. To a man like Abel, who has spent his entire life being moulded for his position, I guarantee he'd rather be dead.

I eye River, thinking of the pain he was in when he lost his wolf, the words he threw at me. The pain he was in. Abel's vampire will rebel, will no longer obey when the truth comes out, and the man will struggle.

Fuck me dead. They don't make this political shit easy, do they?

I understand that he needs to face repercussions for what he did. Eleven of my people lost their lives. He failed to uphold his end of the bargain, and that could've cost his entire family their lives, fucking over the Clan—the people he has sworn to protect—and the rest of the vampire community since Alaric is their monarch.

Abel needs to be punished for that.

But I don't want the man dead.

"Let's push that out of my mind for now." I rub at my temples, feeling a little nauseated. Theo's healing energy is immediately there, his power soothing away the headache and nausea. I'm not sure if he did it unconsciously, or if he's just attuned to my feelings right now, but I appreciate it. If the nausea isn't from this stress, he will not be leaving my side during this pregnancy.

"Good idea," Caden says. "Charles, we're going to be going back and forth over our next steps. Can we call you back when we've got a plan?"

"Of course," the Alpha says. "I'll just be a mind link away if you need anything."

"Thank you," I say, softly. The line goes dead, and we all take a minute to bask in the calm silence, before I break it. "I think option one is our best bet."

"We can gain alliances with the biggest packs—"

"Biggest doesn't mean strongest," Malcolm says, cutting Caden off. Caden tips his head in agreement.

"We've had requests across the entire country," River says holding up Lexie's notebook. "Some of them could be persuaded to hold court together, since they're quite close. I can organise that with Lexie and Lionel."

"Sounds perfect," Noah says, with a nod. "Limits the amount of visits we need to do."

"We need to be prepared for some ambushes," Rhett says, giving me an apologetic look. Silly man. It's not his fault people are trash. "The first visit will probably be fine, but the moment they realise what we're doing..."

"I'm not too concerned about ambushes from other Alphas," I say, with a shrug. It might sound cocky, but I have power pouring through my veins. Sure, they might physically be more powerful, but I've got so much raw energy that they'd be hard-pressed to get an advantage. "I'm concerned with ambushes from King fucking Lobo."

"Do we have to call him that?" Warren asks, and Wyatt laughs. My Beta mate has been a little quiet this meeting, and I don't like it. "What kind of prick goes around claiming to be King of the Wolves and literally names himself King Wolf? It's embarrassing."

"Oh, but don't forget I'm the abomination." My bitter tone has my men snarling, and it does boost my confidence ever so slightly.

"Let's organise for us to leave on Monday," Noah says. "The nine of us will be going pack to pack."

"Nine?" Warren asks, eyeing his brother warily. River tenses, no longer writing on his notepad. I guarantee if the bond still existed, I'd feel a brief dash of hope race through him.

"Nine," Caden confirms, and River goes back to writing. My wolf's curious energy prods at the feeling of warmth in me, not understanding why. *Yeah, me neither wolfie.* "If it weren't so dangerous, I'd suggest bringing Lexie as well."

"Definitely not," I say shaking my head. "She can be here as a liaison for us, but I won't take her from the pack right now."

"I agree," Rhett says, with a nod. "I think it might be worth asking Melinda to come back, too."

"I don't know," Caden says, sitting up properly in his chair. Noah scrunches up his nose, and shakes his head. Warren tenses too, likely thinking of Harper's safety. "I can't... I don't want her bringing Harper back right now, and I really don't want her leaving Harper alone. I know she's with family, but she's a six-year-old girl who needs her mum during this shit time."

"My parents and I can handle the pack," my dad says. He gives Rhett a reassuring smile, but my Alpha doesn't seem to appreciate it. "I'm more than capable of leading my own people."

"I mean this in the nicest way possible"—the thing everyone says before saying something rude and offensive—" but your pack is falling apart." And there it is. Rhett's words are not polite, *or nice*, and of course set my dad's anger off the charts. "You don't have a new Gamma, your people are struggling without a Luna—"

"How fucking dare you," my dad snarls, jumping to his feet to glare at the Alpha across the table. "My mate *died*. Kevin *died*. It's not like they just got fucking fired. I'd be replacing people who have been doing the job *for years*. Fuck, they've been doing the job longer than you've been alive."

"And we understand that. But that doesn't change the state of your pack. If it wasn't for *my* Luna, your people would have nobody supporting them through this transition. They'd be floundering and struggling. They're grieving too, Everett." Rhett's words are an angry snarl, and he's not afraid at all to stand up to my dad. My wolf is torn.

She knows that we owe this duty to our father's pack. Golden

Eclipse are my birth pack, and we feel a tie to those wolves. My mum is the one who passed away, and it would be my duty to step up for my pack, as the only heir.

But she also understands Rhett's concerns, in a way that only wolves can. She doesn't get the full thoughts and feelings behind it, but she wants to be on our mate's side.

"You can't function without help, Everett," Rhett says, quietly.

I don't know if Rhett's plan was to piss my dad off so badly that he would shift and try to attack my mate, but that's exactly what happens. My dad lets out a deep growl, and shifts in mid-air. He dives onto the table, ready to charge at my mate, but with a heavy sigh, I stop him from advancing.

I wrap him in a barrier, moving him to the floor, and give him a dirty look. The wolf whines, giving me a look of pure sadness.

Sadness. As if his upset over *not* being allowed to attack my mate is something I'll give any sympathy to.

"Really?" I demand glaring at my mate. He's easier to handle than my dad. Rhett's unrepentant look pisses me off. This is not the time to be starting fights with allies, even if he is Rhett's father-by-mating.

My dad lost his mate, his life fucking partner, his soul. The only reason he's still alive and functioning is because of me—the pack wouldn't have been enough to save him, no matter how big-headed that sounds. My dad chose to live as only half a person, because he loves me that much, and knows I still need him.

The fact that Rhett can't understand that kind of sacrifice, is somewhat understandable but not truly. His father did the same thing for him, after all.

Sure, I've been struggling a little with Golden Eclipse, but I am more than capable of handling it. It's just an adjustment period. I do not need Rhett throwing this in my father's face on a day like today.

He's more than capable of being Alpha. It was never his job to be the Luna.

So I don't understand Rhett's concerns.

"What?" Rhett demands. His surly attitude is just another black mark against his name right now.

"Are you forgetting that Golden Eclipse is my pack just as much as Rose Moon is?"

"But it's not, Lottie. Right now, whilst your father clings to a pack that he really shouldn't, that's *not your pack*. It's his. You were never part of that pack, and you never will be."

"So what's your game, Alpha?" Malcolm asks, rising to his feet. He gives Everett a look, and the wolf nods. The action confuses me, but Malcolm gains more confidence. "Are you planning on taking our pack as your own? Ousting us and taking over completely?"

"I think it's something Everett needs to hand over, yes." Rhett dusts some imaginary lint off his clothes, and my eyes narrow. "He's no longer fit to be an Alpha."

And that's the final straw. I freeze, my brain genuinely pausing as it tries to process Rhett's words. But they can't.

How fucking dare he.

I stand from the chair, the air feeling a few degrees cooler as I flick my hair over my shoulders. Everyone pays note, and that's before I speak, with a tone so icy I'm surprised there's no visible sign of my breath. "Are you telling me you want me to take over Golden Eclipse before we go on an excursion across the country where we could die? Do you think that's fair for any member of Golden Eclipse to put their trust in people who won't even be there? People who may not even survive long enough to come back to them? Do you think they deserve to be merged with us, thrown directly into the line of fire with the threats we're facing, and be told to just deal with it since we're not going to ease them through the transition?"

Malcolm smirks, which annoys me, but my dad yips in agreement. I give the wolf a dirty look, considering he's not had his words yet he's acting awfully cocky.

I can tell Rhett he's a fucking idiot. Nobody else can.

"Are you really that *unfit to be Alpha* that you'd leave our people to struggle even worse than they are now, just to prove a point?"

Rhett's smugness fades, and he shakes his head. "That's not what I meant, love. I didn't mean that you'd take over now, before all of this. Your dad is struggling to hold onto his pack. The tides are changing and every day that you integrate yourself there, is a day closer to him being pushed out. He cannot hold onto the pack anymore."

"He can't," Caden echoes, giving me a serious look. My dad whines, before shifting back into his human form. He's still angry, but he doesn't seem like he's going to attack my mate, so I let the barrier drop.

"I understand your position," my dad says, with a nod. "But just because I'm not equipped to be Luna for my pack after only a measly couple of months of my mate dying, does *not* mean I am failing my pack. I'm not clinging to the pack for some self-satisfying reason. Like you said, my people are *grieving*. They cannot take losing me as their Alpha right now."

He takes a seat, somehow making the scooting of his chair into the table seem like a strong move. "My daughter is stepping into the role she should've always had, and she will be doing it alongside me and Malcolm. It's an adjustment where they gradually come to accept her more, and once she's settled, I will hand the pack over."

Rhett frowns, cutting in. "And yet, you've given her no support. She's got no Gammas from your pack to aid her *or* the previous Luna."

"And what the fuck did you have?" my dad snarls, slamming his hands onto the table as he jumps back up to his feet. I roll my eyes as the chair falls to the floor.

Dillon flinches, but he's the only one with a visible reaction. I'd have expected those less dominant to my dad's rank to be affected too, but they're not. Elijah's eyes dart to Rhett, a sympathetic expression on the vampire's face, but both Warren and River are relaxed.

"You took over with a Beta who knew nothing and a Gamma who knew even less. People die Rhett. It's a terrible fate, but that's the way of our life. With the current state of this world, with the way fate is playing games with my daughter and those in her life, we're lucky that Grace and I were together long enough for our daughter to be returned to us. But we live, we learn, and we adapt."

"I think that's enough," I say, shaking my head when all eyes fall to me. "Rhett, I love you, but this was not the way to handle this. I started running Lupine Valley without any kind of true guidance, and I stepped in and did the same for Crescent Peak. Even now that we're Rose Moon, I've learned on the job without any guidance."

My feelings are hurt from the reaction Rhett had, almost like he's implied I'm not good enough or able to handle what I was born to do. It's insulting. Especially since he's my Alpha, my partner.

If he can't trust me, how can the pack?

The dark-haired beauty goes to speak, but I hold my hand up and silence him. "I don't appreciate you speaking for me, Rhett, especially in an instance like this. You don't know what I do in a day, and cannot say whether I can handle the job. Poking at my dad isn't going to erase our anxiety over what's coming. He's got my grandparents— huh what's that? Oh yes, *a proper Luna*—who will help him run our pack. They're going to be in very good hands if that's the route we choose."

Rhett clenches his jaw, rolling his eyes a little before sighing. "My intention wasn't to insult you, love. I just thought having more people around to protect our pack would be best." He doesn't break eye contact with me, as he directs his next words to my dad. "I didn't mean to offend you, Alpha."

"I give zero fucks about you offending me," my dad says, with a smirk.

"That's why you dove across the table preparing to attack him?" Malcolm asks, and Warren and Wyatt snicker.

My dad shoots his Beta a dirty look, before turning back to Rhett with an amused smile. "But can you really say the same about offending my daughter?"

Rhett's jaw drops and he turns to me. His eyes widen, and he seems genuinely confused about my anger. "Why are you so mad?"

"You basically said I was a shit Luna, and that you needed Melinda to come and do my job for me," I say, shaking my head when he tries to speak. "But, you're not clear in this," I say, turning to my dad. The man frowns, shaking his head, but it's not good enough. "Have you not learnt your lesson about fighting with my mates?"

"Not something we want to repeat," Noah says.

"No it is not," I retort. "And if your plan was to groom me into the role, talking to me first would've been smart. A Luna is an Alpha's partner—even if that Alpha is her father and not her mate. I cannot be the support you need, the support the pack needs, if I don't know it all."

He nods, rubbing his jaw. "We'll talk."

"Let's." I relax, which causes everyone else to do the same. "Now, we'll put it to a vote."

"I have no doubt that Alpha Mason will be able to lead the two packs in our absence," Caden says, smirking at Rhett. Malcolm grabs a chair, and sits down, since his backup is no longer needed.

"Add in the blood ties that you and he share, the pack will follow him without a doubt," Noah adds, giving Rhett a weird look.

"Motion passed," Wyatt adds. Rhett drops down into the vacant seat next to him, crossing his arms with a petulant look on his face. I hold in my eye roll and do the same, scooting my chair under the table. I take a sip of the water in front of me as we wait for my dad to sit back down.

He surprises me by walking up to the Murder Board of Madness, and tugs off the image of Razor. "You said you were done playing by the rules."

"Yes?" My question is tentative.

"Then I take it we're going to be getting Razor out of the confines of the Council?"

I smirk, and there's some nervous looks. "Dad, when I'm through with my plans, there won't be a Council left to free him from. I meant what I said."

With that microphone dropped, I reach into the centre of the table, and pull the phone closer to me. I call Charles back, and before he can even say hi, I cut in with my request.

"Charles, could you do me a favour and let your mum know that Lexie will be making an appointment with her? I want to chat with her about a few things before I leave."

"Of course," he says, and I'm surprised he doesn't ask any

questions. "We're here to help any way we can. I think... provided things with Abel don't go terribly, it might be worth speaking to Cassie too."

And of course, he immediately understands why I asked this. My mates are worried about the Luna aspect, and honestly, so am I. If Cassie can help, even a little bit, since she's no longer Luna to her own pack, that would ease some of my anxiety.

"Another good suggestion," Rhett says, smiling at me. "Now, are we ready to get down to business?"

"Yes," is echoed around the room. Dillon stands, walking to the murder board, and both River and Wyatt turn to fresh pages in their respective notebooks.

The planning session is underway.

Watch out King Lobo... We're coming for you.

CHAPTER 8

There's nothing quite like the energy when a preparation for a battle is underway. We've been in this position far too many times for it to be new, but the atmosphere is so potent in its determination that it's almost tangible. The air seems to crackle with how close our wolves are to the surface. At this moment in time, we're fully human, but we're using the strength our shifter sides give us.

In one corner is my dad, my grandfather and Caden. They're going over the situation with Abel and the Hearthstone Clan. They know my stance—no killing—but otherwise, they're trying to come up with an outline of the demands we're going to make of Alaric. Caden's more prepared with the political aspect of this, and with the guidance of my dad and granddad, I'm hoping it'll be fair and not too vicious.

Rhett is holding court with Sophie, Callum and Jax in the other corner of the room. The five of them are spread across the table, with paperwork surrounding them. They're discussing the security plans for the pack whilst we're gone and also for us on our trip. The latter is obviously not going to be fully fleshed out until the trip is organised, but they're getting things organised in a way they're comfortable with.

In the room just opposite us, we have Lexie, River, and Lionel going over the different places we'll be visiting. They're going to organise the actual trip outline, making it as easy on travel as they can, but they're also creating documents and binders of important information. Their contribution is not going to be done in a quick hour or two, but once it's done, we'll be able to prepare properly.

Wyatt and Warren are in the room next to River's group, and they're working together on picking apart the other leaders. The two of them are going through the different Alphas we'll be visiting, creating plans of attack and outlining strategies. They're working closely with River's group, but they're focusing more on the Alphas and the packs and going through a thorough list of who we're going to be working with just based on what we know.

This leaves Noah, Dillon and Theo, who are going through the letter King Lobos sent, going through the archives, and just trying to figure out what they can about the attack. I know the least amount of what's going on in there, but the constant state of anger and frustration that I feel from them doesn't bode well.

I'm sitting in my office with Katie, and we're going over the health reviews for the pack. Before the attack, my schedule had me working in the clinic today, going over this information with her, helping those who needed it, and identifying plans of attack for those with chronic issues that keep recurring despite my healing. I healed a lot of the big shit last night without even seeing the people who needed it, but I definitely didn't erase every bump and scrape they had. We're not sure how the powers I have will affect me properly, and with how much of a drain healing those not in my bond usually is, we had limited it to only a couple of people. Now we're trying to prioritise who is in more need and what might not take as much energy.

Elijah is with Scottie doing the same kind of thing, but they're looking at the applications because he's got new people to hire. I know my vampire mate is struggling a lot. I offered to let him stay, and he gave me the dirtiest look I've received in a long time, and honestly, it reminded me of the Elijah I went to school with—the hot and cold asshole. The difference is that this time, he was so offended because he knows being with me is the thing he needs to do, and he was upset I didn't think he'd prioritise me.

That's definitely something we need to talk about once we're done here.

"They'll be fine," Katie says, moving a pregnant woman to the *not-yet* pile. I frown though, and take it from her. She doesn't notice, already going through the next folder. But as I read about the lady who is struggling to shift into her wolf due to exhaustion, I know that we're facing a big issue. She's got plenty of smaller problems that aren't much on their own, but when tied together, it's a lot.

"I want to see Rochelle today," I say, and Katie pauses, reading to look at me with a raised eyebrow. "I think she's got our version of a parasitic pregnancy."

"They don't tend to present this way," Katie says, shaking her head. "Our pregnancies are never that much of an issue. We've got the occasional stillbirth or miscarriage, but nothing like the vampires. Wolves don't tend to struggle until they shift."

"Call it a hunch," I say, shrugging. I've always followed the instincts of my wolf, since her innate sense is the only thing I can trust. I was never taught how to survive in this world, and I was never given the skills to thrive, but my wolf doesn't need any of that.

She trusts in the magic that created her, she trusts in the power of our bloodline, and she's never shy about pushing forth for what she believes in.

My wolf has never led me wrong, and she thinks we need to see this woman.

"Okay, I'll put her in with this group then," Katie says, putting her into the *urgent* pile. I nod, and we continue going through the list. It's not until I see another pregnant lady—this one not too big of a concern, she just needs repeated healing—that I realise I've not shared the news with Katie.

"We're pregnant," I murmur, peeking at her underneath my eyelashes instead of looking properly, just in case she's not as happy for me. I don't know why I'm so nervous, considering she already knows it's a possibility, but my heart is racing, and my palms are sweating.

"What?" she asks, distracted by the file she's reading. "Who is?"

"I am."

Her pupils dilate, and she all but flings the file down. It's almost like a switch flicks inside of her because she then frowns, the excitement being replaced by disbelief. "How do you know? Your scent hasn't changed, and a pregnancy test wouldn't show yet."

"I just do." I look back down at my file, feeling the weight of her chocolate brown eyes piercing into me. I laugh, putting the file down. "Roman confirmed it yesterday. We're having twins."

She grins, pure joy radiating from her, and I laugh. "Fuck babe, that's amazing news. Two babies. Now there's one for your men to fight over, and one for Auntie Katie to cuddle. I'm so fucking happy for you."

"Thank you." I smile, but there's a reason Katie's my best friend.

"What is it?" she demands, showcasing how much she knows me.

"There's some kind of prophecy concerning them."

She rolls her eyes. "Babe, you're one of the most powerful wolves to live. We've never met someone with your power levels, and that's before you took on Conri's curse. Of course, your children are going to be powerful, and of course, there's some kind of prophecy."

"The prophecy is that the world as we know it will be changed," I say, with a frown. I don't like that she'd won playing this. "If we don't fix things, wolves are going to become hunted—they'll become pariahs."

"Oh." Her lips purse, and she sighs. "Okay, fair enough, that's not a *good* one. But it's not that bad."

"No?"

She shakes her head, her brown hair flying around her face, and she smiles gently. "Lottie babe, you're literally tearing the world apart right now. You've got your men making plans to destroy the system we have, and replace the poisoned men with people who are capable and willing to do the job. Don't you think that's changing the world as we know it?"

"Well, yes."

"And don't you think that you'll raise your children to stand up for what they believe in?"

"Well, yes." I can feel the headache forming again and rub at my temples. "I don't want wolves becoming pariahs, though, Katie. It's clearly not a good thing if Roman's been warned of it."

"Maybe not. But I do know you'll figure it out, so that the twins have the best life they deserve." She reaches over and squeezes my hand. "Now, drink some water whilst I get the Guardian to heal you." I nod, and she flounces away before pausing at the door. "Don't get me wrong, it's a good perk, but Sophie's definitely the twin with the better tongue talent."

"Katie!" I moan, and she laughs as she walks away. Theo comes in and heals me, bringing some food and a drink as well, before going back out to join the others. Katie and I continue going through the lists, and it's kind of therapeutic being in here with her.

Every so often, there's an excited shout or some feeling of rage, but for the most part, Katie and I are left alone to do what we need to do.

"Finished," Katie says, with a grin. "We've got four who will be healed today, and then an additional five that can be if you've got the energy to spare. Any you don't get to today, can wait until a few days' time, to give you the chance to recover."

"It doesn't take a few days," I protest.

She frowns at me. "You're pregnant now, missy, you don't push past your limits. It's not just you that you need to worry about anymore."

"You told Katie?" Caden asks, hovering in the doorway. I jump and grin up at him.

"I couldn't let poor Lexie contain the secret," I say, and Katie gasps.

"You bitch. You told my mate you were pregnant before me? Your best friend? *Of twenty-two years*? What kind of loyalty is that?" Katie jumps to her feet, glaring at me. "You better make me the godparent, or I swear to fucking god Lottie—"

"Please don't threaten my pregnant mate," Caden says, a mild chastisement in his tone. Katie rolls her eyes, but leaves the room, and Caden gently closes the door behind him. I narrow my eyes, an amused smile tilting my lips upwards. "What's that look for?"

"Um... why are you here?"

He laughs. "I was coming to check in just on my way for a piss, but then I heard you and Katie talking." He comes to sit down opposite me, in the seat Katie was just in, and undoes the button on his suit. It's such a suave move, and my tummy flutters at the sight of it. "Do you want to tell your dad?"

"Do I tell him now?" I scrunch up my nose, and tilt my head, before slowly shaking it. "I'm not really sure now is the time to drop this on him."

"Drop this on him?" Caden's tone rises, and he gives me a pointed look.

"That's not what I meant. I just think it's a bit rude of me to tell him we're expecting, after my mum—"

"We're still allowed to live our lives, Lottie, just because she's lost hers." His tone is so gentle here, and when he stands up and rounds the table, I'm not surprised when he crouches down in front of me. He takes my hands in his, his head still reaching my shoulders even with him kneeling, and he presses a soft kiss to my hands. "Your dad will be ecstatic."

"Do you think?"

He nods, squeezing my hands once more. "Tell him."

"I will," I say, leaning my head forward to kiss his cheek. "I promise."

"Today," Caden demands, wagging his finger when I go to argue.

"This is our news, baby, and as much as I understand not yet telling the pack—I want to tell my mum when we see her in a few weeks."

"My scent will have changed by then though so it's not like we can hide it," I say, with a frown. I sigh when he gives me another pointed look. "I'm not trying to be a dick here. I don't really know how to go about this. I've still not told my parents that my mum is dead, for fuck's sake. I'm not the best at sharing information."

He nods, rubbing his thumb over my hand in a soothing manner. "I get that. Okay, tell your dad, and Malcolm. We'll schedule dinner with Warren and Elijah's parents, and let them know, and then we'll do a video call with my mum and tell her. You'll need to do the same with Theo's parents, but I think he'll agree that we should wait on that until it's been announced to the world."

I nod slowly. "What about our allies?"

"We don't share with any of them until you're ready, but traditionally the pack would know first," he continues. "Why are you so hesitant? Roman's warning? The health of the babies? The threats?"

"All of that?" I whisper. "I wasn't ready to have kids. I fucked up my birth control shot. But now that they're here, I need to protect them, Caden, and I don't think I can."

"But you're not alone in this, Lottie. It's not you, solely in charge of protecting our children. There are nine dads who are just as powerful, just as capable, and just as defensive as their mother."

"I wouldn't go that far," I mumble, and he laughs.

"We've always come out of this, Lottie, and this time won't be any different. We are stronger together, and we'll make it through."

I nod, and he rises to his feet, now towering over me in a way that makes me feel safe and small. He lifts me into his arms, and sits down on my chair, cuddling me in closer. I inhale his scent and relax ever so slightly.

"Tell me about the plan," I demand.

"Oh, lovely. The demanding part has already started," he teases, kissing my temple. "We're asking for twenty of their men—"

"Only twenty?"

"Are you going to interrupt me before I can even finish a sentence?" His tone is full of exasperation, and I shrug, resting my head on his chest.

"Why change a habit of a lifetime?"

He laughs, and the vibrations from his chest soothe me. "We're asking for twenty of their men to be a scout team for us, for our trip. The logistics haven't been worked out, obviously, but we're in need of support and they owe it to us."

"Oh. That's actually smart."

"I do occasionally have good ideas."

I grin up at him. "I knew I mated you for a reason other than your good looks." He rolls his eyes, but I can see the hint of a blush on his face.

"And then we're asking for a team of around a hundred men, to work in shifts at protecting the pack," Caden says.

"Men?" I ask, sitting forward.

"People," he corrects, and I nod slowly. "Sophie has proved that women are just as capable."

"I think I've proved women are far more fucking capable," I mutter, heaving a sigh. "It bothers me so much how patriarchal this world is. King Lobo seems to think he's entitled to this power more than I am, all because he's got a dick." I shake my head. "So, 120 people?"

"That's just the start, but yes. We also think that, provided Abel is apologetic and we can come to an agreement on Cain, that we keep Abel's fuck-up a secret." He rubs my shoulders. "You've got a strong friendship with Freya, and outside of this instance, Alaric and his Clan have been a good source of loyalty for us."

"I agree, to an extent. I think there needs to be some sort of checks and balances for his behaviour, and a very suitable punishment for it. If he were an Alpha wolf, what would the punishment be?"

"So, for a vow that you made with Abel, which is rare, there's some big punishments. The alliance we share would be broken, and he'd pay the price of that. He'd lose power and strength, just as a result, and likely forfeit his position. We'd be responsible for telling their other allies over the broken vow, and he'd probably lose those too. Another thing would be that he'd likely be punished by fate."

"It sucks being the leader, sometimes."

"It's better being the leader where you can illicit change, than one to suffer because you've got a bad leader." He tucks my hair out my face, and I smile at him. My chest is heavy with hurt, the actions of Abel pissing me off, but Caden's doing a very good job at keeping my anger at bay.

"I agree with keeping it hush. But only if Abel and Alaric are willing to support us in ending Cain."

Caden nods. "That was our opinion of it too."

There's a knock on the door, before it's thrown open, and Theo's standing in the doorway with a strained look on his face.

"What's wrong?" Caden demands, holding onto me as I try to get up.

"We've had another incident with transport," Theo says. I lean forward which is as much as Caden will let me move.

"What kind of incident?"

"The wolves that were being taken into custody are dead." He gives us a small shake of his head. "And so are the transport team."

"Well fuck," I mutter, clenching my fists.

"Mallon's on his way here, with some of his men," Theo continues. "We'll have company in about 12 hours."

"Brilliant," I say, smiling at him as nicely as I can when inside I'm fucking seething. "Why didn't we murder them when they were here again?"

Caden grunts, shaking his head. "I think it's—"

"Shut up," I demand, pushing his arms away and jumping to my feet. Both men frown at me, but I shake my head. I can hear Noah laugh in the other room, so I shout loudly for everyone to shut up. I can feel the tension rising, all of them judging me.

But I need to focus.

I can hear him coming.

His legs pounding as he races through the trees.

His breath in small pants as he conserves oxygen.

But most of all, I can feel his rage, and I just know it's directed at me.

CHAPTER 9

"What's wrong?" Caden whispers.

"Abel is on his way here," I say, and both their eyes widen. I pull all of my power to me, levelling it up ready for the ultimate drop. "Drop the barriers just enough to let him in."

"Are you sure?" Theodore asks.

"No," Caden says, shaking his head. "He's probably coming here to hurt you, Lottie—"

"We do not have the time to argue," I snarl. "Pull down the barriers, or I'll do it myself."

Caden's eyes flash black, and he glares at me. "We are not done talking about this."

"We're really not," I say, with a sigh, as I overpower the barriers surrounding the pack and pull them down. The moment he's in pack boundaries, I shove them back up, transferring the power back to my Alpha mates and Warren. Caden's fuming, and when both Noah and Rhett come charging into the room, I know they can feel it too.

"You can have your pound of flesh," I say, and that pauses them for a second. "But I'll be going first." I walk over to the doorway, looking up at the hulking Alpha who won't budge. "Rhett, move, or I'll move you."

"She's very fucking good at that," Caden snarls, giving me a hurt look. The act tugs at my wolf, a desperate edge to soothe him, but I push it down. This isn't the time to coddle my Alpha's feelings.

It's the time to put an angry vampire in his place.

"We can talk about this *later*," I say, hissing out the word. "But either get on my side, and do this as a united front, or I'll do it by myself."

It takes a beat, which pisses me off because Abel's so close and we don't have the time to debate this. But then Rhett moves, and as I leave the room, Noah and Caden flank my sides. Theo and Rhett are just behind us, with the others coming out of the rooms to assist.

Warren, Elijah, and River can likely feel Abel's energy, recognising him from their time in the Clan, but I know Scottie is here with us too. Before I can warn someone to help her, the door slams below, and there's a whoosh of air.

Abel comes to a stop at the end of the corridor, his eyes pitch black as he looks at me.

"Liar, liar, little Luna."

"Don't make this mistake, Abel," I counter, giving him one chance to concede.

He spits on the floor in front of him, and my wolf has decided that's her limit. We throw a lot of raw power at him, forcing him to submit, going even further than just getting him to show us his neck. He falls to his knees, and lets out a cry of pain, as his vampire rolls over.

I walk forward, keeping my hold on him, and crouch down in front of him. Caden grabs Abel by the hair, tugging his head back, so he looks in my eyes.

"Make no mistake, Abel. Your brother is a dead man," I say, softly. "But your life doesn't need to be over."

"Fuck you," he grunts out.

I shrug, rising to my feet. My nails have shifted into claws, and I'm one breath away from shifting. My legs are shaking, my skin crawling with the urge to shift. My wolf and I are in tune with each other, and our anger. I knew that Abel would come with this attitude, but it doesn't mean I was any further prepared.

"Drag him into the office," Noah demands as Theo and Warren move forward. Abel opens his mouth, and I flood him with more power, cutting off his ability to speak. His body is fighting against me, trying to overpower me no matter how futile it is, but because he's not strong enough, he can't do anything but mentally fight.

He can't speak, and he can't fight against my men carrying him away.

I catch sight of Scottie's face as I turn back around, and I see fear in her face. She's pale, and her eyes are wide.

The problem is... She's not looking at *me* in fear.

But Abel.

"Scottie," I call, but as soon as she looks at me, it's gone. I slowly walk over to her and reach out hesitantly. "Are you okay?"

"Perfect. Could you send Elijah back over once you have a minute?"

I keep my face passive, but I know she's lying. I saw the fear, and I can still see it. Her face might've hardened up, and she might've adopted a forced calm about her, but her eyes still tell the truth.

She's scared of Abel.

"I can," I say, and she nods. "But you can talk to me. Why are you so nervous?"

She shakes her head, a bemused smile tugging across her lips. "Do you know how powerful you are right now? How intimidating that is? My wolf and vampire want to bend over and submit, and you're being *nice* to me. Battling them and trying to ignore the panic, it's a little overwhelming, that's all."

"Right." I want to press her further, and I will, but Abel's not going anywhere for a while. I've got time. "I'll send Elijah in."

She nods, and goes back to the room her and Eli were utilising. It doesn't escape my notice that this time she closes the door. Lexie' watched the interaction, and I gesture with my head to the door. She nods, and I know she'll handle it whilst I can't.

I turn and follow the rest of the men into the room, and I can hear the annoyance from Rhett as he snarls some scathing words at Abel. He can't reply, but there's a lot of hatred in his eyes. If he stopped fighting me, he'd be able to actually fight his case.

As worthless as that would be.

"You had numerous opportunities to fulfil your end of the oath and support your brother," I say, walking into the room. Everyone falls silent, but I ignore all the eyes as I advance into the room.

"We'll be all right in here gentleman," Caden says, and the enforcer heads leave the room. Malcolm and my dad don't budge, but Caden doesn't push it. I'm not sure where Katie and Sophie are, but they're not in the building.

That leaves my mates, my dad, Malcolm, and River in the room with Abel and I, and they spread out covering the spaces near any kind of exits.

"Cain is working with someone called King Lobo," I say, adding a tiny little bit extra power to the attack on Abel's systems. "I'm guessing he's a wolf, but at this point, I don't know. The man is unhinged, and like your brother, wants the power I now hold. It doesn't take a genius to say he's planning on taking it forcibly when I refuse."

Abel fights harder, his vampire writhing and twisting as he tries to shove my power away. His body on the other hand is perfectly still, unable to do more than breathe to keep itself going.

"Cain tried to weaken me with an amulet," I say, and Abel's vampire tightens, the fighting stopping for a brief moment, before fighting harder. I eye Theo, and my mate unsurprisingly pulls it out of his pocket.

"Have you seen this before, Abel?" Theo asks, handing the necklace over to Noah who is right by me.

Abel's eyes dart to it, and his vampire stops fighting completely.

"See, I have never seen it before in my life until we recovered it the day your brother attacked my mate," Noah says.

"So she says." His voice is steady, even through his exhaustion.

"So I say. Did you know it's pure wolfsbane? That, if I were weaker, it could've killed me?" I ask. Abel doesn't react, but I don't need him to. I'm dealing with the vampire within, and the volatile creature is not as good at playing politics as his human. "So, you did. You've seen this before." Another non-answer from Abel, but his vampire reveals the truth. "You know that Cain is the only one who could've brought it here."

"No," Abel says. "Anyone in the family could have."

"I see. So, if not Cain, which of your family brought an instrument onto my lands, in the attempt to hurt one of my wolves? If Cain didn't use it on me, who was it going to be used on? Which member of your family would do something so reckless? Why would they betray the oath?"

Abel rises to his feet unsteadily, and glares at me. "You're trying to twist me, Charlotte, and it won't work. My brother is innocent of your lies."

"Did you go to him, Abel, or did he come to you?" I ask, and he frowns. "We knew it was a vampire far sooner than we knew it was Cain. In fact, we only found it was him the moment he dragged me from my mates and took me to a house just off pack lands. But once there, he admitted everything. He talked about how he deserves the power I hold. He'd never harm Freya, but me? I'm nothing. Your brother is deranged. His death is coming—the question is, who is going to deliver the killing blow?"

"You're a liar. We took you in, we groomed you, we helped you. Over and over, we've endangered ourselves, *our sister*, to help you. And this is what you do to us?" Abel demands.

"You would dare question my mate?" Caden roars, finally losing his cool. He storms forward, and both Rhett and Noah immediately

93

move to flank his sides. I can feel how furious my dad is, a few metres behind them, the antsy edge to him showing how close his shift is, but he knows this isn't his battle to fight.

He maintains a hold on himself as my Alphas take the floor and unleash their rage. The three of them together are formidable, but the Viotto heir doesn't even flinch. The four of them are all roughly the same height, my mates a bit bulkier than him—*a lot bulkier in Rhett's case*—but power wise, they're not too far off being an equal match. Back before I took these powers, before I had completed my mate bonds properly, Abel was securely ranked around River's level in terms of power.

But now that our mating circle is complete, and I've got all this ancient power running through me... I have no doubt each of my Alphas would tear Abel apart alone.

So together? He's got no chance. I think it would be a good fight, if I was into all the blood and gore dripping down their bare chests, but victory would go to my men.

It only shows his foolishness that he's not backing down. He's so far gone, he can't even listen to his own instincts. This isn't a matter of truth anymore—it's a matter of pride. And we all know that men cling to their pride because they're too afraid to apologise.

It's mortifying really.

For the men.

"I'm not questioning your mate's story," Abel says, but where Caden, Noah and Rhett relax ever so slightly, I don't. Instead, I call in the reinforcements we need, because this man isn't playing games. I could drag Cain here to admit the truth and I still don't think Abel would back down. Abel's eyes harden, and he looks at me with a sneer. "I'm flat out calling her a liar."

And then the fight erupts. It's almost like I predicted it coming to blows.

Caden doesn't hesitate in launching himself at the vampire, and I withdraw my influence enough to let him fight back. Abel takes the boon I offered and immediately zooms away. That enrages the wolves, and both Rhett and Noah shift, their large forms growling at the man who smirks at them.

Unsurprisingly, it's Theo who ends it. I just thought he'd let at least one of my Alphas get a hit in first. Even I wasn't going to stop until then—that's why I gave Abel his power back. Theo stamps his feet, yanking all four men to a stop, using barriers to trap them in place.

He can only do this because it's in my defence, which only makes the action that much more attractive. He rolls his sleeves up, showing off those beautifully tanned forearms, and glares at the four men. I don't know whether he forces it or if they do it on their own, but Noah and Rhett shift back into their human forms, crossing their arms in front of their chests in an identical move.

"It's quite easy to prove otherwise," I say, when the room falls silent. I can feel their power, and I'm very reassured now. "Roman's more than capable of searching my mind and sharing my truth with you."

"My sister is lovable, but far too fooled by you."

"Right," I say, with a nod. "Lovable but foolish. At least I know what to say at your funeral."

Freya zooms into the room, her black hair flying behind her, and she comes to a sudden stop in front of her brother. He glares down at his sister, not flinching at her sudden arrival. He really is fucking foolish.

"This is official Viotto business, little sister. Go back to the Clan."

She raises an eyebrow, cocking out her hip. "And I'm no longer a Viotto?"

"This is official *Hearthstone* business."

"So, what? You're kicking me out of the clan?" Freya asks, with a snooty tone of voice. Her mates come in behind her, the twins Hudson and Hunter surprising me the most in their frustration. Roman, Jeremy, and Ambrose are very affiliated with negativity. The twins? They're so much more upbeat.

Right now, they're carrying some dark energy around them— enough to raise even *my* hackles.

They're showing the dark side to their angels, and it's quite thrilling.

Or at least, it is since I know we're on the same side.

They nestle in amongst my men, and I'm surprised when Caden gives them a firm nod. Theo's still holding the Alphas and Abel in a barrier, which at this point is probably best for Abel's safety. Freya's the biggest threat to him. The rest of my mates are tense and ready for a fight, and Malcolm's standing a little too close to my dad for him not to be prepared to pull him back.

"Three of my mates have abilities within the mind," Freya says, tilting her head as she looks at him. Her voice is full of scorn. She's as short as I am, glowering down at a man a foot taller, but we all know she could bring him to his knees. So why is he acting so fucking stupidly? "Four, if you count the dark one."

"We don't," Roman and Jeremy say as one. I personally would count the dark one.

Freya smirks, but doesn't acknowledge their words. "Are you truly saying that I'd choose Lottie over my brother, Abel?"

"Yes."

Freya nods, letting out a small chuckle. "Okay, fair enough. She's the only one I'll have when you lot die, so I need to be nice to her, but still. Cain's my blood. That counts for something. Well, it did before he fucked everything up."

"Freya," Roman soothes, tugging his frantic and angry mate into his arms. "Breathe, little muse, breathe."

"Our brother is worthless," Freya says, quietly. "And if I get my hands on him first, I'll drain him of his blood, leaving just enough so that he's still alive, so that when I do carve his heart out, he'll feel the fucking pain."

Abel glares at her. "That's treason, little sister."

"Try me on it, *big brother*," she spits, pushing away from Roman. The incubus sighs, but lets her go, and she flicks her hair over her shoulder, slapping his face. He smiles indulgently, although I think some of her mates are wary of her snapping and killing her brother. Her aura darkens, her power seeping up, and she's fucking terrifying.

Abel doesn't cower back, but I can see the fear etched on his face. I just don't think he's scared for himself.

"If my word isn't good enough, and my memories tainted," I say. "Then there's no way I'm going to convince you."

"You could—"

"No, you misunderstand," I say, shaking my head as I step up next to Freya. Her vampire is so close to attacking her brother, and I know that would devastate Freya if she actually hurt him. Maybe not immediately, but once she calmed down, she'd be a wreck. "I'm not going to sit here and waste my time and effort on someone who can't understand the truth. For someone who is so stupid, he's letting something as measly as *shared blood* be the thing that costs him everything."

Abel's mouth opens, but I growl at him. I'm not fucking done.

"It's pathetic, Abel. For a man as distrusting as you, to just believe the shit your baby brother spouts. But where is he? Is he here now with you, trying to convince your parents that I'm insane?"

Abel hisses, fighting against the hold he's trapped in. "Cain's terrified."

I scoff, rolling my eyes. "Yeah, terrified that I'm going to kill him."

"Yes, actually."

"I've never killed anyone or anything in my life," I say, stepping forward to glare at him. "Why would he be the one I started with just for shits and giggles?"

Abel hisses again, his eyes flashing black briefly. "Now that you have the power of an original, why wouldn't you go for two?"

"Why would she target Cain if that were the case?" Freya asks, looking at me as if her brother is stupid. I shrug, not really sure how to reply.

"I've had enough of this," Theo says, with a sigh. "Roman, do me a favour and show him the truth, or I'm going to release these three Alpha wolves, and see who comes out on top."

Roman eyes Freya, who nods. He teleports behind Abel and gives Theo an impatient look.

"Do not move," Freya warns her brother. "I mean it. I'll break your fucking legs if you try."

"And I'll rip one from his body and give it to the wolf," Hunter says, with a smile. "We had plans before your family drama interfered."

Freya chuckles, and Abel tenses but doesn't argue. As Theo drops the barrier on all of the men, Noah comes to stand by my side. He reaches for my hand, squeezing it. He seems to need the comfort more than I do.

"I love you," I say silently, stepping a little bit closer to him. Abel grunts when Roman's hands dig into his temple, and based on Freya's snort, he's definitely done that on purpose.

"I love you more. Even when you act foolishly."

"It wasn't foolish." My protests are ignored by Noah, but he tosses me a grin to show he's not truly mad. I eye his twin, who won't look in my direction. *Well, at least one of them isn't mad.*

Abel's face pales as he's still in the vision, and when Roman steps back, Abel's eyes train on me. They're blacker than the night sky, and the vampire within is furious.

"He tried to kill you." His disinterested tone doesn't match his fury. "He tried to hurt those in your pack." He takes a step forward, ignoring the warning growls from my mates. "He tried to harm this pack, *where my mate resides*." He shakes his head. "Cain's dead, Luna. His head will be delivered to you tonight."

And then he's gone.

CHAPTER 10

I could've stopped Abel from leaving, but I don't try. Instead, I lower the barriers for a moment to let him leave our lands. I'm not sure I trust him, and he's definitely not doing this for noble reasons, but if one of my wolves is his mate... I absolutely can't let my mates kill the next leader of the Hearthstone Clan.

Even if I think he still deserves it.

"You fucking asshole," Freya roars, but there's only silence. She turns to me with a smile, most of her anger gone now that her brother is no longer in the room. "Okay, I'll be back, I swear. But I refuse to let Abel hold the fact that he killed Cain over my head for the next fifty years. Imagine the funeral? *Here lies Cain, murdered by Prince Abel, for the saviour of our good friend and ally Luna Montgomery.* Yeah, no, fuck that shit."

"There's some stuff you should know—" I start, but she waves me off. She speeds across the room to Hunter, and he blinks them out of existence. Slightly rude, even if she's excited.

I turn to her more rational mate, but Roman's smile is far too cute for him to be of use.

"We've got mind readers in our camp, Luna," Jeremy says, with a tense smile my way. "I guarantee we already know what you're going to share. I promise, we'll be back soon."

And then the rest of her mating circle are gone too, without even a goodbye.

"They're so fucking cocky," Warren mutters, coming to the centre of the room where Noah and I are standing. He swings his arm around my shoulder, giving me a side-hug. "You good?"

"He's a prick," I say, and Warren laughs. "But yes."

"He's always been that way," River says, shaking his head. "Even when we were kids, he always had that sense of self-superiority."

"He has," Warren agrees, in that snobby way of his where he looks down on those he considers beneath him. In this instance, I'm not going to argue. "But where River means it in a probably nice way, I do not. He's always been a fool, and—"

"How are you feeling?" Theo asks me. Warren rolls his eyes, but nobody pays him much mind. I shrug, smiling at Theo with a sheepish sort of look. He reaches over to heal away that pesky headache that's returned, and I instantly feel the cool relief and lack of pain. I swear, this pregnancy, we're staying joined at the hip.

"Thank you," I say, and he leans in past Noah and Warren to kiss my forehead.

"Don't be doing that in front of me," my dad snaps, and Wyatt smirks.

"Yeah, Toe-odore," Wyatt says, kicking Theo's leg. "Don't be doing that shit in front of her dad."

I roll my eyes and lean into Warren. "Where do we go from here?"

"I'm very curious about this mate of his," Noah says, looking at Caden. "Do you know anything about that?" He shakes his head, but to my surprise Elijah nods.

"Leave that to me," Elijah says, turning and walking out of the room. I frown after him, not liking the distance between us at the moment. We're both being pulled apart by all the things we need to do, and we've not spent much time reconnecting outside of it all.

My wolf whines, and I make a silent promise to her that we'll figure something out going forward. I think this trip, as frustrating as it sounds, is going to be a good thing for my relationship with Elijah. We'll be together with fewer outward distractions.

You know, if you ignore the madman trying to kill us and the hundreds of people that are going to be demanding my attention.

"So, what the fuck do we do now?" Dillon asks, rubbing the back of his neck as he repeats my question in a much less diplomatic way. I eye the former Gamma, and his stress levels are high. My wolf bristles against his, and I send healing. "Ordinarily I'd say let's alert Alaric and Cassie..."

"We'll do that anyway," Rhett says, taking control. "Theo, that's your job. They like you best, and you can navigate the political waters with them." My Guardian nods, but he's clenching his jaw as he does it. "River, go track your brother down and find out what you can about this mate of Abel's. I want answers before he returns." River nods, and with one searing look sent my way, he's gone. My wolf's lack of reaction breaks my heart. But that's okay. I can react enough for us both. "Wyatt, call Charles and let him and Evan know what's gone down. Evan, in particular, might have some advice."

Wyatt nods and gives me a grin, before turning and leaving the room. He hums as he goes, the joyful nature taking me by surprise.

"Good thinking," Noah says, and Rhett sighs and nods.

"I want that family covered, since vampires going rogue is not a good look when they're one of our strongest allies."

"Not when we're the ones who drove them crazy," Warren says with a smirk. I roll my eyes as Theo heads out of the room. "What about the rest of us?"

"Lottie, you and your dad need to talk," Caden says, and I give him a dirty look. Does he really think *now* is the best time for me to drop this news on him? "Or you and I can have that talk about dangerous activities, if you'd rather."

"No, I'm good for now," I mutter, causing Caden to shake his head and Noah to snort. Rhett's impassive, and I get the feeling he'll be on Caden's side when this comes to blows. I turn and smile at my dad, who tries to muster up a smile but fails. He probably thinks I'm going to lay into him further about me acting as Luna for his pack.

I'm going to kill Rhett for that.

"Can we talk?"

"Always," he says, with a small frown. "Malcolm, check in with our pack, and make sure things are okay over there."

"Can do," Malcom says with a nod. He winks at me. "It's always fun with you around, little Luna."

I roll my eyes, and accept my dad's arm as we leave the room together. I'm not sure what my Alphas are going to be doing, but I get the feeling I don't want to know. With Mallon coming tomorrow, we're going to be run off our feet with anxiety. And I'm not borrowing any extra to sprinkle on top of the anxiety-ridden time I'm already suffering through.

We walk down the stairs, both of us lost in our own thoughts, and go sit in the garden attached to the building. It's quite small and peaceful, and I've only been in here one other time. I move to sit on the swinging chair.

"Do I need to be standing for this?" my dad asks, raising an eyebrow.

I laugh and shake my head, patting the seat next to me. "I'm not mad at you, dad."

"You should be. You were right. We should've had a conversation about you taking over as Luna," he says, moving to sit on the chair with me. He rocks us gently, and I'm torn between appreciating it for being soothing, and hating it for spiking a bout of nausea.

Why doesn't the healing Theo do last very long? Why are my pups determined to make me feel ill?

And is this just a placebo effect? I was fine before I knew they were really there.

"Maybe, but we're making do," I say, softly. "Things are just difficult all around right now. I'm handling your pack."

"You are. But, despite the terrible way he went about it, Rhett brought up a good point. Malcolm, your grandparents, and I can handle the pack, *but* we'll probably need some extra help."

"We've got plenty of time to figure it out." He nods, patting my knee. "Do you think mum gets to see us?"

"I know for a fact that she does. I dreamt of her the other week," he says, and I turn to face him properly.

"You did? Why didn't you say?"

"Because it was a dream for me," he says, teasingly. "I'm not sure if it was real or not, but I like to think it was. She's proud of you."

"I know."

"You would," he concedes, grinning. "You're so powerful."

"I am."

"This wasn't the future I planned for you," my dad whispers, tugging me closer to his side. His warmth reassures me, even if his words are a little morbid. He swings his legs a little more, moving the swing a little higher. "I really wanted you to live a good life, Lottie. I wanted you to be happy and thrive, and get everything you wanted." He sounds like he's holding back tears, and it breaks my heart hearing this.

My wolf howls, her upset echoing mine. My dad's wolf doesn't feel this way, so I know this is one of the times where the human emotions are too strong for the wolf.

"I do have a good life," I say softly. "And I mean that. Even with all of the danger and the sadness, all of the pain and suffering... I still have so many good things happening. I'm happy dad. Truly." He nods, sniffling, but doesn't look my way. "Can I tell you something?"

"You can tell me anything." It's such a deep and serious tone, and he pulls away to turn to face me properly. I hate all the tension he's carrying, despise the stress lines marring his face, but the amount of love in his eyes soothes the balm on my soul.

I bite my lip, as his anticipation rises, and I just blurt it out. "I'm pregnant."

And then his jaw drops, literally. His green eyes widen, and he looks at my stomach, before looking back at me, multiple times. I think his brain has frozen. I daren't breathe, just in case, but then he grins. "Really?"

"Really," I whisper, tears pricking at my eyes. I clutch my t-shirt at the neckline, fidgeting with the seam. "We're having twins."

"Twins?" he gasps, tentatively reaching out to touch my stomach but his hand just hovers there. His eyes fill with tears, and I let out some half-laugh sobs as I nod. "You're having babies."

"Babies," I repeat, with a grin.

"Babies." He echoes my word, wiping away a tear. "My baby is having babies."

"Things might be dark, dad, but they're not fully empty. There's brightness coming, we just need to figure out a way to be there to see it."

"Well, that was morbid," he mutters, before jumping to his feet. His exuberant mood is catchy, and I don't even try to wipe the grin off my face. My dad tugs me up with him, squeezing my hands, as he all but bounces up and down. "I'm so proud of you."

Bit of a weird reaction, but still supportive. I launch myself at him, and he swings me around, wrapping his arms tight around me in a hug. He kisses my hair, and I both laugh and cry as I cuddle him just as tight.

"I love you," I whisper, into his chest.

"I love you more," he replies, kissing the top of my head. "Are you sure this is the right move?" And there's my good mood gone. He senses the change and puts me down on my feet, and I skulk back over to the swing. I tuck my feet underneath me, getting comfortable, as I look around the open garden.

"Nope. But it's better than hiding out here, and waiting for them to come to us. At least if we're on the offensive, the ball is in our court."

"But we could have a very strong defence."

"And how many more people will we lose, dad?" I ask.

He shakes his head. "As long as it's not you that I lose, I'd sacrifice everything."

"Good thing I won't then. My pack, my people, they're important to me. I won't play frivolous games with their lives, just to try and make mine less inconvenient. Fate gave me this life because she wants me to make the changes necessary for us to *thrive*."

"You're a mother now, Lottie. You need to put your children first." His words are a plea, the fear pouring out of him, making it apparent why he's acting like all I'm good for is staying home in the kitchen. That's an admirable choice, when it *is* a choice.

But it's never going to be the kind of life I live. "I want to be the kind of mother that my children look up to. I want them to know that the world is a better place because I made it so. If I have daughters, I want them to grow up knowing they're entitled to a place in the world, just like any man is." I rise to my feet, feeling my wolf push forward to merge with me. "If I have sons, they'll be taught that women are to be respected, that they're powerful in their own regard, and they'll be good men."

My power increases, just as the wind picks up ever so slightly. It ruffles my skirt, and teases my hair, and seems to agitate my dad some more.

"But I won't ever *ever* teach my children that it's okay to settle. I have the power to make the changes, and I will make this a better place. It'll be better for the victims abused by their Alphas. It'll be better for the women disregarded and blocked from reaching their full potential. It'll be better for those with *true* power, that the Council then ignores." I raise my hands, the pink glow surprising me, but not scaring me, as I look at my dad who is terrified. "I'm a powerful wolf, dad, and it's my job to end this."

"It never should've been your job."

"Maybe not, but fate seemed to think I'm worthy."

"Fuck, Charlotte, I'm not doubting your worth," my dad gasps, charging towards me despite all the sparks flying off me, despite the raw power that's clinging to my skin. "I want to protect you. That urge you feel to power up your children, to give them the best life possible? That's how I feel right now."

I grimace. "Oops."

"I love your justice rants, but I wish you had some self-preservation."

"I've got self-preservation." My protests are ignored.

He kisses the top of my head. "I'm so proud of you."

And I swear I can hear the echo from my mum, saying the exact same thing.

CHAPTER 11

My dad takes his leave with Malcolm and my grandparents as we head back into the building. As much as he wants to be part of this, he admitted that he's not going to be much help, when all he wants to do is tear Abel's head from his shoulders.

A smart move, to pull himself out of it, and I promised that someone would let him know what's happened.

"Lottie," Elijah calls. I turn, and give him a smile, noticing he's standing with Scottie. The brunette has red-rimmed eyes, but she seems calm enough. "Can we have a minute?"

"Sure," I say, walking past the room that my Alphas seem to be bickering in, and follow them into the office they've been using. "What's going on? Are you okay?"

"Come sit," Elijah commands, and my hackles raise, but I move and slide into the seat next to him. He places a reassuring hand on my knee, squeezing it gently. "Scottie's got something to share, and we're going to listen."

"And not blow our lids, got it."

They both laugh, but I wasn't joking. I know I react first, but sometimes it's too hard to ignore the instincts of my wolf. If she's pushing for justice, who am I to argue?

"Luna," Scottie says. "I... I think I can help you with Abel Viotto."

"I don't mean to be rude—" I start, wincing a little at the look she gives me. I promised to listen, not interrupt, or judge. "How can you help?"

She sighs, fidgeting with her fingers, in a move that's so unlike the woman I've come to know. I admire Scottie because she's so strong, so unabashed about sharing her thoughts and opinions. She went above and beyond to get this job and managed to take out three men, alone.

So, for her to be vulnerable, to show me the fear she's feeling, it pisses my wolf off. In this instance where she can't be strong, I can be strong for her. She's struggling with something, so I can help her.

I will help her.

My mate gives her a reassuring nod, as he squeezes my knee again.

"Abel... Abel is my mate." She sinks into her seat, letting her hair fall forward to cast a shadow over her face. "I don't know what went down between you and him, but I do know that he'll be unsettled with me here." Whether it's fake confidence or not, she tucks her hair back, and sits up straight, giving me a piercing look. "Abel fucked me over, and he's the reason I left my previous pack."

"How so?" I ask, tilting my head.

"Abel's friends with my new Alpha," she says, quietly. "Abel was going to come to the coronation, and I have no doubt he'd make things very uncomfortable for me there."

"Abel? The Alpha?"

"Both?" she immediately counters. "Abel doesn't want me, and if my being there was contingent on my new Alpha getting an alliance with Abel? I'd be removed from the pack, probably given some money as compensation."

"You truly believe he'd do that?" I ask. My heart is racing, my palms sweaty as I wipe them on my skirt.

"He's done it before," she says, quietly. "I was kicked out of my university due to Abel. It's a long story, but the moment he realised who I was to him, he did everything to destroy me and my credibility."

"So why did you come here?" I ask, confused. "It's not been a secret that we have a relationship with the Hearthstone Clan. Hell, Freya's been on pack lands a lot since you've been here."

"Two reasons. The first is that I had no doubt you wouldn't take Abel's shit," she says, giving me a hesitant smile. "And my previous Alpha was debating on approaching you, offering out my services, to try and garner an alliance. Your people were suffering, and it was something I was interested in helping with."

"What would you have done if we had said no that day?" I ask, quietly. My heart aches for the hybrid, her wolf and vampire's pain are so strong. Scottie might be sitting here calmly talking this out, but her other sides are not. They're in agony at the fact that their mate doesn't want them.

That he hurt them, multiple times. The vampire is reluctant to share with my wolf, but her wolf doesn't hide a single thing. She's scared, pained, exhausted.

She just wants her human to be happy.

"I had other plans in the pipeline. Yours were just the desirable one," she says, softly. "So, I have no idea what is truly going on with Abel and the Hearthstone Clan, but my presence at the very least can unsettle him enough that he might... make a mistake? I don't know." Her eyes are filled with her pain, but her smile is bright as she speaks now. "I just... seeing him today, seeing how easily you bested him, it gave me confidence I've not had in a very long time."

"Abel's issue is that her vampire isn't strong enough," Elijah says. "He doesn't want a hybrid mate, especially one who is more dominant as a wolf."

"I see." I sigh. "I'm sorry. It's worthless, but that's all I've got. What we're about to say can *not* leave this room." My words are underlined with a command from my wolf to hers, and she nods. "On the day of the attack, I called Abel and asked for help. He pledged his Clan to me, should I ever need their aid, and he failed to deliver."

"Shit." She's pale, her heart beating erratically, and she clutches at her shirt. "He's... what kind of vow?"

"We're not going to kill your mate, Scottie," Elijah says, softly.

"I really shouldn't care," she mutters, glaring at the table. "I should be happy that I'll get to be free."

"What do you mean that you'll get to be free?" Eli's using his therapist voice here, gently coaxing her into opening up. But I can feel the tension thrumming through him.

"Don't you already know?" she asks, looking at him. "I've met my mate, and just because he doesn't want me, doesn't mean that I don't want him. Logically, I hate the man. My human side knows that and can understand the damage and destruction that he's doing to me. But my wolf and vampire pine after him. I don't find other men attractive, not really, and there's no chance I could move on and be happy with someone, knowing he's out there, potentially going to ruin it. It's weak and pathetic, I know."

I gasp, and look up at Elijah, whose face is passive, but I know he knows the feeling. "That doesn't make you weak Scottie. It makes you strong, that you're still living your life."

She shrugs. "So... can I help, or was this all for nothing?"

"We've found who my stalker is," I say, biting my lip. Elijah leans in and kisses my temple, before taking the lead on this.

"Cain Viotto has been tormenting Lottie under the command of a madman. We haven't shared everything with the pack, but we're identifying the group the best we can, so that we can prevent them from harming Lottie and our pack."

She nods, and it amazes me how she doesn't even flinch. Abel holds command over her fear, and he's the only thing that seems to rattle her. "I understand. I trust in your Luna, I know that we'll be safe."

I grimace, and nod.

"Abel doesn't think that Cain had any involvement," Eli continues. "He refused to send any help to us, because he thought Lottie was lying about Cain's involvement. Even when told the truth, he didn't decide to help until he knew you were here."

"How did he know I was here?" she demands.

Eli and I exchange looks, and I shake my head. Elijah sighs.

"That is a secret the Viotto family hold dear. We can't break our oaths by sharing." Elijah truly does sound apologetic, but Scottie's not very impressed. "However, the moment he knew, he left the pack to track down his brother for us."

"Why?" She's gobsmacked.

"Because Cain was part of the reason we were attacked," I say, softly. "And Abel was not impressed that you were here when it happened."

She slumps back in her seat, shock filling her face. "I don't... I don't understand. That, no, sorry, no. He what?"

"I think his exact words were 'he tried to harm this pack where my mate resides'," I say, and Elijah nods. "I don't know your history, but I want you to be aware that his tune seems to have changed. He's not pushing you away anymore, or at least, I don't think he's going to."

"No, it sounds like he wants me now," she whispers, her hand shaking as she lowers it to her lap. "If I can help, I will, but I won't ever put myself back into his life."

"Nobody would ask you to," Eli reassures her. "Why don't you head home?"

"We've got far too much to do," she replies, shaking her head. "I'll go pick up something for us to eat, then we can continue going through this. We'll need to start interviews as soon as possible, with you guys leaving soon."

"Monday?" Eli asks, looking at me.

"Hopefully, Monday will work," I say. "It depends on how the visit with the Council goes."

"What if we don't do them here at our pack?" Scottie asks.

"Good idea. I can check in with my dad and see if he'd be okay with us using Golden Eclipse. We're not expecting issues from any of the applicants."

Elijah nods. "I'll see how soon people can arrive, but Monday should be doable for everyone. How soon can they start?"

"That's up to you," I say, looking up at him. "Just let me, Lionel or River know." He nods, and Scottie heads out to pick up some food. I think she needs the time alone more than she wants to eat, so neither Eli nor I protest.

"How's today been?" I ask.

"How are things with River working out?" he asks at the same time. I laugh. "Sorry, sunshine. Come here." He lifts me from my chair to his lap, and presses a soft kiss to my lips. "I'm worried about leaving."

"I know. I can imagine why." I cup his cheek, and lean forward to press my lips to his. His kiss was sweet, but I don't want sweet right now. His lips are chapped, the rough feeling tickling me. Our lips meet, and in that instant, a rush of emotion floods through me. His vulnerability and pain intertwine with my own feelings, mirroring them in an unexpected way. It's not just a physical kiss, it's an exchange of our souls.

His hands grab my waist, pulling me closer, and I respond in kind, wrapping my arms around his neck. Our bodies press together, and his rapid heartbeat matches mine. He's so warm, so loving.

"I've missed you," I whisper against his lips. Tears prick at my eyes, but I don't care.

His lips move with a gentle urgency, as if trying to convey all the unspoken words between us. Our souls have merged as one, and the world fades away, leaving only this kiss, this connection. His vampire melds with my wolf so perfectly.

"I've missed you too," he says, through laboured breaths. His pupils are dilated, his lips wet, and he grins at me. "I love you." I pull away from him, and a profound sense of reassurance washes over me. He's here with me. I rest my forehead against his.

"I'm here for you," I whisper, my voice full of sincerity. "Whatever you need."

"Whatever they need," he adds. I nod, and I can feel his gratitude building, as a relieved smile flits across his face. "Go on a date with me."

"What?"

He nods. "We've not done that. I want to change that. Go on a date with me."

"Eli, we've got— "

"I don't care," he says, leaning forward to kiss me once more. "We're always going to have something more. Hell, in nine months, we'll have twins and you'll have ninety more excuses."

"They're not excuses," I whisper, a pang of hurt hitting me.

"Maybe not malicious ones," he counters. "I've been so busy with the pack, that I've neglected you."

"I could say the same about myself."

"I *am* saying the same about you," he teases, and I roll my eyes. "I know you're busy this weekend with Mallon coming, but what about next Friday?"

"Friday it is."

He beams at me. "Thank you." I roll my eyes, but before I can admonish him for thanking me, he takes my breath away.

I don't think this is what they meant by mouth-to-mouth.

"There you are," River says, appearing in the doorway. I freeze, and Elijah lets out a low sigh as he sits back. He's not as unsettled as the rest of my mates would be, but I can feel his vampire bristling. "Sorry."

"Don't be," I say, not looking away from Elijah. My curly-haired mate winks at me, before scooting up properly. "Who were you looking for?"

"Well, both of you really. Caden asked me to come find you once you were done with your dad, and I was tasked with finding out about Abel's mate for Rhett," River says.

"They can't fire you and then boss you about," I mutter, and River laughs as he comes into the room. "I don't let them boss Lionel or Lexie about."

"You're so possessive over your people," Elijah teases, twirling my hair around his finger.

"She's pretty possessive in general," River says, and they both laugh. I roll my eyes, but my wolf seems to nod her head. "So, Scottie?"

"Scottie. She's willing to help us, but she doesn't want to be with him," Elijah says.

"What the hell has he done to make her so angry?"

I move over into my seat, pretending to myself that it's a dignified move. Neither comment, but there's still that air of awkwardness. I don't know if River and I will ever get our bond back, but no matter how hard we try... I'm not sure my mates will ever get over their own unhappiness with the situation.

Sure, they all claimed that they were happy to try, but their animals, their vampires, are not on the same wavelength with that at all. Their wolves see me flirting with another man, their vampires see a man not in our bond receiving my time and blood, and none of them are happy.

I wish it wasn't so awkward.

"He doesn't want her because her wolf is more dominant than her vampire," I say, and River sighs. "Is that... common?"

"Hybrids are often more dominant in one than the other, depending on the strength of their parents. So, I had parents who were powerful, and pretty equal in terms of their dominance. Scottie's wolf is far more powerful than the vampire. She can get by with probably only a glass of blood a week."

"If that," Elijah says. "She's tried to give her vampire more in the past to try and boost her power, but it just makes the vampire ill."

River nods. "It's a delicate balance, especially in someone of her age. She's already had her vampire for over thirty years? How old is she?"

"32," Eli replies, when I don't. I didn't know that.

"So, there you go. She's had her vampire for 32 years and her wolf for 16. They've had this dynamic for so much of their life, and all of their adult life at that. It's not something that can then be changed, not really." River shrugs. "It's not an issue, not really. Unless you're Abel Viotto and think that being a wolf is scummy."

"I know someone is scummy," I mutter, and they both laugh. "Thank you for stepping in for me today."

"Happy to help," he says. "We've covered a lot, but I think it's going to keep us busy for the next couple of weeks."

"Once we pick out when we're going to start this, the better," Elijah says, and I nod.

"I think it'll depend on how things go with Mallon tomorrow, and also whether there are any more... surprises in the meantime. I wish it was something we could just start immediately..."

"You're an action girl," Elijah says, and I tilt my head considering that. "You like immediate results. You're great at planning, but you much prefer when something can be handled immediately."

"In an instance like this, absolutely. Our plan is to uproot the Council, find our enemy, and come home at the end of it all and have our babies," I say.

"And have our babies," River says, glaring at my stomach with a wistful look. I'm not sure how the lack of bond between us will affect his bond with our children, but there's no denying that he's their father, too. Maybe not biologically, but at the time of conception, the bond was there. "I hope we have girls."

"Fuck, I don't," Elijah groans, shaking his head. "Can you imagine any of our mating circle with girls?"

I burst out laughing. "I don't care what we have. They'll be the heir to the pack, though."

"If they're boys," River says, with a nod. He grimaces, knowing I won't agree, but at least he doesn't back down from his own thoughts and opinions.

I snort, rising to my feet. "These children were inside me when I took on the power of the original wolf. They have been prophesied to end the world as we know it. But sure, they're only worthy of running a pack if they've got a penis." I bend down and kiss Elijah's cheek, and round the table. I hesitate before doing the same to River. There's no change in Elijah's bond, but River smiles at me, as if that's made his entire day. "Good to know where their daddy stands."

River's eyes widen. I'm not going to pull punches when it comes to my children. Not now, not ever. I'll fight for them until they're able to fight for themselves, and then I'll fight by their side.

"I'll find out what our Alphas want," I continue. "But then I've got to go to the clinic."

"How long will the clinic take?" Elijah asks. "We're going to need another meeting to go over everything."

I sigh. "It's what time now?"

"Two," River answers.

"Give me until five. I might be a bit useless afterwards, but I'll make sure I'm coherent enough to talk."

"Can you, maybe, not go that far?" River asks. He sends a pleading look to Elijah, but the vampire just smirks and doesn't say anything. He won't either because he's quite willing to trust that I know my limits. River, however, often struggles to believe that I do.

Probably because I often don't.

"How far would you like me to go?"

He rolls his eyes before looking at Elijah again. "Want to weigh in, brother?"

"Not when you're doing such a good job." A very Warren reply from Elijah, and based on the way he winks at me, he knows it too.

"You're pregnant now. You can't exhaust yourself, when that may then affect the children."

"Which I understand," I say, gently. "But don't you think my wolf will be far more knowledgeable about things we can and can't do to protect our pups?"

He growls, his eyes flashing black, but I don't think he's angry. No... I think River likes the idea of me being pregnant. I wink at him, give the brothers a wave, and leave to go track down my other Alpha men. River's not the only one who will have a problem with me pushing limits.

He's just the only one who isn't going to kick up a *massive* fight about it.

CHAPTER 12

"You're late," Katie says, not looking up from her computer. She's changed clothes, no longer wearing the leggings she was when we were going over the files. She's wearing a pale pink blouse that's stolen from my wardrobe and a pair of white trousers. Her white doctor jacket is unbuttoned with the sleeves rolled up to her elbows, and she's got her name badge clipped to her waistband.

That's new. I wonder why that protocol has been implemented.

"You're wearing my blouse."

"Soon enough, you'll be too fat to fit into it," she teases, closing down her computer. I roll my eyes, and she grins. "I can't wait to see them. The mind reader may have ruined my announcement privileges, but please say you'll let me be the midwife?"

"You're a doctor."

"Even better for it."

I laugh. "I'll consider it. Sorry I was late. Rhett and Noah... it doesn't matter." She raises an eyebrow, but I shake my head. There's more than enough drama amongst my mates, that I'm happy enough to sit this one out. They're dealing with the external issues, whilst I handle the pack's well-being right now. "So, who is first again?"

"Kyrie. You wanted to check her over."

"Ah, perfect. Can you grab her whilst I run for a wee?" I ask, already moving to her private bathroom. My best friend laughs, but I ignore her teasing, and go use her toilet. I wash my hands, splash a bit of water on my face, and then head back into the main room.

Kyrie is thirty years old, pregnant with her third pup, and she just seems overall off to me. Her complaints have worried me and my wolf enough that we want to check things out.

"Hi, Kyrie," I say, with a smile.

"Hello, Luna." She dips her head, her voice soft. "Thank you for seeing me today."

"You're welcome. I've heard that you've been having some issues, and I wanted to just check things out."

"Should we be concerned?" Kyrie asks, looking at Katie. "You checked in on things the other day and weren't concerned."

"And I'm still not," Katie reassures her. "Lottie and I sit down and go over all the open cases, so that she can lend her expertise where it's needed. She's not had much experience with shifter pregnancies, and so with your issues, thought she could do two birds and one stone."

"Right," Kyrie says, but her tone wobbles as she drags out the 'i' sound.

"Science is one of my favourite things, and as much as I don't know a lot about human pregnancies, animal pregnancies are very intriguing to me. You have the hormonal changes, which affect so much more than you realise," I say, and she nods, eyeing Katie warily. "You've mentioned your exhaustion four times during this pregnancy."

"Yes, but that's normal," she says. "Right, Katie?"

"We found no abnormalities in your bloodwork."

"That's not the confirmation you gave at my last appointment," Kyrie says. She clutches her bag closer to her chest, and her wolf is in notable distress. I go to soothe her across our pack bond, but then I spot my issue. Well, her issue really.

But I've found what has my wolf wanting to look closer. The tiny pup inside this woman might not have access to his wolf yet, but he's still got the shifter traits, and he's a powerful wolf.

This is just like a parasitic pregnancy; we just didn't realise it. This woman has a baby who is going to be more dominant than she is, a baby which is more dominant than her wolf is prepared to handle. Her baby requires more nutrients, more energy, and more *life* than the mum can safely give.

"Your husband is more dominant than you," I say, and Kyrie frowns but nods. "Sorry, that wasn't a question. Your baby takes after your husband and will likely match or supersede his dominance levels."

"This isn't her first child," Katie argues, knowing where my mind has gone.

"This is your first son, though, correct?" I ask, and she nods. Katie sighs, more at being wrong than at my mind working this way. "Boy shifters are closer in tune with their wolves than females are at this gestation. Females have an additional nine years, roughly, before they get their wolves, whereas some boys only have seven years without a wolf before it makes its appearance."

"I don't understand," Kyrie says. "I'm worried. Can you please explain what's going on?"

"Your son is more powerful than your body is prepared for. This is your third pregnancy, and your wolf knows what to expect by now. However, you've been complaining of exhaustion, weakness, and even hair loss in both forms. Your son is taking so much energy from you, that you barely have enough to sustain yourself."

She flinches. "I've been eating more."

"We'll set you up with the dietician," Katie says. "Which will help make sure that we're getting you the right amount of calories, and even foods, to sustain you both."

"What needs to be done about this?" Kyrie asks.

"I've got two things I want to do," I say, pulling a pair of gloves on. "I want to give you a boost of power that isn't for you but for him. It'll be a reserve so that he takes what he needs from those."

"What's the other thing?" Katie asks.

"I want to check on your pup, to see how powerful he is, so that we can make sure to cover you properly."

She nods, and we get her situated on the bed. I have a feel of her stomach, and the tiny pup kicks in excitement. She flinches, and when I add to her energy, I realise how depleted she was. I leave a little extra, and she genuinely brightens in front of me.

Her light blue eyes were dull, but now there's a spark back in them. Her cheeks were sunken, her eyes littered with bags, but that's all faded away. She's gained some life back, some energy.

"Can you shift for me?" I ask. She's around six months pregnant, so being in her wolf form is still okay for her. Usually, once a woman enters the later stages of the third trimester, it takes too much of a toll on her and her wolf to consistently shift back and forth.

In this instance, she's brimming with energy, so it shouldn't take any toll whatsoever. Her shift is quick and fluid, and her wolf nudges my hand for affection. I grin, offering it in spades. She's mid-size, maybe a little shorter than my own wolf, but a bigger build. She has a tabby coat and is very sweet.

She's got some bald patches, and I can see areas where her coat is thinner. She's struggling. I give her wolf some love as I connect with her pup, and he's such a rambunctious spirit. My wolf is excited at feeling his energy, knowing soon enough, we'll be able to feel our own.

"You'll be okay," I say, stepping back once I've drawn a promise from the wolf to take things easier on his mum and gathered up the stores to protect her in the meantime. She shifts into her human form, and we discuss the signs that she needs another review with me, and Katie reassures her that they'll see each other again next week.

"You're good with them," Katie says once she's gone. "With patients."

"This was meant to be my job," I tease, and Katie laughs. This patient didn't require any healing, just some energy, and that's easily given along the pack bonds. The next patients are going to require actual healing, and I'm not sure how much it's going to take from me.

"You ready for Carmen?" Katie asks, and I nod. She returns a few moments later with an elderly lady within the pack, who has been struggling with recurrent aches and pains after shifting. I can heal it away once it becomes unbearable, and have done twice already for her, but they're repeatedly coming back.

"Hello dear," Carmen says, smiling at me. "I brought you some brownies this time. An entire tray of the salted caramel that you love, and a few blocks of the chocolate orange one that I've made."

"Thank you, Mrs. Taylor." She pops the tray onto the side counter for me, before coming to sit down. "How are we feeling?"

I sit down in the recliner next to her, so that Katie doesn't need to try and catch me if I stumble, and take Carmen's hand. She tells me about her pains, as I slowly heal her. The drain is immediate, even with these powers, but nowhere near as intense as it used to be. The only time I've ever managed to heal a lot of people at once was the night of Midnight Summit's second bombing, when my grief over my mum's death caused my powers to rush out and knocked me unconscious.

Since I'd like to avoid that happening again, I'm taking it slow.

Maybe with time, once I improve my skill with these new powers, it'll take barely anything from me to do this.

But for now, the drain is noticeable and exhausting. Katie manages to remove Carmen from the office quickly, since we're on such a time crunch, but the elderly lady is appreciative and leaves with a spring in her step. I work through the patients that Katie and I identified as having the greatest need, and it's been very different. I'm more powerful now, it's insane how much more powerful I am, but somehow, I'm still feeling drained.

After healing the four patients we've outlined, I can keep going, but I'd have thought I could handle it better. My wolf doesn't have any issues with us continuing so Katie reluctantly brings the next person in. We've got an hour left to go before I said I'd be back with my men, so we're needing to rush more.

One patient blurs into the next. Quite literally, too. My vision has gone fuzzy, and I feel very weak.

"I'm at my limit," I say, once that patient leaves the room. Katie turns to look at me, and groans. "I'm fine, just tired."

"They're going to kill me," Katie mutters. "You healed thirteen people tonight, babe. That's insane, even for you." As she speaks, she hands me a sports drink, uncapping the lid for me. I lift it to my lips, unsteadily, and manage to sip at it. "They weren't easy patients either. I think with some time and practice you'll be able to do double that."

"I agree." My voice portrays my exhaustion, and as I lower my arm, I drop the drink. I watch it roll onto the floor, dribbling juice everywhere. Katie doesn't even flinch.

"Let me call one of your men. Any requests?"

I sigh. "Um, no. Theo might be able to replenish my energy, but he'll probably berate me."

She snorts, as she bends down to pick up the bottle of cherry flavoured juice. "Yeah, probably. I'll call Theo though. He won't berate *me*. What's the plan?"

"We're now going to condense—"I pause to yawn, my body shaking with the extreme exhaustion, and I rest my head back on the chair. "Condense all the information. We've also got to plan for Mallon's visit tomorrow." Three yawns interrupted that sentence. I want a blanket and a nap, but unfortunately, we've got so much shit to cover.

Why would they launch an attack when we're this busy? He's been steadily increasing his efforts into tormenting us—Cain or King Lobo, I'm not really sure—but why did they attack when they did?

"What's that look for?" Katie asks, tucking her phone back in her jeans pocket. She didn't call Theo, which is a surprise. Katie hates texting if she can get away with it.

"I'm just musing things over. Wake me up when the rescue party gets here."

She nods, dimming the lights, and I let my eyes flutter shut. I'm not expecting to actually sleep, but even dozing might help me regain some energy for this discussion we're going to have.

Then again, fate has never, ever given me what I wanted.

"It's nice to see you again, granddaughter," Alpha says. My eyes fly open, and I groan. He's in his wolf form, standing there so majestically. His dark blue fur and tall build show he's nothing at all like a normal wolf, and he trots over to me with endless confidence. I wait for him to say something more, but he doesn't. I'm also surprised that he doesn't shift and talk to me either, since I know he's now allowed to do that.

The rules of this place are so confusing, so contradictory, and far too secret.

I cock my hip, trying to hold onto my annoyance as I look down at him. He plops on his ass in front of me, a foot or two away, and gives me a wolfish grin.

"Why did you bring me here?" I ask. Mentally I'm exhausted, physically I'm exhausted, and even if this realm doesn't permit exhaustion, the moment I'm returned to my body I'll pay for coming here in the first place. It's very frustrating when I didn't ask to be here, and they give me riddles and information I cannot decipher. "I'm not going to lie, but it's very inconvenient timing. My power is already depleted, and we have a lot to do."

"You're one of the most powerful creatures on the entire Earth right now. How does healing a few wolves drain you so badly?"

"Can you heal wolves?" I ask, frowning at his judgemental tone. He yips, and I can feel his indignation. "Yes, yes, you're dead I get it. *Could* you heal wolves before your untimely death?"

He shakes his head, growling low, deep in his throat. *"No."*

"I didn't think so. Healing those in my bond doesn't require much power, if any. Healing those outside my bond takes *a lot*. I healed a lot more today than I normally can handle, because of course there's a giant power increase. But even with doubling my power, my body isn't used to this amount so I can't push too fast, or I'll stall out."

"That makes sense, except you've not just doubled your power, granddaughter. You've gone from having a pint glass's worth, to an ocean. Your power is practically infinite, now."

"Did you just bring me here to lecture me for not being strong enough to utilise the power I was given?"

"I would never class you as weak." I roll my eyes and don't argue with him over technicalities. He didn't say I was weak, but he didn't acknowledge my strength either. *"However, I brought you back to continue our conversation from earlier."*

"Why do I see you now and not Lena?" I ask, and he makes the wolf equivalent of a chuckle sound.

"Now who is being distracted?" His tail wags in his amusement. *"Her role is split between two charges, and since you're comfortable with me too — "*

"Comfortable?" I scoff. He snorts. "Okay. You brought me back to talk to me about what we were discussing yesterday. Loukas brought up the choice thing again. I've told you numerous times that I'll choose my mates."

"No matter the choice?"

"No matter the choice."

"What if it's your pack or your mates?" I flinch, and the wolf nods knowingly. He crouches down low, bowing his head ever so slightly. I wrap my arms around my waist, hunching in on myself a little. It's impossible to feel cold here, and yet my body shivers. *"We're not permitted to share much, but I'd like to offer you one piece of advice."*

"Yes?"

*"Abel Viotto's future is at a crossroads. **You** are the one who will decide his fate."*

"I don't understand. We've already decided not to let him lose his life for making a mistake."

"You're kinder than me, granddaughter. His life would be taken if this were down to me." I flinch once more at the hostility of his words, and he lets out a soft whine that somehow soothes me and my wolf. *"But that's not the choice I'm referring to."*

"So, what's your advice?"

"Don't turn his offer down."

"What offer?" Of course, my words are met with silence, and the vicious way I grind my teeth would have my dentist furious. This is the game we always play. I'm dragged here given such vague advice. How do I know *which* offer that Abel makes is the one I need to accept?

My wolf is just as confused as I am right now, so I doubt she'll be much help when it comes to this *big, life-altering moment.*

"Thank you."

"I know the rules of these lands anger you, Charlotte."

"If you stopped meddling in the lives of the living, we'd probably be a lot less annoyed," I say, with a shrug.

"It's only okay when we help you, as long as it fits your requirements then, is that it?"

I laugh bitterly. "I made the choice I did that night *knowing I would die.* I was happy to have that be my fate. Don't mistake my decisions with yours."

His wolf lifts his head, and his black eyes meet mine. He gives one nod, before shifting into his human form. He's just like the man I saw that first night that I met him, still emitting those vibes of safety and kinship. He's around six-five, and quite muscular considering he's dead. His beard is a light brown colour that's neatly shaved, and contrasts against his honey skin. He's wearing the loafers and shirt that he typically adorns when we meet, but today they're black.

He's never worn anything that doesn't emit positivity.

That's another sign that things are weird here.

"You make a fair point."

"Can I ask you a question?"

"You may." He steps towards me, towering over me as per usual, but he's not intimidating. "Even if it means a dead man may interfere with the lives of the living."

I roll my eyes, but he grins at me, showing he's not truly mad. "Do you know who King Lobo is?" He nods. "Can you offer me anything of use on that subject?"

"He's the true threat you face."

"I guessed that," I mutter, with a sigh.

"He's got a very big weakness that you can manipulate. You just need to—"

"Oh, for fuck's sake," I whimper, my eyes flying open to look into some terrified dark eyes. I reach up and cup his cheek, hoping he misses the way my hands tremble. "I love you with my entire soul, but you couldn't have given me *two more minutes*?" The last three words are a hiss of pure frustration, and Theo sighs, turning his head ever so slightly to kiss the palm of my hand.

"Ancestors?"

"Annoying ones," I mumble, before yawning.

"I'll save the lecture for the state you've gotten yourself into, until we're home and can all lecture you together," Theo says, somehow making the words seem gentle and sweet. I roll my eyes at my wolf, hoping she stops with this mooning. We do not need a lecture. There's a warm energy that fills me, and I know he's trying to heal away my pain.

But it never works in this instance, because I did this damage to myself by healing others.

"Come on, little wolf," he murmurs, walking out of Katie's examination room. I can feel that her energy is still here, but I have no idea where she is. Theo doesn't pause to go and say goodbye though. "You're brilliant, Lottie, even if your recklessness makes me want to lock you in a bubble for the next nine months."

"It's a good thing you're so self-restrained," I mutter, cuddling into him.

He snorts, and drops a kiss to my forehead. "I may be, but we've got eight other men with ties to you. I can guarantee at least four of them are not."

I laugh, tired giggles, as my heart beats erratically at the fact that he included River in that.

The thudding of my heart is just as loud as the howls of my wolf at the implication that River is alive.

When will this pain end, and I can just be happy instead?

CHAPTER 13

"We are not doing this for the entire fucking pregnancy," Rhett snarls, glaring down at me. My Alpha mate towers over me when we're standing, but with me sitting in the comfy armchair, and him standing, it's a notable height difference. His eyes, which are a deep blue, are filled with unhappiness.

He's beautiful, even in his anger. He's been blessed with strong cheekbones, and a perfectly proportionate face, which only makes it that much more annoying that my wolf simpers away in my head about pleasing him whilst he berates us for helping our people.

"You need to take care of yourself, Lottie," Rhett continues. "You're carrying twins—strong twins—who are going to wreak havoc on your body. You can't be running yourself into the ground and not providing them with the nourishment they need."

"That's not fair," Elijah argues, shaking his head. He's sitting opposite me on the less comfortable armchair, with his laptop open on the arm of it. He's been mostly quiet since I got back with Theo, content to just let the more dominant and annoying men get this out of their systems.

My wolf swoons at his defence of me, which he blatantly knows from his sultry wink.

"Lottie is more than capable of stopping when she reaches her limits. Ignoring the fact that, yes, our mate is a little reckless and entirely ignorant— "

"Hey!"

"Can you argue that point?" Elijah asks, and I grumble about not being ignorant. "Anyway, as I was saying. Lottie might be too *naive* about this world, but she's more than capable of listening to her wolf and letting the ancient powers of an entire species guide her. Do you think her wolf would endanger our children?"

"Of course not," Caden says, kicking Rhett when the Alpha goes to argue. "Right, Rhett?"

"Right." It's almost as if the words were dragged out of him with how tightly his jaw is clenched. He sighs, coming to crouch down in front of me. "I'm sorry for the dickish way I acted earlier."

"But not now?" Dillon asks, and there's some snorts.

"Look, your dad's treatment of you lately has been pissing me off."

"Why?" I ask, inching forward despite the aches and pains of my body. My movements are slow and sluggish, but I can do it. "Why does it bother you so badly?"

"Because that's how we treated you when we lost our way," he says, with a deep sigh. I don't look up from my blue-eyed beauty, but I know that the others are feeling a little awkward now. Except Wyatt who is drowning in smugness. "We've evolved and we've mostly worked through our shit. But to me, your dad hasn't, and he's incapable of doing it. It pissed me off seeing him take on so much responsibility, considering he can barely handle the pack he has."

"That's a very good way of explaining yourself," Elijah says. Rhett's head snaps around, likely glaring at the vampire, but Elijah's face radiates with his sincerity. Rhett nods, turning back to me, and I smile at him.

"I get it. I think you were a little... brutish in your explanation during the meeting with my dad, and you hurt my feelings with the implication that I wasn't good enough— "

"You are more than enough, Lottie," Wyatt says, kicking Rhett's thigh as he reaches over to squeeze my hand. He's sitting on the long sofa, right next to my armchair, and has a beer can in his other hand. It's only six, but we're done peopling for the day.

"I know that," I say, giving him a smile. "But Rhett's words, as both my Alpha and mate, put that doubt into both my wolf and I."

"I never *ever* intended to make you feel that way," Rhett says, and I smile and nod. "However, I am not changing my stance on that issue. I do not want your father running our pack."

"Then we'll figure something else out," I say, hoping that my face doesn't display my cringing.

"Not even with the support from Charles's parents?" Caden asks, and Rhett rises to his feet, moving to sit down on the sofa between River and Warren. We're all spread out, with various drinks in our hands. On my left is Wyatt, with Dillon on the same sofa. Elijah's opposite me, on the armchair, and the other sofa is taken up by River, Warren and Rhett.

Rhett, Caden, Noah and Theo have been pacing since I've been home—or standing and bellowing about their tough life with such a reckless mate—and now the latter three find themselves without anywhere to sit, since Wyatt and Dillon aren't moving to share that sofa. The other two armchairs that we have in here are piled with washing, and I doubt one of them is going to move it.

Caden rolls his eyes, and plops down on the floor, causing Wyatt and Warren to laugh. River's unease is palpable, but I'm glad he doesn't move and offer Caden his seat.

"Sit," I demand, tugging my Guardian's hand when he walks past me again. He grumbles, but I scoot over, and he joins me on my chair, leaving Noah alone.

Eli smirks, closing his laptop. "I'd let you sit with me, Noah, but your ass is too big to fit comfortably."

"Noah does have a pretty big ass," Warren agrees. "Poor Melinda. She had to push out Caden's fat head and then Noah's—"

"Are you seriously talking about my mum's vagina?" Caden snarls, jumping to his feet.

"I wasn't, but I could," Warren teases, his eyes flashing purple for a brief second. I much prefer the bright green of his human eyes. *Mostly because the unknown of the purple scares me.*

"Enough," I say, cutting in. "Let's not talk about anybody's vaginas. Or pushing babies out of them."

"As you wish," Rhett says, with a smile. "So, we need to figure shit out with your dad and our pack, we need to prepare for Mallon's lovely visit tomorrow, and we need to come to a consensus about you and your powers."

I sigh. "I get it. You all think I'm reckless and would rather I did nothing."

"We'd rather you were *safe* Charlotte," Theo says, gently. "You've got brand new powers but have no idea how to use them effectively, and with the precarious state you're in, we need to make sure you don't take unnecessary risks and that you learn to protect yourself."

"Have any of you noticed a power increase since I took these powers?"

Dillon sits forward. "I don't think so. But can't you assess that?"

"I haven't," Rhett says, shaking his head. "Not like we did upon bonding, or completing the mating circle properly."

"No, me neither," Elijah says, shaking his head. "Still the weakest Ellis brother."

River smirks at him. "It must be so hard to be you."

"Harder being you, I'd say," Warren says, motioning to River's cock. Each of us watch the action, and as soon as Warren realises we're not on his side, his cheeks darken.

"Did you just..." I trail off, biting my lip as giggles overtake me.

"We might not be biologically related, Warren, but we did grow up as brothers," River says. "Please don't look at my cock, or I'll have to tell our parents."

"You pissed me off earlier," Caden says, cutting off the teasing with his serious tone of voice. "We've been through this—we don't use the pack bonds against each other."

"I understand that I went against your wishes, but I never did that. I used my own power, Caden."

He frowns, and sighs. "That takes some of the hurt away, but it doesn't ease any of my frustration. You disregarded my wishes, didn't give me the chance to make sure we were on the same page —"

"There was no time." My protests are met with multiple shakes of the head.

"There may not have been time, but he'd not have left when he was so intent on getting to you. This isn't about Abel, it's about us and our ability to work together," Caden says. His tone is devoid of emotion, his face hard. "We're a partnership Lottie, and when you go ahead and make decisions unilaterally, you're throwing that in our faces."

"I wouldn't have put it so bluntly, but Caden's not wrong," Noah says, giving his twin a weird look. "We're going to be leaving our pack, only having each other to rely on, and if we can't trust each other, then we're going to be fucked."

"And I'm the blunt one?" Caden mutters.

"We've been struggling with trust," Dillon points out. "Lottie's used to doing things on her own these days, and we're used to charging forward without her. We've been through so much that, of course, we're struggling."

"Lottie and I are going on a date on Friday, and I think over the next few weeks, that this is something we should do," Elijah says. We all exchange looks, me mostly, and Wyatt frowns. "When Lottie's wolf was struggling with the reconnection, we all re-marked her to give her wolf the stability she needed."

"And the fucking," Warren whispers, and Caden and Rhett smirk.

I roll my eyes, ignoring the heat that appears on my cheeks. "Yes, but that was something my wolf needed to feel our reconnection."

"And I think you'll reconnect with dates. You were human for the vast majority of your life, and that's something we've been failing to provide you with. You've needed courting, and we'll be doing that in a way that you deserve."

"And that'll help with her trust issues?" Rhett asks.

"It'll help with *our* trust issues," Elijah corrects, and the Alpha nods. "I've got dibs on Friday, so get planning."

"We do date though," Caden says, eyeing me up. I shrug, because honestly, I'd say we do too. Dating doesn't need to be fancy dinners, or romantic walks. It can be as simple as watching a movie, with a glass of wine.

"Do we?" Dillon asks, quietly. "Because I for one can't remember a day where we did something together without it being interrupted by work."

I flinch, and even though he gives me a reassuring look, his words hit me deeply. "That's fair."

"That's our lives," Caden argues, sitting up properly. "We're never going to be able to shut off for hours and hours."

"A dinner, where we talk about anything that isn't work, is ninety minutes maximum," Dillon points out.

"But having nine of those a week is a lot of time for Lottie not to work," Rhett says. "Or are we meant to do one a week, and wait over two months per date?"

"Scheduling only six dates a year with my mate?" Caden continues.

"Scheduling is hard in any relationship, not least of all a polyamorous one with multiple partners," Elijah says. "But that doesn't mean that it's not doable. Quality time is an important part of a relationship."

"But we do get quality time together," Caden says. "That's my argument. That we do spend the time together."

"I don't think it matters how we feel," River says, gently. His tone is careful, his words deliberately chosen and thought out, so as to not annoy the Alpha wolf. This delicacy in his actions is something that's foreign to River, since he's never had to be this careful before.

But whether his hybrid is guiding him, willing to obey the Alphas and as such not disappoint them or trouble them, or if it's something he's doing consciously, is still unseen. Either way, the atmosphere has been a little off between us all, but the fact that he's still here despite this, is a testament to how hard he's trying to make it work.

Out of all of my mates, River's the one that's put in the most effort lately into nourishing our bonds. We've been stupidly busy, stupidly distracted, and it's honestly a miracle if all nine of us—excluding River, since he moved out—have been home at the same time for longer than five minutes lately.

But River's sent gifts—thoughtful gifts. He's tracked me down and walked me places.

He's tried.

And I haven't.

"I think if Lottie needs more time together to stabilise herself, then we need to give her that," River says. "Especially if it means she's not going to rush headfirst into another situation that could endanger her."

"Risky and reckless should be my tagline," I mutter, and Elijah tuts but everyone else chuckles. "I promise that unless it's an emergency—"

"Define an emergency," Theo says, and I look up at him. He raises a bushy eyebrow, his brown eyes hard. My lips quirk up, but his don't even twitch.

"A situation that requires an immediate reaction—within fifteen minutes."

"Five," he counters.

"*Five?*" I scoff, shaking my head. "Ten."

"Ten," he says, with a nod.

"Any situation that puts your life at risk, no matter the time limit, requires an immediate notification," Caden says, sitting up properly. "We may not have the power you do, baby, but we're still pretty renowned."

I nod, grinning at him. "You're very capable." He laughs. "And I agree to those terms, but I might not be able to tell you that something has happened immediately."

"Then don't rely on the mind link, princess," Warren says. "Tug on our bonds as tight as you can."

River's lips tighten but he stays silent.

"Practice it now, so we all know what it feels like," Dillon says, just as serious as the rest of the men are.

I shrug, and tug on their bonds, even going as far as to pull the pack connection I share with River. I pull it harshly, and all of them tense, and begin to rub at their chests. The physical feeling is apparent in them all, and it gives my wolf satisfaction knowing how deep our bonds go.

"Well fuck, that wasn't nice," Dillon says, rubbing his chest a little more harshly than the others. His eyes flicker to me, and he smiles. "Well done."

"So, it's undeniable," I ask, raising an eyebrow. He nods, and I grin.

"When she does it in a real situation, too, there'll be the emotional twinge that goes along with it," Theo explains. "So, we'll be able to tell if she's fearful, or in pain, or just plain angry."

"You can do that to me too?" River asks, hesitantly.

I nod. "The pack bond is just as easy to manipulate as a mate bond, I assure you. I like the idea of dates, but... I'd like to spend more time together as a group, too," I say, hesitantly raising my hand. "We've got nine months roughly until we've got twins, and I'm hoping this drama will all be sorted out by then."

"There's no hoping, baby girl," Caden says, shaking his head. "King Lobo will be dead before the twins are born."

"So how the fuck are we going to make that happen?" Warren asks.

"We prepare the best we can, for the final showdown," Rhett says, with a shrug. "He's no longer being careful, and so I think the reckoning he promised is coming sooner than expected."

"The longer he waits, the better Lottie will get with the powers she stole," Warren says.

"Hey!" I complain, and he laughs.

"Sorry, princess, but to him you're the villain. You ruined his life, stole his powers, and are doing a better job than him at riling up the Council. Why else would he keep attacking them?"

"We've got far too many things he needs to answer for," River says. "But he's not the only one who owes us answers."

"No, he's not," Warren agrees. "Have you heard from Conri?"

I shake my head. "I'm not expecting to hear from him quickly, but —"

"Why not?" my sort-of vampire mate asks, leaning forward.

"Because he's reconnecting with his mate, who he hasn't seen in *hundreds* of years. I think we can give him more than a day to catch up with her."

Warren rolls his eyes. "Not only does time travel differently in the realm, so he's going to have had much longer than a day with her, but things out here are very tense. He took advantage of that moment to get you to take his power, and we all know it, and as such it's his job to help us as he can."

"My concern is that he's going to be bound by the rules of the land now that he's there," I say, with a sigh. "What do they class as proprietary information? What are they going to allow me to know about?"

"Hopefully, everything," Dillon says before sighing. "I'll look into it tomorrow whilst you're all at your meeting. I've got a bunch of books that I've been reading."

"Thank you."

"Who will be at the meeting tomorrow?" Elijah asks.

"Why do you care?" Rhett asks, with a frown. "You're not usually bothered by this."

"Mainly because Scottie and I have a lot to do for when we all leave, and we want to start organising the visits."

"Shit, I did check with my dad, and he's happy for you to hold interviews there."

"Thank you, sunshine." He blows me a kiss and I grin, pretending to catch it. I ignore the looks Warren and River share. "But if I know who is in the meeting and who isn't, we can direct questions to the right people."

"I'll make sure Lionel is there to assist you both," I say, glancing at River. He remains passive. "River will be in with me. But, your question brings us to the next topic I wanted to discuss."

"What about the Council visit?" Rhett asks, with a frown. "We've finally gotten onto that, and it's pretty important."

"We'll get onto that next," I say, and he nods slowly, giving Caden a weird look. No idea what the two of them are concocting. "The situation we've found ourselves in is shit, and we've had a fair few awkward moments."

"Those moments are only going to increase the more time we spend together," Warren adds, with a sigh.

"Yes, probably," River says. He clears his throat and looks over at me. Without the bond, I may not be able to tell how he's feeling, but the mask on his face is too hard to ignore.

I already know what he's going to say before he says it, and pain hits me like a freight truck. Tears fill my eyes, and I sniffle, as I look down at my lap instead of at him. My heart breaks, knowing that once again he's going to hurt me.

Knowing that once again, River has the power to destroy me.

We don't even need a mate bond for him to hurt me.

"I can step back—" River starts.

"And hurt my mate again?" Warren hisses, glaring at his brother. Rhett's in between them both and moves himself so that he's pressing into the sofa to give Warren the chance to glare at his brother.

"No!" River snarls. The sound sends tingles down my spine, and when he looks at me with black eyes, I gasp. This isn't coming from just him—it's coming from his hybrid too.

Holy fuck.

"I was going to say that I'd step back in a group setting. I know that we all agreed I could court Lottie and try and fix the fuckup I caused in our life. But whilst things are still so..."

"Dramatic?" Dillon suggests.

"Tense?" Wyatt offers.

"Scary?" I add, and Theo squeezes me a little tightly, just reminding me that he's there.

"All of the above," River says with a sigh. "I'm not going anywhere, Lottie. I just know that we're struggling, and I don't want to be the reason why."

"But you are the reason why," Rhett says. I avoid looking at both Rhett and River when this is said, because honestly, that's the truth. I don't want to lose River from my life, even without us having a bond, but that doesn't mean the state of disarray that our relationship is in, isn't his fault.

He broke us.

But he's trying his hardest to fix us.

"He is," Rhett adds, at the dirty look he's given from Wyatt. "River's actions led to the dissolution of the bond, and so the fact that we're all struggling is his fault."

"I know that," River says quietly. "I know that you can't control your responses, which is why I'm offering to step back."

"But not completely, right?" Dillon asks.

"But not completely."

"I think this sounds stupid. When are you seeing a good time for you to step back up and try this properly?" Caden asks, with a raised eyebrow. "When the issues with King Lobo are over and done? When we've had the twins? When they're adults, and we're ten kids—"

"Whoa, whoa, whoa," I demand, rushing to my feet. I stumble, and immediately go back down. If it weren't for the quick save by Theo, I'd be on my ass completely.

"Careful," Theo cajoles, cuddling me in close.

"We're not having ten kids," I mutter, letting my eyes flutter closed.

"But there's ten of us," Caden says, his tone littered with his disappointment. I don't open my eyes, and he sighs. "Something to discuss at a later time then."

"I see your point," River says. "But I don't know what to do about it."

"None of us know what to do about it," Wyatt says. "But we're here each day, putting the effort in and trying."

"That's what you need to do," Noah adds. "Our reactions are ours to deal with. My wolf can't correlate the fact that you used to have a bond but now don't. To him, you're a man outside of our mating circle who wants to touch my pregnant mate." Noah sighs, rubbing the back of his neck. "He's hard to control, which is where some of the reactions come from, but I'm working on it."

"Can you not just bite her again?" Wyatt asks.

"Not when there's no bond there to ignite by biting her," River says, before flashing a cheeky grin my way. "However, if that's something you'd like to try, I'm more than willing."

Three snarls, one hiss, and one laugh. The laugh, surprisingly, came from Caden. Two snarls from the two Alphas, the third coming from Theo. Warren's hiss was another unsurprising reaction.

"How didn't you react?" I ask, opening my eyes to look at Wyatt.

"What?"

"Just there, even the thought of his teeth touching me had Warren, Rhett, Noah, and Theo losing their cool. Elijah and Dillon both bristled, neither liking the implication, but you didn't react in the slightest. How?"

River's eyes widen, also curious.

"Because it was a joke."

"My bristling wasn't because I, or my vampire, were annoyed at him taunting my mate," Elijah adds, and I detect the blush appearing on his cheeks.

"Why were you annoyed then?" Caden asks, confused.

"Why did you laugh?" Elijah replies, the blush darkening and travelling down his neck.

"Basically, we're not all feeling anger at River's existence with our mate," Wyatt says, looking around the room. "Which shows it's something that can be worked on."

"I'm trying," Caden says.

"We all are," Rhett says, before grimacing. "We all *will*. Soon enough we'll be trapped together, and only together, for however long these visits take. We can't make things uncomfortable for you... well we can, but it's a dick move if we do."

"Good to know," River says, with a smile. "Now, before we move on... why were you annoyed Eli?"

"Nobody is questioning Dillon," Elijah protests.

"My wolf was unhappy for a moment at the thought of it," Dillon says, with a shrug. "Nothing deeper than that."

Elijah blows out a huff of air, glaring at his empty bottle of beer on the table. "My annoyance was because he was talking about biting her, which would waste blood if he didn't drink it. My vampire was pissed at the wasting of her blood."

I snort, from where I'm heavily leaning on Theo, and there's more laughter.

"Aw, it's hard being the least possessive man with a possessive vampire," Warren says, winking at the exasperation from his brother. "But I'll work on it. The boundaries with the blood have helped massively, and I just need to get a handle on myself."

"As long as you want him in your life as a mate—with or without the bond—then I shall control my wolf," Theo says, kissing my cheek, before turning to River. "The moment she doesn't? You'd better stay far away."

River nods, keeping his face steady, but I can see the mirth in his eyes, and I'm exhausted. The others will see it clearly.

River might be playing nice guy, since he's the odd man out, but he's not lost his charm.

He's just playing the long game.

"So, now that that's mostly settled, what the fuck are we going to do about the Council visit tomorrow?" Warren asks, resting back on the sofa.

"Well, we came up with a plan whilst Lottie was healing the pack members," Caden says, and Rhett rubs his hands together as his inner child emerges.

"We'll need your help, love."

"I'd have been disappointed if you didn't," I counter, and he grins. "So, tell me, what is the plan?"

CHAPTER 14

*T*here's a wet feeling across my nipples, before some freezing cold air. I groan, wiping at them, waiting for sleep to claim me properly again.

But then there's a sharp bite, and I let out a low hiss as my eyes fly open. The scent of my blood fills the air, the potency of the power teasing the vampire hovering above me.

"Good morning," I say, before yawning properly as I look at the curly brown-haired man with a cheeky grin. "What are you doing up so early?"

"I've got a busy day," he murmurs. He lowers his body down over me, the heat of his naked chest meeting my own, as his tongue darts out to taste the blood. His vampire hums in pleasure across the bond, and the way Elijah's pupils dilate have my wolf rushing around in pleasure.

"Relatable," I reply, reaching out to squeeze his ass. I moan when I feel his bare ass, and I'm so happy about the lack of clothing.

My wetness leaks out of me, no doubt leaving a small pool on the bed, and the desperate edge to my arousal builds.

The only way this could've been a better wake-up, would have been if his dick was inside of me.

My groan when I feel him bite down on my skin with his razor-sharp teeth is involuntary, and my hips thrust up into the air, meeting nothing.

I ache with how empty I am, and my wolf is much *much* more sexually charged.

I grab his thighs, the closest thing to me, and it's with great restraint that I stop my nails from shifting into claws and drawing blood from him right back.

He creates little bites all over my breast, and only when there's blood pooling around them, does he stop biting. He laps at the blood, his moan of ecstasy matching my own.

Once it's all gone—mostly—my fingers tangle into his curls, as I try to pull him up my body. He grins at me, with blood staining his plump lips.

Sure, I'd love to feel them brushing against mine, but pulling him upwards also pulls his dick upwards and I'll get my relief.

"What's taking you so long?" I whine, my hips thrust up into the air, hoping for the first time ever that he might be able to read my mind. He can't. "Eli! You're being so mean to me. You woke me up at" —I check the clock on my side table, groaning dramatically—"five thirty am, and you're not even going to make me feel good."

"Good things come to those who wait, sunshine," he murmurs, trailing down my stomach with one hand. I whimper, goosebumps appearing as he trails it across my skin.

"I'd rather have good things *now*."

He chuckles, and kisses up from my breast to my neck, all without letting those wandering fingers drop below my waistline. He nibbles

—with human teeth this time—and kisses across my cleavage, not even giving my nipples any attention.

My arousal builds, my desire for this man rising as rapidly as my annoyance, and the little wet spot has likely become a fucking puddle.

"Elijah," I plead, willing my body to just let go, and give me the pleasure without the expert hands and well-placed touches. When he chuckles again, I snarl, and move my hands between our bodies, to reach down and touch myself.

But the asshole doesn't allow that.

He uses his hands to grab mine, and he lifts them above my head, holding them in place with one of his hands. The other wanders down my body finally broaching the bundle of nerves that have been begging for attention this whole time.

He kisses the skin of my neck, his warm breaths of air enticing me further.

His thumb brushes over my clit, and my hips buck upwards, pushing into him air for more pressure. He obliges as he bites down on my neck, drawing blood with the sharp pain from his fangs.

He doesn't just bite, he drinks deeply, powering himself up, making himself more attractive to my wolf. Power seeks power and she likes to know our mates are strong, and capable of defending themselves during this troublesome time.

"Elijah." I moan his name in pleasure this time, and I'm so glad that the bond only allows him to feel my lust, because right now, I don't think that I'm able to form full sentences. I'm so close, so desperate for that relief.

But then he pulls his thumb away and withdraws his teeth from my neck. I whimper, my breath coming out in pants.

"Tell me what you need, sunshine," he says, flopping onto his side. I watch as his hand grabs his dick and starts palming it the way he likes. My eyes narrow into slits as I see him touching *my* instrument of pleasure.

Fucking asshole.

"Put your dick inside me and touch me the way I need to be

touched." I grunt when he doesn't immediately move, and reach up to shove the strands of hair off my sweaty forehead. "Seriously, Eli, this is going to be a majorly shit day, and you won't let me cum."

"I'm sorry, sunshine," he murmurs. "I was teasing, but I can see how badly you want me."

I want to be upset that he stopped what he's doing, but the way he's touching himself, lubing up his dick, is a seductive act.

"I don't just want you, Eli, I *need* you. I need you to fuck me as hard as you can, to make it *hurt*."

He pauses in his movements, his green eyes assessing me, before he nods.

"Fuck," he moans, grabbing me roughly by the waist and lifting me so that I'm on top. He's now laid across the middle of the bed with his head resting between our two pillows.

He lifts his cock up gently, pressing it to my entrance, before giving me a *what are you waiting for* look.

I slowly sink down, taking the head of his dick inside me, and a slow grin flits across my face. He snarls, and pushes into me so fast and harshly that I think he's just bruised my cervix.

I let out a whimper, but he just begins to move. The pain of his dick forcing his way inside me like that mixes with the pleasure of his current thrusts, and it sends me into a trembling mess.

I'm on top, and I should be the one to set the pace.

It seems Elijah didn't get the memo.

His pace is painstakingly cruel, my body quivering and bending to let him draw the ultimate pleasure from us.

"How does this feel, sunshine?" he murmurs, his voice low and husky. My hands are resting on his chest, as he thrusts in and out. "Because it feels fucking amazing for me. You always feel so good wrapped around my dick. It's been so long since I've got to fuck you."

I lower down so I'm resting on the side of my arms on his chest, instead of on my hands, which gives him the ability to take one of my pebbled nipples into his mouth.

He bites down, drawing blood, drinking the way a vampire baby probably would.

It hurts in the best way possible, and I'm not sure how long I can last with this rapid pace, and the orgasm that's teetering on releasing.

It's threatening to rip me apart, and Elijah is quickly taking me towards it, his eyes focused on my every movement, his only goal to rip more and more pleasure from me.

"You're close, aren't you, sunshine? I can tell from how tight you keep squeezing me. How badly do you want to come?"

"Badly," I moan, unable to keep my hips still despite him slowing. "Please, Elijah, please."

He reaches up and grabs my hips, faster, harder, pushing past the limit a human body could take, in an effort to give me the orgasm I so desperately crave.

And it doesn't take long. My climax hits, pulling me over the edge, and I scream out his name as I come down from it. My legs are shaking, my pussy spasming, and Elijah *does not stop*.

"Fuck babe," I gasp, when I'm done. He grins at me.

"Was that hard enough for you?"

I tap my chin teasingly, loving the feel of him inside me, even if he's stopped moving. "I don't think so."

"Wyatt is right. You are a little minx." With an animalistic snarl he pulls out of me, turns me from my back to my tummy, and thrusts into me. I'm on my knees with my stomach pressed into the pillow.

"You will tell me if you need me to stop," Elijah silently warns me. I'm not sure why he warns me, until he starts.

He doesn't just thrust in and out at a rapid speed... he does it at a *supernatural* speed. I can barely breathe as he merges with his vampire to fuck me.

He bends down, biting at my shoulder blade and I scream out in pleasure as he draws blood. My body hums on the line of consciousness, every single nerve ending alight with pleasure, my soul totally consumed by this man.

He's the same way across the bond. I can feel nothing but lust from both him and his vampire. It goes down to his very soul, the raw primal feeling consuming him, and me by extension.

I moan over and over, as he continues with this rapid pace, and taunting bites. He kisses and teases, licking and nibbling, drawing my blood all over me. His grip on my hips is so tight I'll have his finger-marks etched into me for days.

"You're mine," Elijah growls out, the words far too deep to have come from him, but they send shivers down my spine anyway.

I orgasm for the second time, my body bent in half, as I scream out his name.

I'm not sure how long we keep this pace, but when I come back to my senses, he's still inside me. His pants are rough against my skin as he breathes on my neck, my lungs labouring to catch my breath.

"Elijah," I moan into the mattress, unable to lift my head. "I want you to cum."

He growls into my ear, and I can feel his breath tickling the loose hair around my ear, the cool sting against the sweaty patch of skin. "Will you cum again for me? Can you cum around my dick?"

I honestly don't know if it's possible, but I nod, lifting my ass higher for him. I'm exhausted, my body fully wrung out. But I won't ever deny him if I can help it.

He growls, ramming into me at that superhuman speed, but from the way his teeth grind together and his ass cheeks clench, I know he's close.

But to my surprise, rather than just letting himself fly off the edge, he pulls out and flips me onto my back. He thrusts back into me, and his right hand slides between our bodies. He presses his thumb against my swollen clit, and adjusts it ever so slightly when I hiss in pain.

Now, all I feel is pleasure.

His mouth encases my nipple, teasing it with small nibbles, before biting down and drawing blood in the way that we both enjoy. He gets my blood, and I get to see him go wild. I don't even try to meet his insanely fast thrusts, and instead just take the pleasure he's giving me.

My nails have shifted into claws as they grip his hip, and I draw his blood too. He doesn't mind, instead moaning into my breast.

His orgasm builds, just as mine does, and I have no idea who is going to fly over the edge first.

My wolf and I are high on the feelings that are flying through his bond. He's so deeply in love with me, so lost to the feral energy of his vampire that he's not thinking properly. I may not be able to read his mind, but if I could, I know that there wouldn't be a single coherent thought.

It's everything.

"Ah," I moan, as an orgasm more powerful than any before it washes over me. My eyes roll back into my head, and my vision goes fuzzy. Those little floaters that appear, seem to take the shape of Elijah's face, the glorious look of his pleasure hovering around my eyesight.

He follows me over the peak, and as he spurts and twitches, I spasm and coax his release further out of him. I'm not sure that my body has got the memo that I'm already pregnant, since I clench so hard, he definitely can't pull out.

The moment our orgasms collectively finish, my body loses consciousness and lets the wave of power rush over me.

Those who said magic sperm isn't a thing, are most definitely wrong.

)) ● ((

I rifle through my wardrobe, trying to find something to wear for today. My clothing has vastly improved since being with my Alphas, and as such, my style has adapted to include far more professional options.

Long dresses with a summery style, ballgowns for the parties, pantsuits for when I need to show patriarchal assholes that my ass looks so much better than theirs in tight-fitting pants.

Well, unless said men are my own. Their asses are pretty damn impressive.

"Fuck," Elijah whispers, the word quiet but filled with his panic. He's been pretty chill since I woke up, not panicked at all, unlike our first time. We cuddled, had some... *touching*, and I've just now decided to get up and grab my clothes before my shower.

I look at him through the mirror, and my frown mirrors his own. His green eyes are still bright with the excitement of what we've just done, but his face doesn't agree. His lips, which are stained red with my blood, are pursed downwards, and his forehead has a few creases in it.

"What?" I ask, spinning to face him properly instead of just looking at him through the mirror. My movements are graceful, but you'd think I just ran in front of a car or some shit with the dirty look he flings my way. "What's wrong?"

"I've marked you."

I nod slowly, not sure of the issue here. "Well, yeah. You all marked me at one point, babe." Sure, my mating bite from Eli is a little red right now, but it only makes my wolf and I feel that much more loved.

"No, I mean I've *bruised* you. I've littered you in bite marks, and *I've hurt you.*" The crack in his voice with the last part of his sentence breaks my heart.

"Whoa, whoa, whoa," I say, shaking my head. I close the door to my wardrobe, not yet having picked my outfit for today.

I was going to ask him to come *shower* with me, before getting ready, but I can't ask him to do that now when he's looking at me as if the world has ended.

We've got a really big day today, and I can't be anything less than perfect when it comes to this visit with the Council. Which means I won't be allowing my mate to torture himself over and over for something I fucking *loved.*

Seriously, I'm demanding that experience from every single one of my men, at least once a month. I feel fantastic.

I got out of my head properly for the entire time we were together, and all I did was take the nourishment the bonds offered. Our physical connection always strengthens our soul bond, and with the added depth to the emotional flares, it was *everything.*

So not only will I not have him ruin this for me, I refuse to let him taint our connection, when I know he needed it just as badly as I did.

"You did not hurt me past what I could take. I *asked* for everything we did. I *enjoyed* what we did." As I speak, I advance closer to him, and even the way he hunches in on himself doesn't deter me. "You do not get to make yourself feel bad for giving me a really amazing morning. It's likely going to be one of the only bright spots in my entire day, and I hate that you feel bad about it."

"I lost myself to the hormones, letting my—"

"Your baser instincts take over? Your vampire have some fun with me? You used me?"

"All of them." He's so miserable here, a pout on his face, that just digs a knife into me. He rubs at his eyes, twisting the knife even further around.

"And do you not think I'm a woman capable of stopping my mate from doing something I wouldn't like?"

He frowns, before looking up at me with tears in his eyes. *Fuck.*

I've been through this before with Wyatt, when it comes to being spanked. I didn't enjoy it then, and I don't now. I hate how badly he feels over this, especially since I don't.

Elijah gave me a gift in the current shitstorm we're in—he gave my mind a reprieve from the endless torment of to-do lists, and he gave my body the release it craved. He's my mate, the other part of my soul, and he used the harmony we share to offer me so much love.

I kneel on the bed, and knee-walk over to him, coming to a stop when I'm practically in his lap.

"I love you," I whisper, and he looks at me in surprise. "Please don't do this to yourself."

"You're pregnant, Lottie."

I sigh. "I can be bled during pregnancy, I can be fucked during pregnancy, and what's more is that I absolutely will be demanding those things even when I'm fat and hideous."

He snarls, gripping my chin so fast, turning my head to face him. "You will never be *hideous.*"

"I'd much rather you disputed the fat claim."

He snorts. "You'll get big, sunshine, but that's because you're the first home our children will ever know."

I gasp, tears filling my eyes, as my wolf howls in my mind. "Why would you say that?" My voice rises in pitch, and I clutch at the base of my throat.

"What? What was wrong with that?"

"It was too... sweet."

He laughs, and cuddles me in tight. "I'm sorry to make you feel badly about what we did," he says once he releases me. "I thoroughly enjoyed myself and would absolutely want to do it again."

"Good. Me too."

"But can you do me a favour?" he asks, cupping my cheek. I nod, not breaking eye contact. "Can you get Theo to heal you?"

"Of course. Um... but since I don't want him to interrupt our *shower* time, could we do it after?"

He smirks, and nods, lifting me into his arms. "Shower you say?"

"A very hot, steamy... *shower*."

And we're out of the bedroom, and into my bathroom before I even blink.

Drama aside, cock's inside. It should be my new motto.

CHAPTER 15

"You look beautiful," Caden says, and I grin as I cross the room to fix his tie. My heels afford me four extra inches, and I can easily reach up to fix that with our height difference.

Caden's hair is surprisingly not in that horrible man-bun combover look that he frequents and instead is down. His shoulder-length wavy hair frames his face gorgeously, and he's tucked his hair behind his right ear. There's a sort of rugged look to his hair, and combined with the stubble across his face, he's very desirable.

My wolf perks her head up, but I bat her back down. Our vagina has been thoroughly taken care of this morning, and now we need to focus on the business we've got.

"You look extremely handsome," I counter, dusting a piece of lint off his dark-blue three-piece suit. The make of it is designer, but I have no idea of the brand. It's fitted to his skin, showing off his muscular physique. "Are you ready?"

"Are *you* ready?"

I sigh, and shrug. "Mostly. I don't think any of us are going to enjoy this. Where's Theo?"

"At the Town Hall." I deflate, and he raises an eyebrow. "What's wrong?"

"Nothing."

"Then why did you want Theo?"

I narrow my eyes his way. "Because he's my mate and I love him?"

Caden laughs, and shakes his head. "No, baby, that's not it. I know your body. I know when you're horny, and wanting some loving. I know when you're lonely, and in need of some reconnection. I know when you're—"

"Yes, yes, I get it." My impatience wins out and he laughs. "I just needed him to heal me."

"Why? Is it our babies? Is something wrong?"

"No," I soothe, reaching out and squeezing his arm. "I just need something healed."

"That's not an explanation."

"I didn't realise I had to provide one."

He chuckles, and reaches out, gripping my chin. He tilts my head up, and gives me a knowing look. "Stop deflecting."

"I had some rough sex, and want to heal my aching thighs," I snap, and he bursts out laughing. I hear two sets of footsteps on the stairs and turn to see Rhett and Noah standing there. Noah's identical to Caden, likely down to the boxers they're wearing. Rhett's suit is the same as theirs—the dark blue three-piece, as a show of solidarity.

They're a unit, a team.

"We look hot," Rhett says, winking at me. "You're beautiful, love."

"Thank you."

"But are we prepared?" Noah asks, stepping out from behind Rhett. "Are you ready for today, baby?"

I nod. "I can do my part."

"That's all we need you to do," Rhett reassures me. "We'll answer their questions honestly, inform them of the threat with King Lobo, and see what they want to do from there."

"But, we're not placing the power in their hands," Caden reminds me. "We need to make sure that we're the ones on the offensive."

"I know," I say softly. "I am more than capable of annoying Mallon enough, that we'll remain the dominant side. He's just..." I trail off shrugging my shoulders.

"A fucking cunt," Noah says, and I snort, not bothering to argue with him. He's not wrong.

"You okay?" Rhett asks, and I nod. He smiles, squeezing my hand.

"Come on, we'll head over to the Town Hall," Noah says. "We'll get this over and done with, then I promise you some sexy time."

"Sexy time that beats whatever you did with Elijah," Caden says quietly, winking at me. I just roll my eyes, causing him to laugh.

"What about Elijah?" I ask, at a volume intended for everyone to hear. Caden sniggers into his fist, turning away from me as if this is the funniest thing that's happened all day. The others exchange looks, so I tug on his bond. Between blinks, he appears in the kitchen in front of us. But instead of the formal attire I expected, he's wearing his normal, everyday outfit—a pair of smart trousers and a shirt—and his hair is, somehow, a messy masterpiece.

"Hey," he says, casually. "What's up?"

"It's time to go," I say, with a small smile. My tummy flutters—*and so does another part of me*—as we make eye contact, and he smirks. "Are you ready to leave?"

"Not yet. I've got a few things to sort out. Just leave without me, and I'll lock everything up and join you over there." My guys nod, and grab their things. Elijah raises an eyebrow at me in silent question, but I shake my head.

Nope, I didn't get healed since Theo's not here. He sighs, and I shrug. I'll get it done as soon as I see Theo; it's not that big of a deal to wait a few minutes rather than calling him here in a panic and drawing a lot of attention to it.

"What was that look between the two of you?" Caden demands, after putting his wallet into his inside pocket.

"Why do you need to publicise this shit?" I counter. "If we wanted to share with the group... we would have."

"I just wanted to tease," Caden says, tugging me into his arms and smothering my cheek in sloppy kisses. My lips may be quirked in annoyance, but my wolf is howling in my head, excited at the contact. She's never bothered by the annoying love they give because it's love, and that's all she cares about.

"Tease how?" I ask, and Elijah purses his lips.

"I just think it's funny that Elijah has been partaking in some extremely rough sex." Caden's amused tone slowly trails off into awkwardness when he sees my expression of annoyance and Eli's of hurt.

"I did not say extreme," I snap. "And I enjoyed it, thank you very much."

Elijah's eyes narrow as he eyes up both me and Caden, and his unease seems to flirt against my own across our bond. But then, he quirks a smile, and laughs. "What I get up to in my bedroom has nothing to do with you."

"That's fair," Caden replies. Noah checks his watch, not hiding his impatience that we're still here. Caden's having far too much fun to care, though. "It does when it's Warren, though, right?"

"Wait, what?" I ask, scrunching up my nose.

"What are you on about?" Elijah echoes.

"I think he's trying to make a joke about you fucking Lottie on Warren's bed," Rhett says, eyeing Caden as if he's just told him Santa isn't real. "Maybe."

"That was me doing it in Warren's room," Elijah says, in a condescending tone.

Caden sighs. "I've just fucked the entire thing up."

I burst out laughing at the complete look of dismay on his face.

"Yes, you did," Rhett says. "Now come on, let's go. I don't want to be late."

"We're not going to be late," Caden says, rolling his eyes. "We've got plenty of time."

"Please?" I say, reaching for his hand. He nods, and pats Eli's shoulder as we pass. As we leave, I wink at the vampire, and a blush forms on his cheeks.

My three Alphas stick close by me as we walk through the town, and I don't know if it's because of the intense energy we're giving off, or if they're feeling bloodthirsty themselves, but we've got a lot more excited looks our way today. The wolves in our pack are submitting to us as we walk, and it makes human me feel nervous, but wolf me is so proud of this.

I try to be friendly and smiley with those who greet us, but my mates don't give us the chance to stop. We're on a mission, and our people seem to know it. It's nice to know we're in solidarity, despite everything that's happened.

"Them seeing us feeling so confident helps them feel reassured," Rhett silently says, squeezing my hand as we walk.

"I'm glad they can't feel my terror."

"You might be scared, love, but you're one of the strongest women I know. There's nothing to fear because you will come out victorious," Rhett says back.

Noah strides forward a few steps to open the door to the Town Hall, and *of course,* he squeezes my ass as I pass. Hannah is on reception, and she grins at us.

"Morning Hannah," Noah says. My nerves have increased now that we're here, and I don't like that we're stopping to chat. It's awkward and uncomfortable, but based on the smiles on everyone else's faces, I think it's only me who feels this way.

"Morning Alphas, Luna," she says. "I've got these—" She stops, and starts to raffle through the cluttered papers on her desk before handing me three sheets.

"What are they?" Rhett asks, leaning over to look.

"Messages," Hannah says pleasantly. "We've had a few different people calling this morning, and most of them were actually quite polite."

"That's great," I say, not genuinely meaning it. I'm glad they were polite, but I'm *not* glad that they're already harassing us for information. I highly doubt that all of these people have positive intentions. "Thank you so much."

"Anytime," she replies. We head over to the lifts, and Caden darts forward to press it before Noah. I barely catch the dirty look Noah throws his brother, since I'm scouring these records to see what names I recognise.

Once we're on our floor, I sigh. "I'm going to drop this in my office."

"Good," Caden says. "I'm going to give your dad a quick ring." He drops a kiss to my temple, before moving down the corridor to his own office with quick haste.

I'm glad he's making the call to my dad instead of me.

I pause on the way to my office and knock on Lexie's office door before letting myself in. She's sitting behind her desk and looks up with a smile on her face as she sees it's me. Lionel and River are sitting opposite her, with laptops in front of them. There's a sort of intense atmosphere, but not hostile, and my wolf is very proud of them.

River's started early and has risen to the occasion, and hasn't even made one snide comment about how he's above the role of Gamma. My wolf is still curious about him, about the differences inside. She recognises the soul of the man, but still doesn't equate him to the one we lost.

That's because we didn't lose him.

He's better now than he was.

He's balanced.

"Good morning," I say, stepping into the room.

"Morning," Lexie says, grinning at me. "How are you doing?"

I shrug. "We're doing okay."

She frowns now, her dark eyes peering at me with something akin to disappointment. "I wasn't asking about everyone."

"I'm a little nervous, but ready," I say, and she nods.

"Good. I've left something on your desk for you."

"Um, thank you." She's smiling so it can't be something terrible, but still.

"What do you need, Luna?" Lionel asks.

"A little less attitude from you, thank you very much," I reply without even looking at him. His tone was abrupt, as if he was humouring me by letting me interrupt. I step towards the desk, stopping between the chairs that Lionel and River are sitting in. The former doesn't react, but the latter tenses, and I brush against his hand that's holding onto the armrest.

Out of the corner of my eye—because fuck being caught watching properly—I see his eyes flash briefly, and his fingertips wiggle, as if he wants to touch me more.

My heart races, and I so desperately want him to do it.

But my wolf isn't sure.

And neither are my mates, despite their insistence otherwise. We're trying, but on a day like today, I refuse to cause tension between us all.

"I have this for you," I say, handing Lexie the document Hannah gave me. "Can you make a note of who has called, the general vibes of their message, and prioritise who I need to get with once this meeting is over, please?"

She nods. "Of course, I can. I'll go through them once we're done here."

"I'm going to be out of the office from five," Lionel says. I nod, looking down at him in confusion. He narrows his own in return. "It's a Saturday."

"I know. I don't expect you to be in at all. If you have plans, feel free to—" I start. River snorts, and Lionel shoots him a dirty look, before looking back at me with one much the same.

"No. This is my job, and you need me here."

"I totally understand that. Well, you have my permission to leave at five." His wolf settles, but the human barely reacts. *Asshole.* "Right, I'm going to go and set up the meeting room. River's going to be in that with us. Lexie, you're staying here, and River will pass on information."

"We know the plan, Luna," Lexie says, gently. "We've got this."

"Okay." I'm not sure if we're missing something, or if this is just general anxiety, but there's a pit in my stomach that won't go away.

Did Conri's powers come with telling the future?

"*L*ottie," River calls. I ignore him for a moment as I continue setting the table, making sure that we've all got everything we need for this meeting. We still don't have an accurate count of how many are coming to this interrogation with the Elder Patriarch, but we've set up in the biggest meeting room anyway.

I'd rather we expect twenty, and he only brings three, than the alternative and have them start off this meeting on uneven footsteps. I know for a fine fact the Elder Patriarch would use that as a power play.

Not today, asshole, not today.

Once I've moved the papers to the right place, I turn to face my very patient Gamma. He's wearing a black suit, and my panties combust here and now, seeing the way his shirt isn't fully buttoned up. I lick my lips, looking away as a blush appears. I can genuinely feel the dampness of my panties, and I pray he can't smell anything.

"What did you need, River?" I ask, tilting my head. My tone is a little abrupt as I try to disguise my arousal, so I soften it when I ask again. "Was everything okay with those numbers?"

"Lexie is working through them, but there are no glaring red flags... Yet. You've got a call."

"Okay, can you take a message? I've got—" I start, and this time, I don't hide the impatience. I've just given Lexie a giant list of people who have tried to call me. Just add this name to the pile, and I'll return it soon.

"No, I can't. The call is from the Elder Patriarch."

My blood runs cold, but I nod, keeping my tone steady. "Of course, it is. Hand it here, please." River doesn't hesitate to cross the room and pass me my phone. I swipe along to answer it, and I'm surprised that River doesn't move away from me. No, instead, he lets the heat of his body soothe me, in the way our bond used to.

My wolf sits up, paying attention to this. She's not angry, but she's also not supportive of it either. She's strangely inquisitive. River's hybrid, on the other hand, is very eager and very excited. His hybrid doesn't care that the bond is gone, whereas my wolf isn't sure that anything exists without it.

I shake my head, washing these hopeful thoughts away, and put the phone to my ear. "Charlotte Montgomery speaking. How may I help you, Elder Patriarch?"

"Oh, um, hi, I am so sorry. This isn't him, this... I am... this is Vicki. I'm one of the assistants for the Wolf Council, and since Elder Mallon's normal assistant is on leave, he asked me to help him out for a couple of weeks. I'm just wondering if you had the time to take a call from him?"

I bite my lip to keep the annoyance in check, since I can sense her nervousness. I let my wolf probe her a little, and she seems to have some kind of hero worship—towards *me*—instead of anything nefarious. Fair enough. Oversharing due to nerves, I can handle.

"Of course, I can. Thank you for reaching out so politely."

"Always, Luna Montgomery," she says, sounding a little breathless. "I'll just transfer him through to you now."

"Thank you."

"Um, be careful."

And the line clicks before I can ask her what she meant by that. Her words were hushed, as if she shouldn't have said them, and the rapid transfer of the call doesn't help matters. River's eyebrows raise, and he taps his temple.

"*What?*" I ask.

"*I'll have a look into her, and see what we can find out.*"

"*We have resources within the Council?*"

"*If you know where to look, angel, we have resources everywhere.*"

I nod, but before I can reply, there's another click on the line. The breathing of the man who is really starting to piss me off sounds down the line, and my wolf bristles. She's so violent since we've accepted our destiny from Conri, and it's kind of startling.

Are bloodshed and destruction part of our destiny?

"Charlotte Montgomery here, how may I help you, *Mallon*?" I spit his name at him, showing the absolute disrespect I have for him and his sham of a position.

He doesn't value me or my wolves. That's fine. Because I don't value him or his pathetic attempts at leadership.

"That was a very disrespectful way to acknowledge the leader of your people, Luna Montgomery," he says back, also emphasising my name.

"Oh, sorry, I didn't realise we were back to playing nice. I'm still reeling from yesterday's discussion, where you told me you wished I was dead." River's sharp inhale goes ignored. His grip on my hand is an attempt to warn me to be careful, but I'm done treading carefully around men whose egos have far more reach than their power.

I am the most powerful wolf alive. Who is he to treat me like I'm nothing because I have a vagina?

River's attempts to corral me aren't going to stop me.

"I would never say such a thing to one of our most esteemed wolves."

"I'm sure you wouldn't, Elder Mallon," I say, forcing a polite tone. We both know it's fake, but he doesn't call me out on it. "And may I ask, who else is on this call?"

"It's just you and I for now." And there we go, his tone changes, going from the pleasant—but arrogant—man to his true nature. His nasty tone prevails, like the fucking viper that he is. A viper with a wolf. A dangerous combination.

I hate him.

"So, I wanted to let you know that we won't be attending our meeting today." His tone is back to that fake pleasant shit, and it riles me and my wolf up so badly.

We know the truth about him. Why is he hiding under this mask?

"I presumed we weren't since you have yet to even leave the South," I say, looking around the room that I've set up perfectly ready for his arrival. There's water, papers, notepads, hell, I even brought out the good china for tea. *Okay, fine, it's all good china.*

"Your assumed smarts is one of my least favourite things about you," he says, and I hold in my snort. "Unfortunately, we've come into a bit of an issue."

"You have?" My tone is dripping with fake shock, and I roll my eyes. I've spent all morning churning with anxiety, struggling with the weight of this visit and what it will mean for me and my mates, and they had no intention of even coming here. It is another one of their power trips, and I'm seething.

River taps my thigh, and I turn to look at him. The full weight of my glower hits him, but he shakes his head, warning me to tread carefully.

I nod firmly, but I don't need a controller right now. Especially not from my Gamma, of all people.

"What do you mean you've run into a bit of a problem, Elder Patriarch?"

"We're currently on a full council lockdown."

"Wait, what?" This time, my shock is genuine. What does a full Council lockdown entail? Why would this happen? I nudge River, and he nods, his eyes going distant as he loops someone else in.

"You don't already know?" he sneers. I shake my head, and when I remember he can't see me, I verbalise the no. He sighs, and I can imagine him now, with the scrunched-up face as he tries to decipher my lies. Well, this time there isn't one. "We received a letter last night from someone who calls himself—"

"King Lobo," I whisper at the same time he said it.

"Yes. What do you know of it?"

"We received a letter too." River tenses, and I look up at him. The hybrid shakes his head, and this time I listen to the warning. "Well, I did. He's taking a bit of a fancy to me. But you'd know all about that, right?"

"Oh, did you now? Well, we were not aware of that."

I roll my eyes, knowing that he's a liar.

"I'm sure you didn't." I wait a beat, and he doesn't share what I want to know. "What did your letter say?"

"Unfortunately, due to the threat to the Council, *among other things*, that remains confidential," he says. Among other things? What other things? "But since we are unable to leave our confines, we're not going to be able to have our conference."

"Our conference."

"We're very important people, you see, Charlotte, and so we need to make sure that *we're* safe."

"I totally understand," I say, my tone dripping with honey. He's a patronising asshole, and we both know it. He's trying to rile me up, ready for whatever news he's about to drop. "So, how may I be of assistance to you?"

"Well, we can't do the interrogation"—how quick this changed from a *conference* to an *interrogation*—"face to face, since we're not permitting anybody who could harm us onto Council property."

I laugh, cutting him off. Is he for real? Anyone who could harm them? I'm very cutting with my words, but they're not at risk of physical harm from me.

Yet.

"Well, at least you acknowledge my power," I say.

"Is it your power we're acknowledging, Charlotte, or your ties to a terrorist?"

"What?" My jaw drops, and even River stills next to me. *My ties to a terrorist?*

"I wish I could say it surprises me that you're working with King Lobo, and I truly wanted to bring you in then and there." I flinch, and River's hand rises to rub my lower back softly. I lean into him, breathing in his scent. We're alone. I refuse to feel ashamed for still wanting him. "Alas, I was overruled by the Council. So, the compromise is that we'll be doing a full Council-wide meeting with you, your three Alphas, and any you wish to bring at 11:30 am today."

I check my watch with a frown. "And what are we discussing?"

"Well, the attack that this... King Lobo launched upon your pack, *according to you*. The same attack, which resulted in some *rogue wolves* and the death of some of our people. In fact, since the moment you decided to return from the dead, and involve yourself in a world that doesn't want you, you've been involved in several controversies and attacks."

"I see."

"So, Charlotte Mason, the topic of discussion is *you*."

My wolf is furious. She's seething, and I can feel the desire within me to shift. It's like a second skin, the energy dancing across my body, my nerves prepared to commit to the change. But I try to hold it off. This is not the time to let her take control. We need to ignore our more volatile emotions and try to be logical. We need to know what's going on.

Especially since I'm the current threat.

My body is still tense from the idea that, once again, I am being put into the Council's cruel games. But my wolf has retreated ever so slightly.

"Well. When will this be taking place?"

River frowns at me, and when Mallon's annoyance rings across the line, I understand why. "We just said that it will take place at 11:30 today."

"And what would the outcome of this inquiry be?"

"Well, either we find you innocent, or we find you guilty." He sounds very amused now, and I'm not impressed by that in the slightest.

"Innocent means you'll leave us alone, correct?"

"In this instance, yes," Elder Patriarch Mallon says, but I can hear the smirk in his words, and I'm not stupid enough to not read deeper into them.

"And if we're guilty?" I close my eyes briefly as I ask the question, letting the fear take grip of my heart for one second before pushing it outwards.

I don't have the luxury of being scared right now.

I need to be the Luna of this pack.

"We'll have no choice but to seize you, your mating circle and your pack."

"And what will happen to my pack?" My words are deathly calm here, with no hint of the turbulent emotions that are raging rampant within. They're free from the howls of my wolf, and the terror of myself. I'm speaking like a leader.

But then I look up at River, and he sees the truth. He and I, may be lacking a mating bond, but we've still got the friendship bond we've formed—we've still got the love. He knows me just as well as I know myself; he rubs my back, leans in closer, and gives me a small pleading nod.

I yank on my mating bonds with everything I have in me.

This isn't a drill.

This is the time to panic.

I know they'll be heading our way immediately, so we don't have a lot of time.

"Your pack will be given a true Alpha to lead them, and anyone who is sympathetic to you will be held for questioning."

"I see." My hands are shaking, and I hope he can't hear the trembling of my voice. "And what about my mates and I?"

"Well, that depends on how the trial finds you. It'll likely either be life imprisonment or death." Then the line goes dead, but the pounding of my heart echoes so loudly in my brain. The door flies open, and my mates barge into the room, their faces ranging from annoyance to anger to fear.

"What is going on?" Rhett demands, his tone firm and hard, as his eyes rake over me with an intensity I can't bear.

"Lottie's just been handed a death sentence by the Council," River says, somehow managing to sound calm.

But it's a good thing he was.

Since everybody else loses it.

CHAPTER 16

"What is going on in here?" a feminine voice calls. I don't know if anyone, other than me, heard it and I unsteadily rise to my feet. I have no idea when I collapsed to the ground, but nobody felt it was appropriate to help me up. It's a good thing nobody heard the voice though, because in the doorway of the room stands Freya—who is welcome here whenever—Abel and Alaric Viotto. The latter two are *not* welcome here at all.

My heart speeds up, and I swear I'm one second away from having my heart burst from the ferocity of it.

"What are you doing here?" I ask, inching towards the trio in the doorway. Freya gives me a grim smile and I just know they're not here for a good reason.

My men stop shouting, each of them looking at me in surprise.

Whether it's because of the panic I'm feeling or the rising dread, I have no idea. I ignore their looks, and step forward again, to advance towards my friend and her family. She's in pain, and I've got a good guess as to why.

But as I side-step around Warren to get to the Viotto's, Theo grabs hold of my arm, giving me a concerned look. "What is *who* doing here? Who do you see, Charlotte?"

"Freya," I reply, shaking my arm so that he gets the hint and lets go of me. He doesn't, and instead scans the room. I can feel his power pulsing out, but for whatever reason, he can't feel her. I scrunch up my nose, pointing to the doorway. "She's right there, babe."

"There's nobody here, Lottie," Noah says, and his tone is gentle, but I can feel the undercurrent of his annoyance through our shared bond. His wolf is concerned since he, too, can't find the power. But I'm beat out of replying by the vampire with the additional powers. Warren throws out a beam of purple energy towards where I pointed. I flinch, even though my wolf recognises the power as belonging to our family line, because it's a very powerful display.

It's unnatural. Scary. New.

And so fucking hot.

And yet, Warren's power bounces off the barrier that's surrounding the three vampires, disintegrating into the air.

"Why did you do that?" Theo demands, glaring at Warren as he gently tugs me closer to his side. I hold in my eye roll at that, and even Freya's lips quirk up in amusement. Warren could never—*would never*—hurt me physically.

"Can't you feel it?" Warren counters, gesturing once more to the doorway. "Can't you feel the presence of something?"

"I can," I say, smiling at him softly. "But I don't understand how *you* can when none of the others are able to." And by the others, I mean Elijah, River, and Theo. I don't expect my wolf mates to be able to sense the energies of the vampires, even if they are powerful, because they're not too familiar with it. However, my vampire mates were part of their clan. They should be able to recognise the energies belonging to their leaders. And Theo, well, he's so connected to me—

a part of my soul, an extension of my entire being—that I'm so used to him being in tune with me and knowing what I do.

Has me taking the power of Conri fucked us beyond repair? Are we no longer as strong as we used to be together?

I don't like the thought of that. It causes my stomach to churn, and my throat to burn. My body is physically rejecting the idea that Theo and I are no longer in a harmonious sync.

Warren shrugs, and grins. "I've always been the better man in this room, princess. It makes sense."

Everyone else rolls their eyes, and nobody bothers rising to the bait.

"What can you see?" Theo demands, still holding onto me.

"Can you drop the barrier, please," I say, turning to the vampires. "This isn't working."

"Very tactful Charlotte," Theo says, pinching the bridge of his nose. He doesn't let go of me to do so. I can feel how unsettled his wolf is, feel his desire to shift and protect me from this unknown danger. But I can also sense the annoyance from my Guardian, knowing how badly he hates being caught unaware when it comes to my protection.

"Calm down, Guardian," I soothe, sending love and reassurance along our bond. Freya has brought her father and brother here for a reason, and I know it's not to do us any harm. Alaric is wary but also apologetic. The elder Viotto wants to help; he wants to make amends.

And Abel... he actually seems remorseful.

So clearly, something has gone down with Cain.

"So, what *is* going on in here?" Freya asks, giving me a wink when I roll my eyes.

"Fuck me, that was creepy," Caden whispers, but his voice echoes across the room.

"Right?" Warren says, nudging Wyatt, who is right next to him. Wyatt steps backwards, and I hide my amusement at his nerves.

"How did you get here?" Rhett asks, with a frown. My Alpha is, of course, worried about our safety since the barriers should be up, stopping anyone coming on our lands.

"Roman dropped us off," Freya says. "But when we felt the disturbance in the air, we decided to wrap ourselves in a barrier until we determined the cause."

"Smart," Theo says, and she grins at him.

"I have my moments."

"This was my idea," Abel mutters, which is ignored by all of us.

"We're fine," I say, and Freya narrows her eyes. "The Council are playing their twisted games once more and have decided that I have..." I blow out a small huff of air, eyeing my mates, before revealing it anyway. Freya knows me, she knows the truth, even if they don't. "They've decided I'm a terrorist."

"Ha," Abel snorts, rolling his eyes.

Once more, he's ignored, and he purses his lips. I can feel his unease, but it's hard to know much more when his vampire is as secretive as he is.

"Where is Roman?" I ask, changing the subject.

Freya gives her dad a dirty look, and I look away from it. "At home."

"What we're here for is a meeting between the three of us and you," Alaric says, diplomatically. "If you have the time—"

"I'm not going to lie, but we really don't," I say, cutting him off. Alaric dims, but he gives a nod. Freya frowns, and Abel's head snaps up as he looks at me.

"I understand that I fucked up—" the Viotto heir starts, and surprisingly he's both dropped his usual pompous decorum and the distant tone. He's not ashamed to practically beg.

"We don't," I say, softly. "This isn't because I want to be rude, or throw some kind of power around just because I can. We've got things to do, and..."

"Speak freely, young Luna," Alaric says. "You can always speak freely."

"Well, you dropped in without warning, and unfortunately, you've practically demolished the allies' bond we share. We can only trust a certain amount of people right now, and you're not it anymore."

"You're not wrong," Rhett says, and both Caden and Noah step into my space, showing they back me.

"If you go back to Clan lands, Primus Viotto, we can arrange something for another day," Rhett says, and I notice Theo steps away, sort of surrendering me to the care of my Alphas. "But we have family business right now."

"This is important," Abel insists.

"Are you really so desperate to cause more unrest among us that you're going to ignore what we've asked of you? Do you really want me to attack you the way you've earned, and take the life you haven't?" Rhett asks, snarling deeply.

Abel clenches his jaw, but doesn't back down.

"Why are you here?" Caden asks.

"My brother is dead," Abel says, stepping forward from the confines of his sister and father. The former probably wouldn't protect him immediately should one of us attack, but Alaric probably would.

I sigh, and drop into a seat at the table. I blink, and Freya is sitting opposite me.

"Are you okay?"

"I should be asking you that question," she counters. *"A fucking death threat?"*

"One of many, babe."

"The same could be said for my brother," she replies, and I snort, even though we both know it's not funny. I reach across the table and squeeze her hand, which she returns with just as much effort.

"Of course he is," Dillon says, with a roll of his eyes. There's a few clearing throats, and Dillon shrugs.

"Are you okay?" Wyatt asks me, and I shake my head gently.

How can I be okay?

I've got the Council breathing down our necks, and they've just threatened to take me, my mating circle *and* my entire pack in for questioning, whilst also in the same exact breath, telling me that if that happens, I won't be leaving their premises alive.

And then we've got the shit show that's happened with Abel

Viotto. There are so many ramifications of his actions, but the biggest one is that it has led to Cain dying. If it weren't for his reckless behaviours, we might've been able to actually question Cain and get some answers.

"Who killed him?" Noah asks, either reading my mind, or just still knowing.

"None of us," Freya mutters with a pout. Her dad gives her a warning look, probably for the utter dejection in her tone, but she shrugs. "Come on, Dad, we all know that he was going to die. Cain was heading that way."

"That does not change the fact that he is your brother, and your mother is upset," Alaric says. Theo mouthes the word 'was' but thankfully doesn't say it out loud.

"It also doesn't change the fact that he was an asshole who tried to kill my pregnant mate and hurt my people," Caden says. "I'm very glad your son is dead, no matter how your mate feels."

Alaric lets out a sigh. "It's not *just* about it being an upset for my mate. It's about the loss of life—the loss of a life who could've answered some big questions that we have. There was a benefit in having him alive."

"Wow, devious," Rhett says, with an appreciative look. "And about your own son, too."

"He was disowned," Alaric says slowly, dragging out the words as if he wasn't sure of them.

My mates and I exchange looks, but it's Elijah who breaks the silence.

"*I don't think it would hurt to bring them in on this,*" Elijah says, bringing us all into one telepathic connection. I note wryly that he included River, too.

"*No, it wouldn't,*" Wyatt adds. Rhett frowns, and Wyatt shakes his head at him. "*Alaric's a very good ally to have at a time like this.*"

"*And when we can't rely on them?*" Caden asks. Freya narrows her eyes at me, and I wink. If Roman were here, she'd know what we were talking about, but she can't right now.

"*Is our mate's life something we're willing to risk for our pride?*" Noah counters.

"*We risked our pack's life when asking for their help,*" Theo says quietly.

"*And I'd argue that right now, our pregnant mate is absolutely a bigger risk than our pack,*" Noah says. He and Theo exchange nods, but I'm looking around the room at each of the others.

"*They're here, and they're willing,*" Elijah continues. "*Even if they're not reliable completely, aid right now is needed.*"

"*Especially when it comes to keeping our mate out of their hands,*" Warren says. The brothers nod, and even River seems to agree with that.

"*Bring them in on this.*" My decision is the final one, and they all nod as Elijah dissolves our connection.

"It would be helpful if you could bring Roman here for this," I say, and Freya's grin is overshadowed by Alaric's frown. "Not to overhear whatever we need to figure out between us, but because at this moment in time, you are one of our strongest allies, and I've got a situation I need advice on. I don't have the time to cover all the intricacies that come along with it."

"I see," Alaric says. Abel frowns, but Alaric nods. "Whatever you need."

"Perfect." I look up at my mates, and they're all tense, ready for a fight that isn't coming just yet. "This is one of those instances where I tell you what to do, and you just do it. We can talk things out soon, but we're running against the clock here."

"We've got until 11:30," River says.

"For what?" Noah asks.

"For the meeting to take place that decides our fate," I say, with a smile. There are more frowns around the room, and I sigh. "The entire Council wants me to answer for the actions of a fucking madman."

"Fucking hell," Rhett snarls.

"They've decided that if I don't manage to convince them of my innocence, then I'm going to die."

"Your innocence for what?" Freya asks. "Because we've done some sketchy shit."

I laugh, but the smile disappears just as fast as it came. "This is why I need Roman. I don't have the time to go into it all."

"When will all this fucking shit end?" Wyatt mutters.

"When King Lobo, is dead," Noah says.

"Well, on that note, let's split everything up. River, can you send everyone off on tasks whilst Freya and I fill in the others?"

He nods, and starts sending people off. There's a lot of bristling and general unhappiness from the more dominant males, but thankfully, they bite their tongues. At the end of the day, my Alphas no longer wanted to work with River, so I did.

He might not be my mate any longer.

He may not ever have a real bond with me again, but he is still *mine*.

My Gamma, my friend, my love.

But at this moment in time, he's one of the three people that I trust to handle work situations for me.

"He's on his way," Freya reassures me gently, and I nod. Caden's on the phone with my dad, whilst Elijah silently communicates with Evie. I have no idea what the others are doing, but I know they can handle it.

"What do you need from me, little muse?" Roman asks, teleporting into the room, and immediately focusing on Freya. His back is to the rest of us, but I have no doubt the incubus is aware of where every single person is standing, just in case he needs to act to protect her.

"Lottie needs to share some things with my dad. Can you help her?"

He nods, and turns to me. There's a blank expression on his face, but he dips his head in respect. "May I have a chair to sit in, please? I'm a little drained, and will probably go down once I share this."

"Take from me," Freya demands, giving her mate a dirty look. He shakes his head, and she glowers at him in a way that's both frightening and amusing. "Ugh. Someone get him a chair. He's more malleable when he's drained of energy."

"Please don't be announcing that," Abel says, with a sigh. "I do not need my baby sister going to jail for doing *unwanted things* to people when they're too weak to fight her off."

"Fuck, that was actually funny," Caden says, with a grin at him. Noah and Rhett nudge Caden, and he frowns, clutching at his stomach, and turns away from Abel. I roll my eyes.

I drag a chair out from the table for Roman, before sitting down to the left of it. Roman sits in the middle, and Alaric sits to the right of him. Abel and Freya both stand behind Roman, and each puts a hand on his shoulders.

I still don't know enough about the incubus my best friend is mated to know why he's going to struggle this time when he doesn't usually, but the fact that he opened up about a vulnerability highlights how deeply it's going to affect him.

"Are you ready?" he asks, and I nod. I know I don't need to do anything really. Instead, I just sit here, and let him rifle through my brain to pull up what he needs to see. I can feel his presence, but my wolf doesn't fight against it, as he easily shares my memories with Alaric and Abel.

What would take me a good fifteen, twenty minutes to explain everything and answer all of their questions takes Roman less than a minute to broadcast everything. It's time we just don't have.

"Mallon is an idiot," Alaric hisses, as his bright red eyes meet mine. His hands are clenched into fists, and I can feel how unsettled his vampire is.

Roman slumps in the chair, his eyes fluttering closed. There's a sheen over his skin, and he seems clammy, even without me touching him. His eyes are flashing a bright gold under his eyelids, and they're moving a little rapidly, before they just stop.

"He's exhausted," I murmur, reaching over to him, but he's out. I place my hand on his forearm, sending a little bit of healing energy into him.

"He's drained," Freya says, shoving Abel out of the way so that she can get to her mate. She places both hands on his shoulders, and starts to power share with him. I don't see the energy transfer, but I can feel it in the air. There's this tingling sense that both my wolf and I are tuned in on, alerting us to the power. I know she's a vampire, we can detect that, but her powers are *more*.

Like mine, her powers are an ethereal sense of a deep and old origin. She's the descendent of the original vampire and the bond we share reassures me that there's no danger. I'm not foolish enough to think that all the other originals are as nice, but Freya and I are a team.

The difference is that she's had her powers for years, and is slowly learning how to harness them with the help of her mates. I've only just been granted mine, and have no idea how long it'll take to master them. Freya's only a few years younger than me and still doesn't have full control.

"That's rude," Roman says, half asleep.

"Yes, it was," Freya says, winking at me. She drops a kiss on Roman's head, before moving to sit down. He looks drained still, but nowhere near as badly. "So, where are we with your shit?"

I flinch, and look around the room, not having realised a lot of my men are no longer here. It's only been a minute or two, but they're in different areas of the building. I can detect others here, too, Evie from my dad's pack, as well as some of the other lawyers that I know of, but have yet to meet.

"Your mates have done a very good job of splitting themselves up to share the tasks around, but I don't think it's going to be enough," Alaric says.

"No, neither do I."

"Stop being so cynical," Freya says, with a glare. "Worst case, you can just flee. Fuck everything, and go live in Canada or some shit."

I give her a soft smile, but we know that's not an option. Not really.

"As far as I'm aware, you've got two choices," Alaric says.

"And they are?" I ask, raising an eyebrow.

"Show that you are the Original Wolf, and you take the power that your lineage affords you," Alaric says.

"What's the other option?" I ask, to all of their disappointment. "I'm not sure we're yet ready for the nuclear option."

"You go rogue. You let your pack go, go on the run, prepare your allies, organise what needs to be organised, and prepare. A fight is coming, and you prepare for it, letting yourselves be the ones on the offensive."

Abel's jaw drops, and he gives his father a shocked look. I can feel his anger brimming, but it's not directed at us. He's mad *for* me, I think. It's weird, since he's never been a fan of me—never even been an ally. "Are you taking the piss?"

"What?" Alaric asks, his voice dropping as he returns the look. "I'm not wrong."

"No, but you're telling her to become a fugitive. You're telling her to run away from her problems."

"No, I am not, son. Only one of us in this room has run from their problems repeatedly, as far as I'm aware," Alaric says, with a deliberately calm tone of voice. "Lottie's move would be a strategic one to prepare herself for doing the right thing."

Abel's lips are pressed firmly together in a thin line, his disapproval evident. But for some reason, he doesn't argue any further.

"I don't see how making ourselves criminals is going to help," I say, and Freya sighs. She's just excited for the fun of it all, whereas I don't have that level of detachment. I've got to think strategically because it's my pack, *my people,* who would pay the price. "But we're also not yet in the position to take the Council by force."

"Not yet is very different from never," Roman says quietly.

"That's very true. Our plan is to take the Council by force and rid the wolves of the oppression figureheads who aren't doing their job," I say. I can hear footsteps along the corridor, feeling people approaching us. Hopefully, they've got some better ideas.

"I can't deal with this," Abel says, shaking his head. "You can't—"

"Oh, dear brother," Freya says, rolling her eyes. "For somebody who was more than willing to disobey the rules that are set out by the vows you had taken so that you could protect our pathetically dead brother, it's a little judgmental that you can't do the same for someone who is fighting for her life."

Abel sighs, resting his head in his hands. "I really don't know what to do," he mutters. "I really don't know what to do."

"You've given some advice Primus," Evie says, stepping into the room. She's wearing a gorgeous grey pantsuit, and she grins at me. Caden, Noah and Wyatt are here with her, and they all make their way over to the table and slide into some of the open seats. My Alphas seem calm and reassured, but Wyatt seems very unsettled. "But I've got a different idea, if you're willing, Luna."

"What's your idea?" I ask. "Because I'm willing to do almost anything. I really don't want to be a fugitive. Not with everything that we've got going on."

"What you do is fight their law, with the law." Evie's words seem simple in theory, but I don't truly understand what she means. "The Council are currently on lockdown, which means everything shuts down. They should not be interrogating you when they're not permitted to be in service. Technically, every single proceeding should stop."

"What does that even mean?" Caden asks, with a frown. My father and Malcolm join us, the former kissing the top of my head as he walks past to sit down. The latter winks at his mate but gets ignored.

"Does it really surprise you that they're, once again, choosing to ignore the laws they set?" I ask, rolling my eyes. "Because it doesn't surprise me in the slightest."

"I was going to explain if you didn't interrupt," Evie says, her words sharp as a whip, as she gives my mate an impatient look. He hangs his head low, a blush coating his cheeks. I laugh, but she turns that scowl my way and I fall silent. I don't want to piss off the people helping us. "We're in a precarious position right now as a species, and our leaders have decided that because of some threat they've not shared with anyone, they've got to lock themselves down to remain safe. One of the requirements with this act, is that they inform every Alpha and Luna within a set timeframe, which, as far as we're aware, they've not done."

We all shake our heads, because even if they classed that terrible call as a notification to me, neither Charles nor my dad received a report either.

"And their first act in this shutdown is to haul you in for a formal interrogation. They've done their required part for that, giving you the time and the date, and even giving advanced notice. For something of this calibre, they only need to give you sixty minutes' notice."

"Sixty fucking minutes?" Malcolm demands, echoed by Wyatt.

"Sixty minutes," Evie confirms, giving her mate a dirty look. He holds his hands up in defence, but Wyatt is smug that he didn't get lectured. "I know it's not much of a notification, but that's the law. However, they are breaking the law since they're not following the rules of their self-imposed shutdown. They need to decide whether to put their shutdown on hold to give you a trial or whether they're going to keep themselves safe and delay things."

"That's ingenious," Alaric says, with a smile. "I can get Edgar to come down and help out if that would be of any use."

"Absolutely," Evie and I answer at the same time. Edgar is someone I respect for the help he gave us at Midnight Summit, and he's faster than us wolves.

"Thank you," I finish alone. Alaric nods, maintaining the cool façade. I can feel the pride from his vampire, though, and it's a nice feeling to have. "So, what is your plan, Evie?"

"My plan is to use the law against them. If we can force them to push the date of this back until their shutdown ends, it gives us a lot of time to organise." She purses her lips, meeting my eyes. "The plan is for you to form more allies, correct?"

I nod. "We've got visits to make over the next few weeks, and it'll be really imperative that we do that without me being a fugitive."

"Us," Caden says, leaning forward to look at me properly. "Without *us* being fugitives."

I nod, and connect with him mentally as Alaric asks Evie a question about the specific law that shows this. Edgar's going to read up on it.

"I sort of like the idea of you being a little criminal, baby."

He puffs his chest out as he meets my eyes once more, a delicious grin appearing across his face that enhances the twinkling in his baby-blue eyes. *"Me, you, tonight."*

"Tonight."

"Do not look at my child like that," my dad hisses, and Caden groans as my dad kicks him under the table. *Immature, as fuck.* "I already know far too much about what you do to her."

"It might not have been me," Caden argues, rubbing his shin.

I roll my eyes, and turn to Evie. "So, how far back can we legally push it?"

"We negotiate it. Four to six weeks would give us plenty of time to organise our defence."

"Is that all we can get?" I ask, exchanging nervous looks with my Alphas.

She frowns. "Depending on the threat level, we might be able to get it to twelve weeks."

I nod, sighing, and I'm not the only one. My dad's frown is deep, but my Alpha's is deeper. Freya and Roman are still in the room, but they're definitely not partaking in this conversation, and Abel's holding his tongue, but taking everything in. Alaric's still chatting with Edgar—I think—but I have no doubt he's actively listening.

My dad leans forward, clasping his hands together, and gives me a look across the table.

"Lottie is pregnant," Caden says, taking that decision from me. I smile, and he relaxes. "So, three months from now will put us close to the four-month mark, and we can't delay it further than that."

"Probably closer to the three month mark than four," Noah says, but he nods to his brother. "Which means that'll put you in the second trimester, right? Giving you only two or maybe three more months of shifting since you're pregnant with twins."

"Twins?" Evie mouths, delight filling her gaze. I ignore that reaction.

"I don't know what you're getting at here," I say, giving my twin Alphas an apologetic look. Is this baby brain, or are they being obtuse?

"After we handle the Council, we've got this fight with King Lobo," Caden says, and Noah nods. My eyes widen. "So the longer we delay the Council, the less time we'll have to handle him."

"Well fuck," I mutter, closing my eyes briefly.

"I doubt it'll be this clear cut," Wyatt says. "But that's the gist of a plan. The ancestors told you to wrap up the problem with the Council so that you can focus on the attack from King Lobo."

"Well fuck," my dad echoes.

Who thought getting pregnant right before a war was a good idea?

Oh yes, my sex-deprived vagina, that's who.

CHAPTER 17

"It's time," Theo says, resting the small of his hand against my back. "Are you ready?"

I bite my lip, and nod. He either doesn't realise he's doing it, or is content to offer me the healing without a chastisement for drawing blood.

"That doesn't convince me."

"I'm terrified, Theo," I whisper, finally turning to look at him. He pulls me into his arms, lowering his head to rest his forehead against mine.

"I promise you, little wolf, that no matter the situation, you will thrive. I will not allow the Council to take you away from us, Charlotte, and I most definitely won't be settling here as a fugitive."

"You can't promise that."

"I can, and I have."

I giggle, just a little pathetic one, but it's enough for him. He presses a soft kiss to my lips.

"Be strong. Be bold. Be you. Fuck the patriarchy, Charlotte."

I laugh properly this time. "It's not necessarily the patriarchy that's the issue this time. It's King Lobo and his desire to fuck with my life."

"Because you're a woman with something he wants," Noah says, from the doorway. I pull away from Theo, the wolf not letting go of me properly, and smile at Noah. "Now, we've got a plan. We're ready to do this, okay?"

"You'll be there?"

"We'll *all* be there, baby," Noah reassures me. He outstretches his hand, and Theo squeezes my hip once before letting go. I reach out and take Noah's hand, and the three of us leave my office and go through to the large meeting room we had originally set up for the in-person meeting earlier this morning.

We've moved the room around, so instead of the one long table, we've broken it up into segments. At the top of the room are three separate smaller tables. On the far left, are my three Alpha mates. On the far right are River, Wyatt, Warren and Theo.

The table in the centre is also set up for four—me, Alaric, and my two lawyers.

Alaric is sitting at the head of the table, with a spot for me right next to him. On my other side are Evie and Edgar, the vampire from Alaric's clan who helped me during my questioning after the events at Charles's pack. I'm glad Alaric managed to get him to come since he and Evie work amazingly well together.

We've brought in a large screen, and that's hooked up to the computer so we can do this properly. Elijah's not in the room with us, although I can feel him in the building, and neither is Dillon. He's not in the building, though, and is instead at the library trying to piece together some of the advice we've been given by the ancestors.

Lionel and Lexie are sitting behind the screen, but we're not going to announce their presence, and the same goes for the three other lawyers Evie brought. Lionel is in charge of keeping Charles up to date, and Lexie is taking notes of the information shared, in case it's relevant to the other Alphas and Lunas we're going to be visiting. Abel, Freya and Roman are sitting at another table, again just wanting to be involved, and helping keep things calm.

The room is large but packed, and we are all anxious. Or maybe I'm so anxious I can't feel anybody else's emotions.

"It's eleven twenty-eight," Noah says, taking his seat. He's in the middle of Rhett and Caden, and he gives me a small smile. "Take a deep breath, baby; we're hooking it up now."

"Nothing will happen that you can't come back from," Alaric reassures me, and I nod slowly. My head feels empty, as if it's full of nothing, but yet so chaotic that I can't breathe.

My heart is pounding, my palms are sweaty, and I can feel the goosebumps breaking out across my skin.

The worst that happens is we'll need to go on the run forever, lose our pack and the stability, and let them all go under the control of a Council who doesn't want to—

"Breathe," Evie whispers. She reaches under the table and squeezes my thigh, and I jolt. It wasn't a soft pinch; it was a nip that hurt, but it did the job of centring me. "Breathe, Luna."

I nod my head and watch as the person in charge of the screen inputs the code, enabling us to join the Council's call.

I close my eyes, and merge with my wolf, needing the stability of her to get through this.

Give me the strength.

Give me the calm.

Give me the power.

And when my eyes re-open, I'm a lot calmer, and ready to do this. We're one.

There's some crackling on the screen, which is louder in this merged form, but I hold off on the cringe. I also hold back the snarl when Mallon's face appears in front of me.

There's a flash, and then more viewpoints appear, and I cringe internally. Mallon's standing at the front of the room. It's the same room we were in for my official appointment as Luna, I think, except this time, there is a wide podium in front of him. There's a microphone atop it for sure, but it also looks like he has books on there. I can't see well enough, even with the enhanced senses of my wolf, due to the camera quality, but the podium is wide enough that Rhett, River and I could sit and have breakfast on it.

Or do rude things to each other with one of us laid across it...

The connection my wolf and I share tenses, and I know it's because I thought his name. I resist the urge to turn and look at the man, but my wolf doesn't try to corral herself from reaching out to touch his hybrid.

I leave them to the mental inquisition and start scanning the crowd on the screen.

I wish the quality was better, but I still see some familiar faces. I just can't tell how they're feeling. It's very frustrating, and doesn't help my anxiety.

Mallon clears his throat, silencing the room he's in. We were already silent, waiting for him to begin.

"Please bear with us one moment, Luna Montgomery, Alpha Simmons, Alphas' Jameson. We're just getting ourselves settled."

"There's no rush, Elder Patriarch," Noah says, smoothly. I can feel the anger across my mates' bonds, and so it makes sense he's speaking. Neither Caden nor Rhett could hide their disdain.

There's a loud beep, and the cameras move around on the screen. Mallon comes centre stage on a full-sized screen, whereas the others decrease in size to be smaller ones surrounding him.

It makes it even harder for us to assess the audience, but makes us have to look at him even further.

It doesn't help the rage we're all feeling.

Just behind the screen, I see Lionel nudge the laptop he's got open over to Abel, who nods. Lionel then tugs it back to himself and starts furiously typing away. I'm not sure what's going on, but I appreciate their diligence.

We were a little unsure about allowing Abel to partake in this meeting, but he came to me alone and asked to be part of it. He wants to talk to me about something once this meeting is over, and apparently, being here will aid that.

I've got no idea if that's the truth, but as the heir to the biggest vampire clan in the UK—the heir to the monarchy here, really—he's likely got a lot he can offer us.

"Are you all ready for the proceedings to begin?" Elder Patriarch Mallon asks. His question pisses me off for two reasons.

The first is that he was the one who needed more time so that they could all get themselves sorted.

The second is that his tone is one I have *never* heard from him. Not even during the meeting where they were deciding whether I was worthy of being Luna.

He's putting on the show now, pretending to the Council and the rest of our people since this is recorded for the archives, that he's a good man, that he's not the asshole that we know him to be.

"We're here at your request," I say, softly.

"Please do not address the Council unless directly asked a question by name, Luna Montgomery," the Elder Patriarch replies, without breaking this fake polite tone. My face must show my surprise, because he explains. "In matters like this, it is your Alphas who speak on your behalf. You should defer to them as the powerhead of your pack, and of your mating."

My jaw would drop if I allowed it, but instead, I purse my lips. I'm not the only angry party here, even Alaric is seething.

But that's my own fault for not guessing this would be the way of it, I suppose.

"Objection," Evie says, rising to her feet.

"We don't do that here," the Elder Patriarch says, amongst all the snorting and laughing from the Elders in the crowd. "But we appreciate the effort."

"I see," Evie says, although her tone shows how adamantly she does *not* see. "So how do I voice my unhappiness with what you've just said?"

"You do not," he says. "We do not recognise you as a party to these proceedings."

Evie's wolf is tense, but I think the human is even more tense. She doesn't know where to go from here, and honestly, neither do I.

"Unfortunately, Elder Patriarch, we've got cause to register this objection. Our client is the one on trial, is the powerhead of both her mating *and* her pack, and there is legal precedent for her to speak on her own behalf."

"And who may you be?" Mallon demands. He lost composure for a moment there, letting his annoyance seep into his tone, but he immediately fixes his attitude.

"My name is Edgar Whitmore, Elder Patriarch. I have intimate knowledge of your court and have met with a few of the Elders in attendance," Edgar says calmly.

"I see," Elder Patriarch says. "And your position here is?"

"I am here as legal counsel to Alpha Simmons, Alphas Jameson and Jameson, and Luna Montgomery."

A hand raises in the crowd, someone I don't recognise on the grainy screen, but even without Elder Mallon recognising him, I would've as soon as he spoke.

"And what gives you that right?" Elder Brooks asks.

"As part of the official ally vow my clan—Hearthstone—has with Rose Moon, I am duty-bound to provide them the support that they need."

Elder Patriarch Mallon quickly disguises his smirk, and I know that Edgar's words were phrased that way deliberately.

Or at least, I hope that they were.

"Good to know. So, who else may we be introduced to," Elder Patriarch says. "We're at a very unfair advantage."

Noah rises to his feet, and goes through the list of introductions. It's not until we reach Alaric that there's some discomfort across the Elders.

"It's nice that there's such a big party on your side," the Elder Patriarch says, gathering some laughter amongst the crowd. "Considering the summons was only for Luna Montgomery."

There's a growl from Caden, but I don't turn and look, trusting that they'll keep him contained.

"And yet you just told my mate she cannot speak unless directly spoken to," Noah replies.

"Since she's a woman," Caden adds in.

"It's not because she's a woman," Mallon says, patronisingly. He titters as if we're so dumb, and there's laughter in the crowd. We've got people watching this feed, and I hope they can gather more information than I currently am, so that we can be a little more prepared when it comes to meeting them face to face.

"No?"

"Of course not. We'd never judge someone for their... *parts*, no matter how inferior." There's some hollering in the background and lots of laughter at Mallon's words. I roll my eyes, and I'm not the only one, but I've got to hand it to him.

He truly knows how to play the game and secure his alliances. He's not *this* sexist, not really, but in front of this audience—both the full group of Elders and the camera, which will be made public record and definitely announced to everyone depending on how — he's playing it up.

"May we ask for some decorum in the chambers, Elder Patriarch?" Edgar asks smoothly.

"Of course, you may." Mallon clears his throat, and then, in the most condescending tone possible, he calls out, "Quiet, quiet everybody. Thank you for that. Luna Montgomery is getting her feelings hurt that we're so joyful." There's an increase in the laughter, and he allows it for a moment before holding up his hand. The entire room falls silent at the act, almost as if they practised it. "Now, before we start with the proceedings, is there anything the defence would like to say?"

Evie's lips purse, and I can sense the surprise from her inner wolf. Is this not normally how it goes?

"We'd like to propose a motion to request this hearing be delayed until a time when the Council is no longer in shutdown," Edgar says.

"We're still in action," Elder Patriarch Mallon says.

"Then this meeting should take place in person, by law," Edgar says. "Shall we reconvene until that time can be met?"

"Unfortunately, for our safety, we are on lockdown," Mallon says, once more with that patronising tone. "But we're all here, and we're all willing to do this through the video. It's probably more efficient."

I'm sure it is. *Even my thoughts can't hide the sarcasm.*

"We're all ready to make a judgement on Luna Montgomery's status and her affiliation with the traitor that we've come to know as King Lobo."

"Unfortunately," Edgar says, enunciating the word with the same inflictions that Mallon did. "As per your laws, if you are in shutdown —which lockdown is the first step of—every single Alpha and Luna must be notified within the first twelve hours of that being declared. Rose Moon did not receive word of this notification, and neither did the nearest packs."

Mallon's eye twitches, barely, but since I'm watching him so closely, it's clear to see. His lips seem to tighten—or maybe he's holding back a snarl—as he regards my lawyer. Edgar really was a good idea, and I'm grateful to Alaric for suggesting it.

"Official lockdown was only announced at 8 am this morning. We wanted to cover this before going through the official notifications so as to not waste our time during this very troubling time," Mallon says. His words are pleasant enough, but his tone is biting. I have no doubt we'd smell his anger if we were there. "We have our plans in place already to let every single pack know of this before the deadline the law demands."

"Good to know," Edgar says, with a nod. "But that brings us to our motion. If you are in shutdown, that means you cannot operate with this interrogation, and if you're not in lockdown, we need to do this in person. It's quite the legal conundrum."

"Objection," an Elder, shouts from the audience. "We're only in a shutdown because of her. If she weren't spreading her legs for any man, our lives would not be in danger. This is the only safe way to apprehend this traitor."

"The floor does not recognise you, Elder," Mallon says, without even looking at him, but there's a smirk on his face as he says it. I guarantee he didn't name the bastard deliberately, too.

Dickhead.

"I completely understand your position," Mallon says to Edgar. "However, we've deemed the matter concerning Luna Montgomery as a matter of great urgency. Our laws grant us an exemption when it comes to terrorist attacks."

"And where is your proof that Charlotte Montgomery is part of a terrorist attack?" Edgar asks, as my eyes widen.

Terrorism? They're blaming me for *terrorism*?

"It'll never *stand up,"* Roman reassures me, and I'm surprised he's the one reassuring me.

"Never. I'll wipe them all out first," Freya adds, winking at me. *"Now relax, because I can see the murder in your eyes, which means he can too."*

I relax my jaw and nod once but keep it as a tiny movement so Mallon won't see it.

"We've got plenty of evidence that Charlotte *Montgomery* was part of a terrorist attack," the Elder Patriarch says. "She's consistently in the middle of these attacks and the centre of every problem. Not only did King Lobo call her out directly, but she was also there the night the Council were attacked."

"The night the *Council* were attacked?" I hiss, glaring at him. "That attack was—"

"Were you asked a direct question, Charlotte *Montgomery*?" he asks, spitting my surname at me in that disrespectful and condescending tone of his.

I shake my head, clenching my jaw.

"I didn't think so, please remain silent until such a time occurs." He waits for a beat. "Perfect."

"Well, since I've yet to be greeted, Mallon, I'd like to the floor," Alaric says, rising to his feet. "For those of you on the Council who do not know me, I am Alaric Viotto, the reigning monarch for all vampire kind. I'm here today as we have an alliance with Luna Montgomery, and her bonded Alphas."

A hand rises in the audience, and Mallon calls upon them. "The floor hears you, Elder Parkinson."

Elder Parkinson rises to his feet. "Thank you, Elder Patriarch. I wish to know how you and Luna Montgomery came to be acquainted."

"Unfortunately, that's something my client will not be answering today," Edgar says. "How long do you anticipate the lockdown to be for?"

"Likely ten weeks or so," the Elder Patriarch says. "We will not be explaining our safety protocols, to you, but rest assured that we are handling this situation to the letter of the law."

"I completely understand and have the utmost faith in you and your capabilities of following the law," Edgar says. "However, ten weeks is plenty of time for us to organise transport down there and making sure that everyone is safe. It'll give us the ability to submit ourselves to this interrogation, legally, so that the outcome cannot be contested."

There's silence, but I recognise the look on Mallon's face to know that they're silently communicating. My heart is pounding as we wait, and I don't know if I'll hear him when he does speak.

"What do you think the possibility of this is?" Caden asks, drawing me into a silent connection with Evie, and whoever else. I can feel multiple energies across the link, but since we share a bond too, I'm not sure.

"No idea. I'd like to say highly probable."

"We'll get back to you with our decision in thirty minutes," Elder Patriarch Mallon says, before hanging up the call. All the screens go black, as a pit forms in my stomach.

"What does that mean?" Caden snarls. "He's going to *get back to us in thirty minutes*?"

"These white men are really rude," Freya says, from across the room. I nod at her, but her dad sighs.

"So, we're pushing for a meeting date in twelve weeks, right?" Edgar asks.

"Yes. Twelve is the max amount of time that we can push this," Noah says. Edgar nods, jotting that down on his document.

"I'd prefer the ten," I say, before sighing. "But of course, I'm not allowed to ask about that."

"Thank you for stepping up when my vagina became an issue," Evie says, and Edgar just nods, not saying something one way or another.

I reach over and squeeze Evie's hand. "Fuck the men, Evie. You're so smart and powerful and knowledgeable."

"Fat lot of good it does though, when they won't even hear my arguments because I'm a woman." She blows out a breath of air, before patting my hand. "Sorry. This isn't my pity party. So, ten weeks?"

I sigh, but we all debate it back and forth. Two weeks is a massive difference, but I'm nervous about pushing it that far, when I've got the twins to think about. We don't reach our consensus before there's an alert, and the cameras come back on.

"Charlotte Montgomery, please stand before the Council," the Elder Patriarch says. I rise to my feet, holding in the eye roll at his tone. "We're willing to grant the motion of your Alphas, provided that you follow some conditions."

I nod, not bothering to speak as I wait for him to outline those.

"You must make yourself available to the police and special team that are handling this threat. You must be honest and help them with their investigation in any way they deem fit."

"Clarification on that one, please, Elder Patriarch," Edgar says, rising to his feet.

"Nothing that would put you or your pack in danger," Elder Patriarch Mallon says, but I can see the annoyance. He hoped we wouldn't ask for that clarification. "But anything you withhold that is then found out about during your interrogation, you will be prosecuted for."

I nod.

"We will be having a full council debrief on the 18th of October, as we predict our shutdown will be over by then," the Elder Patriarch says.

I nod my head, again. That's about nine weeks away, give or take, and gives us a decent amount of time to get things sorted.

"That works for me," I say. "But I want to make one thing very clear—"

"You were not asked a direct question," he interrupts.

"I give zero shits about that. You'll learn to respect me, vagina and all, or this will not be a meeting that ends well for you."

"I thought I made it very clear how the meeting will end," he says, and there's that vicious smirk that he's tried to hide. "You'll lose your life if you are found to be guilty in any way, shape or form. And it might not be terrorism, the way you're threatening your Head of State, but it is treason. I'd be careful, Charlotte."

"Trust me, Elder Patriarch, if there's death to be had, I will not be the willing sacrifice," I say, sweetly. Edgar gives me a dirty look, but Alaric's booming laughter makes Mallon smile.

"Something funny, *Primus*?" Mallon asks, the title for the monarch on my side is sneered.

"We're very proud to have Charlotte as an ally," Alaric says, standing and patting my shoulder. "Trust me on this, *Elder Patriarch*, you do not want to make an enemy of her, because you *will* make an enemy of us all. We honour our allies." Alaric gives me a sad look, before turning back to the camera.

"King Lobo, what can you tell us about him, Charlotte?" Elder Patriarch Mallon asks.

"Not much," I reply.

"Nothing at all, actually," Rhett interjects. "Everything we know we've already told your people. Remember, when we tried to call to tell you about the issues we were having, and you left us to ourselves?"

"I do," Mallon snarls. "Unfortunately, the safety of one pack is not *my* priority when I have an entire race to look after. You should follow the correct procedures, instead of thinking you're above the law. If

you have issues, you'll need to talk to your council representatives."
He grins. "You know, after the shutdown."

"Trust me, we will be," I snarl, and the line goes dead.

But with that win, our room erupts into cheers.

We got what we wanted.

Now it's time to plan on how we're going to end the Council in just under ten weeks.

It's been a long time coming.

CHAPTER 18

"Well, thank fuck that's over," Caden says, coming to sit on the table in front of me. He reaches out, smoothing out my loose hair, and smiles at me. "How are you feeling after it?"

"Not great," I say with a sigh. Alaric reaches over and pats my arm, before going over to sit where Freya, Roman and Abel are.

I look around the room, an overwhelming sense of guilt filling me, as I see everyone sitting tensely.

The joy we felt at our victory only a few moments ago has disappeared, and the burden of what we need to do fills the air.

I hate that I've brought this into their lives.

"This new motion gives us what, nine weeks to get everything planned?"

"Nine weeks is plenty of time to get it all outlined," she says.

"Nine weeks to plan a revolution," Theo says, coming to stand with us. "Aren't we lucky?"

"Don't be an asshole," Caden says, as I give my Guardian a dirty look. He laughs, and comes to stand behind me, squeezing my shoulders.

The bond between us hums in pleasure, and I lean into his touches, wanting more even with my terrible mood.

He's trying to make light of this situation, likely in a way to reassure me, but it doesn't help. I'm the reason we're in this mess.

They've branded *me* as a terrorist, for fuck's sake, and what am I doing? Committing the treason they accused me of.

I'm not a terrorist, but I *am* a traitor.

My wolf howls, and I sit up a little straighter. I'm being so ridiculously hard on myself, when this is a move I *want* to make.

I want to use the powers I've been given to end the Council's reign and fix the problems they've been causing.

I just want to do it as quickly—*and legally*—as possible.

My wolf, on the other hand, is so bloodthirsty that she wants to storm down there today and take control of the Council as violently as possible—no matter how ill-prepared we are.

"Nine weeks is plenty of time," Caden says. "Let's just hope that King Lobo doesn't have any plans in place before then."

"If he does, we will handle it together as a team," Theo says, squeezing my shoulders gently. "We can do this."

"We'll sit down and create a plan," Evie says. "Are you available as counsel, Edgar?"

The vampire checks with his Primus, who nods, and then nods himself. "I'll be as available as I can, alongside my normal duties to the Clan."

"Good. I'm missing the parts that would grant me permission to speak when it comes to the Council," Evie mutters.

"We'll need to make sure we've got adequate time to travel the country within this plan," I say.

"We know, little control freak," Caden says, smirking at me. "This was a win, baby. Stressful, sure, but it's a win."

"Is it a win, though?" I mutter, shaking my head. "We have so much that we have to do. We've got to outline everything that needs to be done, and we have such a limited window to do it all in. We've got to travel—"

"Enough," Theo says, crouching down as he squeezes my shoulders a little bit harder. "I understand you're stressed, little wolf, I get it. It's scary, and we've got so much resting on this."

"But where's the girl that used to see the danger, and throw herself into it? You'd plan, and prepare, and not just sit here so defeated," Caden says.

I frown, and shrug. "I think after everything, I'm entitled to sit here and take a beat to feel like the weight of the world is on my shoulders."

"We're just not used to that from you," Evie says, and flinches when both Caden and Theo glare at her. I give her a smile, knowing she didn't mean it offensively.

"Well, we're not going to change anything today," Theo says. "So let's go out."

"Go out?" I frown, and shake my head. "We've got way too much to do to take the day off."

"I didn't say we were going to take the day off work," Theo counters, rubbing my shoulders in a way that I don't know whether it is meant to be reassuring or he's just trying to touch me. "Dillon's over at the library now, let's head over there."

"All of us? Why?"

"Not all of us," Caden says, shaking his head. "We'll handle the shit show that's brewing over here, whilst you go and play swot with Dillon."

I roll my eyes, but laugh. It doesn't last long, and the sombre mood fills me once more. I bite my lip. "I don't think I can play hooky."

"The workload isn't going to change between today and tomorrow."

"I mean, it absolutely is," I say, scrunching my nose up. "It loses us an entire day."

"Half a day where we're barely focused," Caden says. He leans over and presses a kiss to my forehead, cupping my cheek. "As your Alpha, I am ordering you—"

"Oh, that's not going to go the way you think it is," I say, with a smirk.

"Maybe not," Caden replies, his lips quirking up. "But you are going to go with Theo to see Dillon, and find out what he's doing over there. We'll handle Alaric and the wonder twins."

"Hey," Freya protests.

"Stop eavesdropping," Alaric lectures her.

"And then we're all going to meet at home. I've got a plan for relaxing."

"A plan for relaxing," Theo says.

"Don't sound so sceptical, Toe-odore," Caden says, and Theo groans. Freya bursts out laughing, and thanks Roman for the mental image. "I'll see you soon."

I sigh, and wave to everyone, as Theo all but drags me out of the room. Freya winks at me as I pass, muttering dirty things in my head.

Roman's words are a lot more helpful, and he promises he'll be over at the library in a little bit with Freya in tow.

Which is both great, and a little disappointing. My mates are going to sit down with Alaric and Abel and determine the fate of the vow Abel broke, and it would've been nice to have Freya there.

But I have faith my men can handle it.

"Hey," I call, knocking on the edge of the table lightly. Dillon's gaze jumps up from the book he's reading, and he grins at Theo and me.

"Hi. How did the meeting really go?"

I sigh, and shrug. "Well enough. We got the delay we needed, meaning, for now I am not a fugitive. That's all I needed, really."

We both know that's not the truth. There is so *so* much more I'd have loved to get from the meeting.

"That's good news." Dillon's relief is felt across the bond immediately, and I send some love his way. We let him know the outcome of the meeting, but with our own debrief, we didn't sit and go into the ins and outs with him.

I just don't have the mental capacity to do so now, so hopefully, Theo will go over it with him.

"What are you researching right now?" Theo asks, pulling out a chair for me.

"I've got three things. The first is Warren's powers. Sure, he's been working more at getting them under control, but control isn't the thing I'm most interested in."

"What are you most interested in?" I ask, cocking my head. Theo sits down next to me, tilting his chair towards me subconsciously.

"How he can best utilise them," Theo says, with a grin in his words. Dillon nods, and the two of them share a knowing look. "That's very fucking smart of you. What else?"

"The second thing is the 'Guardian of All' that you came across. I want to know everything."

"Another smart move," I say, with a sigh. "Will our to-do list ever disappear?"

"You're very melodramatic today," Theo says, narrowing his eyes at me. "Do we need to do something about that?"

"Like what?" I hear the pout this time, and he laughs.

"I was thinking of feeding you and giving you something to do so that you can relax." He tugs my chair forward, my wheels crashing into his, as he grabs me by the nape and tugs my head forward.

His breath is warm on my cheek, but he connects our lips faster than I can do something about it. It's a rough and fast kiss that sends tingles down to my toes.

When he pulls back, he grins at me. "Feeling better?"

"Slightly." I turn towards Dillon, my desires clearly shown on my face, as Theo releases me.

Dillon winks at me. "After. I'm in work mode, and if you're here, you can join me."

"What do you need me to do?"

"The third thing I've been looking into... is the bond you and River once shared, and the creature that he now is." He's tentative here, not sure if he should say it, but saying it anyway.

"I'll take over that. I've got a few areas to look anyway," Theo says, tugging that binder from Dillon.

"Then it's your choice, baby," Dillon says, moving past the awkwardness.

I'm half-tempted to demand answers, to know if he's figured out a way to return the bond River and I once shared.

But I know that's not the thing that's going to help me right now.

"Give me this Guardian of All," I say, and he nods, pushing the content over to me. I can't handle reading something negative about Warren's situation, and blaming myself.

I'll just read up on this woman and find out what we can about her. Surely, there's information somewhere.

I read up on Dillon's information, which is basically nothing, and grab the nearest book, ready to settle in for what's surely going to be some long and drawn-out text that reveals absolutely nothing.

And I was right. I skim the book, rubbing my temples as I go, and sigh when I feel the powerful energy of my friend.

"You good?" Freya asks, startling Dillon and Theo. I just nod, and she comes to sit down with me. "Pass it here."

"Why?" Dillon asks.

"I read a whole lot faster than you do," she says. Her tone is undeniably cocky.

"And you couldn't have helped us with any of our research previously?" Dillon demands, and I give him a look of pure exasperation. Dillon shrugs.

"We did. We sent you books, and have been helping facilitate what you're doing," Freya says.

"But why didn't you help us by reading the books faster?"

"I don't see any of your vampires here," my friend counters.

Roman snorts, but as always, when I look at him, I see no evidence of the fact. "Why should I be the only one wasting my time?"

"How are we wasting our time?" Dillon asks. "This is a book from your library."

"This book isn't truly useless," Roman says, taking the book from Freya. "You gave us two things you were looking into—River, and the Ancestral Realm. This book ties into both, kind of."

"We've got one more item now," Theo says. "The Guardian of All."

"Well, that's not ominous or anything," Freya murmurs, rubbing at her arms. I spot the goosebumps that have appeared across her skin.

"It gets worse, babe," I say, getting comfortable in this chair. "She's apparently the one responsible for the creation of supernatural creatures."

"As in, my dad?" she asks, her eyes narrowing. I nod. "Don't you think my dad might have some insight on that?"

I cock an eyebrow at her, feeling a little defensive. "Don't you think we would have asked if everything didn't go to shit?"

She sighs, kicking out at the chair opposite her. "Fucking Abel."

"How did things go earlier?" I ask. She sighs.

"Nope," Theo says, shaking his head. "That's not our purpose right now. We can discuss that tomorrow. Today, we're researching."

"Well, to research this Guardian, this book is absolutely useless," Freya says, plucking the book out of Roman's hands and putting it down. "However, there may be something of use in my dad's personal archives."

"He has a personal collection?" Dillon asks eagerly.

"Doesn't any self-respecting immortal have a private collection?"

"Wouldn't know," I say, before laughing. Freya rolls her eyes.

"Well, if we want something from it, we're going to have to steal it."

"Are we actually though, or can we just ask him if we can take a look?" Theo asks, giving Freya a firm stare. "I know your game, but we're not trying to play a game here."

She lets out a mock huff of indignation but then nods. "Yeah, we do actually have to steal from it. The books in his collection are things that should've been burned, so that the knowledge doesn't fall into the wrong hands."

"Which is why it makes total sense that he's keeping hold of them," Dillon mutters, rubbing his temples. I can feel the excitement pouring off him at the idea that there's hidden knowledge that he'll get to see.

"So why didn't he?" I ask, and when I get four identical looks, I realise my naivety is showing.

"The only thing more powerful than lost knowledge, is knowledge held by only one person."

"Fair enough." But is it though?

"Has your dad ever mentioned this Guardian to you?" I ask, and she shakes her head.

"Nope. I have no idea if any records even exist, but if they do, that's where they'll be."

"I bet Conri had a secret stash of books once upon a time," Dillon says. "A shame he's dead."

"Fine, let's go to the clan and rob your dad," I say, and Freya grins, clapping her hands.

"How about the two of you stay here, and Roman and I can go commit this heist?" Theo asks, very unsubtly.

Roman nods, and reaches out to Theo, seconds before they disappear.

"Ugh. So boring," Freya mutters.

"Dillon?" I ask, and he raises his eyebrows. "Could you do me a favour?"

"Always, baby," Dillon replies. "But you don't need to create a favour, just to tell me to fuck off."

"Okay, fuck off," Freya says.

Dillon laughs and rises to his feet "Do you want some tea, Lottie?"

I nod. "Decaf, please."

He grins, and turns and heads through the other stacks of books.

"So why did you get rid of him?" Freya asks, leaning towards me.

"What happened with Cain?"

She sighs, bringing her knees up to her chest, balancing her feet on the edge of the chair. "He's dead, and it really wasn't pretty how we found him."

"Fuck."

She's a little pale, and she tries to give me a brave smile, but it doesn't truly hide her pain. I reach out and squeeze her hand.

She rests her head on my shoulder, and we sit in silence for a moment. I can't offer apologies, not with knowing what he has done to me, but I hate that she's suffering.

"I joked, mostly, about killing him myself. I wanted to, of course, but I don't think I could have. To see him like that..."

"You never should've had to see that."

She nods, and sighs. "I am so sorry."

"For what?"

"Everything. Between me breaking out of the confinement I shouldn't have left, Abel disregarding the rules he created... and even Cain."

"Okay but you breaking out of confinement was one of the best things to happen," I whisper. "I'd never have managed to get this far without you."

"And the rest of the bullshit I've brought?"

"That's not your fault. We're living in a crappy world, playing a crappy game to entertain fate. I won't blame the wrong people for the mistakes of others," I say, squeezing her shoulder. "There's enough bad shit happening that we don't need to create any."

"My dad is going to offer your mates a lot," she says.

"I'm sure he is. I just don't know if they'll take it."

"They'll figure it out."

And we fall back into silence, this time a little more comfortable than the last. It doesn't last too long, before she pushes up to a proper sitting position.

"What?" I ask, seeing the look on her face.

"Caden was right. Where has your spark gone?" She gasps. "Where has *mine* gone?"

I laugh. "We're allowed to take a beat."

"A beat, sure. But I refuse to sit here and be a whiny girl, doing fuck all, when I'm so much better than that. I have the capacity to make change, and I will do so."

"You've got the capacity for mayhem."

She snorts, wagging her finger my way. "Yeah, but you have the capacity for change. So, get off your ass, stop moping, and enact it."

"Tomorrow. Today, I'm going to whine." I dust off my lap, and grin at her. "And maybe get some good sex."

"Good sex is the cure for every bad mood."

"It's a good thing since the men who deliver it often cause said bad mood."

We both dissolve into a fit of giggles as Dillon returns with four mugs. He places his coffee down in front of his seat, hands me my decaf, and offers Freya both a cup of tea and a mug of blood, warmed.

"You're so good to me, Dillon," Freya grins, taking my blood.

"I robbed River's supplies, don't stress." He looks at me. "Did I give you enough time?"

"You did. Thank you," I say, and he winks. I turn back to Freya. "Want to know a secret?"

She nods, her pupils dilating a little.

"I've found Abel's mate."

And now her jaw drops properly. "You have?"

"I have," I reply, smirking at her.

I won't betray Scottie's confidence, but maybe she'll be able to give me that extra bit of insight.

Scottie deserves to know everything, and I'll do my best to make that happen.

CHAPTER 19

"We've got it and, we're fine," Theo exclaims, dropping back into view with Roman. There's a weird feeling, just before Freya's twin angel mates appear in front of us too. "But they need to be healed."

My power flies out much faster than Freya's does, but she won't be able to heal them like I can. I force my way past their shields, appreciative that neither of them put up much of a fight, and let my powers do their job. I heal the burns across Hudson's hands and restore the feeling to them once that's done.

Hunter's worse off, but it's just as easy to fix him, since nothing is truly life-threatening. The problem comes the moment I pull back. The exhaustion seeps in from healing those not in my bond, and I'm struggling to keep myself awake since they're vastly powerful. My head feels very light, and I lean forward to rest it on my hands, so that it doesn't just flop around.

I can understand why babies struggle to hold their heads up, they're extremely heavy.

"Here," Freya murmurs, gently placing her hand on my arm. I feel her sharing energy with me, the cool, comforting aura washes over me. "You saved mine, let me help you not feel the strain so much."

"Thanks," I mumble, not moving from my position as her power slowly soothes some of the exhaustion from me. Sadly, it's nowhere near enough to replenish what I lost.

"This reaction is definitely something we need to work on," Theo says, assessing me with that watchful eye of his. Dillon nods, or at least, I think he does. I can feel his agreement through the bond, but I can't turn and see. "We can't have you suffering with this giant weakness with what we've got coming up."

"Then maybe she doesn't heal those outside her bond," Freya says, without a hint of shame.

"That's what I've been doing with Katie." I hope my words are decipherable through my yawn, but Theo seems to be paying attention. "I'm pushing myself to try and get my tolerance up, without pushing past my bounds too much. I should not be this weak after healing two people, no matter how powerful they are."

"Very, very powerful," Hudson says, with a big grin.

"And I'm very, *very* powerful plus one," Hunter adds, winking at me as he nudges his brother. They both start playfully slapping each other, acting like the squabbling siblings they are—albeit a good fifteen years older.

"How bad was it?" I ask, looking up at my Guardian. The twins huff about not being given any attention, but they're Freya's problem. Roman snorts, which incites another round of bickering, but I tune them out.

"Heavily warded," Theo says, with a sigh. "But the wonder twins handled that for us, so I'm good on that front."

"Perfect." I reach over and squeeze his hand, offering him a little top-up anyway. He rolls his eyes, as his lips tilt up, and he drops a kiss onto my forehead. *"I love you."*

"I love you more, little wolf." I scrunch my nose up and he laughs, before addressing the group. "I don't think he'll notice they're missing immediately."

"He will," Freya says, and Theo deflates ever so slightly. "So, let's get it read before he returns home."

"Great plan, little muse," Roman says. "Can you read it and I'll share it with the group?"

Freya sighs but nods, rubbing at her temples as Roman gently places the very old book in front of her. It's a little decrepit, but I have no doubt Alaric's taken care of it whilst it's been in his possession. There's a sort of musty smell coming off it that turns my stomach.

"Why the sigh?" Dillon asks her.

"I can read really fast, but my understanding of what I'm reading does not process at the same speed. So Roman sharing the information will take that burden from me since I won't need to process it at all." Dillon nods, as Freya opens up the first page, gesturing to a language I cannot read. "But since it's written in Latin, which I can't actually read—"

"I can," Theo says.

"So can I," Roman replies.

"Which doesn't really help Freya, though, since neither of you are as fast as her," Dillon says, and Freya nods.

"Which is why when I share it, I can help with the translations," Roman adds, reassuringly.

"But that doesn't erase my headaches," she pouts. Roman crouches down and must say something silently because she nods, and leans in to kiss him.

"Do either Warren or Elijah speak Latin?" I ask, giving them their privacy. Dillon shakes his head.

"Elijah?" Theo snorts, shaking his head. "He wouldn't know—"

"Enough," I say, giving my Guardian a stern look. "Not only is he not here to defend himself, so this is just mean and uncalled for, but you need to get over the past. I have."

"And you've not treated Lottie the best, either," Dillon says, with a shit-stirring grin that really doesn't suit him.

"I'll be fine," Freya says, and Roman squeezes her shoulder.

"I can heal the headache as soon as you're done," I reassure her.

"Won't heal the exhaustion," Freya murmurs, before shrugging. "It's fine, I'm just whining."

"Explains why we didn't use you before now," Dillon teases. Freya hisses at him, before turning and grabbing the book properly.

My eyes widen when she starts to actually read, because it's incredible. Her eyes fly across the page, her hands darting out to turn pages just a little faster than my eyes can track, and yet I know for a fact that she's reading. Roman's eyes are closed, as are the twin's although I'm not sure if they're able to understand Latin. Her mates are taking in the information she's sharing and processing it at inhuman speeds.

Seeing her abilities in this area have me so curious, and also a little jealous. It's one of those things that I dreamed of having, when I was still unaware of the supernatural world, especially during exam periods.

I'm watching in awe as she devours the book in front of her. It's thick, maybe five to six hundred pages, and in a language, she doesn't even understand, and yet still, as she closes the book, it's been less than five minutes.

"You're done now," Roman soothes, pushing the book forward. Freya nods, and her eyes are bloodshot, before she rests her head on her arms, much like I was only a little while ago. I reach over to soothe her, not caring about the drain it'll have on me, and I soothe as much of the physical pain as I can.

It'll help the strain of her eyes, and the pain in her head. She's right, though, it doesn't fix the exhaustion.

"Do you want some fresh blood?" Dillon asks, keeping his tone soft so as to not hurt her head.

"Remember when she was drinking from mere mortals and couldn't stomach it unless it was from the vein?" Hudson whispers.

Why he whispers this, I have no idea, since his words carry through the nearly silent library.

"Now I get blood of an absolute goddess," Freya says, smirking at me.

"And us!" Hunter and Hudson protest. Hunter continues alone. "My blood is far better than Lottie's, Freya, and we both know it." Dillon and Theo let out identical snarls, that makes me smile.

"Sorry, Luna," Hudson says, glaring at his brother. "No disrespect meant, but angel blood just doesn't compare to that of a wolf."

I snort. "Absolutely none taken. You're both very powerful, but we both know, that you're not as powerful as me. Don't worry, I don't need the ego stroking to know the truth."

"Take as much as you want. Directly from the vein," Hunter says, offering his mate his wrist. He's glaring at me, and Freya laughs.

I shift my teeth, bring my wrist to my mouth, and sink them in. There's a brief moment of pain, but Theo reaches over and heals me without breaking from his conversation with Roman.

"Take as much as you want," I tease, holding my wrist out in front of Freya.

"You're evil," Hunter says, shaking his head as Freya pulls my wrist to her mouth instead of his. In his defence, I had at least broken the skin so she could smell my blood, and I can feel his exhaustion from whatever he did to get the book, so I have no doubt that she can too. "I can give her better orgasms than you ever could."

"I mean, if you're dealing in the hypotheticals, that doesn't ring true," Dillon says, grinning at the angel. "As a woman with a—"

"Nope," I say, cutting that conversation topic off. Dillon's lips quirk up in a smile, despite him trying to hide the amusement, but the twins don't even try. I turn my attention to my Guardian and Roman, since they're both still going over the contents of the book. "How are you two doing?"

"Holy shit," Theo whispers, his eyes filled with awe as he looks at me. "This is... insane."

"Have you seen this?" Roman asks, seemingly just as awestruck as he points out a passage.

"They're very cute together," Freya murmurs, pulling away from my wrist. Again, without thinking about it, Theo reaches over and heals the wounds. "Nerding out."

"If only I knew Latin fluently," Dillon sighs, leaning back in his chair.

"How much do you know?" Freya asks, with a raised eyebrow. Dillon shrugs, and as they talk about languages, I watch my Guardian engaging with the incubus. They're both extremely smart men, and the way they're working together truly is cute.

"Look," Theo says, moving the book closer to him, and pointing something out. "Do you think that's true?"

"I'm not sure, but I'm leaning towards yes," Roman says, his eyes bright pink. I still don't understand what his eye colours mean, but this one doesn't seem to be a negative feeling. He's excited and engaged.

"What can you share?" I ask. My curiosity is burning, and I wish I knew Latin so that I could just read the damn thing myself. I've always loved learning and being able to learn more about a world I've barely scratched the surface of, is thrilling.

"According to the author of this text, the Guardian of All is believed to be a Goddess," Theo tells me. "And not a Guardian like me."

"An actual goddess?" Freya asks, tilting her head before shaking it. "Not sure I believe it."

Dillon laughs, shaking his head too. "You believe in vampires and wolves, but not gods and goddesses?"

"I see a vampire in the mirror every single day. I live with vampires. My best friend is a wolf—"

"Poor Remy," Hudson says, as Hunter and Roman snicker. "Not even first on the list when it comes to the wolves in your life."

"You know what I mean," Freya mutters. Based on the way Hunter's fingers are flying across the keyboard of his phone, I don't think that's something that's getting dropped. "It just seems a little... farfetched to believe in mystical beings that way."

"Well, she's not the only goddess around," Theo says, and Roman nods. "I'm sure we can investigate things a bit more now that we've got some basis, but this text outlines her as one of the only remaining goddesses to this day. Many have been forgotten, or their duties are no longer required in this current day."

"When was this text written?" Dillon asks. Of course, my mate is jotting all of this down, and it gives me a warm feeling.

"About fifteen hundred years ago."

Dillon nods, jotting that down, with a question mark around it.

"So, what does she do?" I ask, sipping at my tea. Unlike Freya, I'm not immediately doubting this revelation. I grew up in a human world, and I've seen how many people believe in religion and gods, and how many different ones there are.

We have mythologies with the Roman gods and goddesses and the Greeks, and the crossovers they have.

Why wouldn't we have some legendary creator from an elevated status?

I've been around her and felt her power, and it's different to that of the ancestors I've seen and felt. A goddess isn't that farfetched to me.

"Is she dangerous?" Dillon asks.

"Everything has the potential to be dangerous, Dillon," I say. The twins laugh, and Freya turns and gives them a dirty look.

"If you can't behave, I'm sending you back to work on that issue with Ambrose," she warns, they both grumble and move to sit down at the table with us. She shoots me an apologetic look, and I wave it off. They're not being disruptive, and their jovial nature isn't a bad thing. The angel twins can be serious when it calls for it.

"This text is very helpful, but it's also very hard to read," Theo says. "It's hard to discern what is the truth and what is exaggerated because the author... well, he doesn't seem very stable."

"There's got to be something of importance in here that is true enough, or Alaric wouldn't have removed it from the general public," Roman says, and Theo nods. "We just need to identify what that is specifically."

"Does there need to be one specific thing?" Hudson asks. "Can it not just be the mention of her or the vibe of the text?"

"Potentially," Roman says.

"So, rumour has it that she is the creator of every supernatural creature in the world," Theo says, and Dillon shivers. The twins narrow their eyes, giving off identical looks of distaste, whereas Roman and Freya seem interested.

"She did say that same thing to me," I say, a little hesitantly, because Theo doesn't seem like this is a good thing. I can see his argument, even before he shares it—is it right for one person, goddess or not, to have power this grand? I just don't have the answers to it.

Theo sighs, giving me an intense look. "She's not the only supernatural goddess thing, which is where the confusion comes in with her motives."

"What do you mean?" Dillon asks.

"Wait your turn, wolfie," Hudson says. "Clearly, he was going to explain."

"Clearly," Dillon mutters, with an eye roll.

"She's in charge of everything living, everything dead—"

"We got that based on the Guardian of *All* title that she holds, Ro," Freya says, squeezing his forearm and cutting him off.

"Not only is the wolf Ancestral Realm—a place where you have a lot of problems, Lottie—part of her purview, but so is every single otherworldly realm," Roman finishes.

"And unsurprisingly, she's taken an interest in you, Luna," Hunter says, his voice devoid of his usual teasing.

"Nice of you to point it out," Dillon snarls.

"It doesn't do any of us any good to hide from the truth," Hunter says, with a shrug. "She's a dangerous creature who has fixated on your mate, and no matter how powerful you may be now, Luna, you are *not* more powerful than a goddess."

"No, I can't imagine I am," I say, gently. "But thank you for putting it into perspective. If I can work with her... I will try."

"Actually try," Theo says with a teasing smirk that doesn't reach the worry in his eyes. "I was with you when we spoke to her that time, remember? You're a little... abrasive with the dead."

I snort, shaking my head. "And I'm not with the living?"

"Good point," Theo replies. "I think this is an avenue we might just leave alone and try to survive any future visits with her."

"It seems a little too dangerous to prod at something like that," Roman agrees, and it's with his words that it becomes a finality.

"In terms of Warren and River, though, if you need anything to assist with them, we can help the best we can," Freya offers, and I give her a hesitant smile. She reads my mind, and squeezes my hand. "I don't mean my father, and the Clan's resources. I mean me, and my mating circle."

"What are your plans for the near future?" Theo asks.

Freya shrugs, eyeing her men. "We're handling the traitors amongst our midst who are targeting my mate and his brother, but for the most part, nothing. We're on call whenever you need it—and I expect you to use that."

"I've never hesitated in the past," I remind her. I've dragged Freya into far too many situations that don't concern her, and we've reaped the benefits of it every time.

"Maybe not," Hunter says, still using that same tone of voice. "But you did reach out to Freya's second worst brother, instead of her, and look at the shit it's caused."

"You've ranked them?" Dillon asks, with a grin. Smart of him to intervene that way before Theo can, because my Guardian is not impressed with the implication.

"You're right," Theo says. *"I'm not."*

"He's not blaming me for the situation we're currently in. He's just upset that his mate is upset, and wants to know that next time, he wants us to fuck off protocol." I reach over and rub my thumb over the back of his hand. *"Wouldn't you do the same thing for me?"*

He grunts, and doesn't reply, because we both know he will.

"Evan is first," the twins say as one, as I tune back into the conversation. I laugh because I completely agree. Evan is the best of the Viotto men. "Blade is second, Devin third, Abel fourth and the lovely Cain is last. If we bring Charles and Landon into it, well, Abel becomes sixth."

"You rank Charles underneath Blade and Devin?" I ask, in surprise.

"You might love the Alpha, Luna, but we do not," Hunter says. "Stop popping in unannounced Hunter."

"Stop stealing our food, Hudson," Hudson says, rolling his eyes.

"Stop groping my sister-by-mating," Roman adds, in that same tone of voice.

"Charles lectured you on that?" I gasp, mentally scheduling a call with my friend so that we can chat some shit, and not just to have his help on the political dramas we're still wading our way through.

"You're still fools, with this ranking," Theo says. "Devin's the best one to have on your side."

"Ugh," Freya groans, holding her head.

"What's wrong?" Theo asks, his wolf immediately on alert. I can feel him gathering his power, building it within him, as he scans the area for danger. I'm amused, but my wolf is full of pride to have such a dedicated mate.

"My dad is calling for me. It seems their meeting is over," she says, rising to her feet.

"We'll get this delivered back there before he returns. Hopefully, he won't know we broke in," Hudson says, yanking the text into his arms as the identical men disappear.

"And we'll head over to your dad," Roman says, reaching for Freya's hand.

"How does... how does he feel?" I ask, before they disappear.

"Relieved," Freya says gently. "A little annoyed, some guilt, but mostly relieved. I think it went well."

"Which sets the tone brilliantly for us for tonight," Theo says. "Let's kick these people out and go home. We've accomplished more than enough for today."

I eye Dillon, not sure he'll agree, but he nods and gives me a warm smile. "We really have, Lottie. We've crossed off a massive research task."

"Did we cross it off because we finished it, though, or did we cross it off because we're unable to do anything else about it?" I ask, with a weary sigh. Freya shrugs, and her and Roman disappear.

"Little pessimist, stop," Theo says, squeezing my hand. "We discovered enough to know that's not something we want to get ourselves involved in. It was a success."

"It was," Dillon echoes. "Now, let me just tidy up here a little before we go."

My phone rings before he moves, and I reach over for it. Rhett's name flashes on the screen, and I smile, sliding along to answer.

"Hi, love, sorry to interrupt," Rhett says.

"Never an interruption."

Theo groans, but I don't care. I can just imagine the beautiful smile on Rhett's face at my words. "We've just finished up with Alaric and Abel, and it went well enough. We'll discuss it more in person, but I just wanted to reassure you."

"I wanted to," I hear Caden shout down the line, before grunting.

"Ignore him," Rhett says. "He lost the coin toss." I snort, and Theo laughs. "We've got a few things to go over, and then need to send him some paperwork, but we'll be done in an hour max."

"Works for us," I say, looking at Theo and Dillon, who both nod. "You're all good though, right?"

"Absolutely. I love you."

"Love you too."

He clicks off the line.

"Let's go home anyway," Dillon says, rising to his feet. "An hour is plenty of time."

"For what?" I ask, taking Theo's hands and letting him pull me up to my feet.

"Well, I did promise you later," Dillon says, waggling his brows.

"Then let's shift and get there faster," I hiss, excitement thrumming through me. I charge away from Theo towards the library door, and shift into my wolf. I dart through the street, hearing the two of them coming after me, and it's exhilarating.

It's also accurate—they're all very good at making sure I cum first.

CHAPTER 20

"Hello," Caden calls, barely giving me the chance to sit up, before he mutters, "I can feel that she's home."

"She's not hiding from us," Warren says, and there's some laughter and jokes as they tease Caden.

My wolf is as excited as me that they're all coming in, and she's excited to go and see them. I move out of the bed, ignoring the way Dillon tries to reach for me to stay. I'd love to hide away with my two men for the rest of the night, but with everything we've got coming up, I'd much rather hide away with *all* of my men. I spot my bra to the left of the bed, and bend down to grab it, and based on the way Theo groans, I'm sure I gave him an eyeful.

"A bra is most definitely not needed," Dillon says, as I stand up properly.

I turn, thread my arms through the bra, and take them both in. They're both under the covers, a Lottie-sized gap between them, as they show off their very fit bodies. Their faces have a lazy look, but also so much contentment thrumming through the bond.

My wolf takes their shirtless state, their skin marked by me, and the combination of our scents as an invitation to go for round two. My body is desperate for it, fluid once again leaking down my thighs. *And Theo had already cleaned his cum out from inside me.*

"Lottie," Caden shouts again. I can hear his footsteps coming up the stairs, and both Theo and Dillon laugh as I crouch down to tug my panties on. In my haste, I stumble, and give myself a wedgie. I'm pulling out some shorts from the dresser when Caden barges into the room.

His nostrils flare, and his eyes dart between the two shirtless men, and a nearly naked me. Caden groans, the disappointment that he missed out clear across his face. "I knew I could smell sex."

"It was very good sex," I say, with a grin. Caden smirks, dropping his head down to press his lips to mine. One of his hands reaches down to cup my ass, and his other tangles in my hair. I press our bodies together, as we share a very heated kiss, with a very good audience.

I can feel the desire pulsing from both Dillon and Theo, and combining that with the arousal from Caden and I, I'm a very turned-on girl.

The bonds between us all are singing with pleasure, and my wolf is ecstatic.

"I don't doubt it," he replies, pulling away from me once I'm breathless. I tug the shorts up my thighs, using him for support so I don't stumble again, and then yank the t-shirt over my head. It's one of theirs—Warren's, I think, based on the design, but it's freshly clean, so I can't scent him—that I stole because it's baggy and comfortable on me.

Caden helps me put my cardi on, being especially sweet with his soft touches that nourish our bond. He then encourages me to sit on the bed as he grabs a pair of fluffy socks from the dresser. When I move to take them from him, he shakes his head and crouches down, putting them on for me.

"I can do this," I say softly, not wanting to break the peaceful atmosphere between us.

"In a few months' time, you're not going to be able to," Caden says. "This is my pleasure. You're growing our children; what the fuck am I doing?"

"I love you," I say, pressing a kiss to his chin. He grins.

"Well after Caden put us both to shame, I better get up and start pulling my weight," Dillon says, causing me to laugh.

"Fuck it, I suppose I'll put some clothes on as well then," Theo says, with a sigh.

"If you want to stay naked in bed with Dillon, who are we to judge?" Caden asks.

Theo rolls his eyes and grabs his boxers from the bottom of the bed. Our clothes are all strewn about my room, but mine can stay there. I'll sort it out later.

"We've had a lovely afternoon. Caden didn't put anyone to shame," I say, before looking up at the man in question. "How was yours?"

"We're not talking about what me and the others did," Caden says. I gasp, and Dillon laughs.

"I told you," Theo says. "Tonight, is for relaxing. We've all agreed on this. So, let's stop trying to sneak answers out of him whilst his blood is in the wrong location."

"It's not relaxing to be forced to relax," I say. How am I meant to relax when there's so much to do? When I don't know what's been done?

Trust, Lottie, you have to trust your mates.

"Oh, believe me, little wolf, we both know that I can make you relax," Theo says, cupping my ass. I jump, not having felt him behind me, and he laughs.

"Okay, but I've already had my orgasms for the day. How else are you going to force me to relax?" I raise my eyebrows at him, as my core clenches, at the thought of more orgasms.

"You think that's all you're getting today?" Dillon asks, waggling his brows when my head snaps to his direction.

"What's that supposed to mean?" I ask. *Can my vagina not take a hint? We do not need to have something inside us every moment of the day.* My wolf howls inside my mind, the primal energy of us bonding exciting her.

"All you need to know is that it'll be fun," Caden tells me, squeezing my hand.

"Now, go downstairs with the others," Theo says. "Caden, Dillon and I will join you in a few. And no questioning the others."

"If they're weak enough to give up, then that's on them," I say, charging away from Caden. I giggle as he lets out a low snarl, the sound encouraging my wolf that much more. Surprisingly though, he doesn't follow after me.

I know, for a fact, he's going to tell Theo and Dillon about the meeting they've had today with the Viotto's, whilst still keeping it from me. I'm frustrated, even if I know their motives are pure, because just telling me how it went would solve my problems with being unable to relax.

But I need to try and trust that they've got this handled. My mates are so determined to let me relax, and I'm going to stop trying to fight them on it. I've been nothing but broody and miserable today, and as much as it's understandable, it's not the kind of person I usually am.

The rest of tonight, we're going to have fun, and relax, and then from tomorrow we're going to start handling shit.

As I go down the stairs, I grin because Elijah comes to a stop at the bottom, his dimples on show. I pounce a few steps from the bottom, and he catches me in his arms. He presses lips to mine as I wrap my legs around his waist.

The kiss is soft and gentle, and when he pulls back, he tucks some loose strands of hair behind my ears.

"How are you feeling?" he asks, and I shrug, still smiling.

"I'm feeling okay. Freya and I had some fun this afternoon with our research."

"Of course you did. What were you researching?" he asks.

I wink. "Well, you're keeping your daily tasks a secret. I think I'll do the same."

He laughs, the furrowing of his brows disappearing. "I love you, sunshine."

"I love you too, Elijah." I kiss him deeply, gently tracing my nails at the back of his neck.

"Stop hogging her!" Wyatt shouts, and I laugh, pecking Elijah's lips once more before pulling away completely.

He slides me down the length of his body, helping steady me on the ground.

"So, what's the plan for tonight?" I ask, taking Elijah's hand and leading him to the living room where the others are. They're spread across the sofas and chairs, and I get a bunch of smiles as we join them.

I smile at River, a little startled to see him here. I'm glad he is, even if I am a little reserved about it.

"We've ordered some food," Noah says. "But it's not here yet. Pizza and Chinese."

"Very different cuisines."

"Astute observation," Warren teases, and I stick my fingers up at him.

"Couldn't decide what we wanted," Noah explains.

"What about a coin toss?" I tease. Rhett's booming laughter makes me smile.

"We played rock paper scissors," Rhett says. "We both got some bruises, so we ordered both."

I roll my eyes, plopping down on the sofa next to Wyatt. "Well, I did fancy some noodles, so good job to whoever wanted Chinese."

"There'll be plenty of food for you, love," Wyatt reassures me. He presses a kiss to my cheek, and I cuddle into his side.

"Anyone want a drink?" Warren asks, getting up. He might've made it open-ended, but he's looking at me when he asks.

"Apple juice, please," I say, and he nods, before going to the kitchen. Not to be deterred, everyone shouts through their orders.

Warren groans but doesn't complain as he makes a couple trips, but my wolf is preening at the fact he brought us ours first.

She's not as impressed that every single one of our mates, and River are drinking beer. *Beer.* We can't have anything alcoholic, which wouldn't be the end of the world if wine was rightfully classed as the fruit that it is.

But I draw the line when Warren comes in next with three wine glasses and a bottle of a deliciously dark red. Immediately, my smile drops.

"What's wrong?" Wyatt asks, rubbing at my arms. "You've just completely tensed up."

"No," I say, glaring at Warren. He stops, and his eyes dart to mine guiltily. "You are *not* having that in front of me." I wag my finger when he moves to step forward and ignore me.

"Really?" he asks. I can hear his exasperation, which only annoys me further.

How *dare* he taunt me this way.

"You're—" I cut myself off, waving my hands in the air, unable to even continue my sentence through my annoyance.

"Come on," Warren whines.

"Come on?" River asks, raising an eyebrow. "That's the mother of our children. She doesn't want us drinking wine, get used to it."

"Let's not ruin this night by fighting," Rhett says with a sigh.

"Fighting?" I hiss, glaring at him too. "There'd be *no fighting* if Mr. Grumpy over there weren't a selfish—"

"Lottie," Rhett cajoles.

"You fuckers knocked me up and set me up with this wine ban," I hiss. "You've dragged me to a forced relaxation night, and you think I want to watch you *savour* my very nice, very expensive, *delicious fucking wine*? Not a chance."

"I mean, technically, you were the one to forget your birth control," Wyatt says, teasingly. I elbow him in the ribs hard, then move away from him to go and sit on the other sofa with Noah instead. I press a soft kiss to the underside of his jaw as he lectures

Wyatt, and once he's done, he kisses the top of my head, and snuggles me in close.

"We're putting a lock on the cellar until the babies are born," Noah says, squeezing me tight. My wolf purrs in pleasure, and I kiss Noah's neck. He's a good man.

"A very good idea," I say with a smile and send mass smug feelings towards Warren. His eyes flash black, but I can tell his vampire is pissed at him for trying to upset me.

"But what about my blood," Warren asks sadly.

"Lottie's blood, you mean?" Elijah asks, teasingly. Wyatt and Rhett snort, but since Wyatt was rude, I don't share in his laughter.

"Drink it as it is," I say. "Lap at a vein. Fucking starve for all I care."

"Wow, pregnancy has made you heartless," Warren gasps.

"I don't think it's the pregnancy that made her heartless," Wyatt says, winking at me. I narrow my eyes at the playful Beta. "I think it's the lack of wine for our alcoholic mate."

"Withdrawals are hard," Elijah agrees. I glare at him now, but the bastard isn't even looking my way. Noah commands Warren to get rid of the wine, and he does it within seconds.

Doesn't change that he's an asshole, though.

Wyatt laughs once more, sniggering still about his rubbish joke.

I stand corrected. *They're all assholes.*

"What are we doing for entertainment?" I demand, and rub at my stomach to ease the hunger pangs. Rhett follows the movement, but now I'm the one to pretend not to notice. I'm hungry, and it's permitted.

"You've got two choices," Elijah says, grinning at me. "We're going to the fun old days."

"The fun days?" Warren mouths to River, who snorts.

"Oh, choices," I say, still glaring at Warren. "How fun."

"Stop being so mopey," Dillon says, coming down the stairs with Theo and Caden. "I'm excited to play."

"Play?" I ask, my wolf perking up ever so slightly.

"Elijah's elected himself as the game master or something like that," Wyatt says. "We're intrigued."

"Don't be. Elijah's not very fun," I reply.

The brunette rolls his eyes. "We're either going to play *Truth or Dare* or the classic, *Never Have I Ever*."

"Why limit ourselves," River asks, taking the offered mug of my blood. It's room temperature and probably tastes like crap without the wine to pair it with.

What a shame.

"I like your thinking," Elijah says, beaming at his younger brother. "Everyone get a drink, and we'll start with Never Have I Ever. You okay with your apple juice, sunshine?"

I nod, just as the front door goes. Caden walks over to it, the only one of us who hadn't yet sat down, and hands the young wolf at the door the cash before coming over with six pizza boxes and at least one kebab wrap.

"Pizza, love?" Rhett asks, and I shrug before nodding. He opens one of the boxes and puts a slice of cheese and a slice of pepperoni on my plate. They're piping hot, and I'm very grateful for that. Rhett doesn't touch the pizza, and neither does Elijah, but everyone else has at least one slice in front of them.

"Never have I ever... kissed a man," Caden says, teasingly as he winks at me. I roll my eyes and sip my apple juice. I'm not the only one to drink, and some of the men surprise me. Theo's sip, though, doesn't shock me in the slightest.

$$)) \bullet (($$

"*H*ere?" I ask, my face bright red. I'm the only one who hasn't touched a drop of alcohol during this game night of ours. I wouldn't say any of my men are drunk, but they've, most assuredly, lost some inhibitions. Warren definitely has, to be suggesting something like this.

We played Never Have I Ever for a good hour or so as we ate—I got my noodles—and it brought out some very surprising details.

Mostly from me.

But once the food was cleared away, we moved on to the Truth or Dare portion of the night. It started off tame—as tame as it can be with a bunch of tipsy men—but we're now getting into the more... risqué portion.

"Here," Warren confirms, licking a droplet of blood wine from his lips. I only relented on it because he begged so *so* prettily. But I told him tonight is the only time. He smirks at me, likely guessing where my thoughts went.

But his smirk does more than just aggravate me. It sends a tingling feeling coursing through my veins, as goosebumps rise across my skin. My wolf is preening at the eyes of our mates on us, and she can feel my nervous energy and my underlying arousal which only excites her that much more.

"But..." I trail off, not even sure why I'm complaining. I don't look at River, not sure how he or any of the others will handle having him in the room whilst I complete this dare. Hopefully, they can handle it without violence.

Because as much as I could take a group truth to get out of it... there's honestly something so hot about undressing here in front of everyone.

"Fine," I say, rising to my feet with a shrug.

"Ah, ah, ah," Warren says, and I frown. "In front of *me*."

"What?" My question is accompanied by laughter from me because, surely, he's not being serious. He shrugs, smirking at me with that annoyingly *pretty* look.

It drives me fucking crazy.

Both how much I love it, and how I hate it.

"It was my dare." Pure fucking smugness radiates through his side of the bond, and I'd be so tempted to tell him to fuck off, but I can feel how excited he is and how my other mates feel, too. "Time is ticking, princess."

I roll my eyes, stomping over to where he's sat, my unamused look showing my displeasure. Not at the dare itself, just his cockiness.

"Perfect," Warren says, giving me a genuine smile. I've already shed my cardigan throughout the night, so I grab my T-shirt and rip it over my head.

Warren tuts, slowly wagging his finger back and forth. "Slowly."

"Did anybody else hear him say slowly?" I demand, looking around at the onlookers. Why I thought they'd agree with me, when they can get a slow and *sensual* striptease, I don't know. They all say yes, and I roll my eyes, but I can't deny how their desire makes me feel.

I bend at the waist.

"Ah, ah," Warren says, still using that condescending tone.

"What the fuck do you want," I hiss, turning to glare at him. "Outline the entire damn dare."

"So testy, love," Wyatt says, with a smirk.

"I think we'll have to do something about that," Caden says, with a knowing grin.

"Turn around if you're going to bend over," Warren commands.

Fuck me.

I turn so that I'm now facing Rhett and Caden, with my back towards Warren and Wyatt. I bend down at the waist, practically shoving my ass in Warren's face. My hair falls forward to cover my bra, and even I know that's unfair to those opposite me. I'm the one smirking now as I stand back up, and I quickly tie my hair up into a messy bun.

I then bend over for the third time tonight—but most definitely not the last—as I slowly pull my shorts down my waist. I even go as far as giving a booty wiggle, no matter how stupid it makes me feel. My very appreciative audience gives me the praise I need, though. Warren sends me love and affection through the bond, as his hunger literally pulsates in the air.

"Is this good enough?" I ask, turning to look at him over my shoulder.

"You're always perfect," Warren says, with a grin. "You did account for the dare, I suppose."

"Well, if you want to get more off me, you best get another dare," I say, with a wink. He laughs, and I move to go and sit down in the space between him and Wyatt. Warren tugs me into his lap instead, and not to be undone, Wyatt scoots closer and pulls my feet into his lap.

"Do I need a dare to get these off you?" Wyatt murmurs, heat filling his eyes.

I tap my chin teasingly. "Depends on if you're going to rub them, or not."

"If rubbing things is the requirement to get you out of your clothes, I'll more than happily rise to the challenge," Rhett says.

"Seconded," Caden adds.

"How's that?" Wyatt asks, pulling my socks off, before rubbing my feet. I hum approvingly and cuddle into Warren more.

"So, whose turn is it now?"

"Yours, angel," River says, with a husky voice. I chance a look in his direction and give him a small smile, which he returns. There's not an ounce of uncomfortableness in his face as he sips at his beer. If I'm kidding myself, there might even be some lust there.

I look around the room and spot my favourite target.

"Dillon," I say, with a smile. He doesn't sound as excited as I am. Maybe it's because the dares have gotten dirty, maybe it's not. Either way, I'm not going to spare him. "Truth or dare, babe?"

He sighs, eyeing up the rest of the room, and I can feel his nervousness. "Truth."

"Boring fucker!" Elijah says, and there's a lot of laughter. A few rounds ago, Caden said that to Elijah, so it's amusing to hear it echoed once more.

Dillon rolls his eyes, and grins at me. "What truth do you want from me, baby?"

I could ruin the mood and demand a real truth. There are so many questions I have for my previous Gamma. I want to know if he's content with his life of research. I want to know if he regrets anything. Hell, I want to know—

I shake my head, cutting those thoughts off. I'm sticking with my vow to keep the fun atmosphere going. I get the feeling now that I'm sitting here in only my bra and knickers sprawled across Warren's lap, that they're going to target me with a lot of fun and dirty dares. I wouldn't want it any other way.

But I may as well have my fun right back.

And of course... I am a little curious about the answers.

"Of all the men in the room," I pause, just for a second, to let them all get excited. "Which one would you fuck if you had no other choice?"

"Why would I not have a choice?" Dillon says, scrunching his nose up in distaste. His logical brain wins out and he wants to analyse this properly. "What would happen that I couldn't just masturbate if I got horny?"

"Aw, little Dillon looking for some relief," Warren says, with a smirk as Wyatt stops for a second to make some lewd movements. I would kick him, but he's gone back to rubbing my feet, so I leave Dillon to fight his own battles this time. "No girl to touch him, so he has to touch himself."

"You'd know all about that, wouldn't you?" I say, giving my vampire mate a dirty look, making the implication very clear. He's not giving me some nice foot rubs. The cheeky fucker just brings my wrist to his lips and nibbles me instead. Those pointy teeth of his are teasing me, my veins throbbing with the idea that he wants my blood, instead of biting down like I'd prefer. He gives one sharper nibble, but doesn't even nick me, before he drops my wrist.

I sigh and turn back to Dillon. "I don't know, babe, maybe the government lets out a decree that men now must be in same-sex relationships because the world is ending. It's just a fun question."

"Not very well thought out one," Theo says, with a smirk. Dillon laughs and looks around the room with a more assessing eye now.

"To be honest, no fuck it, let's do this properly," Dillon says, and I bounce in Warren's lap, excitement filling me. He smiles, kissing my neck, once again targeting a spot he usually bites. "We all know that River would break me. I'd rule out the Alphas for that reason, too."

"Nah, he's ruling me out because I'm far too pretty for him," Rhett says, and Caden snorts.

"I've also never had a man in my ass before, so I need someone who is going to be sweet to me," Dillon continues.

"You're looking for someone who is sweet to you?"

"To *it*," Dillon hastily corrects. Sadly, that only incites more laughter and teasing, so many jokes thrown out over the top of each other, all in increasingly loud tones. I can't even tell who made the funniest joke.

"That's so adorable," I say, and I'm the only one not making fun of him right now, so he latches onto it like a lifeline, giving me a big smile. How short his memory is, considering I was the one to put him in this position. "So, who is the one?"

"I think I need to rule myself out," Warren says, with a shrug. "I don't think I qualify for *sweet*."

"You can be," I say, turning to smile up at Warren. "You're normally such an asshole, that your sweet moments are appreciated so much more."

"I'm not sure that's the compliment you think it is, mate," Caden says, only slightly dimming the grin on Warren's face.

"Elijah, it is," Dillon says.

"No, thank you," Elijah immediately replies. There's so much laughter that Elijah's, "No offence" is nearly missed.

"No, thank you?" Dillon gasps, with shock filling him. "No, thank you? We are *lawfully fucking obliged* to do this. Do you think I wanted you because you're you? No, you were just the best of the bunch. *No, thank you*. Asshole."

"Well, no, *you* had no choice," Elijah says, and the look on his face is identical to the one on Warren's. They're both smirking with excited looks in their eyes.

"Well, who would you choose?" Dillon demands.

"Of course, my betting pool has been massively decreased considering, you know, relations."

"Me too," Caden says. "Identical twins."

"We know," Elijah says, rolling his eyes.

"The law didn't say no incest," Theo points out, and there's some laughter, but those who are related look disgusted. Noah turns a pet lip to me, and I smile.

"No incest." My decision is final since it was my strange scenario.

"Fine," Elijah says, looking at them. "Since it's not my truth, I choose not to answer."

"Fine," Dillon says, in the exact same tone. "Truth or Dare, Elijah."

Elijah groans, but the humour doesn't fade from his face. "Truth. But I want it on the record that you missed out on giving our mate some very fun dares."

Dillon shrugs nonchalantly, but I can feel the disappointment from his end of the bond. "If you could fuck any man in this room, who would you choose?"

"I'm not going to choose any," Elijah says, and there's some laughter. "But I'll take pity on you and answer. I'm not an idiot, and if I'm going to do it, I want to do it properly. I want someone who can make me feel really good." Elijah winks at my Alpha, who is extremely cocky. "I choose Rhett."

"Second that," Wyatt says. "I've already seen him naked—"

"Who hasn't?" I mutter. We eventually go around the room, each of them using their turn to question someone else. Elijah was one of the most popular men, but Theo surprised me by choosing Warren over the others.

"And now it's my turn once more," Elijah says, rubbing his hands together and winking at me. "I dare you—"

"What if I wanted a truth?" I demand, with a pout.

"Fine. Truth or *dare*," Elijah asks, waggling his brows. "I can promise something fun for the latter option."

I stick my tongue out at him, before putting him out of his misery. "Dare, please."

"I dare you, to get naked. Completely naked," Elijah says, and I rise from Warren's lap with help from both the vampire and the wolf. They're so eager to see me displayed fully that they practically threw me on the floor. "And then—"

"No two-part dares you cheat," Theo calls, and they all laugh. I swear they find themselves so funny right now, with such mediocre jokes at that, that it's got to be alcohol. There's not usually this much camaraderie between them all. The only one who loves it more than me, is my wolf. She's imagining the end of the night, where we all shift into our wolves and cuddle in between Elijah and Warren.

There's still no River in her picture of eternal happiness.

"I'll allow it," I reply, cocking my head at Elijah. "What's the next part of your dare?"

"I want you to sit in my lap, sunshine, and let me feed from you in a location of my choosing."

"Not fair," Theo protests, a slight whine in his voice.

"Why not this time?" Elijah asks. Theo flounders, causing me to laugh. I don't know why he's complaining, but as soon as I unclasp my bra, all the dramatics fade away.

I bend in front of Elijah this time, having learnt my lesson from Warren, and I make eye contact with River, who is directly opposite. I can feel my cheeks heating up because it feels a little bit weird to be doing something this intimate with him here.

My wolf's not opposed to it, but she's not happy with it either, whereas, to me, he's just as much a part of me as the rest of them.

There's just not a tie proving it.

I don't know why I feel so self-conscious, considering that this man has seen every part of me, and he's even been inside all *three* of my available holes. His hands have brushed across my skin, his tongue tasting all of me, and yet I'm *shy* to undress in front of him.

The father of my children, a man I was soul-bonded to, and now... I can barely look at him.

I feel his presence in my mind, requesting access to form a mind link. I allow it, my heart pounding in my ears louder than the men chatting. But rather than adding to my anxiety, he calmly says, "I won't touch you. I won't do anything to you without permission."

There's no heat in his gaze, even though I can hear it in the voice inside my head, and he's trying to be as polite and understanding about this as he can.

I doubt I'm the only one to feel weird.

I lost one bond. He lost nine.

I give one firm nod, tug my panties down my thighs, and step out of them all in one fluid moment. I throw them across the room, not sure who won them, because I turn and straddle Elijah's lap. He tucks the loose strands of my hair behind my ears and tilts my head to the side. He trails his tongue down my shoulder, the heat of it burning my skin in the best way possible.

"Fuck me, how is this hot?" Wyatt whispers to someone.

"Right?" Rhett replies. "Then again, Lottie's hot."

"Everything she does is hot," Caden confirms. What a lovely boost to my confidence that is.

But it's Elijah's turn to keep my attention right now, and he's feeling rather selfish over it. His tongue trails across my chest, finding a path towards the left boob. He circles the nipple, before bringing it in his mouth and biting down.

I let out a small whimper, but the sound is pure need. I'm dripping with desire, desperate for him to touch me properly—for them all to touch me. This teasing is great. But I wish there was more.

"I love you," Elijah whispers in my mind as he drinks from me. I've got one hand holding his nape in place, stopping him from moving. I can feel my wetness dripping onto Elijah's leg, and although I know he notices, he doesn't complain.

If when I move, one of them points out a wet mark, I'll make them sit this entire night out.

When Elijah's had his fill, he pulls back and draws my head towards his, connecting our lips in a passionate kiss. I can feel his arousal through the bond, and I can taste the coppery tang of my own blood on his tongue. For someone who doesn't drink blood, it's weirdly erotic.

"I love you more than life," I reply, cupping his cheek.

"You love us all more than life, right?" Rhett demands.

I don't break from my stare with Elijah, and I notice the laugh lines around his eyes are so prominent this close. It's very sweet.

"Lottie, tell us you love us all," Rhett whines.

"Yeah, Lottie," Caden teases. Noah and Wyatt burst out laughing, and I'm struggling to break from my connection with Elijah to give them what they need.

"No, no, this is a valid demand," Theo says, when Dillon takes the piss. Rhett fist bumps Theo.

"Yes, obviously," I say rolling my eyes. Elijah turns me around on his lap, placing one leg over each of his. He then spreads his legs a little, putting me on a clear display. River's in the position here to get a very good show.

"So," I say, with a big grin. "Who wants to be my willing victim?"

I'm not surprised when multiple hands shoot in the air.

CHAPTER 21

"Please," I whimper, looking at Rhett. I can only imagine the look of pure want on my face, but I don't bother trying to dampen my pleas. He glances at Noah, who is standing to the side of us, who nods. I don't know why I'm surprised Noah is in charge right now. From the dominance fights, Noah was the first Alpha knocked out of them, so maybe a tiny part of me has assumed he's not as dominant as Rhett and Caden.

Wrongly, clearly, since he's doing an excellent job of it right now.

Rhett and Caden have stepped back, deferring to Noah as the one in charge. If it were me, I'd not be complaining. Being the conductor of our sex life is a very good role to have. But it's more than that—I can feel how into this situation Noah is.

He's loving the level of trust that I and the rest of our mates are putting into him, and it's fuelling his arousal.

Noah demanded that the coffee table be moved before things progressed to this level, but the sofas remained where they were. I'm currently spread out in the gap, where someone has thrown a blanket down to protect the rug at Rhett's insistence, and I'm thoroughly enjoying myself. I've been teased and pleasured with tongues and hands, but I'm missing what my body truly craves.

Not a single one of them has *actually* fucked me yet.

Noah's getting off on the power, and so far, it's brought him great joy to deny me.

"Open your mouth, baby," Noah commands.

I immediately do as he says, and Rhett grins.

"Good girl," Rhett murmurs, stroking my cheek with his thumb before he gently pulls me up so that I'm sitting, then pulling me up further when I try to stop. Kneeling now, with my back facing River, I watch as Rhett smoothly gets onto his feet. He stands before me and nods to get me to open my mouth again. "Open, baby."

I obey, and he immediately pushes into my mouth. My bond with him hums in pleasure, although honestly, that might be Rhett himself. There's no hesitation on his end; he slowly and steadily advances as I tease the metal in his cock.

That piercing was one of the best things Rhett ever got for me. Teasing it heightens his pleasure when his cock is this sensitive. But for me, it doesn't have the same impact when it's in my mouth as it does inside my pussy.

Speaking of... I feel very empty right now. My pussy is dripping, desperate to be filled, and I've even clenched my ass a few times.

"Did I hear someone is feeling empty down here?" Elijah murmurs, and I gasp around Rhett's dick, the man pushing in deeper as I do. I didn't hear Elijah's approach since the vampire is very fluid that way. It's something I'm envious of since we wolves can't. I think it's their speed.

"Her mind is wandering," Theo calls. I'm sick of that fucking Guardian bonds we share right now. He's been verbalising all of my inner thoughts, *ruining* my pleasure.

I feel two sharp spanks on my ass, and I have no idea who delivered them since far too many of my men are aroused and delighted by the view.

"Take me deeper, baby girl," Rhett pleads.

Noah's commands must have moved from the verbal realm to the silent one because I now feel two sets of hands on me, trailing over my chest. They move towards my nipples, but I can't see them since Rhett's commandeering the use of my face.

Warren is one of them since I can feel his bite on my nipples drawing blood, but I don't know who the other mouth belongs—oh. It's Dillon—my gorgeous male with the gentle firmness that always feels amazing.

Elijah's at my back, teasing my pussy, but not once going inside me the way I'm craving. At this point, I'd even take his *fingers* if it meant I got to throw myself off the cliff into the pool of pleasure. He teases my clit, pressing down firmly with his thumb, but the moment I grind into it, he pulls away and leaves me desperate for more.

I glare at him, but it's not even glaring at him. It's glaring at Rhett's chest.

"Ah, ah, ah," Rhett says. They've all been mimicking Warren, and it's pissing me right off.

"I'll *ah, ah, ah* you," I snarl into his mind, pulling off from his dick.

"Put him back in your mouth, Lottie," Noah calls, and everyone stills. Warren and Dillon stop with their teasing, and I can't even feel Elijah next to me anymore.

"Put me back into your mouth, little minx," Rhett says, his words like a soft caress. Before his tone then hardens, *"Or you'll get nothing at all."*

I whimper and then moan, reaching forward to take his cock back in my mouth. I hum ever so lightly, determining to make this the best blow job he's had.

At least then, one of us will have a good orgasm.

But the moment I decide that, Elijah's fingers push inside of me, and I whimper once more. Warren and Dillon are eagerly lapping and teasing my nipples, and I genuinely think I could cum without them touching my clit.

Everyone is watching, and having this much of an audience excites me in the best way. One pair of eyes burns hotter than all the rest, but I'm too terrified to look his way.

I'm also curious about what Theo and Caden are doing since they —other than Noah—are still the only two fully clothed.

Rhett's hand grips my hair, the other cupping my cheek, and I open my mouth a little wider to let him take over for a moment. This always kills my jaw, but fuck, is it worth it to see the absolute ecstasy on his face as he uses me for his pleasure.

Elijah withdraws his fingers, and my wolf protests vehemently, until we feel Wyatt taking his place. We hum in pleasure, the vibration making Rhett growl in pleasure, as the heat of Wyatt's body presses against us.

Rhett weaves his hands through my hair, his head falling back, a curse falling from his lips as I moan again. His roughness sends a thrill of satisfaction down my spine.

"Straddle my hips, little minx," Wyatt pleads, and when I don't move fast enough, Noah echoes the words in a much more demanding tone. I move to do as they say, and Wyatt helps, lifting me down over him. I spread my thighs, opening myself up so I'm more comfortable, but as I lower myself, down, he doesn't give me what we both crave.

We're in a reverse cowgirl position, but Wyatt's cock just teases my pussy, not once entering. I can feel the heat of him through my folds, but he's not actively going into me.

Rhett, Warren and Dillon are still touching me in the delicious way I wanted. There's some blood dripping down my chest from Warren's messy play, although he's been doing his best to lick it up.

I can feel something wet and cold brushing against my ass, and I flinch, as Rhett stills his movements.

I can't look to see who is touching me, but based on the way the bond lights up, I know it's Elijah. He's preparing my ass, as Wyatt slowly teases me. Rhett continues with using my mouth, as Warren and Dillon up the ante of the nipple stimulation.

I'm feeling so sensitised, and yet I'm not getting touched the way I need to be able to cum.

They're driving me crazy.

"She's ready," Elijah murmurs a few moments later. It could've been minutes, or hours, as far as I'm concerned. I can't really keep track with how delirious this pleasure is making me.

"So am I," Rhett murmurs, looking down at me. "Are you going to swallow, baby?"

I nod the best I can with the position we're in. Rhett really doesn't last any longer than that, and the salty taste of him fills my mouth.

The others are patient enough to let him savour his release, but when Rhett steps back, both Warren and Dillon pull away, and I'm flipped over so that I'm now facing Wyatt.

Elijah appears at my back again, and the two of them press in me at the same time. I gasp, and then push against Wyatt's chest trying to move away.

"No, no, no," I chant.

"Stop," Theo, Noah and Rhett call simultaneously.

"What's wrong, baby?" Noah asks, crouching next to me.

"Not at the same time," I whimper. "It hurts too much." I don't explain very well, but Theo takes over and shares what I mean. It's the first time tonight I've been grateful for his spying ways.

Elijah pulls away, and Wyatt presses in first. Once he's bottomed out inside of me, Elijah gently pushes in too. There's a burn, but it's nowhere near as bad as the pain I had just felt.

"Fuck," Wyatt groans, as Elijah slowly pushes inside of me. The two of them strike up movements between the two of them, that elicit moans and whimpers from me. It's electrifying.

"More," I beg, rocking gently between them both. Warren and Dillon move back to my nipples, and I love it.

I fucking love being the centre of this.

Why didn't we play as a bigger group before now?

"More what, baby?" Noah asks, and I open my mouth. He grins, and Theo moves to stand in front of me. I don't immediately take him inside, instead I circle his head, teasing him. My Guardian threads his fingers through my hair, and it's perfect.

Mostly. If someone reached up to touch my clit, I think I could die a happy woman right now.

Wyatt's thumb presses there once again, and I know I've got Theo to thank for that. So I do, in making his blow job the best I can.

I am honestly living my best life.

"You're gorgeous," Noah says, stepping closer to us all. "Can you show us how you ride those two cocks, baby?"

"She's full of cocks," Dillon says, licking at my nipple, as my orgasm starts to build. Wyatt presses in a little firmer, and they time their movements better to draw out my release.

Dillon's right, I'm full off cock and just about to... *oh fuck.*

My orgasm is an avalanche, drawing me

This is the best way to live.

☽ ☾ ● ❨ ❩

"*I* don't want you like this," Warren says, and my eyes fill with tears as my wolf howls in pain. Does he... does he think we're dirty for how we've been playing?

I take a step back, and his jaw drops, as he seems to understand how his words affected me, how terrible I feel.

"Shit, princess, no," he gasps, pulling me into him. He lifts me into his arms, so that we're eye to eye. "I just don't want you in this *position.* Do you think you look any less beautiful to me now, because of what we're doing?"

I shrug, not sure what I'm feeling to be honest. My wolf isn't mollified by the attention and touch he's showering us with, and it's hard to tune her out when we're this connected.

"Oh, princess," he murmurs, his voice taking on a husky edge to it. "The fact that you're literally dripping with cum, soaked in the scents of our mating circle, turns me on so badly." He presses a kiss to the pulse on my neck, which makes my heart speed up. "You've never been more desirable to me—you're beautiful, princess, so fucking beautiful. I'm so lucky to have you as mine."

"Ah, Warren's being selfish," Caden says. I glance at the Alpha wolf, and he's spread out in the arm chair, still fully clothed, but with his cock out. He's stroking himself back and forth at a very leisurely pace. He refuses to get involved just yet, because he has plans for me.

These plans haven't been disclosed, but he has shared that I need to be thoroughly fucked before he takes part.

He said he has plans for me, and he wants me thoroughly fucked before he takes part.

It's a little weird, but I've got enough dicks to keep me occupied— both in the literal and the insulting way.

"I want you bent over this table," Warren says, motioning to the coffee table. *The coffee table?* It really doesn't seem stable enough to hold my weight, never mind hold my weight as I'm fucked over it. "And whilst I'm fucking your pretty little pussy, I want someone doing the same thing to your mouth."

"It's a dirty job," Theo says stepping into my vision. "But I don't mind taking the mantle."

"I just bet you don't," Dillon says, with a smirk. "I'm exhausted, or I'd fight you for it."

"If you had enough stamina to keep up with the talented men," Theo says, winking at Dillon. "Then you wouldn't be missing out on our mate's very delicious mouth."

"Theo, stop antagonising the weak wolves," Warren says, patting Theo's back. Dillon's jaw drops and I let out a small giggle. "Get your dick out, and let our mate worship it, whilst I do the same to her."

Things move pretty quickly after that, and I get spread out across the coffee table. I'm on top of the table, on my back, and I hope that Warren can be gentle enough he doesn't break this thing. He kneels down next to the table, and we're at a perfect height for him to easily slide inside of me.

My legs are hanging down off the side, but he lifts them up, pressing my knees into my chest.

Theo turns my head to the side, and his cock is right there in my face. He's also kneeling, but the angle isn't the same for my mouth as it is.

"I want to be in your mouth," Theo says. "I want to be buried in your throat for as long as you can take. I want to be deep inside of you, little wolf."

I nod, opening my mouth, and letting him push past my lips. His cock is leaking pre-cum, and the salty tase explodes over my tongue. My wolf is obsessed with the taste of him, and she'd absolutely request his cum as one of her last meals on Earth if she had to.

The two of them begin to fuck me in tandem. I whimper around Theo's cock and he fills my mind with praise, lathering it on deeper than I'm taking him.

Warren's pounding shakes the table, and it makes me feel amazing with how deeply he's managing to hit. My own orgasm is still very far out of reach, but I'm more focused on helping Theo get off.

He deserves the pleasure and I *need* his cum.

"Come and touch her," Warren demands, and a thrill races through me. "Seriously, Noah?"

"I was just enjoying the show," my Alpha replies without a hint of the annoyance Warren's tone had.

There's rustling before I feel numerous sets of hands touching my skin. One gently brushes against my stomach, another touches my thigh. Warren slows his thrusting for a moment to adjust my position —this time letting my legs hang over the sides of the coffee table.

The edges aren't sharp, but they do dig into my thighs—*something to consider when buying our next coffee table, I suppose.*

Out of my peripheral vision I can see Wyatt and Elijah all crouched down. I have no doubt there's men on the other side of the table too, based on the excitement through the bond.

Gently hands reach out and touch me, teasing me with their featherlight brushes. Someone's tongue—Wyatt's or Elijah's I think— traces my skin, and it's warm at first before becoming cold when another blows on it. The sensations that act brings is intense, and each time it happens, I gasp around Theo who thrusts inside of me that much deeper.

"You're such a good cocksucker, Charlotte." Theo groans as he fucks my mouth.

Warren grips my hips hard, the hold definitely going to bruise, and as everyone participates in this fun, my brain is in complete overdrive. It's a mindfuck from Warren, one that I'm not sure is meant to encourage my pleasure or steal it from me.

I love it equally.

I can spot River just behind us all, sitting on the armchair, not taking part fully. His cock's out, his pants still mostly covering him as he strokes himself. His eyes have been trained on me this entire time, and sure he's said a few words here and there but for the most part he's not been very active.

There's a distance between us, and it shows in his hesitance. He's not yet been brave enough to touch me, he's been too unwilling to broach the barrier of separation between us.

It hurts.

A lot.

A man I love, a man who loves me, is unable to fully show that love in the physical way I crave—*the way we both crave*—because he lacks a bond with me that protects him from the anger and jealousy from my mates.

So now, where we're having a good time, I think he's scared to do anything that might disrupt it.

Should I push him? Should I beg for him? Plead for him to come and participate?

Or should I let him have his distance? Do I leave this to his terms?

"Worrying during sex means we're not fucking you hard enough," Theo says, just as Warren increases his tempo. Theo matches it, and I lose the capability to even breathe, never mind worry.

Someone gives my nipples little bites, not drawing blood so it could be anyone, that feel intense. Rhett bites down just under my ribcage, and it would hurt, if it wasn't for the pleasure of the sting.

This is perfection. It's nearly everything I could've wanted.

My mates are giving me the ultimate pleasure, whilst some of them take the pleasure I am offering.

I feel like a Queen.

I love the way they're ravishing me.

239

Warren calls me princess, and right now, he's got me laid out on the table like a fucking buffet. He's taking his rightful spot, as he lets the peasants—in his mind—take whatever small scraps he's offering.

Theo tenses in my mouth, seconds before his cum spurts down my throat. He's gently holding my head in place so that it doesn't get too overwhelming for me.

As if the taste of him could ever be overwhelming.

He steps back once I've cleaned him fully, and then Warren truly takes his treatment to the next level.

"Give us all your screams, love," Wyatt murmurs, his breath tickling my ear, as someone reaches down to press on my clit.

I don't know if I pull Warren over the edge, or if he was already there, but we join as one, both our orgasms crashing over the other.

I get lost in the bliss of the moment, floating in the sea of pleasure. There's so much lust and desire surrounding me, the feelings in my chest alluring and adding to the desperation I feel.

The sex is amazing, the connections we share powerful, but the love is what enhances this moment.

I'm left spent and shattered as Warren pulls away, falling down onto his ass. Wyatt rises to his feet, and lifts me into his arms, kissing my sweaty shoulder softly.

A blanket is pulled round me, as someone demands a water break. I laugh though the exhaustion, but even this here shows how well they take care of me.

I eye the men I've not yet touched at all, and know this is *break* in the fun, and not the end of it.

Even if they're willing to stop here, I'm not and neither is my wolf.

"*T*ogether," I whisper, eyeing them both up and down with hesitance. My heart races, as my core tightens. Sure, I want to take them, and my wolf is insistent that we'll manage, that we *need* this. But she's a hussy at the best of times.

My eyes dart between the two identical men. Is it... isn't it just a little bit incestuous?

"Like, both of you want to be inside my vagina... at the same time?" I ask, not sure if they meant the same thing.

"Vagina is such a... clinical word," Caden says, reaching down to cup me. His thumb presses down on my clit eliciting a gasp and a full body shiver from me, but his tone is *clinical*. "This pretty cunt should never be so impartially spoken of."

His fingers slide up and down now, moving away from my clit in what feels like a punishment. The sounds of my wetness is mortifying to me, but another gasp leaves me when another set of fingers touches me.

Noah's face appear in my vision, and he winks, as he gives me back the pleasure Caden so rudely took away. My legs quiver, and my pussy clenches in anticipation.

"Caden and I work very *very* well together, baby," Noah says, with a dangerous smile. "But if you don't want to—"

"No, I really do," I say, pressing in closer to their hands, gripping them both just in case they try and take this away from me.

They gave me the offer.

They are *not* backing out now.

"Of course you do," Warren says, with a laugh in his words. He's exhausted from our... *bonding session*, but he's sitting stroking his mostly soft cock.

I have no doubt he'll cum again before this is all over, despite the fact that seem to have a one time fuck rule in place.

Which is fair considering there are nine of them, and only one of me.

I was initially worried about that, but my men have reassured me multiple times that they're enjoying this—that they're *loving* this.

They've described this as live porn, with a deeper emotional connection, so it's so much better.

Apparently—it may just be an ego boost for me though.

But this way they get to be involved, they got touch, to talk and direct. They're loving it, which boosts my confidence that much further, and enhances the experience.

Once I'm done with Caden and Noah they've all had a turn. Well... everyone except River and I'm not sure if that's happening.

My wolf isn't going to be settled until we've had our fill of them all. She's been desperate, and eager, keeping me going and powering me up. Honestly, I feel the exact same way.

It's like a marathon, but a sex marathon—the only kind I'd willingly participate in—but I think once we're done here with Noah and Caden, she's going to be too exhausted to continue.

I don't think she's counting River.

I don't think she's going to want to nourish the bonds that we no longer share with River, even if I do.

But that's fine, because I will.

"Are you ready?" Noah asks, and I nod slightly. I can feel his excitement racing through the bond, and it's only matched by that of Caden's.

"Right, how do you want to do this?" Caden asks, and the pair of them look a little bit hesitant.

"Well, I don't know," I say, with a small laugh. "I've never done this before."

Theo laughs, too, and takes over with the directions. "Lottie on your back." His deep voice is laced with desire.

"Lottie on your back," I mutter, in a high-pitched voice, before bending down and doing what he says. My wolf will never deny an order from them when it comes to our sex life, it seems.

Hussy.

"That's not going to work," Warren says, shaking his head. "Caden, you get on *your* back."

"Why him?" I ask, curiously.

"Do you know what, that's a good point," Warren says, with a shrug as if it doesn't matter to him either way. "Noah, you get on your back."

"Caden should be the one on his back," Noah says, but then lays down next to me without putting up much of a real fight. We're now both on our back on the living room floor, and he gives me a small smile as his eyes twinkle.

I think he's enjoying being told what to do, almost as much as he enjoyed telling them what to do.

"Lottie straddle him," Warren commands, and that's an order I'm eager to follow. I hover over him, and reach down to take hold of Noah's thick cock.

"Do not put that dick inside your pussy," Theo says, stroking his hand down my back, eliciting shivers from me. I whimper, and rock against Noah, letting his cock slide between my folds, silently begging to let him fuck me.

He moans, and I grin as I continue doing it.

My tits are jiggling, and they're only noticeable really because Wyatt's eyes are trained on them. He starts beating his cock a little bit faster, and I get distracted watching.

There's so many dicks and I sadly only have two eyes so I can't look at everyone.

Maybe next time we need to record this.

"Caden, crouch down behind her, and Noah, keep your legs together," Theo says, and when Noah doesn't do it fast enough, Warren kicks them into place.

I continue with my movements to try and keep the lust-filled mood that I need, instead of letting my anxiety creep in. I leave my men to the directions, and it's interesting how the two Alphas are listening to Theo and Warren.

It's a weird change of dynamics especially since it's not Rhett who has stepped up, and our usual dynamics revolve around our wolves, since that's when we're all most comfortable.

Theo and Warren working together though is extremely hot. *It'll do.*

"Okay, Caden you're gonna have to do it gently and slowly so we can avoid hurting her," The says, his tone soft as he coaches my guys on how to fuck me best. "Noah, you go in first but not all the way. Caden needs room to get in as well."

"Enough, Lottie," Warren demands, and I whine, but stop. Noah presses in, and it feels amazing as he sheathes himself mostly in.

"There, stop," Theo says, and Noah obeys. I rock a little trying to get a little bit more friction. He's so close to being at the perfect spot, but Theo has decided to take it all away from me.

"No," Warren says, amused as he holds me still. I swear all this anticipation is only enhancing the moment, but damn am I needy. "Wait for it, impatient one." *Easy for him to say—he's not the one being taunted.*

"I told you she was a minx," Wyatt says, sounding like he's in pain. My eyes dart to him, and he's enjoying this so fucking much.

They all are.

Shit.

"Okay, Caden, you're up," Theo says, and Caden nods, and there's some fiddling as they line him up properly.

I'm aroused when Theo gets intimately involved in the lining up process, but he's so clinical that it's just me being so dirty minded.

But the moment he presses inside, I gasp because it fucking *burns.* Tears prick at my eyes, and I tense up. Warren's fingers gently trace up and down my spine, but that's not helping.

"Keep going," Theo says, when Caden stops right at the entrance. Caden begins to protest, but Theo shakes his head. "Trust me. This part will be uncomfortable, but you're all plenty lubed, and it'll be fine once you're inside of her properly."

"Lottie?" Warren asks, softly. "What do you, need princess?"

"More," I plead, terrified Caden's going to stop. "Touch me."

"Keep going," Warren says, and he looks at Noah. "Noah press down on her clit, circle it, enhance this moment for her. She's the one suffering, and we can all see how good even just this part feels for you."

Noah blushes a little but then does as Warren demands. It helps with the pain I'm feeling, the combination of the pleasure and the burn actually balancing each other out.

It doesn't feel *good* but it's no longer terrible.

Caden moves in a little more stretching me further, and tears drip down my cheeks.

"Press a little harder, Noah," Warren coaches. "You want it to feel good." Noah's touching me so good.

I'm going to cum. My hips start to move on their own accord, as I try and chase the pleasure I'm being given.

"Lottie, sweetheart, gently," Noah gasps.

"Don't thrust at all, love," Rhett adds from the sofa. I whine and there's a bunch of laughs.

"It'll hurt you if they don't do it properly," Theo says. "Be patient, and you'll get the pleasure you deserve."

I nod, my breath catching in my throat. My orgasm is there, desperate to be given.

"Warren bend down and take her tit in your mouth," Theo demands, and Warren does. His cock is right in Noah's face, and I'm so tempted to touch it.

Fuck me.

Warren teases my nipple biting it ever so gently but sucking on it providing pleasure. Between that and the feeling of my clit, it's easy enough to ignore the pain of Caden.

But not the pain of denying my orgasm.

"How... how much more?" I stutter.

"Not much more," Theo reassures me, and I nod, ignoring the pleas from my wolf to just take what is mine.

She's so impatient.

"I'm all in," Caden says a moment later.

"Noah, your turn," Theo says. "Thrust into her properly, now."

And *fuck.*

"Holy shit," I scream, my words barely discernible, as my orgasm crashes through me. My body is on fire, every single touch and feeling so sensitive, so enjoyable, so fucking overwhelming.

I can't stop the tears from falling, the pleasure is *that* good.

"Move," someone demands, and I can feel the dicks inside me dragging my orgasm out as they take it in turns to move in and out.

My orgasm only ends when Caden accidentally withdraws too much, but there's no pain as he thrusts back inside of me.

"And she's back," someone says, and my eyes widen as the overall pleasure dims, and I can feel each moment more clearly.

"Are you full, sunshine?" Elijah asks from the soda.

I nod. "So full. I don't think I've ever been this full before."

"You won't have been," Theo says, as Warren bites down properly, drinking from me. "You're full with two Alpha cocks, little wolf. You're taking them so beautifully, isn't she?"

"So fucking beautifully, angel," River says, and my eyes dart up to his. *Fuck.* The desire from him knocks the breath out of me, and I have to look away.

I shiver, and Caden gasps.

"Fuck, baby, do that again," he pleads. "Please do that again."

"What did I do?" I ask through my own panting breaths.

"You clenched around us," Noah says, sounding as distressed as Caden is.

I do my best to clench my inner walls, and the pair of them grunt, moaning loudly.

"Yeah, I'm not going to fucking last long," Caden says, pressing into my back but somehow not moving too much inside me, as he lets Noah take the brunt of the movements.

It feels fucking incise, having Caden pressing against my g-spot, as Noah fucks good enough for the three of us.

I'm not ready for Caden to cum. I, selfishly, want another orgasm before I even think about letting him leave me.

Theo must hear that, because he asks the audience for a willing volunteer, and Elijah drops down to his knees on the other side of me. My eyes widen when he licks blood from my chest following the trail down.

My moans and whimpers would terrify our neighbours if we had any.

"I'd love to fuck your pretty little mouth , right now," Rhett says brushing across my bottom lip with this thumb. "But I don't think you can take another cock in you right now."

"Oh, no, definitely do not do that," River says, looking at me with those intense eyes of his. "I want to hear your screams, angel. I want you to bring the house down with your pleasure."

"Fuck," I gasp, shivering under all of their attention. Goosebumps coat my skin, and I know for a fact that it's not because I'm cold.

"More," I demand, and Noah nods, looking over my head towards Caden.

They both start to pull out of me, and I can feel myself whimpering as the empty feeling builds. But then the assholes both thrust into me at the same time, and I scream.

Noah's moan is barely heard, although I can feel the intensity of his feelings through the bond, as I let my pleasure be known.

The orgasm that's building is so intense, so powerful, so fucking needed.

"More!" I scream through my pants, and my pleads and my begs. "More."

Over and over I just beg for more. It's the only word I think I know. My men are giving me their all, and I can barely fucking breathe, it's that good.

It goes deeper than just the pleasure they're giving my body. My wolf and I are in harmony with Noah, and Caden, and Theo and Warren and Elijah.

Even the men not actively touching me are on the same wavelength as far as our bonds go.

Warren and Elijah bite down on my nipples, and blood is coating my body. I know the blood doesn't turn on the wolves, not really anyway, but it's giving River the best show of his fucking life. And I think that's why they're doing it.

The vampires are being antagonistic on purpose because they're just as eager as me to bring their brother back into our dynamics.

They're doing their best to wind him and try to push him past this tight control he seems to have over himself, all to ensure he gets his turn.

That I get my turn with him.

I don't know if my men can handle it, but I fucking hope they can. Between the drinks they've all been less snarly with each other, River included, so I have hope. I'm lit on fire right now, but my soul won't rest until I reconnect with River too.

"I'm going to cum," Noah grunts.

"Don't you dare!" Caden snarls, and I shake my head. I *need* Noah's cum "We do it together or we don't do it at all."

Okay, that's intriguing, and I'll allow it.

"Are you close, Lottie?" Theo asks, and I nod and then shake my head and then nod again.

"It's intense." I say this through the bond, unable to speak aloud.

"Okay, then that means they're likely giving you too much stimulation and not enough relief," Dillon says. "Noah, remove your thumb."

He does and that calms things a little bit, so that I can enjoy the building pleasure that was just hovering there.

It was so intense, but as soon as he's removed that one thing, it calms a little.

My pussy quivers around their cocks, teasing and taunting them the way they both like.

I revel in the feeling of this intense orgasm that is right there, and I know I'm seconds away from going over the edge.

"Are you close?" Caden grunts in my ear, and I nod.

He bites down on my shoulder blade just as my orgasm unleashes. The three of us are quivering, moaning, screaming messes as we ride out each other's ecstasy together.

Our bond is pulsing with love, as the connection we share deepens.

Sex is always the best way to connect with each other, and I will be demanding this occurs far more frequently than it has.

I rest my head back on Caden's chest, who somehow manages to support me even despite the fact that he's unleashing a tidal wave of cum inside of me.

As things die down, Caden gently pulls out, and flops back onto his ass. Noah is far less gentle as he pulls out, and cum coats his stomach.

Neither of them seems to care, they're both exhausted with sweat covering them.

But I'm not done.

I've got one more cock in mind.

One more mate to connect with.

I unsteadily rise to my feet, bloating literally dripping down my body, as cum does the same thing.

I'm a vampire's wet dream... or at the very least, a hybrids.

I take a hesitant step forward, still on top of Noah as cum runs down my thighs. River lets out a snarl, glancing around the room and somehow in the time it takes me to blink, I'm in his lap.

"Please, I beg you," I whimper, reaching up to cup his cheeks. I won't take this without his permission, but as soon as he nods, I sheath myself on his dick.

His piercings touch me in all the right ways, but River's not the gentle man. He fucks into me at a rapid pace.

His touch though is gentle and soft, so tender and loving.

River doesn't kiss my lips despite my attempts—he doesn't even kiss me at all. He's focused on fucking my pussy as hard as he can, as he lays his own claim to the moment.

My wolf is surprisingly silent. She's not in support of this, but she's also not yelling at me in denial.

She's giving her weird blessing, despite the fact that this is something she can't understand.

I take the initiative, gripping his face harder as I tug it down to me.

Tears drip down my face, of joy and sadness, as he kisses me softly. Our kiss feels like coming home after a long work day.

There's still so much baggage between us, something we both need to work out, but there's something so important about having him here for this right now.

We need to fix our relationship, but I take everything from him now that he's offering.

I take it all, because at the core of him, River Bextor-Ellis is mine.

He fucks me into oblivion, and nobody is surprised that once River and I come for one last time, I pass out.

There's too much power, too much lust, and too much fear that I've fucked everything, for me to remain awake.

But damn, do I feel good.

CHAPTER 22

"We've got a lot that needs to be organised over the next few days," I say, looking around the breakfast table. Dillon was up early and went to grab us some breakfast with Theo and Elijah. I've got hot food—a cooked breakfast, with extra hash browns—and they were smart enough to get some cold items too, for when my meal eventually gets past the acceptable level of warm. "But one thing I do want—"

"Anything," Rhett says, patting my stomach gently. I roll my eyes, scooting my chair further away from his, and he frowns at me. I can feel the hurt through the bond, which wasn't my intention. "I was being sweet. Why would you move away?"

"I'm sorry, I really do appreciate the gesture." I reach over and squeeze his knee, sending some love through the bond to soothe the rejection. It doesn't work on the man, but his wolf appreciates the gesture. "I'm not pregnant enough where there is even a heartbeat for our tiny humans."

"Right," Rhett says, raising his eyebrows as he looks at the rest of my mates, who all share the same confused look. Well, it's probably best to address it to the group as a whole. "What's that got to do with anything?"

Warren snorts, as he reaches into the middle of the table to grab some of the grapes.

"You're just patting my stomach, Rhett. If you wanted to be sweet, you could've squeezed my hand, tucked my hair behind my ear, or kissed my forehead, or done *anything* that wasn't just whacking my stomach."

"I didn't whack it," Rhett mutters, a little sullenly.

I laugh, but I'm the only one who does. I squeeze his hand this time, getting his attention, before giving him a gentle look. "I know that you're all excited, and so am I. Even if the timing isn't perfect, I love that we're pregnant. But until there's an actual baby bump, can we chill with the tummy patting?"

"Fair enough," Noah says, with a smirk. Rhett frowns, but nods, still a little sullen.

"Just let her have this," Theo grumbles, and I look around, unsure who complained. My Guardian grins at me across the table, not revealing the source. "But the moment there's a bump?"

"The moment there's a bump you can fight over touching me until the sun goes down," I confirm. He beams, and he's not the only one. *I hope they didn't take the fighting comment literally.*

We fall silent for a few beats whilst we eat, and I pour myself another glass of apple juice.

"So, what is it that you'd like?" Noah asks, bringing us back to the discussion we were having.

"I want us to have the party."

"The party?" Dillon echoes, narrowing his eyes.

"The party?" Wyatt's tone is vastly different to Dillon's. Wyatt seems excited, and he has a smile on his face as he says it.

"The pack wanted to throw me one, remember? For being Luna officially?"

"Oh shit!" Warren says, with a nod. "I completely forgot about that."

"I didn't, but I don't understand why you want to throw one," Rhett says. "It's not like it's a joyous time right now."

"Okay, Mr. Killjoy," I say, and he shrugs, giving me an apologetic look. I took the day yesterday to mope and be a miserable defeatist. Today, my attitude is vastly different. Getting really great sex can do that—and I refuse to let anything, or anyone take away the good in my life.

"I just think it'll be a good moral booster. Not only are we going to be away for several weeks, but when we return, it will be to face a trial where I may get exonerated or end up executed. With everything we've got going on, it would be a good for us, for the *pack*, to have a moment, however brief, to celebrate. Think of it as a sendoff and a promise that we'll be back."

"I see your point," Rhett says, but his face is twisted up in a way that I think the answer is going to be no.

"We took that time for us last night," I say, dejectedly. "Remember?"

There are a *lot* of smirks, but Rhett's face heats up.

"Last night was great."

"Great?" Caden demands, leaning over to me. "I can handle not patting your tummy and throwing a majorly expensive party with barely any notice, but you referring to last night as *great* is not going to fly."

I bite my lip, hiding my amusement, but the others don't bother. Caden's nostrils flare, and I smooth out my grin.

"Last night was hot and brilliant, and I'm still quivering from it now," I say, only slightly mollifying my mate. "And I'm desperate to repeat it all again."

"Again?" Caden asks. I nod. "Okay."

"Simp," Rhett mouths, and I pretend not to see it.

"I really loved the time we all had together, and I think we need to do something similar with the pack."

"Explain it to me," Rhett says. "Because to me, it still makes very little sense. There's *nothing* to celebrate."

So, I try and explain to my very against this idea, Alpha, that we should throw a very expensive party. But in the end, the thing that convinces him is something I think he was angling for this whole time.

"I also think we should announce the pregnancy." I bite my lip, and they all grin.

"You should've led with that," Caden teases. "We'll absolutely throw a party to celebrate."

"What do you actually celebrate when it comes to pregnancy announcements?" Wyatt asks. "It's not like your dad is going to be excited we fucked you—"

"No," Rhett says, reaching over to smack Wyatt's hand with the back of his spoon. "We celebrate the new life."

"I still think it's weird that everyone knows what we did to make them," Wyatt says with a laugh.

"Maybe, but the worst thing," Elijah says, leaning into Wyatt like he's telling him a secret. "Is that you're the evidence of your parents —"

"Don't even go there," Wyatt snarls, pushing Elijah back. Elijah doesn't fall to the floor only due to his speed, but that doesn't quell his annoyance.

"Whoa, what the fuck?" Elijah demands. "It was a joke."

"Not a very funny one," Wyatt snarls.

I look over at Rhett, whose face is pinched together in concern, but he minutely shakes his head at me.

"Okay, well... we all know what we're doing today, right?" I ask, changing the subject. Wyatt withdraws even further as we try to move past that explosive outburst.

It's weird. Wyatt is *never* one to blow up like this, and it's over a subject I never realised was an issue.

Which is stupid, because now that I think about it, Wyatt's parents have never been mentioned. I've never seen them in the Ancestral Realm, so they're either not dead or not interested in meeting me.

I get the feeling it's the former, though.

"*Later,*" Rhett says, giving me a soft smile.

"Do *you* know what you're doing today?" Caden asks, smirking at me. "We all worked when you ran away for some *fun* yesterday."

"Yes, yes, I left the office. However, *unlike you*, I do have a very amazing personal assistant who will have my entire day planned out for me."

Noah laughs, nudging his twin. "Your jealousy is showing." And it is. Caden lets out a huff.

"She's perfect, I know. Definitely, be jealous."

"Yeah, yeah," Caden says, good-naturedly. "But how are you feeling? Yesterday was a lot."

"We didn't really help," Noah says, with a sigh. I now understand the guilt I've been feeling from him.

"Yes, you did," I reply, looking at Noah in particular. "I was... not myself yesterday. I was feeling a little defeated, but mostly I'm tired of the unfairness of it all."

"You've been dealt a shit hand," Elijah says. "But you're doing an amazing job at compartmentalising and organising yourself so that you're not drowning. I'm so proud of you, sunshine."

I grin at him, but I don't fully feel deserving of that praise right now, so I change the topic. "What's the plan in terms of the party?"

"I am not sorting that out," Caden says. I roll my eyes.

"Dibs, not me," Noah says, immediately pressing his finger to his nose.

Rhett groans. "I don't want to do it either."

I snort. Child one through three, showing their true colours. "I can sort that."

My offer is genuine, but all of my mates shake their heads.

"You don't have the time," Rhett says.

"And we're trying to keep your stress as low as possible," Warren adds.

"And I appreciate that, but I don't need to actually do anything," I say, and Wyatt asks how. "Well, as long as I get Lexie to organise a meeting for either Lionel or River with Judith, then they can organise it for me. All I need to do is get Lexie to make sure it's on our list, and she'll coordinate everything."

"Please, please, please do me a favour," Warren begs. I raise an eyebrow, waiting for the request. "Please, make River the party planner."

"Yes!" Caden laughs, clapping his hands. "Fuck, Lottie, please. That'll be fucking gold."

"I'm not making either of them actually *plan* the party," I say, with a frown between the two of my mates. "I'm just going to get them to speak to Judith about it."

Warren shrugs. "Still, that'll be funny enough. Make him do that."

"What's your obsession with punishing your brother?

"I just find it funny," Warren says, before dropping his lips into the most adorable pout. *Seriously, it should be illegal to look that good whilst being a brat.* "We're going through such a terrible time—"

"Ha!" Rhett's booming laughter fills the room as he mostly drowns out Wyatt's snickers.

"You're trying to use the fact that we're facing an enemy who literally wants us dead, to try and convince me to make your brother plan our party?"

Warren doesn't even have the decency to look ashamed. "At the end of the day, I'm doing my part for the pack now. You know how amazing I've done with our Delta's in readying them for a working role. He needs to do his part."

"I'll think about it," I say, feeling the genuine happiness inside Warren. *Surely River won't mind that much... right?* "And we do appreciate you."

"Suck up," Wyatt teases. "I can do my job without getting rimmed out by—"

"It's breakfast," I groan, and Theo and Dillon nudge Wyatt.

"But for now," Noah says, when Warren goes to say something

else. "Let's finish breakfast, and we'll head down to the offices, ready for the lovely day we're going to have."

"Your day might be lovely," I say, spearing a mushroom with my fork. "But mine is going to be filled with relentless men who are going to be demanding a lot of answers they're not entitled to. I can promise you they're not going to enjoy our discussions."

"Fuck catering to the patriarchy," Theo says, and I snort.

"I'm going to have a great day with it, though," I reply, with a secret smile.

"I'm sure you will," Dillon says. "I'm heading back to the library. If anyone is free, and by anyone, I mean Elijah or Warren, feel free to join me.'

"Why us?" Elijah asks, before shaking his head. "Either way, I'm not. Scottie and I have a lot to sort out ready for this upcoming week."

"You sure are spending a lot of time with her," Warren says, eyeing his brother up.

"And your implication is what, brother?" Elijah's eyes are black as he glares at Warren.

"No implication," Warren replies. "Just wondering if she's said anything about Abel."

"I bet you were," Elijah hisses. He doesn't bother to respond and shoves a spoonful of beans into his mouth. I've never seen anyone chew beans so angrily, but that's not something I want to be involved with.

"Warren probably won't be much help," Theo says. Warren frowns, and Theo explains what Dillon wanted. He's right in his observations that Warren couldn't help. He's not the most studious, and since he won't process the information at the same speed, and so will still need to actually work.

"Yeah, no fuck that," Warren says, with a small laugh.

"What are you all handling today?" I ask, curiously.

"I'm going to be preparing the Delta's for this upcoming week," Warren says. "Abel's going to be bringing forty of their men over tomorrow so they can learn the ropes before we leave."

"Perfect. I'll be handling that with you tomorrow, so if anything crops up, come and get me," Rhett says, and Warren promises he will.

"Have the enforcers all forgiven you?" Wyatt teases. Rhett rolls his eyes, but nods. "I'm going to be assisting Noah, right?"

"Right. We're going to be going the information Lexie and whoever started to outline about the packs, and identify and security issues," Noah says. "We are going to liaison with Landon and your dad too."

"My plans for today are to work with Theo on the security plans for the trip," Rhett says. "I think your dad planned on coming down to help."

I try not to worry about them being in the same room.

"I'm all yours, baby," Caden says, grinning at me when I turn to him. I roll my eyes, now understanding about the teasing from him earlier. I, of course, didn't know "We're going to share these calls and whatnot. Unless you'd rather do it alone."

"No, you're perfect," I say.

"We're all perfect, though, right?" Rhett says, and I burst out laughing. I don't give him an answer as I scoot my chair back and get up from the table.

"I need to grab my cardi, then we can go," I say, leaving the room.

"We're all perfect, right, love?" Rhett calls, and I continue giggling.

I made the right decision last night, trusting that they had everything handled. It's healed a little of my soul, being able to trust in them and then have them rise to the occasion.

King Lobo might've attempted to destroy our bonds, but all he's done, is give us the chance to grow and develop *stronger* bonds.

These men are parts of my soul. The most important parts. We're never going to lose each other.

CHAPTER 23

"*D*id you get my present?" River asks, and I pause in my writing to look up at him. There's an uncertain look on his face, almost as if he doesn't know where we now stand after last night.

"I did. Thank you," I say, grinning at him as tears fill my eyes once more. When I went to grab my cardi from my room this morning, there was a large gift on the bed, wrapped up in angel wrapping paper that I'm sure is meant for Christmas. My heart raced, but there was a giant note that I could see from the doorway, in River's handwriting, promising that the gift was safe.

The gift in question was a photo frame with a lot of different photos inside it. I don't even know how he found so many of them. There was a photo from the day I moved in where we were all at dinner, and I can't even remember us *taking* a photo, which means it was probably from one of the pack members who were at the restaurant.

There was another photo of us from when we were at the new house, and I'm grinning with my arms wrapped around Warren as the others watch on with similar goofy grins. Dillon must've taken that photo since he's not in it.

My favourite, though, was the one of us at the night of the Council ball, all dressed up, looking fierce.

"My favourite was the one from last night," River says, softly. *Oh yes, the dirty photo.* It's somehow pretty tasteful considering what's going on in it; my legs are spread wide, with Theo crouched between them, cutting off the view of anything dirty. It's heavily implied what he's doing, though. My fingers are laced in his hair, holding him in place. Behind me is Rhett, and he's kissing my neck, with one hand teasing my nipples. My head is turned to the right, as I kiss Dillon, and he's got his hand in my hair, not giving me any room to breathe.

I can see the pure lust on my face, but more than that, when I saw the image, the love and contentment I felt last night, comes back to me.

Caden and Noah are a little off away from us, since they were planning on doing... well, me, together. Caden's stroking his cock, which hasn't been cut off, and Noah's still fully clothed. Elijah's exhausted, but is laying on his side, watching. Whereas the other Ellis brother is watching with lust in his eyes.

Wyatt's sitting on the armchair, watching, and waiting for his turn, with pre-cum glistening on his cock.

River's the mastermind of this photo, having had the perfect angle to capture it all.

"I, yes," I say, blushing. At least the talk of the dirty photo stopped my teary happiness over the gift. "River, that was everything. Thank you."

"I left the blank square for the day we leave," he continues, giving me a piercing look.

"Why? We're all going to come out of this alive."

He nods. "I know, but I think seeing us prepared and ready, will be something you treasure when it's all over."

"Okay," I whisper, and he smiles before turning to leave. "River?"

"Yes?" He doesn't fully turn around.

"I don't regret last night."

Some of the tension fades out of his shoulders, and he turns back to me. For a brief moment, his eyes turn a deep, inky black—darker than ever—before settling back to their regular dark hue.

"It's obvious that I wasn't in the right headspace before we broke our bond. We've talked about it, and I've apologised," River says, and I nod slowly. "But it's not enough. It won't ever be enough. I hurt you, so badly, and I'm trying to prove I'm a better man—"

"I don't need you to prove that you're a better man," I say, softly. I rise to my full height, although it has nothing on River and round the desk. "I don't need you to be different than the man I first met. The quiet calm, the sarcastic mate, the loving and devoted man you were. I don't expect you to completely change your personality to try and give me something you think I want."

"I made a lot of mistakes."

I nod. "So did I. But you paid the price for the actions of a madman. Our bond will never be returned, but... last night shows we can still have a future."

"I want that."

"We deserve that," I add, coming to a stop in front of him. "But I'm not quite there yet. I need... I need us to put the past behind us. I need you to forgive yourself, *truly forgive yourself*, and then we can move forward."

"I... I have."

"You haven't," I whisper, shaking my head. Tears drip down his cheeks, and I wish I could reach up and wipe them away. "You're giving me these gifts to try and grovel. You're holding back from me and the group because you don't feel like you deserve to be part of us. You're trying so desperately to be everything you're not because, in your guilt and self-hatred, you don't think you deserve my love."

"Because I don't," he snarls. The man is in pain still, desperate for the love of his life—me—to just love him, but he can't love himself and won't ever accept my love as anything more than pity. The hybrid cries, and tries to reach for my wolf, who won't connect with him.

"And until the day you can accept that you deserve my love, there is no future here," I say, softly. "We can't have a relationship built on these foundations."

"We can."

"Then let's correct. *I do not want a relationship built on these foundations,*" I say, enunciating the words so he knows that I'm serious. "I love you, so just let me know when you're ready to accept my love for what it is."

"And what is your love?" His breath catches in his throat, his words coming out husky and sad.

"My love is pure and encompassing." I squeeze his hand. "Not full of pity."

With that I turn and walk back over to my desk. I take the ten seconds that I have where I'm not facing him to smooth out my face, so that when I sit back down at my desk, and smile at him, he's a little unsettled.

"Now, I've got a task for you."

"I... what is it?"

"I need you to check with Lexie for what time she's organised it for, but we're going ahead with the pack party. The Alphas approved it and have given us a very generous budget, so we want to go all out. It's going to be the night before we leave, and it's going to be a triple announcement."

"The pregnancy announcement?" he asks, and I nod. A grin appears on his face, a genuine one that smooths out some of the upset he's had. "I think that's a lovely idea."

"Good. We'll also be readying us for the send-off, and then celebrating that I'm officially Luna," I say, and he nods. "One last thing?"

"Yes?"

"Can you pretend to Warren like this is the worst assignment you've been given?" I ask, and River snorts.

"No need to pretend. I've been downgraded from Beta to a party planner."

I laugh, and he winks at me. A sombre expression fills his face again. "I'll... I'll talk to my therapist about what you said. You're right. I love you, down to my soul, but I can't trust that you've fully moved past what I've done, because I can't forgive myself for it." He heaves a sigh. "I'll not bring this up again, until I'm fully whole."

"You are whole, River," I say, softly. "You're just not yet sure how to love yourself."

He nods, and grins once more. "But on our trip, whilst I figure myself out, if you ever want a voyeur..."

I burst into giggles as he lets himself out of my office, and instead of going back to what I was doing, I call Charles. Unsurprisingly, he answers on the first ring.

"What's the drama now?"

"Well, I've just told River I can't love him until he loves himself," I whisper.

"Oh fuck," he says, softly. There's another ringing on my phone as he requests to switch it from an audio to a video call. "You look beautiful. I'd have thought you'd look like shit after ripping his heart out."

I snort, and shake my head. "One of us had to be strong."

He nods. "How do you feel?"

"I know that it was the right decision. After last night—"

"Last night?" Charles waggles his brows when I blush. I can see the redness appearing on my pale cheeks. "Oh, wow, this is dirty."

"I've got so much to tell you. You don't get all the *dirty details*, but... we had a very emotionally charged time last night."

He bursts out laughing. "You fucked them all?"

"Some of them together," I say, and he laughs again. "Also, what do you think about being a godparent to my children?"

"Children?" His eyes widen, and the humour fades from his face. "Are you...?"

"We're pregnant," I say, with a grin. My mates promised I could pick the godparents since anyone they'd have chosen individually

—bar Lionel—is one of my mates. I'm not going to deny that. "Twins."

"Motherfucker," he gasps. He shakes his head. "Are you... seriously?"

"I want you to be their godfather."

"Me?" He grins, and nods. "Of course I will. Fucking hell. You are my favourite wolf, you know?"

"Hey!" Landon complains, coming into the room. "Who are you gifting that title to?"

"Hey, Landon," I call, raising my voice even though it's unnecessary, and he grunts out a hello. "Promise me, though, Charles, that you won't let Landon teach them how to talk."

"Teach who how to talk?" Landon asks, peering at me on the screen. "Why are we teaching people how to talk?"

"My godchildren," Charles says, proudly. "Lottie is having twins."

"Holy shit," Landon gasps. "Congratulations, Luna. None of the men mentioned it."

"And now they'll live until dinner time," I laugh. "We've not fully announced it yet, so please keep it on the down low until we tell our pack."

"Of course. Can I tell Evan?" he asks, and I nod. Charles then turns to his mate. "What do you need?"

"You didn't answer your phone, and Noah needs your help with something."

"Of course he does," I say, with a pout. "Fine, last thing before I let you go play with my men."

"You better not be playing with her men," Landon warns, and Charles grunts. I don't want to know what Landon did or where he touched to elicit Charles's look, but a small part of me is curious. "Did you know Freya's mates have ranked you all?"

"Oh, trust me, we know. The group chat was popping off with that a lot yesterday," Charles says, with a strained laugh. Not because of the topic but likely because of the wandering hands of his Beta mate. "But I'm not bothered about that. I get to be your children's godparent. Fuck the peasants, Lottie, they don't get that privilege."

I laugh, and he blows a kiss as he makes his goodbyes. It was a short conversation, but it really helped boost my mood. Which is good because Alpha Redhead is going to be a massive pain in the ass.

I finish jotting down the notes from the last Alpha conversation before calling him.

$$)) \bullet (($$

"*H*ey, beautiful," Noah says, gently knocking on my door. I sit up, yawning, and he grins. Of course, he'd come and find me during the few minutes break I was awarding myself. "How are you doing?"

"A little tired, but overall, I'm doing well."

"Good. How has your day been?" He moves to come and sit down opposite me. He's wearing a shirt and some smart trousers, and he kicks one leg over the other, resting his ankle just at the knee. His shirt sleeves are drawn up to the elbow, showing off his forearms, and his sandy blonde hair is a little messy but still remains tied up in the bun. He's gorgeous.

"Pretty productive." I stretch my arms, and he eyes my boobs as I do. "Yours?"

"Somewhat productive. We've identified a few security threats and ruled out a good few. Most of them are sitting in that middle realm, where there will be some posturing, and they could go either way. I don't think we're going to be harmed by them, but we'll still need to be wary."

"We're not staying in their pack lands at any point, are we?"

"No. We won't be spending the night at any pack lands," Noah says. "But there's a danger with that as well. We've got it handled, though."

"I have no doubt of that. I got a call earlier from the police, and they're wondering if it's okay for them to come up on Tuesday."

Noah frowns but nods. "Tuesday is fine."

"Well, I told them that I'd check with my Alphas and get one of you to give them a callback," I say, biting my lip.

Noah's eyes light up, and his wolf preens. "Sounds perfect. I'll double-check with Caden and Rhett, then call them back."

"Thanks, baby."

He blows me a kiss. "I was just dropping in with some files from Lexie and another from Evie."

I nod, taking them from him and moving them to my to-do list. "I've got to call over to the clinic, but I was thinking about leaving that closer to the end of the day since I'm likely going to crash once it's done."

"What time is the end of your day?" Noah asks, checking his watch. "I think we still have a decent amount of hours in here. It's going to be a late one for Wyatt and me."

"Do you still have a lot to do?"

He nods, rolling his shoulders. "We're about halfway through this stage, and we need to finish today so that tomorrow we can start plotting out the route."

"How's everyone else doing? Nobody has really interrupted my bubble time," I say, although that's not true. River, Caden and Noah have all dropped by, but I've also spoken to Dillon via our mind link a few times to answer his questions.

Noah fills me in on their progress. Although Rhett and Theo are still alive and working well with my dad, their progress isn't much. Warren's prepared the Delta's, and they're all willing to work with the vampires and be the in-between they need. He's now running through drills with them and Sophie.

Dillon is doing his part and hasn't found much, but that's to be expected.

Caden and I are making good progress, and he's still got a couple of calls to take since he took the worst of the bunch. And once he's done, he's going to go join the others.

So we're all on track.

"I probably won't be home until about eight," I answer his original question. Noah nods. "And I'll probably crash immediately."

"Make sure to eat," Noah says, and I nod. "And if I don't see you before you leave, I love you."

"I love you more," I murmur, and he grins. As he disappears, I open the file that Evie has prepared. She's going over our legal defence, but we'll talk on Thursday so she and her team can start looking into the legalities of my position within our current legal system.

I've got a half-thought-out plan that needs refining, but I will rid the Council of the dangerous men who should have never been elected. I just don't think it will be as simple as I'd like, so the more we can do legally, the better.

What's the point of being this powerful if we're not going to do anything about it?

CHAPTER 24

"*Y*ou did amazing last night," Katie says, bumping my shoulder when I scoff. "An extra four people healed is not something to scoff at."

"Four people should not drain me to that extent," I say, with a sigh. "I have so much power."

"You're also growing very powerful twins. The first trimester is a *bitch* and that's without all the extra stress you have," she says, softly. "Be kind to yourself."

"I'm trying." She nods. "Your mate destroyed me this morning, by the way."

"For what?" Katie asks, with a frown.

"Not Lexie. *Sophie*." But now I'm the one to frown. "Wait, what would Lexie be annoyed with me?"

"She's not," Katie says. "That's why I was confused. Sophie's far too excited about all this extra fighting she gets to do. It's been a big source of frustration between us."

"How come?"

As Katie explains, my mind wanders a little to that conversation Sophie and I had about her upbringing. Sophie's so excited to be able to provide a worth to our pack, to help prepare our members for the chance that the fight is brought to them. She's always been made to feel less than for not being a Guardian like Theo.

But for Katie and Lexie, this is a terrifying time. Katie's scared for me, my children, and the fight I have to undergo. But she's also frightened for the pack because she's still helping some of them with the abuse they suffered during their time at Shadow King. Some of those people have chronic issues I can't fully heal away, and they're still undergoing mental health treatment with Elijah.

It makes sense why they'd be upset and struggling with this, but I know they'll figure it out. The two of us chat, whilst drinking our tea, until Lexie comes to get me.

"They're all here?" I ask, and she nods.

"Who is all here?" Katie asks, with a frown.

"I've already told you this. The vampires are here from the Hearthstone clan. They will be moving into the second pack house and staying here as protection until we're back."

"How many?"

"Forty today and another forty next week," I say. "Then more will be brought in as needed."

She nods. "I'm not sure if you sorted out healthcare for them, but it might be worth asking for some kind of doctor to come stay too."

"Oh, shit, that's not something we considered," I say, and Katie winks at me. "Thanks. I'll get that sorted."

"What are they doing for blood?" Katie asks.

"We actually did sort that," I reassure her. "We've not just yanked forty vampires from their homes. Those with mates are bringing them, and Alaric's organised for blood to be brought here as needed. Each of them will have their rooms stocked with it, and the pack house will be regularly stocked. There's a list of people willing to donate in an emergency, too."

Katie nods. "Good thinking."

"Okay, I'll answer any further questions you have," Lexie says, giving her mate a look of pure adoration. "That's the second time you've been requested, Luna."

"I'm going, I'm going," I say, waving to them both as I leave the offices. I shift into my wolf as I leave the building and race over to the clearing where they are. I can feel the heavy presence of vampires, but I can also sense Warren, Caden and Abel there as well.

When I arrive, I can sense a little bit of tension in the air, although I don't understand why. According to my mates, the men who are here volunteered to protect our pack. Lionel has arranged accommodations for them at the pack house, just as he did for the people from Shadow King and those we saved from other packs. They don't have any bags or anything, so I'm not sure what's going on in that regard.

But the vampires don't seem very... pleased. Abel's vampire is frustrated, as is Caden, whereas Warren is amused.

"There she is," Warren says, grinning at me. My wolf pushes forward in our mind, and I step back to let her have this brief moment. She bounds over to Warren and jumps at him, knocking him to the ground. He laughs, running his fingers through my white fur. "Shift back, princess."

My wolf licks his face before relinquishing control to me, and I shift.

"For those of you who haven't yet met Luna Montgomery, here she is," Abel says, gesturing to me. "Lottie, could you display your power to them please?"

I glance up at Caden, who nods and I kiss his jaw before stepping forward. "The full lot, Abel, or?"

"Do it gradually, but yes, give the whole lot," Abel says, eyeing his people.

I nod and turn back to the people in front of me. "At first, it'll feel like a tingle that your inner vampires will want to pay attention to, but eventually, it'll be so overwhelming you can't do anything but submit. I'm not sure you're powerful enough to withstand the full weight of my power without damaging you physically, so once we reach that point, I *will* stop."

"I highly doubt—" the man saying that is cut off as my power fills the air. Even with it at such a low magnitude, they can all feel it, and as predicted, their vampires are ready for it.

Some of them lean towards it for two different reasons. There's the group trying to make themselves seem more desirable, and then there's the curious folk. Neither of them can resist the call of true power.

Then there's the other reaction—the people who are smart enough to back away from a true predator. They don't move far, just a few steps, as they try to make themselves seem small to avoid making an enemy of me.

The unconscious reactions from their vampires tell me a lot about them. It's intriguing and something I will absolutely examine at a much later date.

As I amp up my power, it's easy for me to identify their power levels based on how quickly they submit to me. I'm not even displaying the level of intensity I used have, before Conri gave me his power, that is, when they're all on their knees, baring their throats at me.

I walk through the group, and as promised, I don't increase my power further than they can handle. That doesn't stop me from poking and prodding their vampires just to see if there's any unease or anything malicious in their psyche. Abel and Caden are probably doing the exact same thing, neither one wanting to risk bringing something here that would upset the balance we've struck between our pack and the Clan.

I doubt Warren is, though. He already knows some of these people and is probably amused at how he's now ranked higher than they are.

I don't sense anybody here with a sinister motive or anyone who is too interested or too disgusted. Abel's claim that they volunteered rings true, which is a huge relief. There are a few men who aren't too impressed with what I'm showing them, but because they thought I was stronger.

"And now I release you," I say, drawing my power back to myself, immediately releasing them from my hold. I barely notice the power returning to me, it was that little in the mass I now hold.

"Was that your entire power, Luna?" Abel calls, a mocking sort of tinge to his words.

I turn around, my hair whipping around me, and grin at the vampire. It's not a nice grin, and he realises. We are never going to be friends, he and I, but we're not yet enemies either.

"It was not, Abel."

He grins. "Unleash it on me."

"Honestly, Abel, you couldn't withstand her," Caden says, and I grin at my mate, who winks in return.

But then there's a slight disturbance in the air just before Freya and Roman appear. The vampires flinch in surprise, but I can feel their happiness at seeing her. Abel sighs, pinching the bridge of his nose, and both Caden and Warren seem unsurprised.

"I could," Freya says, grinning at me. I smile back. "You all know how powerful I am?" Her question is directed to the awed vampires behind her, who nod quickly. "Then do me, *Luna*." She waggles her brows, and Roman lets out a small sigh. "We all know you can best me."

"No way," someone whispers, and a quick look confirms that their jaws have gone slack in shock.

It's been publicised how close we are, the ties Freya and I have with one another, so it's amusing that even members of her own Clan are surprised by it. Freya and I both know that I can take her. Her bonds are not yet all complete, and she's not taken all of the power from her dad. And honestly, I think wolves are so much stronger than vampires.

Roman snorts, not even hiding it from me this time, as he shares with Freya what I said. I don't bother doing it gradually like I did with the vampires. Instead, I throw as much at her as I think she can take and then add a little more just in case.

She gracefully drops down to her knee, baring her throat my way. There's no crumbling or shaking of her decorum, and I am so jealous of her natural grace.

I nod my head in return, acknowledging us as friends and equals. My power might be greater than hers right now, but one day, we will be mostly equal.

"Lottie hasn't even unleashed her entire power here," Caden says, and there's some whispered shock because nobody seems to agree. I might not be utilising my full power, but I can feel the strain on what I am using. "You know what Alaric Viotto is to vampires and what Freya will become." He waits until there are some nods. "Alaric is the first ever vampire—the original."

"They know this," Abel says, with a taunt.

"It needed to be built properly," Caden hisses back.

"Meet the first true descendant of the original wolf," Warren says, stealing Caden's limelight. I pull my power back from Freya and wink at her.

"The first?" someone queries within the crowd.

"The first female," I reply. "It seems that this is the era for female domination. After so many years suffering under a patriarchy, I think it's time." Freya fist bumps me. "So, we've got the pack house prepared for you. Your mates are, of course, welcome to be here whenever they're being brought over. I'm not sure when that is."

"We're handling that," Roman says, nodding his head.

"Of course you are," I reply, with a smile. "In terms of the pack structure, Warren here will be matching you up with one of our Deltas, who will then help you get acquainted with the pack properly. This will only last a few days, so unless there are serious issues with your partner, please try to stick it out. Warren will be your main point of contact."

Warren grins, and comes to take over from me, wasting no time addressing his new charges. Oh yes, there's a lot of smug amusement from him, and I wonder if there's one in particular he wants to target.

I step back into the line with Abel, Caden, Freya and Roman.

"Was that all I was needed for?" I murmur, looking up at my mate. He shrugs, and nods.

"I know it wasn't in the plan, but we had a bit of unsettledness because some of them did not appreciate the welcome wagon they were given."

I glance at Abel, who sighs and shakes his head. "They... they thought they'd be meeting the pack immediately and may or may not have thought there might be some... hero worship involved." I snort, and Abel gives me a weak smile.

"Sexually frustrated empires," Caden mutters, with a laugh.

"What are you doing here?" Abel demands, raising his eyebrow at his sister.

"None of your business," she replies.

"We got the idea that we were needed," Roman says, tapping at his temple. Abel's brows furrow, but he nods.

"Whilst we are here, though, do you mind if we borrow something from you?" Freya asks. I nod. "Perfect. I'll be back later this evening, and I need you to come and heal some things for me."

"Heal what?" Abel demands. His tone shows his fear and concern.

"None of your business," Freya smugly repeats.

"Course I can," I reply. "I had been planning on going to the clinic to help out, but there's nothing that can't wait another day.

"Thank you. Also, I need a book."

"Dillon's at the library," I say, squeezing her hand. "He'll be able to give you whatever you need."

She beams, radiating pure excitement as she grabs Roman's hand, and they both disappear. The vampires behind us, who Warren is currently drilling into, didn't notice. They're very focused on Warren, which is a very good thing for me. It reassures me.

"This friendship you and my sister share is very strange." I glare at him, but he's not even looking at me. "Can we talk?"

I hold in my sigh and check my watch before nodding. "I've got some time."

"Perfect," he says. "Lead the way."

I squeeze Caden's hand, but he shakes his head when I try to let go. "I've got a meeting in fifteen. I'll walk back over there with you both. Warren's got these in good hands."

"Fair enough," I say, with a shrug.

"I think it helps that he's one of them," Abel says.

"Mostly." Now, I'm the smug one, but Abel sadly doesn't try to demand answers from me like he did for his sister. "Now, why is Freya's relationship with me weird? You seem scared of it."

"Well, at first, I thought you were the kind of person who only *took*." Caden snarls, but Abel shakes his head. "I've now seen very, *very* different."

"That's good to know."

"You give my sister just as much as she gives to you," he continues. "You didn't demand answers like I did; you just promised to be there."

"Your sister is very special."

"And so is Lottie," Caden says, and I burst out laughing. Both men smile, and it breaks a little bit of the tension. Don't get me wrong, it's understandable. I've barely been a wolf for a year and am vastly more powerful than him. Caden, Noah, and even Rhett have been wolves only for about fifteen years, compared to Abel's forty. It won't be that big of a deal in a hundred years or so, but right now... We're still children to him.

"Do you think they'll all be okay?" I ask, referring to the new vampires we're housing. Abel nods.

"Yes. They were all vetted by me, my dad and Freya before we brought them here," Abel says. "This is their first real assignment—"

"How capable are they that you're giving us *newbies*?" Caden hisses the word *newbies* as if it's a dirty word, and I elbow him in the ribs.

"We wouldn't give you anybody that wasn't capable," Abel replies. "What I meant is that this is their first real assignment where they're not doing baby duties or just training. These people are strong and capable. A good few of the men are young and single and thought they'd..." He trails off, and I can see his cheeks redden ever so slightly.

"They want to show off to the other unmated members of the

pack," I say. "And thought the welcome wagon would be a good time for them to do so."

"Yes."

I laugh. "It's fine, Abel. We can handle some sleeping around. Nobody is policing what they, or our wolves, do in their free time."

"You might not be," Abel mutters, rubbing the back of his neck. "Our people might not be aware that this is just one of many reparations which we're giving you, but we do not want them to badly represent the kind of vampires our Clan has."

"We know the type of vampires your clan has," Caden says gently. *Well, as gently as he can be when not talking to me or someone he cares about.* "And we're not judging them for finding a release."

I snort at the look on Abel's face.

"If there are any issues, please don't hesitate to reach out to the Clan. We'll deal with it and handle any reparations owed," Abel says.

"You're good at handing out reparations, aren't you?" Caden teases, waggling his brows.

I roll my eyes, grateful we're close enough to the town centre that they both need to shut up. We don't want to air any of our dirty laundry out to the pack. The walk through town is filled with smiles and waves before we make it into the office.

Caden kisses my forehead, heading to his office as I lead Abel to a meeting room. I close the door and raise an eyebrow at him. "So, what do you want to talk about?"

CHAPTER 25

"He's gone. My brother is gone." Abel's voice rings with disappointment. There's a defeated nature as he hangs his head in shame. "I thought..." Abel shakes his head, before looking at me properly. "I thought my brother was telling me the truth. I thought you were the liar, and for that, I'm sorry."

"You thought, or you hoped?"

He cocks a brow at me. "Is there a difference?"

"One is vastly more forgivable than the other," I say, and he sighs, but stays silent. I let that rest, not bothering to waste my time in pushing further. "My mates and your father have come to a very good agreement, and I'm content to let it rest there."

"If you were happy with that, why would you still let me speak with you?" Abel asks.

"Because I don't think you're a lost cause yet," I reply. "I think there's still hope of a strong alliance between us both, and I want to give you that chance." I didn't, but the ancestors have pushed me, and I'm not ignoring their warnings when they're as straightforward as that.

"How can I be the man you think I can be?"

"That's something you should probably unpack in a therapy session."

"It's a shame the only therapist I'd want hates my guts," he says, waving me off when I go to complain. "Tell me your thoughts."

"I'm happy with the restitutions and the reparations that you and your dad have organised, but I am still very displeased with the decision you made," I say.

"I can never apologise enough for that." There's a haunted look in his eye.

"No, you can't," I say. "But the ancestors came to me and gave me a warning."

"Another one?"

"Can you drop the arrogance because this isn't going to be a fun conversation for you if I have to pin you to the floor as you submit for the entire conversation, now is it?" I demand.

"I do apologise." He nods once, but honestly, I don't believe it. "I'm in a very tenuous position and taking it out on the wrong person yet again."

"Yes, you are." I shake my head with a sigh. "But I'm willing to move past it." *Being the bigger person, again, is fucking exhausting.* "The ancestors told me that I have the fate of your life in my hands, pretty much. You're at a crossroads, and I am the deciding factor. I have no idea what they mean, but you're going to come to me with a choice, and I need to be careful about how I answer."

"I see."

We fall to silence, and it's not uncomfortable. His vampire is as pensive as the man as he considers what I said, and I'm content to let the silence heal some of my headache. It's the only sign I've had of this pregnancy so far, although admittedly, it could be stress-related, but it is still very annoying. Especially when Theo isn't around to help me with it.

Not being able to heal myself is horrible.

A smile grows on Abel's face, and his eyes widen. "I know what it may be."

"Oh, do you now?" Now, I'm the sarcastic one.

"I do, but I think you'll want to call all of your mates here for this. This is something I want to do, I think I can truly help with, but I also know that it's something you might not appreciate."

I sigh, and tug on my mating bonds to get them here. Sure, I'm bringing them here to hear this, but it also brings Theo to me, and means my headache will be gone. I send reassurance along the bond, promising them it's nothing terrible, and that I'd just like them here when they can spare a moment.

"How explosive is their reaction going to be?" I ask Abel.

He laughs, sounding far more carefree than I've ever seen him. "Significant, probably."

Perfect.

"Okay, we're all here," Rhett says, glancing between me and Abel with a lot of frustration. He was the first to show up, but I refused to share what was going on until they were all here. "What do you need, love?"

"Abel has something he wants to discuss with us all, and I figured it would be best if we were all here and handling it together."

"What do you want?" Noah asks, looking at Abel.

"It's not something that *I* want, but rather, something I can offer you," Abel replies. Caden snorts, and Dillon mutters something about Abel not being able to provide us anything. "I'll lead your pack whilst you're gone."

I frown, but my Alpha mates burst out laughing, sniggering away at each other as if this is the funniest thing they've ever heard. Wyatt snorts, but then tries to smooth out his expression when I give him a dirty look. I get it from the Alpha's, but not him. He's never usually this rude.

Warren, however, doesn't even crack a smile. I can feel his bristling anger, his vampire side not impressed with the heir. His eyes flash purple as his hands shift into miniature claws. As I have been doing, I reach over and soothe Warren's ire, topping his power level up that little bit further. Warren's powers seem to have the potential to be limitless, but they're hindered by his natural abilities and limitations on his power.

So, each day, I boost his power ever so slightly, strengthening his bond with the Ancestral Realm. Soon enough, he'll rival my Alphas, then my Guardian... and then I'll be the only true match for him.

"Good joke," Rhett says, wiping his eyes. "Seriously, I needed that laugh after sitting around and waiting."

"Agreed, my day has been pretty boring," Warren says, eyeing him up and down with disdain. He's only barely retained his cool, and I know he's itching for a fight. I'm pretty confident Warren would win. "Now fuck off with your bullshit whilst we deal with the issue you refused to help with."

Abel's frown now mirrors mine, and he seems a little... disappointed. "I was not joking. We are allies—"

"For now," Caden says, with a smirk.

"And I'm their heir to the most powerful vampire clan—"

"For now," Noah adds, with a little laugh.

Abel's frown deepens. "My mate is in your pack—"

"For now," Warren says with a grin. "She's already approached us about a transfer."

"No!" Abel roars, jumping to his feet in anger. He slams his hands down on the table and shakes his head. "No. I told you not to approve that in our last meeting. Scottie is my mate, and once we reunite, you will see that."

I frown even further now, not sure how he doesn't understand that Scottie does *not* feel the same way. Fuck, that's going to be an explosive reunion.

"I'm not in the position of holding my pack members hostage,"

Rhett says. All traces of humour have disappeared from his tone as he looks across the table at the Viotto heir. "If Scottie doesn't feel safe here, it's our job as her leaders to find her a safe haven and give her the guaranteed safety that we cannot."

"She's running from me," Abel snarls, a look of desperation filling him. "Time and time again, she's running away." Something seems to come over him, some silent conversation with his vampire that I'm not privy to, I think. He sits back down and nods, clasping his hands together. "I understand your position, and I appreciate the means you're willing to go to to protect *my* mate."

The emphasis on his tie to her wasn't missed by any of us.

"Scottie is an important member of our pack," I say, gently. "I don't want to lose her, Abel, not after seeing the good she can do and knowing she's *happy* here. But I won't keep her in Rose Moon if she no longer wants to be here. Rhett is right—we don't hold people hostage."

Especially not after the lengths we went to in order to *free* people who were being held hostage.

"We told her that we wouldn't be in a position to find her a new pack until we had returned from our trip. But make no mistake, we *will* be using said trip to find her some new options. Her only requirement was that these places be free of your influence, and we'll make that happen," Caden says, and Noah nods. They've been silently debating on whether to share that bit of information with Abel.

Scottie has become a friend to Elijah and a vital woman to many of my pack, and I meant it when I said we didn't want to lose her. But I suppose this is just another Abel Viotto fuck up that we need to deal with.

Abel's breath hitches, and he nods slowly. "I fucked up, there's no denying that."

"Anymore," I say, a little pettily. Eleven of my people died, and he said some very disgusting things. I am more than entitled to be petty.

"Anymore," he acquiesces, nodding his head. "I was blinded by... I won't make excuses. I should've tracked Cain down myself *whilst sending support.* I failed you, our most important ally, but I cost your people their lives."

"We don't know that," Rhett says gently, in a way that's very surprising to me. "You made a terrible, *terrible* call, but you being here might not have saved their lives."

"I owe a debt to your pack, and sure, we've outlined some reparations from my Clan, but we've not outlined anything from me personally," Abel continues, almost as if he didn't hear Rhett speaking in the first place. "This is one *tiny* way for me to repay it. The only reason I haven't taken over the Clan is because my dad is still holding onto the powers he was afforded. Once the curse fully transfers to Freya, I will be more than ready to take the mantle from him. I already run most of the Clan as it is, and I am more than powerful enough to protect your people."

It sounds arrogant, but my wolf and I appreciate his outlining his exact uses to us.

"Especially now that you're around your mate," Noah adds, almost snidely.

Abel gives a tense nod. "I can protect your people. I can lead your people. I can make sure that nothing goes wrong, and I can assist with all the issues you have going on from both a legal and political standpoint. You're concerned about leaving, especially since you've not outlined a true leader."

"I—" I start.

"Yes, your dad was going to take over, and you had support from my mum and blah blah blah." He waves his hand dismissively, which grates on me. "But I promise you, that with me at the head, nothing will enter these borders without my permission. Your people will be safe."

I nod slowly, but it's my three Alphas that need to make this call. I'm far too soft-hearted and would be pretty willing to give him this, even with what he's done. I think he's made some excellent points, and putting him at the head and having our pack be underneath the vampire monarchy whilst we're gone effectively removes them from the Council's hands.

Abel made a mistake; sure, he's arrogant and cocky, but he's also trying.

Even if it's just for Scottie's sake.

Maybe that's actually the reason I'm so tempted to say yes. Nothing hurts me as Luna more than seeing my people unhappy.

"You've never hidden the fact that you don't like our Luna," Caden says, with a sneer. "Why the hell would we trust you after you've done this?"

"After you betrayed our people, the alliance you formed, why would our *people* trust you?" Noah asks. He and Caden have identical looks on their faces right now, their baby blue eyes trained on Abel, their wolves emanating the same amount of power.

It's freaky.

And kind of hot.

"They shouldn't," Abel says. The words, if said by me, probably would've been pretty pitiful, but from Abel, they're just the truth. There's no emotional infliction, and especially no anger. He's taking accountability. "But I'm trying to make amends for the damage I've caused. If I could go back in time, there is so much I'd do differently."

I note wryly that he doesn't say exactly what he would do differently, but that's the politics at play once more.

"It's hard when time travel isn't a thing," Rhett says, with a smirk. Abel laughs, but it wasn't a humorous noise.

"Let me do this. Let me do this for your people. Please."

"Give us fifteen minutes to talk this out," Rhett says, taking my hand in his. I give Abel a warm smile and let Rhett tug me out of the room. He's so careful in his manhandling of me, that it's very sweet, even if unnecessary. We go into the next meeting room, and Caden and Noah join us. Then Wyatt, and then Theo. Just when I think the door is about to close, Warren comes in, too.

"Why didn't we just make this a group meeting?" I mutter.

"Lots of people have a say in the security matters of the pack, princess," Warren teases. "And we couldn't all come; someone had to watch over him."

I roll my eyes. "He's not a risk." I take a seat at the table, and Rhett slides into the seat next to me and asks my feelings on the topic.

"I think it's a perfect idea. Abel is a leader and has the political mind space to do this," I say. "Putting our pack under his lead ties our pack to Alaric and the vampire monarchy, which then limits the Council's reach whilst we're not here to protect them."

"And can we trust that he'll protect our people?" Noah asks. "If it comes down to him or them, who do you think he'll choose?"

"I think he'll protect our pack for as long as Scottie is in it."

"I don't like that he's just doing it for Scottie, though," Caden protests.

"You wait your damn turn," Noah says, looking at his brother. Caden laughs.

"No, I get his point," I say, reassuring. "I just think this is an advantage that we have, and it's one we'd be fools to not take advantage of."

"I can see your point," Noah says. "I'm just not sold."

"What happened to waiting your turn?" Caden mutters to Wyatt, who laughs.

"I think this is what the ancestors were talking about, and I'm scared to make the wrong choice."

"We don't know that for sure," Rhett says.

"No, we don't," I agree.

"I think using Abel this way is the best thing. Lottie makes the most sense," Warren says.

"Because nobody else has had the chance to speak," Caden says, and Wyatt snorts.

"Then speak," I hiss. "I was asked my thoughts, so I answered the question."

"I agree with you," Caden replies. "Even if his motives aren't pure... they're still good." I roll my eyes but can't deny that my wolf feels pretty smug.

"Exactly," Warren says. It beats using Everett, who—no offence, princess—isn't handling life very well, and asking for assistance from others who can't be here full time and are at risk when popping in and out."

"Then I think we do it," Noah says, and I nod.

"We don't really have the time to give him a trial run," Wyatt says, hesitantly. "And what of the pack?"

"They don't know that he betrayed us," Theo says, with a shrug. "And if they're not going to accept being under a vampire for the time we're gone, it looks like they're not a good fit for this pack when things stabilise."

"Agreed," Rhett says. "Any stipulations?"

"I mean, it goes without saying that he doesn't change anything," I say, and they all laugh. "But none that I can think of."

"None for me right now either," Rhett says.

"Let's schedule a meeting with him in a week or so," Caden says, sitting back in his chair. "And we'll outline what we're expecting of him and where we're up to with everything."

"That's fair," Wyatt says. "I can sit down and outline what I do to pass on to... whoever."

"I think if Abel comes, he'll bring a second with him," Noah says. "And if not, we can outline it as a requirement."

"It still doesn't include my share of the duties," I say, raising my hand.

"They'll figure it out. They've got Lexie and Lionel, who can assist with your duties," Rhett reassures me.

"Then let's do it," I say with a shrug. A feeling of *rightness* fills me at the decision, and I know that, deep down, this was the right call to make.

CHAPTER 26

*A*bel was very pleased when we told him he could take over the pack when we're gone, and he readily agreed to the meeting next week. He said Blade would come here with him for the few months, and I think he's kind of excited to be out from underneath his parents for a while and sort of... trial it out alone.

His relief at being able to aid us didn't go unnoticed, though, and for that, I am hopeful. He's desperate to make amends.

But I'm a little hesitant about this next part of the... discussion. Abel wanted to head off and leave so he could start making preparations with his dad, but Elijah said Scottie wanted to come and talk to Abel.

"What's this about?" he asks, tensely. "We've sat in silence after you *begged* me to stay here."

"I've got something... someone who wants to talk to you," I say, literally seconds before the door opens and the woman in question is standing in the doorway. Scottie's face is painted in a perfect calm, and if I couldn't feel her wolf, I'd believe it.

"Scottie," Abel whispers, his voice hoarse as he has eyes on his mate for the first time in years—as far as I'm aware. She steps into the room but doesn't approach him properly, not how he wants if his vampire's longing is anything to go off. She crosses her arms in front of her chest and meets his gaze head-on. "What... what are you doing at this pack? I thought you were still further South."

"No surprise that you are still keeping track of me. I've been part of this pack—*this amazing pack*—for all of a week before you come along and fuck it up for me," she says bitterly. Her hair is braided down her back, and she has bright red lipstick on. It's the first time I've seen her with a colour that bright, and I'm not sure if it's a shield or a fuck you to Abel. *Maybe both.*

Her leather jacket and pants, combined with her snarky attitude, already show him that he will have to work for her time and affection. I just hope that the Viotto heir will put the work in. I don't know Scottie very well, but she's provided Elijah with a strong support system and has really eased the burden on him.

"But ruining my life is your standard MO, right?" she asks, still holding onto her anger. I'm impressed, especially seeing the usually composed Abel lose his composure in front of her. He's almost begging with his eyes for her to drop the anger, to just love him.

He flinches, his eyes flashing black as the vampire within him writhes in agony. The vampire can feel how her wolf and vampire do, and it's breaking him to not be able to connect with them like he wants. "That's... I was young."

"So was I," she scoffs, shaking her head. Her wolf is howling inside her mind, begging her to go forward and mark her mate. I can only imagine that her vampire is doing the exact same thing. I don't have a connection with her vampire, so I can never hear her that clearly, and with her wolf being more dominant, her vampire gets drowned out a lot.

But Abel, surprisingly, hasn't even tried to put the barriers up and stop me from mentally spying. The desperation and pain he's feeling breaks me, and I'm glad Freya wasn't here to witness this since it would *destroy* her.

The fact that Scottie isn't giving in shows her strength. She's ignoring the wants of her wolf and vampire and is putting herself first. She's not going to allow herself to accept any less than she deserves. *I fucking commend her for it.*

"I'm sorry," he whispers. The room falls silent briefly before she laughs in his face. It's such a bitter sound, showing her pain, too. I shouldn't be here for this. It's not my fight to witness. But as soon as I take a step back, Scottie gives a tiny shake of her head as she pleads with me to stay.

For whatever reason, she wants me to be here for this moment. I don't leave, giving her the support she needs, but that means I'm stuck here watching the two of them reunite in a way that really should not have occurred.

They're mates, and Abel's spent years not treating her like one.

"How have I been fucking things up for you?" Abel asks.

"You know exactly how you've been fucking things up for me," she says, shaking her head. "But I'm telling you now, I'm not letting you fuck this one up for me. You will fuck off. You'll go because you're not allowed to be here anymore. I want *nothing* to do with you, Abel Viotto." She shoves a barrier in her mind, cutting off the whimpers from her wolf and vampire. "If you remain here, I will leave, and I'll make it so that you do not find me the next time."

"Scottie, please—"

"Do not Scottie me," she snarls. "You do not deserve a single thing from me." She bitterly laughs again, and Abel visibly flinches. "You chose to help your brother, and fuck us over, and you only decided to help us now because of him endangering the pack that I reside in." She scoffs. "Did it escape your notice, *mate*, that I'm only in this pack to be endangered in the first place because you were there? Because you caused this? It's down to you, Abel. Time and time again, your failures to be a good mate have destroyed my life, and now... You're facing an opponent who won't accept mediocrity from you."

Fucking hell.

She's brutal.

"You should have done your part," Scottie continues. "When my Luna requested help, you should have given it. No questions asked. But you didn't. Maybe"—she tugs her shirt up, displaying a scar on her side, and my eyes widen at the implication— "if you had, I wouldn't be permanently marked like this." She shakes her head at him. "This is the only mark I'll ever allow you to put on my body, Abel Viotto. I hope it was worth it."

She turns around and goes to leave the room, her hand resting on the doorknob for a moment. "Also, I hear condolences are in order. I'd say it was a shame, but I'm not one to lie." And then she's gone.

My jaw drops, and my wolf is stunned silent. *Holy fuck.*

There are tears in his eyes, as he stares at the back of the door. I can feel how hopeful his vampire is, almost as if he's expecting her to walk back through the door and say it was all a lie.

"I'm sorry," I whisper, and he shakes his head, turning away from me to compose himself.

"I did this. She's right. This is all me," he says, looking out the window. I don't hear him sniffle, but I watch him wipe his nose with his handkerchief. "Scottie is more than entitled to her anger. I was a stupid fucking kid, and I've spent so long trying to track her down to redeem what I've done that it clearly hasn't translated well since I've been too cowardly to approach her." He sighs, and turns to me, with a sigh. "You get it. You've got your own mate who fucked up, and you're not letting him fix it."

"Excuse me?" I snarl, flinging a dose of dominance and dropping him to the floor with zero hesitation. Abel immediately bares his throat, but I'm tempted to claw it out after that. "Fuck you, Abel. You're in a position right now where you can *work for her*; you can show her *you are worthy*. We're giving you *months* to sit here and plan how you're going to win her back. *Months to earn her love.* But what do you do? Stand here and snivel like a pathetic male who still doesn't understand the depth of what he's done. You're pathetic and have *nothing* on my mate.

"You have terrorised your own for years. You've sent Scottie running from multiple homes, stopping her from feeling safe and content, which is the exact thing that a mate *shouldn't* do. River chose to sever our bond so he would no longer tarnish me. I've not rejected him or stopped him from fixing it. He's taking the required fucking time to *heal* and process something *traumatic*. Do not ever talk of my mate's Abel, or so help me, you won't be alive long enough to apologise.

"Take the chance you've been given, or I will help your mate hide somewhere you will never *ever* find her, and I'll give her the option to sever the bond the two of you share. I won't let you trap such an amazing woman in your web of disappointment and fuck-ups. So pull your head out of your ass, or go fuck yourself. It's not like anyone else is willing to do it for you."

I turn and storm from the room, my hands shaking in my anger, and rather than lose it on someone else, I head out the front and shift into my wolf, charging through town as fast as I can.

I can feel the concern from my men, but I don't answer them.

I can't.

Not when I'm *this* angry.

How fucking dare he presume anything.

And how the fuck does he know? Has River said something? One of the others?

I hate that more than I hate Abel's big mouth and smarmy attitude, and right now, that's a hard thing to beat.

"*A*re you feeling calmer now?" Theo asks, stilling with the rubbing of my shoulder. He goes to move his hands away, but I quickly reach back to grab them. He laughs when I bring them back to my shoulders. "Want something, little wolf."

"Please keep going."

He laughs and continues with the rubs. He waits for another beat before he asks if I want to talk about whatever is bothering me yet.

I sigh. "I've already told you. Abel was a prick.'

"And you've not yet elaborated on how." My Guardian raises his eyebrow, giving me a piercing look.

"I know. He was just..." I tail off with another sigh. "I don't really want to talk about it. He's just really pissed me off."

"I love you," Theo says.

"And I love you," I reply, turning around properly, to press my lips to his.

"How are you feeling with everything that's going on?" Theo asks.

"Ugh," I mutter, with a shrug. "It is what it is."

"We've accomplished a lot in a short amount of time."

"There still feels like a lot needs to be done."

"So we can do something productive?" he offers. "What were your plans for today?"

"To go to the clinic, but now Freya needs me," I say.

"Then why don't you go to the clinic anyway? You can just help out—no magical healing needed."

I shake my head. "I can't just sit back and not touch someone who needs the help."

"That's fair. You and that moral compass of yours," he teases, and I laugh. "Why don't we go back to the office?"

"I appreciate it, but I'm just going to sit and wait for Freya." I lean into his chest, taking comfort in his scent and warmth. Our bond is lit up in contentment, our wolves mindlessly flirting. "What's happening out there?"

He laughs, and drops a kiss to the top of my head. "Sophie is currently working with Warren, going over the plans for the vampires. They're going to run them through some drills tomorrow along with the Delta's, I think, just to see where things are with them. Sophie's really excited to be working with them."

"She was a good ask to put in charge whilst we're handling things," I say, and Theo nods.

"She really was. Warren's obviously better suited since he is a vampire—"

"Don't do that. Sophie's more than capable. She's smart and powerful."

"You're right. I was apprehensive when she came here, but I'm glad she's found her place," Theo murmurs, and I squeeze his hand. "She... she's never had it very easy being my sister. You'd never think we were biological siblings with the differences in how our parents treat us."

"Would that bother you?" I blurt the question out, feeling shame for even asking it.

"Would what bother me?"

"If the children I'm carrying are not yours biologically."

Theo tugs me away from him and holds my eyes. "No. Not even a little bit."

"Do you think..." I can't even voice it.

"Talk to me," he pleads, rubbing his thumb across my jaw.

"River's definitely not the biological dad. Sure, he's the... he's connected to them."

"But there's no biological tie to him or even to seven of the rest of us," Theo says, and I nod. "Is this something you've been worrying about for a while?"

"Yes? No? Both, maybe?" I shrug. "I'm borrowing trouble, I think."

"Genetics is not something I care about. These children are yours, so they are mine. We might not have mating bonds with each other, but we're all still connected. Even without being the biological parent, we will have a tie to our kids, more than a human parent would."

"Okay."

"And if you're done after these two, we will be more than happy with that decision," Theo continues. "And if you want ten children, then we'll absolutely try, and try again, to keep you gorgeous and round."

"I'm not even round yet."

He smirks, looking so much unlike himself with the relaxed aura around him. "Ah, but I can't wait for the day that you are."

His wolf is so enthralled with the idea that it gives me tingles.

"And Lottie?" Theo murmurs, his voice dropping to a soft cajole.

"Yes?"

"It doesn't bother the others either."

"How do you know?"

"Because this is already a discussion we've all had."

"Without me?" I gasp, and he laughs.

"Without you. What do you think we discuss at guys' night?"

My cheeks definitely heat up here, and I say a bald-faced lie. "I mean, I presumed that I wouldn't be a discussion topic.'

He snorts. "That was silly of you. Not only are you a topic..., but you're the *main* topic. We are all obsessed with you, little wolf. Why wouldn't we talk about you?"

He leans in, pressing his lips to mine, and I lose track of the time we spend together. Who cares about watching the clock when it's so much more fun to count the moans I manage to elicit from him?

"Holy shit," Freya gasps, as I fling myself away from my mate. Roman's face is passive, but Freya's is lit up in amusement.

Mine is surely mortified, but Theo just looks proud.

I think our time together the other night really unleashed an exhibitionist kink in him.

"You've caught me at a terrible time," I say.

Freya snorts, before sighing. "I'm sorry for coming."

"Don't be silly," I say, turning to give her my full attention. But I freeze when I see her properly. She's wearing a bright red dress with bright red lipstick to match. I just missed the dark shades for what they are—blood. She's covered, head to toe.

"The healing," she murmurs. "I need it now."

"Then let's go," I say. "Do you need me to bring anything?"

She's full of anxiety and pain, the depth of it going deeper than her. As I guessed, there's something wrong with her mates.

"Just you to heal me," she says.

I nod and turn to Theo. His cock has gone down, and he groans when I make eye contact. *"Stop looking at him."*

I snort, but so does Freya.

"Do you think resorting to the mind link is going to work?" She eyes her nails, feigning a bored look. "I'm sorry my mate, who is *dying,* ruined your *erection*, Theodore."

"I'm not," Roman replies, and I hide my face to hide the laugh.

"Can you let everyone know that I'm with Freya?" I ask, and Theo shakes his head.

"Guardian." Freya's smirk is not a nice one. "Don't make me hurt you." Some of Freya's anxiety has faded now that she knows I will be coming with... or maybe it's at the prospect of causing physical harm to my Guardian.

"You couldn't take me," Theo replies, dismissing her and turning to me properly. "No. You're not leaving with them." Theo shakes his head when I open my mouth to argue. "You and her are *not* running off together when she looks like *that*."

"What?" My eyebrows are in my hairline, and I'm so confused. Clearly, she was covered in blood when one of her mates was hurt.

"At least not alone," he continues.

"She's not in any danger," Roman says. "Freya and I are more than capable of keeping her safe, but we also have her entire mating circle with us."

"See," I tease. "There's plenty of them to keep me safe."

Theo growls, but Freya meets him head-on with a hiss. "You're forgetting, Guardian, that not only am I in the process of becoming the original vampire, but your Luna is the new original wolf. We're pretty harsh opponents to go up against."

"I know that," Theo says, solemnly. He steps forward and shrugs with one shoulder. "I just know I'm expendable, and she is not."

My heart shatters into a million little pieces.

That's not fucking true.

I look up at my Guardian, and he shakes his head. "We are one, Lottie. My soul and your soul, we couldn't live without the other."

"Then don't make me," I hiss.

"You're the one going somewhere dangerous in your condition *alone*. You're the one making me."

"Fine," Freya says, as if she's making a giant sacrifice on her behalf. "You may come with us."

"We're going to the Clan," Roman says, taking pity on my Guardian. "She'll be safe."

I feel through Freya once more, probing deeper to assess her mates. Her inner vampire isn't best impressed, but she recognises my energy, so she doesn't fight. The twins are hurt, but it's not anything life-threatening. But her vampire is in a *lot* of pain.

Critical condition, really.

"Let's go," Theo says, hearing that from my mind. I reach over and take Freya's hand as Theo grasps mine. Roman must connect with us somewhere because then we disappear.

We reappear in a room I've never been in before. The floor is hard stone, and the walls are the same. It's not decorated, besides a table that the vampire is on. The room is deafening and chaotic as Freya's mates panic.

The vampire is grunting and moaning quite dramatically if I must say. By his side is a younger man, a few years at least, and he's very quiet and unsure. The vampire within him is... strange.

"Are you okay?" I ask, taking a hesitant step towards him as I drop both Freya and Theo's hands.

"He's not why you're here," Freya says, gently. "But I'd appreciate the help if you can offer it."

I tilt my head because she's never once mentioned him to me. Who is the vampire, and how does he tie in? I can't get much from him since his inner vampire is very broken, even with her assistance, but he's definitely not one of hers.

"Luna," Jeremy murmurs, nodding his head my way as he barges past the angels. He bares his throat.

"We need to chat later," I say, and he frowns.

"What have I done now?" he demands.

Freya snorts. "Way too much that you don't want to tell your Luna about."

"Way too much you don't want to tell your *cousins* about," Theo echoes. The two of them laugh, and Jeremy rolls his eyes.

"Let me know when," Jeremy murmurs, blending back into the background.

"Smart boy," Hunter, I think, whispers in my mind.

"Can you help him, Luna?" Roman asks, directing me forward.

"Absolutely. I need a chair, though." One appears in front of me before my blink is even complete, and I smile as I ease myself down into it. Theo moves with me, still hovering close.

"Can I have a hand?" I ask, looking over at Freya. "And any power you're willing to offer?"

She heaves a sigh and moves forward. "I suppose so." She presses down on one of Ambrose's wounds, causing the vampire to scream. The younger vampire flinches, looking down at his feet, and I can feel the terror pouring off him.

I don't know who reacts first, but Freya and I reach out to him to soothe him the best we can. I don't think my wolf offers him much, but his pain is evident.

Does he... does this vampire have feelings for Freya's mate?

"They're brothers," Roman says, and my eyes widen. *Fucking hell.*

"I am not giving Lottie this power for *your* sake," she warns her mate. "I'm giving it for the sake of my tiny little niece and nephews."

"No," I immediately say, and she looks at me. "Your nieces *or* your nephews. Or one of each. Don't be wishing more children into my womb. There's two.'"

Freya laughs. "Technicalities, my good friend. Now come on, use my power so that my *useless fucking mate* doesn't die. Not that he deserves to live."

"Or will want to once we get our hands on him," Hunter adds, with a glare.

I eye Theo, who shrugs. Clearly, there's some tension between them that we're not aware of.

"What happened?" I ask, before immediately moving to do what Freya says.

"Don't make this fast or easy," Freya asks, and I nod slowly.

What the fuck?

"Just the normal," Freya says. "We had set up a potential raid to try and draw more players out of the woods so we could figure out who was targeting the brothers. We had a plan outlined, but someone decided to go rogue instead."

"Fuck," Theo says, with a groan. "You don't change the plan when it could put your mate at risk."

"No, you really don't," Jeremy says, nodding at Theo.

Ambrose doesn't seem phased by the conversation, not even caring that he messed up. His brother, on the other hand, is slowly relaxing as he sees his brother being healed in front of him.

"The plan was to try and figure out who is behind it all," Freya continues.

"And did you figure out who might that be?" Theo eagerly interjects.

"None of your business," Freya and I say simultaneously. I turn to glare at my Guardian, and Freya's angel twins snigger.

"You two are next, so you probably don't want to piss me off," I warn.

"Yes, ma'am," Hudson says, with a nod. I know for a fact they're mentally taking the piss, but I don't care.

"Yes, ma'am," Hudson says, with a nod. I know for a fact they're mentally taking the piss, but I don't care. We fall silent for a few moments as I continue gradually healing Ambrose.

He's glaring at the ceiling, and he feels so hostile.

"So, we were attacked, and what does the fucking dipshit do?" Hudson snarls. "He jumps in the way to try and protect Freya."

"And that's a bad thing because?" Theo asks, with narrowed eyes. He jumped into things two minutes ago, preaching about protecting your mate, and yet, from this story, that's what Ambrose did. He looks at me in confusion.

"Have you seen Freya?" I ask.

"Well, yes. I know she's very powerful, but it's a mating instinct to protect."

"Not this mate," Roman says, anger lacing his tone. His eyes are pale red, and I can feel his low-simmering anger. He's got it tampered down, but he can't hide it from Freya, whose power I am channelling. "This mate would never do a single thing to help Freya, especially not if it would put him in harm's way."

Theo's frown deepens, but he turns the glower to the vampire.

"The bond between them... can you not feel it?" Roman asks me.

"Believe it or not, Roman, but I don't probe where it's not needed," I say, with a shrug. "They're connected, and I've never felt more than that."

"The bond between us isn't real," Ambrose says.

"The bond between us is... strained," Freya says, shaking her head. "Ambrose did this on purpose to cause more tension, and now we've had to take out a man who could've been an ally. He also lost us an important bit of leverage."

Hunter snarls. "Leverage, I nearly died to get in the first place. But hey, good job on the teamwork, Brose. We truly appreciate it."

"Cunt," Hudson mutters.

"He was not an ally," Ambrose snarls. "And that leverage—" He's cut off when Roman reaches over and presses a finger into the wound on his thigh. Ambrose flinches away but doesn't cry out this time.

"You're a fool. I told you he could have helped us," Roman says. "And I do not make mistakes."

Ambrose falls silent, throwing his head back down onto the table. He doesn't argue any further, but Freya and I can both feel his distrust of the situation—of them.

"Heal him properly now, please," Freya asks, so I increase the power behind the act, and he's healed within minutes.

"You're all done now," I say. I'm still exhausted, but it's not bad at all. It's much like when we healed Marielle. But since we were healing her mate, it took practically nothing out of her. It's nice when nature works with us instead of against us.

"You two," I command, turning to face the twins. "Hands." There's no hesitation as they each offer me one.

"Fuck, we should've done this last time," Freya gasps.

"Hindsight is a real bitch," I say, having thought of that myself. I steal from Freya's power reserves and send the healing energy through them both. It takes seconds since their injuries weren't too bad.

Hudson had a kidney that was beginning to fail, and Hunter had some internal bleeding. Not bad at all.

"Thank you," they say together.

"Well, this was an excitement," Theo mutters, shaking his head. "I think we'll now leave you to it." He turns to me. "Want to call in and see Alaric?"

"Is that something I... have to do?"

"Why don't you want to see my dad?" Freya asks. "I thought things were all sorted now."

"What do you mean things are sorted?" Hunter asks.

"They were fighting because of Abel," Jeremy says.

"You're all so nosy," I say, rolling my eyes and looking at Freya. "Are my men all like this?"

"No," she says, with a smirk. "Your men are all pretty good at holding their tongues."

We hold in our amusement, knowing that's so *not* true. Theo's a prime example of that, with his questions about Freya's current task. It's not like his getting the answers would be beneficial—we genuinely cannot help her more than we are right now.

"No, it's not your dad that I'm avoiding. Abel and I did not leave things on good terms."

"What did my dipshit of a brother do now?"

"What was he like when he came home?"

"No idea," Freya says, with a shrug. "I've not been home yet."

"Is this what the two of them are always like together?" Ambrose mutters. "Ignorant and rude?"

"Brother," the younger vampire warns.

"Oh, shit, I didn't introduce Bennie," Freya says, with a grin. "This is Benedict. The absolute *darling* of the family. He's been a little... abused."

"You're either abused or you're not," I say, gently. I rise to my feet and gently reach out to shake Benedict's hand. He eyes Freya with fear, but she nods.

"If you can help, I'd really appreciate it," Freya says. "But I'm not sure if it's something that lies outside your usual realm." I examine the man as Freya continues speaking. "He was tortured and abused by his dad, and whilst I've powered him the best I can, it's not helped as much as I'd like."

"You'll not be able to help him, will you?" I say, and she shakes her head. "Even with your help, I think this kind of healing would require multiple tries."

"Not like I can with my men. He is a vampire with a tie to me, so I can offer my energy like we did with Marielle, but I can't afford to be drained right now." She's a little embarrassed as she says this. "We've got a big target on our backs because of that fucker."

I nod. "This is extensive." I look at the vampire, and he flinches. "How are you even alive?"

"Vampire healing," he whispers.

"I can feel that. This is my confusion. When I probe at some of the problems, your body doesn't recognise them as such. It thinks you're healed correctly."

"But what about his pain?" Freya demands.

"So, the way things tend to work," Theo starts, "is that when something is healed, correctly or not, it's not something you can undo with your powers. You work with the body to heal injuries, deformities, etc. You heal broken things, Lottie. You heal the bad and the painful."

"But this is both bad and painful," I argue, but I can see by the expression on Theo's face that it's a weak argument.

"You can't heal what the body thinks is healed," Theo says, quietly. He gives Benedict a pained expression. "It doesn't hurt to try... once you have the power and time."

"So, you're leaving my brother—" Ambrose starts, anger racing through him.

"She might let you get away with that," I snarl, flinging dominance to the rude asshole, who immediately submits. "But I will not. Leaving him in this amount of pain is *disgusting*. It physically pains me, and that was when I only felt the echo of his pain from your mate. But for Freya? This is *destroying* her."

Benedict flinches at the implication, but I squeeze his hand.

"But right now, she's trying to save both your lives. Sure, he's in pain, but Benedict is *alive* and *out of danger*, so get off your fucking high horse, follow the damn plans that have been outlined when it comes to these missions, and put someone other than yourself first.

"I'd love to spend the next few days, or week, or however long it takes right here, to heal your brother." I pause, and turn to the younger vampire, giving Benedict an apologetic look. "I'd love to heal you, Benedict, but I cannot spare the time or power right now."

I drop his hand and advance to the asshole vampire.

"Not only am I in an extremely vulnerable position with my life, but I'm also pregnant with twins. So, draining myself day after day to heal your brother *could kill my children*, which is a risk I absolutely will not take. Ignoring all of that, I have the problem of being the sole target of a crazy man who wants to steal my power and kill me.

"Said madman has blown up an entire pack, killed a random human, and a shit tonne of other things. Do you really think my pack would be safe whilst I hid out here? My people? No, they wouldn't. Benedict is clearly a loyal brother, but he is not worth more than the entirety of my pack. So yes, I will be leaving your brother for a while in the state he's in. Any more questions?"

He's still held under my power and can't fight against it, so there are no more questions. *Asshole.*

"Well said," Freya says, quietly.

"I understand, Luna," Benedict says. "I truly do, and when your fight is over, I would welcome any help you could give."

"Absolutely," I say, softly. I turn to Roman, and he gives me a nod. "I think we're done here. Could you drop us back home?"

"Of course. Thank you for coming." Roman turns to Freya, and she raises an eyebrow. "Do me a favour, little muse, and get him out of here before I return."

My influence over the bastard disappears the moment Theo and I are teleported away.

"He's lucky," Roman says, as we arrive back in my living room. Dillon shouts out in surprise, spilling his tea over the sofa. "Theo was about to claw the man's throat out if you didn't intervene."

I gasp, looking at my Guardian, who just shrugs. Roman disappears.

"What the fuck?" Dillon demands.

"It's a long story," Theo says, and I laugh, heading upstairs to shower.

It is a long story, but it's one I don't want to hear again. Benedict's pain... it's immense, and I hate that we can't help him right now.

To win the war, you have to prioritise.

No matter how badly it hurts.

CHAPTER 27

"*A*lpha, Luna," Hannah calls, gently knocking on the open door. I turn in my chair and see two familiar officers behind her.

Oh, thank fuck.

Not that they were overly friendly with us when we were at Midnight Summit, but Officer Hall and Officer Watson were only there to do their job.

They don't—*didn't*—care about politics and just wanted to find the ones responsible.

I can work with that.

"I have Officer James Hall and Officer Oliver Watson here. I checked their identification before bringing them up," she adds.

"Thank you so much, Hannah," I say, as warmly as I can muster.

"Welcome to Rose Moon," Rhett says, stepping towards them. Hannah makes her exit as Rhett's dominance emits out strongly. He's making it clear that should it come to it, he's not afraid to put them down.

Their wolves both submit to the Alpha out of respect, but I can tell neither are concerned.

"We're used to the posturing from Alpha males, Luna," Officer Hall says, with a smile. "If we submitted to every Alpha and let our wolves guide us, we'd never make it far in our profession."

"So, how do you resist?" I ask, curiously. Rhett lowers the dominance and invites them to sit down with us.

"We're trained to. We've been tested repeatedly by many powerful wolves, vampires, and everything in between until we can mostly resist the lure."

"Very interesting," Rhett murmurs, eyeing me thoughtfully. I nod, understanding what they're saying without actively saying it.

"It is," Officer Watson says, scooting his chair closer to the desk. Officer Hall starts unpacking his bag, pulling out recording equipment and stationary. "We're not loyal to any but the institution and, of course, the people we've served to protect."

"It's our job to get to the bottom of the relationship between you and King Lobo," Officer Hall says. "And unfortunately, this interview will become part of public record."

"So, you need to be wary of what you say on the video—"

"Is it a videotape?" Edgar interrupts.

"No, sorry. It's just an audio tape," Officer Watson says, and Edgar nods. "So, you need to be wary of what you say on that audio tape that could implicate yourself in whatever proceedings you have going on with the Council."

"You're not supposed to tell us that, are you?" Rhett asks, and both officers shake their heads no.

"We appreciate the help you're giving us," I say, placing a hand on Rhett's thigh under the table. My Alpha mate is not as impressed as I am.

"We wish we could do more," Officer Hall says. "But what we can offer is something that might be of value."

That piques my curiosity.

"Just like your interview here will become part of the public record, the same will happen for anything else we come across." I frown, but Officer Watson ploughs on. "With this being a public matter of danger and—"

"So, wait a second," I say, interrupting. I give them all apologetic looks. "Sorry for interrupting." Everyone waves me off, waiting to hear what I say. "If every part of the proceedings is going to become part of public record, what's to stop King Lobo from getting access to the investigation?"

"That's the problem with a public inquiry," Officer Hall sighs. "Someone would need to request the information, but with a case like this, so many people are going to be requesting the information so they can stay appraised of the situation. None the least, Alphas who are wanting to protect their packs so nothing like what happened at Midnight Summit would happen to them."

"Sadly, we can't track everyone who will be watching the case," Officer Watson says. "If a red flag appears, we'll look into it... but for the most part, I doubt King Lobo is stupid enough to use someone that would raise our suspicions."

"And if he did, it's likely not an avenue you'd want to explore," Rhett says, and the officers nod with a heavy sigh.

"Could you not petition the Council?" I ask, even though I know it's futile. The Council don't care about anyone but themselves.

"Unfortunately, they're not in the mood to listen to us. Those of us working this investigation have all lodged a formal complaint with our bosses, who have petitioned the Council, but it made no difference."

"Off the record," I say slowly, eyeing Rhett, who gives me an encouraging nod. "Is there anything you can help us with?"

"Depending on how this interview here goes, we might be able to," Officer Watson says, eyeing Officer Hall, who nods. It seems Officer Watson's taking the lead on this. "I don't want this to be seen as a quid pro quo—"

"Then don't make it that way, Officers," Edgar says. "Tell my client what she may receive if you like her answers."

"It's not about liking your answers, Luna," Officer Hall hastily rushes to admit. "It's about erasing your guilt."

"Not that we think you're guilty, but we still have bosses to appease," Officer Watson adds. "But your lawyer is correct. We can give you a head start on any tips we receive. If we get wind of an attack, sighting, of anything—before it's put onto the record officially, we can make sure you receive it."

"That would be extremely helpful," Rhett says, and I nod. "And what would you like in return?"

"The same. If you have anything you can share, do. We won't put it into the public record unless we have to, but if anything you give us helps, it will go a long way."

"Are we talking days here? Hours?" Rhett asks, raising an eyebrow.

"Hours, more than likely," Officer Hall says.

"We met with you last time at Midnight Summit," Officer Watson says. "And we pushed to be the ones to come and interview you today."

"Why?" Rhett's demand is laced with his dominance.

But just like before, it doesn't truly affect the officers.

"We've all had training to undergo resistance to the power of those more dominant," Officer Hall says, wryly.

"And, obviously, as you can both tell, I'm not the most dominant of wolves around," Officer Watson says.

"You're not," Rhett says, sounding almost amused. "You're probably not as strong as our top enforcer."

"Exactly," Officer Watson says. "That's another benefit of my position. I am not a naturally powerful wolf, but I am very adept at shifting, fighting, and holding my own in the political minefield."

"But we're not strong in terms of just raw power level," Officer Hall says. My wolf sits up to pay attention, and honestly, I feel the exact same way.

This is a part of things that I am very interested in learning about.

"So, this training was important," Officer Watson says.

"I don't get the point," Rhett says, looking at me, and I shrug, too. I bet if Noah or Theo were here, they'd have figured it out, but I'm not that aware of this world.

"We may be able to resist the call of a more powerful man, but our people are not above being bribed. And trust me when I say that politics is a dangerous game," Officer Hall says, as Officer Watson has a whole body shiver.

"We understand," I say, resting a hand on Rhett's forearm. "But I do have a question to ask, that will probably show my naivety as a wolf."

"You're still very young and new to this world. Anyone who sees that as a weakness is a *fool*," Edgar says.

"Correctly said," Rhett says, nodding at Edgar. "What's your question, love?"

"Is that the kind of thing any wolf can undergo? Isn't that a very big... breach, for lack of a better word?"

"Okay, we don't have much time to go over this since we'll need to start the proceedings soon, but I'll give you the cliff notes," Officer Watson says. "Our wolves have a natural inclination to submit around those more powerful. In being trained to resist that, we're only being trained to resist orders that go against the vow we had taken as officers of the law."

"So, if you asked me to disclose information of a case and used your dominance to do so, I'd be able to ignore you, Alpha," Officer Hall says. I note, and I'm sure so did Rhett and Edgar, that he specifically singled Rhett out there. Interesting to know. "But if you tried to force me to submit, I likely would do that. If you demanded to know my favourite colour, I wouldn't waste the energy to fight."

"What if I asked you?" I ask, and they both fall silent.

"We've never trained against someone of your power, Luna," Officer Hall says, and there's a red tinge to his cheeks.

"And even if we had," Officer Watson says, almost morbidly. "I don't think my wolf would even attempt to resist you."

"Understood," I say, softly. "And we appreciate all the help you're offering."

"Now, let's get down to business," Officer Hall says, grabbing his bag. He starts to pull out recording equipment and stationery.

"We've seen the letter you received, Luna Montgomery, and it was made very clear that this fight is yours," Officer Watson says. "But we're not fools, and we're here to help the best we can. If it were up to me and my boss, we'd take you into protective custody, surround you in a barrier, as we draw the bastard out. We'd have the battle that is required, but it would be with you *safe* as we utilised *all* of the resources at our disposal."

My wolf can sense no lies from either of these men, just a genuine desire to do their jobs to the best of their ability.

It's very reassuring.

"I appreciate that," Rhett says, raising his hand to stroke my stomach. I don't protest, knowing that just this time, he needs it.

"The recorder is nearly set up," Officer Watson says. "And when it's live, we'll be going through some standard questions. If there is anything you do not want to answer because you don't want it on tape, then please switch to the mind link with me. We would appreciate any information—and as long as it's not on tape, we do not need to submit it to the record."

Once again, they're going against the rules to help me, and it gives me more faith that the entirety of the shifter world aren't bad people.

"Is this something you have authorisation for, boys?" Edger asks, sitting forward in his seat.

"We do," Officer Hall says. "We had surmised that you would be here for this as well." He grins. "Or at least my boss did."

Edgar gives a wry smile. "You can tell your boss that, yes, I will be here acting as Luna Montgomery's legal counsel and her Alphas for as long as is necessary. And, if, for whatever reason, her pack members need a lawyer, I will be here for them too."

"Don't you have your own team of solicitors?" Officer Hall asks.

"Not that it's any of your concern—" Rhett begins.

"My solicitors are missing a very key component," I say, and their eyes widen. "Most of my solicitors are *female* and, as such, don't have penises."

Officer Hall pales as Officer Watson snorts.

"Oh, I wish I was joking," I say, glaring at Officer Watson. "Unfortunately, my female lawyer was not allowed to talk in front of the Council. So ultimately, we have to play the patriarchal game to ensure I don't go to jail." Rhett gives me a very indulgent look, knowing exactly where my mind has gone.

We've got to submit to the patriarchy for now, but that time will be coming to an end very soon.

"Are you okay with Alpha Rhett being here?" Officer Watson says, moving on from the touchy conversation.

Touchy for him, that is.

For me, it's my reality. But my body grows the next generation, whilst theirs does fuck all.

"Alpha *Simmons*," Rhett says, emphasising his surname. "But yes, my mate is more than happy with me here."

Both Officers look at me almost hesitantly.

"Are you..."

"I'm more than fine with it," I say, patting Rhett's thigh under the table. "Out of my three Alpha mates, I decided Rhett was the best one to be here with me."

Mainly because Caden was feeling a little too keyed up and wasn't sure he'd be able to behave, and Noah had to handle something in my place, which left Rhett.

Theo, River, and Warren all tried to plead their cases as to why they should be here with me. But, in no particular order, one promised to gut the officers who arrived, and one offered to steal the recording tape once it was conducted. The other offered to be my *representative* and tell some very creative lies.

Needless to say, the promise I elicited from Rhett to do no harm to anybody was really helpful.

"As soon as we start, we will go through your legal information. Your name, your date of birth, your pack, your status and so on before we go into the questions. Do you understand?"

"I understand."

Officer Hall reaches forward and turns the tape on. "Interview Recording 3957 begins at 10:57 a.m." He lists his name and badge number, and then Officer Watson does the same.

"The suspect, Charlotte Montgomery Mason, is in attendance with her Alpha mate, Rhett Simmons, and her legal counsel, Edgar Whitmore, of Vampiric Origin."

"Objection," Edgar says, and both of the officers hold in their sighs. "My name is Edgar Whitmore, and I am a *vampire*. I'm older than everybody in this room and belong to the Clan reigned by the leading monarch of my kind. You will *not* demean me that way."

"I'm, um—" Officer Hall starts.

"Let the record be amended to show that the third person in attendance is the legal counsel Edgar Whitmore, a vampire associated with Rose Moon. He belongs to the Hearthstone Clan, which is in a formal alliance with Charlotte Montgomery's pack."

There's a brief pause as the two officers wait for Edgar to complain, but he doesn't.

"Now, Charlotte Montgomery, your Alpha mate, is permitted to be here on your behalf but must remain silent unless asked a direct question. Is that understood, Alpha Simmons?" Officer Watson asks.

"I understand," Rhett growls.

"All questions are directed to you, Charlotte Montgomery, and you must answer to the best of your ability. If we find out you lied at a later stage, that will only impact your official trial. Do you understand?" Officer Watson asks, not even making eye contact with me. I can feel the shame of his wolf for even asking this question.

"I understand," I say out loud. But to Rhett, across our mind link, I mutter, *"Fucking hell."*

"I know, right? I hope they won't be this pompous the entire time."

"I don't think they have a choice," I reply.

"What is your full legal name?" Officer Watson asks, and so it begins. I answer questions on my name, my date of birth, my appearance, my mating marks, my fucking weight.

I'm not stupid enough to disclose my pregnancy, despite them questioning me about that being a possibility, but other than that, I've answered very honestly.

I love that all of this information is both on my police record *and* made clear to the public.

"Thank you for answering those questions. Now we can get into the real reason we're here," Officer Watson says. The audio tape has been recording for seventeen minutes and 12 seconds at this point. "Do you understand that we are here to question you regarding an allegation of terrorism?"

"Yes."

"Perfect. In your own words, can you please describe the nature of the relationship between you and the man called King Lobo," Officer Watson says.

"We have absolutely no true relationship. In fact, King Lobo only identified himself a week ago to us."

"And how did he do that?" Officer Watson asks. Rhett's jaw clenches together, and I can hear the ferocity behind how he grins his teeth.

"He sent us a letter, which is in your possession, and it outlined his plans to end me," I say, sharp as a whip.

"How was this letter delivered to you?"

I rub soothing circles into Rhett's thigh as Edgar jots down notes from this session.

"We were having a pack meeting after the attack we suffered, and a vampire in his command came to us with the letter. He killed himself during our pack meeting, terrifying some of my pack."

"I see," Officer Watson says. "And still, you deny having a relationship with King Lobo?"

"We definitely don't have a willing relationship, at least not on my end. The man is crazy and has been harassing me since I learnt about the supernatural world," I say, not genuinely sure if that's true. Cain has definitely had a hand in things, but was he acting as a servant, or did he go rogue? "King Lobo orchestrated this attack on my pack, but at the time, we thought Cain Viotto —"

"Cain Viotto, the son of Primus Alaric Viotto, the Clan you have a steadfast alliance with?"

"Yes," I say, with all the grace I can muster. "Alaric was extremely apologetic and has made the correct amends for his son being a traitor. Unfortunately, Cain Viotto has been found dead, so neither us, the Council, nor Alaric can question him."

"And you would have wanted to question him?" Officer Watson and Officer Hall exchange looks here, putting me on edge.

Rhett's now the one offering me soothing touches because he's so fucking perfect.

"Absolutely. The man kidnapped me and tried to forcefully take my power. He brought a family heirloom—a red amulet laced with wolfsbane—to subdue me. Sadly, for him, I was far too powerful.

"And no, that's not a brag. Cain Viotto was a powerful vampire, but he had nothing on me or even my mating circle. That particular family heirloom is only as powerful as the man to wield it, and so it was easy for me to overpower it.

"I easily overpowered Cain, returned to my pack, and sadly lost sight of him before he died. But, King Lobo executed Cain, which led to us connecting the two of them together."

"Seems like a bit of a stretch," Officer Watson says.

"Did you read the letter that was handed into your office?" I ask. My innocent tone causes Rhett to laugh, and he receives an admonishment from Officer Hall, which Edgar objects to.

So much fun.

"We did not," Officer Hall admits.

"Then that's something you may want to do. The letter clearly outlined the attempts on my life at his demand and the link between him and Cain."

"I see." They exchange looks, and Officer Hall jots something down on his notepad.

"Is this the only time you've been a target of King Lobo?" Officer Watson asks, reading the question off his sheet.

"No. There were the bombings that occurred at Midnight Summit. There were two that night—one designed specifically to target the Council. They took *five hours* to arrive, and I had to drain myself to help heal the healer wolves."

The two Officers exchange a look of surprise.

"There have been many smaller attacks within my pack that have come from members of my pack, who have both ended up dead, so they cannot be questioned properly. A bit of a trend where King Lobo is concerned," I say, with a small sigh.

"Do you know why he's targeting you specifically?" Officer Hall asks, and I'm surprised since this is the first time he's asked a question.

"We're not certain," I say, not yet ready to drop the status of me being an original into the woodwork. No, this is a surprise I need to give the Council properly. "But according to the letter, he's off my bloodline." I frown. "Or, more accurately, I'm of his, and he thinks he's entitled to my power for that reason."

"And what power may you be referring to?"

"I'm a very dominant wolf, and I think that fact makes him feel emasculated. I have nine mates"—*technically, I have eight right now*—"and I'm Luna to a very large pack and the only living heir to a second."

"It's hard not to see why he'd feel emasculated," Officer Watson says, with a slight smirk.

The rest of the questions continue in a similar fashion. They query everything, probe where it is necessary, and are willing to chat along the mind link when needed. They've tried to catch me a few times, but since I've not told a single lie, this game of theirs has never worked.

This interview was as much as to clear my guilt—for them, not the Council—as it was to find out more information, and I'm pretty sure I've shown I'm not the terrible person the Council have painted me out to be.

At least, I hope that's the case.

Finally, the interview comes to an end, and the audio recording is turned off

"So, how did you find that?" Officer Hall asks.

"Annoying and invasive," I immediately reply, and there are some chuckles. "I tried to be as honest as possible, whether mentally or verbally, and I hope it helps. I'm actually really glad we're going to be out of the office for the next few weeks."

"Oh yes, me too," Rhett adds, dropping a kiss to the top of my head.

"I don't want King Lobo to realise what we're going to be doing since the plan is to end him," I say. "But if he knows where we're up to..." I trail off, not sure how to finish.

"But if he knows where we're up to, then it takes away our element of surprise," Rhett says. "This man is crazy and broken, so the sooner we can find him and get this over with, the better."

"I agree," Officer Hall says. "Which is why we'll let you know whenever we come across something that can help."

"Which my client appreciates," Edgar says.

"He's dealt far too much damage and destruction," I whisper. "We don't want to add anything else to his tally."

"Thank you for your time, Luna, and I'm sorry that this interview felt so invasive."

"It is what it is when you're suspected of terrorism," I quip.

Edgar rolls his eyes, and it's one of the most laidback responses I've seen from him to date. He eyes both officers before focusing on Officer Hall. "I'd like a copy of that audio recording once you file it."

"I can do that. I'll get my boss to forward it to your office."

"That's appreciated."

"I'll see our guests out," Rhett says, and I move to stand, but he gently shoves me back down. "Sit, relax. I've got this."

He kisses my temple and leads both police officers and Edgar out of the room.

I could've put up a bigger fight, but I'm exhausted. I rest my head on my arms, leaning across the table, and let my mind wander.

My head is pounding, which my Guardian will heal, from all the questions.

I'm glad it's done, and I just hope I didn't say something that King Lobo can use against us.

Knowing my luck, though, that will definitely not be the case.

CHAPTER 28

The last two weeks have been a flurry of organisation, which has been great, but it's been silent from King Lobo *and* the Council. There's not been a hide nor peep from either of their followers, which makes me very, *very* nervous. We have been outlining our plan of attack, and it makes sense that he is, too. Everything before King Lobo's full-scale attack on my pack the other week had been done secretly. And it wasn't small problems that he caused whilst in hiding.

They murdered a girl and put her in my home. They bombed a reception, killing and harming so many people. They set up a second bomb, attacking the Council specifically. They somehow had connections to people in my pack and used them to do damage.

We have no idea how my kidnapping plays into this because

Conri has still not shown his face and given me the answers he promised me.

So now that King Lobo no longer wants to hide, he's got the potential to do plenty of more risky things. The nearly three-week break he's had to sit and plan this attack out *terrifies* me. But our country-wide trip starts tomorrow, and we're going to be away from the security of our pack.

Abel's prepared and ready to take over as Alpha—although I doubt he's going to be called such—and Blade is going to come here as his second. Abel's spent a lot of time with us, but Blade hasn't since he's been finishing up things he's doing for the Clan.

"You done with that?" Theo asks, with a grin. I close the file and nod. I'm content enough with the plan we've outlined. Nothing ever goes right down to plan, so we've covered exactly what we want to accomplish, including finding as many allies as possible, whilst informing the people of what is going on since I know for a fact that the Council gave very little information on the looming threats.

Sure, I'm the target, but King Lobo has already shown he has no qualms about attacking anyone and everyone who stands in his way, which the Council knows and should've put plans in place to handle.

Our journey ends with us finishing up at the Council headquarters, ready to right the wrongs they've been committing. Conri was limited in what he could do because of them, but I won't be. I plan to rip out every single piece of badness from those walls.

"Badness?" Theo mentally teases. *"So eloquent."*

I shrug, winking at him. Eloquent, maybe not, but vengeful? I'd say so. Everything is going to go down, and it's not going to be pretty. Sure, I'm scared, but more than that... we're prepared.

I hand Theo the file, and he kisses my forehead before disappearing into his own bedroom. We're working from home today, he and I, since I keep getting distracted when at the office. I open my laptop and get lost in answering the emails Lexie has prioritised for me.

"Beautiful," Noah calls. I turn and smile at him, before going back to what I was doing. He's probably coming to drag me from work under the guise of an early night, and I am not quite ready yet. I have two more emails to answer before I'm finished. "Can you do me a favour?"

I nod, not really paying him much attention. We've had an offer from one of the school suppliers for a bunch of free technology, provided that—

"Lottie, can you please turn and face me?" Noah demands, a little sterner now. I sigh, and turn to look at him before gasping. There are tears in his eyes and my heart cracks.

"Noah, baby, what—" I start speaking as I scoot off the bed. I walk towards him, but he shakes his head, holding his hand up so that I stop.

"Just stay where you are," he pleads, and I nod as panic fills me. I feel a tugging on our bonds, so powerful and intense, but I'm not the one doing it.

"Please talk to me," I beg, cradling my stomach. I want to run to him, but I'm scared. He's crying openly now, and whilst the tugging of the bonds was strong... he seems *happy*. "What's going on, Noah?"

"I'd like to know that too," Warren demands. He glares at Noah, before freezing for a moment. He inhales deeply, and then his head snaps in my direction, and he cocks his head. "Holy fuck."

"Holy fuck," Noah repeats, with a big watery smile.

"Tell me what's happening," I demand.

"Really?" Warren whispers.

"Really," Noah confirms, just as Caden arrives. One by one, they have the same reaction, each getting more and more excited. I've still not moved, as they talk about things being real now.

"What the fuck is real?" I demand.

"Your pregnancy," River whispers from the doorway. His eyes are black, and there's a lot of euphoria on his face. He zooms over to my side, hesitantly reaching out to touch me. He stops when there's a snarl.

"No," Theo snaps, glaring at Rhett, before I can. "We are *not* going to be selfish, immature, and reckless when our child is involved."

"Children," Dillon whispers.

"We already knew I was pregnant," I say, rolling my eyes as some exasperation leaks into my tone. "Why are you all acting like this is brand new news?"

"Because your scent has now changed, angel," River says.

"Okay? I can't smell anything different," I say, with a frown. I sniff the air but only smell them, like usual.

"We can tell you're pregnant now," Noah says.

"Fuck," I whisper, hiding my head in my hands. "You know I'm pregnant now? You can smell it?" There are many nods as I peek through my fingers and whimper, bringing my hands to my stomach. "Why the fuck is that a thing that happens? Do you think this is a weakness I want to share with *the world*?"

Theo's the only one brave enough to step forward—River actually moves away. "Charlotte," he says, in his commanding tone.

"Take a deep breath, love," Wyatt soothes, moving past Theo to get to me. My Guardian is not pleased that he's been replaced as my confidant. But Wyatt has always been one to help explain this world to me—he and Dillon seem to understand me in ways the others don't.

He bridges the gap between the human and the supernatural— the human and our life.

"That's not how it is," Wyatt continues, reaching for my hands. "Only the fathers can smell the difference in your scent."

"Oh," I whisper, glancing at River, who gives me one slow now. I burst into tears, and they're all surprised. Nobody tries to calm me down, which I'm grateful for since I can't even truly identify what's happening with myself.

I'm pregnant, and I knew that deep down. But now, for my guys, this pregnancy is *real* to them. They've got their confirmation now, and I still don't.

Is it wrong that I'm bitter?

But then, I'm so excited that River can scent the change. There was a small bit of doubt, especially after my conversation with Theo weeks ago, but now, knowing there is actually a connection, my heart is healed.

"Your thoughts are a little bit of a mess," Theo says. "But I've got an idea for that."

"Me too," Elijah says, and Theo sighs. "Give me two minutes."

Elijah disappears and reappears back in front of me, handing me a plastic bag.

I take it and check inside before smiling. There's a bunch of pregnancy tests inside, and it warms my heart completely.

"Thank you," I say, grinning at Elijah, who returns it.

"What is it?" Noah demands, and Caden reaches over to snatch the bag.

"Pregnancy tests? Where did you get those?"

"We've still got a few people who use them," Warren says, snatching the bag from Caden and handing it back to me.

"Excellent idea," Wyatt says, fist-bumping Elijah.

"And these will show just like the human ones do?" I ask, and they all nod. "Perfect. I'm off to wee on some sticks then."

My heart beats wildly as I clutch the bag to my chest and head to the bathroom. Because as much as this is real to them, and I know Roman's confirmed it... to me, taking these tests will be the thing that makes it real for me.

There are bangs on the door the moment that I flush the toilet, but I'm too terrified to dip the tests in the wee and check.

I can feel his presence on the other side of the door, and, even without that feeling, it's obvious who it is based on the impatient knocks. But I can't bring myself to go and open it.

"Come on, let me in," he begs, but my legs aren't working enough to get me there.

What if it doesn't come back as positive?

Yes, I know they can smell the difference and that Roman's seen it... but that doesn't stop my fear. There's so much negativity regarding my children that I just... *what the fuck do I do?*

Do I take a deep breath?

"Take a deep breath," Theo commands, his tone is calm and soothing. I do as he says, but it does nothing. What the fuck is breathing meant to do?

Instead of trying, I let my wolf push forward and retreat into my mind. She's excited, so excited. If she were in her shifted form, she'd be wagging her tail and nudging at her stomach. I can feel it within me–a little bundle of life.

I can only really feel one bundle of life, and yet... I'm pregnant with twins. Is it just one feeling for being pregnant, no matter how many children are inside me?

I don't know. I'm already worrying, and they're not even born yet.

It's hard work being a parent. My wolf whines, another excited sound, and I relax a little more. She's right. I am more than strong enough to face my reality.

I stalk over to the counter, continuing to ignore the knocks from Caden and dip the tests one by one. I lay them out, appreciating that there are both digital and non-digital brands and a few different brands. Elijah was thorough, and I'm very grateful.

"Nine tests?" I raise my voice, shouting down the stairs. A tiny part of me is sad—I would have liked one.

This is my first baby—*first pregnancy*—and I want to remember it all.

"I wanted one," Warren shouts up the stairs, reinforcing that I don't get one.

"Here," Theo shouts.

"Perfect. Hand it here," Caden demands, charging over to where Theo must be standing. He's back at the door moments later and knocks more gently this time. "I've got a present for you, baby."

"From me!" Theo shouts, and I roll my eyes. It's a good thing I'm hidden away; they can't see my smile.

They're really not that funny at all.

Walking to the locked door, I open it for Caden, and he bends down, dropping a kiss on the top of my head. He grins, shoving two more tests at me.

"I wasn't sure which one you'd prefer," Theo says, sending a little love my way. I grin and rip the packages open before dipping them both in the cup.

I turn to see Caden still standing in the doorway, with a pretty pitiful look on his face. "Please, can I come in?"

"Fine," I relent. "But you better stand still and not interfere."

"You get to do all the fun parts," Caden whines, kicking his feet dramatically as he storms over to where I pointed. "You get to grow the babies, you get to feel their kicks first, you get to do all of it."

"I didn't get to scent the change," I argue, and he tilts his head.

"Growing the children is better than smelling them."

"Well, just think, I'm going to have to push them out of me. They'll spread my vagina open further than it should ever go, probably ripping it to pieces," I say.

"Yeah, but you get two tiny pups at the end of it."

I laugh. "And so do you. *Without the pain.*" He has the decency to look ashamed now. As we've been talking, the tests have slowly started to show up. "You get the easy part, so stop the complaining."

"Fine. How long until the lines show up?"

"Two minutes," I reply. "But I don't think it will take that long."

"Why not?" he asks.

"Because they're already showing as positive," I whisper. Three say *pregnant*, two have two lines, and the others are still processing.

But it's confirmed.

I'm pregnant.

And I can't fucking wait until the day I get to meet them.

CHAPTER 29

"*I*t's time!" Katie yells, and I'm so fucking grateful none of the others are home.

I do not need them around for this.

Not even a little bit.

"Come up," I shout, not wanting to move from my very comfortable bed. The blankets are warm but not too hot, the position I'm in is great for the nausea, and everything is just perfection.

I'm the only one with very little to do this afternoon, so I came home to nap while they were running around to prepare things for the party. We're leaving tomorrow for our voyage, so I'm not arguing with the take-it-easy order.

"Can't," she shouts back. "I've got an ultrasound machine here so we can get eyes on those little bundles of joy. You have to come down here."

"You brought it here?" My voice is shocked. How the fuck did she manage to steal an ultrasound machine from the clinic? *Fucking hell.* I get out of bed, the world spinning a little, and I hold in the urge to throw up.

Whoever said morning sickness only occurred in the morning was a fucking liar, and Theo's not here right now to help ease the side effects of my hormones battling against each other. Usually, he's here to take the edge off, so it's not been too bad, but he's not been around since this morning.

I slowly walk down the stairs, holding onto the rail so I don't fall, and grimace at the frazzled look on my best friend's face. Her chocolate brown hair is styled around her face, and the highlights she's added make it seem lighter overall. Her eyes are the same colour, and they're lit up in excitement as she practically bounces on her fucking toes.

She's wearing one of my dresses, which pisses me off since it both looks better on her and probably doesn't fit me anymore. I'm not really showing, but I am already gaining weight. She spots the glowers and smirks, doing a spin to cause the red dress to spin out.

Bitch.

"It's time," she repeats, and I grin and nod. "Now, I know we're just trusting the word of the telepath here, so I figured—"

"I'm pregnant."

Her smile drops, some disappointment leaking into her words. "Are you sure?" I nod, and she frowns as she looks at her ultrasound machine with a hint of sadness. I hold in my laughter as she turns to me with a pleading smile. "How sure are you?"

"Well, between the eleven different positive pregnancy tests, the eight males who have smelt the difference in my scent, the constant morning sickness when Theo's not around, and my wolf who is being extra fucking dramatic whenever my stomach even brushes against something, I'm pretty fucking sure."

She squeals, clapping her hands excitedly. "Fucking hell, babe, I'm so thrilled for you."

"Yeah, me too," I mutter, feeling a little less than, to be honest. I wish I could enjoy her excitement, but I'm torn between my body wanting to pass out and throw up at the same time. It's exhausting. "We can still do the scan, though. I want to see if the little pups are healthy."

"You just want me to stick my big stick in you, right?" she asks with a smirk. "How long has it been since one of them has touched you?"

"Not too long," I say, thinking of last night with Elijah and Wyatt. "Although, some of them are concerned that they'll hurt the baby."

"As if women haven't been birthing babies for years whilst maintaining active sex lives."

I nod, and we head through to the living room. I arrange cushions so I can lay on the sofa as she drags the stolen ultrasound machine through. I yank my t-shirt off as Katie plugs it in, and I can feel the stirring of excitement building.

Katie brings the machine closer, gelling up the large wand that will find my children.

I tug my shorts down just as the front door opens. Katie and I freeze, me with my literal pants down, and I hear multiple footsteps coming into the room.

"Whoa!" Noah gasps, his eyebrows at his forehead.

"Are we interrupting something?" Caden asks, with a smirk on his face.

"What are you doing home?" I demand, cocking a hip as I glare at them. How I can hold the power balance even now, with my pants around my ankles, is hilarious, but Noah rubs the back of his neck in confusion. I hear more footsteps as more of my stupid mates enter the room, and my excitement turns into frustration.

"Did you really think we'd miss this?" Dillon asks, giving me a smile. I roll my eyes, but I'm sure deep down, I'll appreciate it eventually. I suppose it's not really fair to get to see them for the first time without them all.

I let out a sigh and throw myself down onto the sofa dramatically. I'm not sure why pregnancy is making me so mad at them all, but seriously, nine fucking mates and not a single one of them has a uterus?

It pisses me off, and when Caden asks what's wrong, I repeat my annoyance.

"You're not bisexual, love," Rhett murmurs, dropping a kiss on my forehead before doing the same with my stomach. I can't wait for the day my little pup starts kicking him in the face for doing that.

Hmm, maybe I am a supporter of violence.

"Where's River and Elijah?" I ask, noticing that they're the only two missing. Dillon gently eases my trousers off as Caden places a blanket over my stomach. I don't argue, feeling this feigned attempt at modesty is more for their benefit than mine.

Katie's seen my vagina many times, and she's going to get a very good look at it when I push the twins out. But I'll let them have their moment.

"We're here!" River says, appearing a second or two before Elijah does. "I got you this."

He hands over a chocolate doughnut, and I immediately burst into tears. There are some groans, some laughter, and two frantic sets of arms trying to reassure me, but there's no need. I push both Rhett and River away the best I can with one hand, the other protectively holding onto my doughnut.

"Nobody will take your doughnut, angel," River says gently before giving the others a very vicious look, in warning.

"Heal me," I command, looking at Theo insistently. He raises an eyebrow, maybe at my tone, before obliging me as I deserve. The sickness disappears, the headache retreats, and my body relaxes, ready for me to demolish this doughnut.

"Okay, baby mama," Katie says, grinning at me. "Eat your doughnut whilst you can, and then let's get looking at my little nieces!"

"Nephews," Elijah says, shaking his head. "We're definitely having boys."

"I'm team girl," Noah says, shrugging.

"One of each," Wyatt says, sitting next to the machine to get the best view.

"Well, we'll start a betting pool to make our guesses. We're still a ways off finding out," Katie says, with a smile. "For now, let's look at them."

She leans in towards me with the wand, and to the credit of my guys, not a single one makes a joke about the giant stick going inside of me. I had some very fun responses rehearsed on the off chance.

"It'll be a little uncomfortable, but we're just... and there we go," she says, excitedly.

"Keep still," Rhett says, gently placing a hand on Katie. My best friend winces, giving me an apologetic look. In her bouncing, she moved the wand, moving our view of the tiny pups inside me.

"So, we've got Baby A here," she says, showing off the tiny bundle that is our child. My eyes widen as my wolf howls in excitement. There's a sort of *I told you,* combined with protective mama vibes. But I can't even listen to her properly in my excitement. "And we've got Baby B here." She moves the cursor and zooms in a little.

But unlike the rest of my mates, I immediately see why. My blood runs cold, and my legs are trembling.

"What's wrong?" Theo demands.

"This is Baby C," Katie says, quietly.

"Three?" River asks, looking around at us all in surprise. "Who the fuck has triplets in their genes?"

"Four," Katie says. Her excitement has dimmed, as shock has overtaken her. "Baby C and Baby D were hiding between them all." I see where she motions, and she's right.

"Four?" I whisper, rubbing my stomach gently as if my touch could hurt them. "There's four in here?"

I connect with my wolf once more, feeling her absolute smugness, as now inside me... there are four bundles of life. I don't understand that. Yesterday, I *knew* we were having twins but could only feel one, and now there are four.

"Four," Theo confirms, a touch of anxiety in his gaze. Titling my head, I try to uncover his secrets, but his mental block is strong, and he's not looking my way. "Four healthy little pups."

"Four. Four is two more than I expected," I whisper, and there's laughter across the room from my men.

"Four is more than you expected," Dillon teases, reaching over to kiss my forehead. *"Thank you, baby. Thank you for giving us this gift."*

Dillon's not the only one to share the sentiment with me, but he beat the others out for it.

"Can you show us them all again?" Caden asks, and my best friend nods, walking us through each baby. They're tiny little blobs, nothing showing off the fact that they're pups, except the attachment I have to them.

Four babies.

Four pups.

Four.

"Let me clean this off, and I'll get you some photos." We all know she's just giving us a few moments alone, and I appreciate it more than anything.

"Dibs on naming Baby C," Caden says.

"Dibs on Baby D," Noah echoes.

I roll my eyes as laughter bubbles out of me. "Four babies."

"Four," Theo adds, not sounding as excited or nervous as me. I can feel each of my guys, and they all vary in their responses, but underneath their primary reaction, they are *all* excited.

Except Theo. He's a hard, stone wall with a forced calm.

Something is going on, and I don't like it.

"Okay, babe, you're good to go," Katie says, coming back into the room with a smile. "It might be worth getting Freya to have a spy just in case they're vampires since I've still not had any experience with those. I know you two are well-versed in pregnancies at this point, but there's nothing I see that concerns me, so don't panic."

"Except the third and fourth child?" I scoff, and she laughs.

"You've always been an overachiever. At least this way, you get it all done at once," she replies. The tension in the room rises as all my men look around at each other. As much as Theo reassured me they'd be done now if I was, I know we're still too out of our depth to commit to that.

I'm not going to lie to them or myself, but I'm unsure if I'm done after this pregnancy. I'm making zero promises.

"You're going to be a great mum," Katie reassures me.

"Love, there's nothing to be worried about regarding your parenting," Wyatt soothes, pressing gentle kisses across the top of my head. "You are a mother to an entire pack, and they all adore you. You're more than capable of doing this."

"You really are," Warren adds. "Remember when I doubted you could sustain the three of us?" I hiss at him, and he snorts. "Well, this is just like that. You're the perfect home for our pups until they're ready to be out in the world."

"Okay, but you're forgetting that I need to push out these four babies so they can join us in this fucking world," I snarl, and he roars with laughter.

Theo squeezes my hand. "You won't be alone throughout this pregnancy or in the after part. We're all here, and we'll all continue to be here."

For a man who can read my mind, he missed my main concern very easily. Despite being here physically, he's mentally not. I narrow my eyes, but he turns to Katie and starts to ask questions about the babies. Questions I don't truly understand why they are important.

"We're barely five weeks, babe," I say, and he nods.

"I know," he replies. "But I just want to know the gestational age of each baby, if possible."

"I mean, we'll be able to tell that a little later, but they're quads, Theo," Katie says, patting his arm. "Triplets and a singleton, to be precise. They're all fine and healthy, so let's not worry."

"Yeah," he mutters, looking upset for a reason I don't understand.

"Okay, since Daddy is being a Debbie Downer," Katie says, glaring at him with pure hatred, she turns to the rest of my mates. "Why don't you guys let the rest of the important people know? I'm not the best with secrets of this magnitude, and considering that one of my mates is dickhead's sister, she will want to hear it from all of you."

"I'm going to call Freya here first," I say, and my men nod. Everyone except Theo, who seems so blank and unhappy. "Just to check and see if there is a vampire."

"I don't think there is," Warren says.

"And can you tell they're wolves then?" Noah asks.

"No," Warren replies.

I laugh, despite it not being that funny and lay back down. I connect with Freya, and it takes her a minute to let me in. *"Hi."*

"Hi," she replies. *"What do you need?"*

"We're pregnant with four children."

"Fucking hell."

I laugh at her bluntness. *"I want you to see if they're of vampiric origin,"* I say. *"I can't really feel anything that would say one way or the other."*

"I can try, but it might not show this quickly," she says, seconds before she appears in front of us. Theo frowns, as does River, but neither of them moves. "Hi."

"Hi," I say, nodding my head to Hunter. He waves at me. "What do you need?"

"Want the big stick?" Caden asks.

Freya snorts. "No, I'm good." She comes forward and touches my stomach before shrugging. "So far, nothing. I can tell there's life, but not what said lives are."

"Werewolf and vampire babies both grow faster than humans despite taking the same gestational growth," Katie shares.

"I'll see you all later, but congratulations on having quads," Freya says, beaming at us all. She and Hunter, who weirdly remained silent this entire time, disappear.

"Well, looks like it's time to tell the family," Rhett says, with a smile. "Theo, want to call Sophie over?"

"Not yet," he says, with a frown.

"I shall see myself out," Katie murmurs, eyeing her machine.

"I can get it to the clinic for you," I promise, and she nods before letting herself out.

"What's going on?" Noah demands. "You've been miserable ever since she said we were having four."

"Because he knows that we weren't having four originally," Dillon says, meeting Theo's gaze head-on. Theo flinches but nods. Dillon sighs. "You're having at least one Guardian baby, Lottie."

"A Guardian having the next Guardian?" Warren asks. "I thought that didn't happen."

"Did you really think the chosen one would not have special children?" Caden teases, but there's no heat in his words.

"You've known before, she said, right?" I ask, looking at Theo.

He nods. "Since you mentioned that yesterday, you felt one life, and today there's four."

"That's how fast it happens?" Noah demands, and Theo nods. "Why?"

"We've got a singleton and a set of triplets."

"You were originally a triplet, right?" Wyatt demands. "How likely is it that Lottie will lose one of the babies?"

Theo shakes his head. "I don't know."

"I think all along Freya and her men knew we were having more than two," I say slowly.

"Freya mentioned a niece and her nephews," Theo says, and I nod. "One girl, three boys. Seems plausible."

"Well. I'm adding Guardian babies to the research list," Dillon says, and I nod appreciatively. "Sure, it's a little concerning, but we can still celebrate for now."

"But only if we all feel comfortable doing so," I say, giving Theo a pointed look.

He sighs. "It's not a bad thing. It's just... concerning."

"Concerning regarding Lottie's health?" Wyatt asks, and Theo shakes his head. "Then, for now, let's not worry."

"Then let's divvy up the calls," I say, grinning, but then a more sombre mood fills me. "Actually... I'll let you guys handle the supernatural family."

"Who are you going to call?" Theo asks, carefully.

"The human ones," I murmur, thinking of my mum and dad. They... they deserve to know.

Even if I haven't yet told them everything that's going on.

A parent's love is unconditional, right?

I hope that's true with all the lies I'm keeping from them.

Or I'll lose them, too.

CHAPTER 30

"*I*t's nearly time!" I exclaim, seeing Elijah walk down the stairs and join the rest of the group.

His curly brown hair is freshly washed and very fluffy from his use of the hairdryer. Like the rest of my men, he's dressed smartly in nice trousers and a shirt, but he's not taken it to the extreme of being overdressed. He's wearing a pair of nice trainers and grabs an offered beer from Rhett.

All of them look amazing, and I'm buzzing with the excitement of what we're going to do. Sure, there's a little bit of underlying anxiety, but for the most part, my wolf and I are in harmony with our decision to share with our people.

"You ready?" Caden asks, very indulgently. I nod, and he takes my hand, leading me out of the house without speaking to the others.

They realise, obviously, and follow up after us with their drinks. The atmosphere is jovial and sweet, and I'm not sure if any of them are as excited as me.

But as we reach the open field where we're having the party, my nerves overtake me. I cling to Caden's hand as we get up on the stage, and Rhett lets out a small howl that draws the crowd over to us properly. It takes them all around fifteen minutes to quieten down and for me to feel like everyone is here, and I had a very riveting pep talk from Rhett, Noah, and Caden whilst that was happening.

I'm ready.

It's time to announce my children to the world... *well,* our *world, that is.*

"We've got a lot of news to announce," I say, standing before my pack. There's some general anxiety amongst the crowd, but there's also some excitement. We've got everyone here—the young, the old, and everything in between.

They're nervous because something big is about to happen, and they don't know the outcome. But it will always be that way, even without significant threats hanging over our heads. There's not much that is certain about life.

The main goal of this fight is to let my pack have a future where they don't need to be scared to procreate or send their children to school.

I don't want them running around in fear, trying their best to put trust in us as leaders when they're so scared for themselves, their families, and even us as their leaders.

"We're going to party to celebrate our wins and to prepare ourselves for a short goodbye. Because—"

"From tomorrow, we'll not be here for a good few weeks," Noah says, stepping forward. When I gape at my Alpha, he winks at me before addressing the crowd once more. "So this is partly a send-off for us all."

Everyone seems to be waiting with bated breaths to see what's going to be said. We did announce this party, and most of the crowd are in party clothes, but I don't know if they've fully understood how much we've thrown into this.

"A send-off as we head into battle," Caden says, taking over from his twin with such easy camaraderie. "The Council may have appointed Lottie as our Luna"—there are a few cheers here, which makes me smile—"which we definitely need to celebrate, but that was only one of the political battles we have to handle."

"Along with the Council, we've got the upcoming fight that is King Lobo," Rhett adds, patting Caden's shoulder as he takes the stage. Each of my twin Alphas now step back, each of them taking my hand on the side that they're on, squeezing gently. "There is a man who wants to destroy our Luna, take her power, and break her. He seeks to take what she has."

"But the thing about Lottie is that it's not just her power that makes her so brilliant. It's just her," Theo says, grinning at me. "But she is not broken. Not when she carries the heirs to this pack inside her right now."

There's a loud collective gasp before hollers and cheers fill the air. Tears fill my eyes as my pack all drop to their knees, even the very young who don't truly understand why they're doing it. But I do, though. I understand the respect they're giving me.

My pack are honouring my children... and they're honouring me.

"Not when she's pregnant with not one, but four children," Wyatt continues, and a deafening collective howl fills the air my wolf silently joins in on. Happy tears drip down my cheeks as I feel the empowered air, supercharged with joy.

It makes me breathless to feel the level of their excitement.

My pack respect me, but more importantly, they value me as their leader. Ever since I discovered this world, this is what I needed. I needed my pack to understand that I would do anything and everything for them.

"We may not know the gender of our future children, but our future Alpha is already growing, ready inside my mate, and they'll be here in eight months. Whether we're graced with little boys or girls, they'll lead this pack to victory one day."

"As will we," River finishes, and my heart stalls as he gives me a beautiful grin before he turns to the crowd. "We'll be home before my children are born, victorious and ready to live a long life free of threats, danger and panic."

"So, we're having a party to celebrate the good news and all of the good things we have going on," I say softly, my words carrying across the crowd. "And because I know there's no doubt within me that we'll all survive this battle and be back here in a few months ready to live the rest of our lives. So, come say your goodbyes, but most importantly, drink, dance, and enjoy yourselves. Enjoy this for what it is—a celebration for the future, for safety. It's our first official party with me as Luna, but it won't be the last."

"As my mate commanded it, let the party begin!" Noah's voice is a booming demand, and the music starts, and people are stunned me momentarily as lights fill the area. They're overjoyed as they disperse, and I hope the cheerful atmosphere continues throughout the night.

I don't think the pack realised how much we'd put into this party since nobody other than Judith and her crew seemed relaxed. We've got plenty of food, drinks and enough entertainment to last the adults through sunrise.

People merge into groups, and the overall mood has changed from being tense and unsure to an atmosphere worthy of a celebration.

"That was a good speech," I say, smirking at my men. I'm glad they included River in it, but I am surprised they did, not because of the lack of mate bond but because he's *mine* and not one of theirs.

I reach up and kiss Theo, who is closest to me, and his hands start to wander. Warren hollers as the twins steal me from him. My lips are likely as red and rosy as Theo's, and I'm half-tempted to call off the celebration so we can have a more *adult and private celebration*.

"Your speech was good," I repeat, listening to the desires of my wolf. For once, she's not being led by her hormones. My wolf is desperate to be around our people and to soak up their love. "But stealing the spotlight from me was a little rude."

They all laugh, and Noah bends down to brush a soft kiss across my lips. "We could never steal the spotlight from you, baby."

I grin, and as soon as I step off the stage, my dad is there, wrapping me up in his arms. Our wolves are in sync, taking comfort in the familiar, and I relax in his embrace. My dad is everything to me.

"Again, Lottie?" he whispers, sounding tortured, and I tense. "Please take pity on an old man, and don't make me see you having to do *those* things to your men. Sure, you're carrying the proof, but let me pretend this was an *immaculate* conception."

My panic immediately fades, and I snort, trying to hide my amusement in his chest. My dad's chest vibrates with his own laughter, and I tighten my hold on him. His tears drip into my hair, and I get the feeling he's both proud and sad right now.

His wolf shows his melancholy at the thought of his mate—*my mum*—not being here for this moment, but he's also excited at the idea of grandpups. It's a prideful thing for my dad's wolf to know I was both strong enough to take the burden of the immortal line and that I'm capable of furthering our line.

"I am so, so proud of you," he whispers, tightening his hold on me. "I love you so much, sweetheart, even though she's not here... I know she's so proud of you, too."

"I love you too, Dad," I say, adding the silent love to my mum. She'll hear it; I know she will.

"I'm so excited to meet them." He relents on the hug, and his hands press over my stomach. "Four babies."

"Four babies," I repeat, pulling away from him. His eyes widen, but I give him a sad smile. "I told my parents about the pregnancy earlier today."

"You did?" he asks, and I nod. "How did it go?"

I sigh, huddling in on myself a little. His wolf doesn't like that I'm upset and is desperate to comfort me, but he doesn't understand why that's needed. "They were excited for me, especially since this will be their first grandchild. But they were also a little hesitant that I'm pregnant so soon."

"Soon?" my dad echoes, a look of pure confusion on his face.

"For humans, yes. We've not even been together a year yet, Dad," I shrug. He still seems confused. "I didn't mention the quadruplet aspect just yet but did keep to the truth the best I could. We're only a few weeks along, and we're excited. They were proud and promised to call over at some point during the pregnancy."

"Oh, love," he says, sadly. I lean into him, taking comfort in his embrace once more.

The solemn moment doesn't last long since Malcolm pops up at his side with Evie. I smile at the pair, and Evie's grin is much less devious than her mate's.

"I hope one of those babies is getting named after me," Malcolm says, clicking his fingers at me. I roll my eyes. "The cutest one, preferably."

"Wait, what? I'm the granddad! If anyone is getting a baby named after them, it should be me," my dad protests, giving me a pleading look.

"Which is why you don't need the babies named after you," Malcolm replies without flinching. "You're already tied to them as a granddad."

I laugh and reach forward to hug Evie. She whispers a soft congratulations before letting me go. Then I turn to Malcolm, raising an eyebrow and keeping my tone stern. "I already banned junior names. You are not getting a child named after you."

"But..." He groans when his mate elbows him, but the disappointment doesn't last too long. "Fine. I'm sure they'll still have cool names." I laugh, and he leans in to sweep me up in a hug. "Congrats, little Luna." He hugs me tighter and whispers, "We're so fucking proud of you."

"Thank you," I murmur back. He releases me, and I grin at my family before waving and dancing away from them. I don't make it far before Judith pulls me into a conversation and hugs me.

She showers me with congratulations and belly touches. Rhett sticks close by as we are moved to the next group and the next, and he never drops the smug smile on his face when people touch me. He's so excited to see his pack excited about our pups, and so am I.

"Congratulations, sister," Sophie says, grabbing me in a hug. She's very tipsy and very free with her love right now. I've seen her dancing —*gyrating against*—with Katie in positions that made *Lexie* blush, and now she's here showering me with love. "I am so excited to be an auntie."

"Can we talk before I go?" I murmur, and she tilts her head but nods. "Thank you."

"You okay?" Rhett asks, me.

I nod, and grin up at him. "Want to dance?"

He smirks, tugging me into his arms, and sways us side to side. "Like this?"

"If that's what you'd prefer," I murmur, and although I step on my tiptoes, I can't reach his ears to whisper until he ducks his head. "Or we could do some of the very... *salacious* moves that Sophie seems to be fond of."

His eyes fill with lust, as he gulps. No words are said as I tug him into the crowd.

There's no need, after all, when his erection says everything for him.

)) ● ((

"*L*et's get you into bed," Dillon whispers, gently laying me under the covers. He stripped me off not even fifteen minutes ago and helped me brush my teeth since I was too exhausted to do so myself. Someone has readied the bed for me, but I can't keep my eyes open long enough to thank them.

I'm asleep before Dillon tugs my blankets over me, and I don't feel him or any of the others joining me in bed. But, of course, my well-deserved sleep doesn't last for long.

I wake up in the middle of the Ancestral Realm, the serene energy not soothing my annoyance. I'm fucking wrecked, and with our busy day tomorrow, I *need* the sleep tonight. I cannot be fucked with dealing with a rude as fuck Alpha—*more than likely*—as I have some kind of shit show to handle—*almost a guarantee*—whilst running on no sleep.

That annoyance is only amplified the moment a familiar cough sounds. I whirl around and glare at him, unable to hold in the absolute fury on my face. I mean, I suppose I *could*, but I don't try.

"You told me you'd be in touch," I say, glaring at Conri. He shrugs, and I growl, unable to hold in my frustration at the lack of shame on his face. Things have gone to literal shit out in the real world—the one he was desperate to leave, despite being in a prime position to help—and now he's taking the piss with reaching out to me.

"Time works differently in this realm."

"Oh, fuck off with that bullshit," I hiss, and he laughs, but it's a bitter sound.

He sighs, hunching in on himself. I can see a weariness fill his face, almost as if he's unsure if I will accept what he says. "I've yet to find my mate."

"Oh." I blink in surprise, this not having been something that I thought could ever be wrong. "I don't understand. How?"

"I don't know. They're hiding her from me, but I don't know why," he replies, with a heavy sigh.

"I know that feeling," I mutter, thinking about my desperation to see my mum when they blocked me from doing so. "Why are they keeping her from you? A punishment?"

"I don't think so. I was—" He suddenly stops and frowns, rubbing his chest. "It seems I'm not allowed to talk about that without causing myself pain. Fine. When I first arrived, I went through some kind of *onboarding* course."

"I take it questions about the realm will only fuck you over?"

He laughs, and nods. "I think so, Lottie. As long as things are kept vague, I can answer them."

"So, to you, how long have you been here?"

"A few days," he says.

"It's been three weeks," I reply, and he flinches. "I'm sorry, Conri."

"I'm sorry too," he says. "If I knew it had been this long, I'd have worked harder to—" He jolts and shakes his head. "I'd have worked harder to get here to help."

"Good. In the time you've been gone, the threat has been identified. He calls himself King Lobo."

"What of Cain?"

"He's been murdered," I reply, without a care. I frown. "Shouldn't you know this?"

"Not yet. I've been caught up on the—" He flinches, and barks loudly. "I can't fucking say. Let's just stick with the answer being no, I don't."

"Well, King Lobo, or more likely one of his followers, got to Cain before Abel and Freya could. He's gone, and so can't answer any questions." I give the dead man a piercing look. "You've got a lot to answer for."

"I know I do, and I am so sorry." He looks around the realm, and I get the feeling he can see far more than I can. He looks back at me, his face full of remorse. "This visit isn't going to be as long as you need it to be, and I won't be giving you the answers you so desperately seek."

"What? Why?"

"Because you're about to be woken up in three... two..."

Fucking bastard.

CHAPTER 31

*M*y eyes fly open, and I look into the exhausted face of Wyatt. He tilts his head in concern, and I can only imagine how I look right now for him to feel that strongly. "Are you okay, love?"

"No."

He crouches down next to me, gently stroking my hair out of my eyes as he takes on a gentle and soothing tone. "Did you have a bad dream? Are you suffering from morning sickness?"

"Neither." That only causes his brows to furrow. "Conri finally made an appearance last night, but I was pulled away after what only felt like a few minutes with him." I sigh, and shrug. "It's not your fault. The realm was not very forthcoming." Which is no different from usual, I suppose.

"Oh, fuck. Maybe you could try going to bed earlier tonight?" Wyatt offers, and I scowl at him because that was very fucking unhelpful. He sighs. "Sorry. Maybe we can try and get Warren to help you get back there tonight now that Conri is willing to assist."

"We've tried that, and so far, it hasn't worked," I murmur, stretching myself out. I feel my back crack, and it feels amazing, but Wyatt flinches. "It doesn't hurt to try again, though."

"Good. The annoying duo and Lexie are here for breakfast, along with Scottie and River. Can you stomach eating something this morning, or would you prefer I packed you something for the road?"

"No, I can eat, but it won't hurt to pack something either." He nods, and I smile. "But if you send Theo up here to work his magic, I would not complain."

Wyatt snorts, and kisses me softly. "I love you, and everything is going to be okay."

"I know," I reply, squeezing his hand. I scoot out of bed, not having realised I was naked. I briefly think back to last night and Dillon trying to get me dressed, but I was adamant that naked was better. Wyatt's eyes immediately rake over me, and I shiver. My skin erupts in goosebumps, and I am so tempted to say fuck the schedule... and fuck Wyatt instead.

"Give me ten, and I'll join you all," I say, ignoring the building desire inside me.

"Absolutely." Wyatt kisses my cheek, then disappears, and neither of us mentions the tent in his pants. *Sigh.* I grab the outfit I laid out yesterday afternoon and get myself dressed. All of our clothes are packed and already put away in our transport.

However, we're definitely going to need to either buy clothes or be on top of our washing every time we stop because we can't show the people we're visiting anything less than perfection.

Theo meets me on the stairs, healing the pregnancy sickness away as we descend back down to the kitchen, and I can feel the difference by the time we arrive in the kitchen. Our four guests are spread around the room, merged in with our family.

Scottie and Elijah are sitting in the corner, drinking coffee and reviewing last-minute information. Lexie is sitting with River, and they're murmuring very quietly to each other. Sophie's talking with Warren and Rhett, but like her mate, she's chatting quietly.

But the third part of their trio is bouncing on the heels of her feet, grinning at me. I can feel how excited her wolf is, but I don't understand why.

"Morning, babe," Katie shouts, giving me a little wave. Her mates flinch, their dark eyes and hunched-over bodies showing their hungover states. *Ah, that explains it.*

"Morning," I murmur, squeezing her tight in a hug. "You're not hungover."

"No, unlike those two, I can handle my alcohol," Katie says, laughing loudly.

"You're a bitch, Kitty," Warren says, with a smirk. He raises her voice, and ignores the dirty look from Sophie. "Morning, princess. How are you feeling?"

"Good," I say, with a nod. "I'm going to need to steal Sophie for a few!"

"Can I steal you after?" Scottie asks, almost nervously.

"Of course," I reassure her. I send some energy along the pack bond, soothing her wolf, and she relaxes marginally. It's easy to understand why she's stressed since Abel will arrive soon.

The asshole better behave himself when we're gone, or else he'll have hell to pay.

And not from me.

No, Scottie will be the force behind his reckoning.

I'm just not happy I won't be around to see it.

Abel and I have tiptoed around each other since his big confrontation with Scottie, and he's been nothing but polite. Very smart of him because if he even tried to bring it up, I think I'd do some physical damage that I could never take back.

Oh well.

"Me? Why?" Sophie whines, and Theo kicks her on her way past. She clenches her fist, but I tug Theo out of the way before she can try and land one on him. She grunts, and grabs my hand. "Come on, Lottie. I refuse to sit here if this is the case."

"Not my fault you're too weak to hold your alcohol," Theo taunts.

"Fuck off, Toe-odore," Rhett hisses, as the door closes behind Sophie and me. I'm mourning the loss of my breakfast since she's dragging us further away from the house.

"What's wrong?" she demands, giving me a stern look.

"Whoa, nothing," I say, holding my hands up. "I just wanted to talk to you about the pregnancy."

"Why?"

I give her a soft smile. "Because... I'm pregnant with Guardians."

Her face pales, tears filling her eyes as she turns from me. "Theo never said."

"I don't think your brother has come to terms with it yet," I say, gently. "But I figured it was something you should know."

"Do they know yet?" Her words are barely louder than a whisper. I can feel her devastation, the pain inside her growing, and even her wolf feels inferior.

"No." My tone is strong and final. "But they'll know eventually."

She sighs, and turns back to me, giving me a watery smile. "I'm so excited that you're pregnant. I'm excited to be an aunt. I am... I really am."

"I know." I reach for her hand, squeezing it in mine. "But I also understand why you feel so upset. This has never happened before. Theo couldn't have—"

"Predicated it?" she snarls, and I know she's not angry at me, but that doesn't stop the barrier my wolf throws up to protect our stomach. Sophie doesn't realise, and I'm so fucking grateful for that because I think that simple act would have done *a lot* of damage to my sister-by-mating.

"No, Lottie, he wouldn't have. But he is the favourite son. The golden boy who is the Guardian not only to a very powerful wolf but to the new *Original Wolf*. You are the most magnificent wolf in the entire fucking world, which only makes Theo's part in your life that much more of a *boon* to my family. A brag as if they did anything more than have a fucking child."

"I'm sorry."

"Promise me," she begs, turning to look my way with tears streaming down her cheeks. "Promise me they—he or she—won't ever be made to feel *less than* for not being the special one. Promise me."

"My love is not based on their traits," I say, stepping forward. "I promise my children will be treated fairly, loved the same, and one will never feel *less than* for not being a Guardian."

"I know," she says, and she's the one to pull me in for a hug this time. "I just know this is going to be marked down as another failure against me. How much of a terrible fucking sister am I that I'm throwing myself a *pity party* instead of congratulating my brother?"

"You're not," I whisper into her chest. "You're really fucking not. Your parents are trash for doing this to you, for making you feel this way. I might never understand the feelings you're going through, but I do respect them."

"I know," she says, squeezing gently before pulling away. "I'm glad we spoke about this. I really appreciate you."

"I'm pretty perfect, I know," I tease, hip-bumping her. She laughs, and it's not as light as her normal carefree one, but it's not as dark as her current mood, either. "I'm sorry Theo didn't tell you."

"I'm glad he didn't. I needed the chance to have this upset without him having to carry the burden of it."

"You're the auntie, so I wasn't going to ask you to be a godparent, but would you be opposed if Katie was?" I murmur.

She shakes her head. "Of course not. My mate has been desperately waiting for you to *formally* ask her. Alpha Charles has already taunted her a few times about his status. You should've seen her texting him last night once you announced it to the pack."

I laugh. "That's why my phone has been blowing up all day. I've not checked it."

"I wouldn't. Just delete and move on," she says. "What about Freya?"

"I love Freya," I say, slowly. "But she's not yet prepared to take on the burden of caring for my children if I die, and since that's a very real possibility... I'll just let her be the fun, crazy aunt that drops in with inappropriate presents."

"Smart," Sophie says. "I'll probably be a little... uptight whenever they come for a visit."

"Me and you both," I mutter, and she snorts. "I'll make your brother give you a proper heads up."

"Good. Do you mind if I go for a run? Katie and Lexie are both uptight with you leaving, and I want to process my feelings properly so I can support them."

A grin appears on my face, and she groans, and shifts into her wolf. She bounds away, and I laugh before heading back into the house.

"Where's Soph?" Theo asks, the moment I step through the front door. I can hear the others still in the kitchen, but I can feel his underlying anxiety.

"She's okay, just gone for a run," I say, reaching up to kiss his cheek. "You could probably catch her if you wanted."

"I need to tell her about..." He trails off and sighs. "Of course you told her."

"She deserved to know," I say, gently. "And I think it was for the best that I told her."

"I know, which is why I didn't tell her," he says, sighing. "I had hoped you would."

"And I did. But next time, tell me that since I'm not a mind reader." I squeeze his hand, then go off in search of Scottie. She's exactly where I left her, but there's an empty plate of food in front of her. She grins at me as I approach.

"My turn?"

I laugh. "Yes, but please let me get something to eat first." She nods, and Dillon jumps up to make me a bacon sandwich. I convince him to add an egg as well.

Scottie and I are back in the same spot Sophie and I were in only ten minutes ago, but we're sitting down together so I can eat.

"You're a good Luna, you know? I didn't just say that to Abel to make a point. I mean it."

"You're an amazing pack member, and I'd hate to lose you to another pack," I say, gaining at her. "I didn't just say that to Abel to make a point either."

"I'm not sure how things will go for the next few months."

"We're going to look into all the other packs and do our best to find you somewhere," I reassure her. "And the offer for you to transfer to Golden Eclipse whilst he's here is still there. My dad is willing to admit you to his pack and even house you until I return."

She nods. "Having that escape plan if things become too much is very helpful. For the sake of my long-term mental health, though, I'm going to try and have a conversation with him. I hate him, but my wolf and vampire *love* him. The distance between us all these years has not been kind to us."

"You know yourself best."

She nods, and looks out at the trees as I take another bite of my food. I get the feeling she's got something else to say, but I'm not sure what. Abel's an asshole; understandably, she's not happy about him coming, but her hesitance here seems to go deeper than that.

"The day I saw Abel, he ran out of this room after talking to you, and it was as if..." she trails off.

"You're wondering if I laid into him?" I ask, and she nods. "I did, but not on your behalf. He compared himself to an issue I've been having with—"

"River," she murmurs, and I nod.

"The two are not the same, as far as I'm concerned, and he tried to get my sympathy," I growl the words, my anger filling me once more. "I held him under my dominance and explained why he was wrong and how much of a prick he was for even thinking otherwise."

"Which is fair," she says, slowly.

"He's determined to do right by you this time. It's your choice, Scottie, and nobody will judge you."

She sighs. "A part of me trusts in the bond fate gave, and I know that without her meddling, I'd have missed out on so much *good* that

347

I've since done. But... that doesn't mean I want to forgive him for making the last two decades so fucking miserable. We've got longer lives than humans, but he and I? We're not immortal."

"But your love could be," I whisper, and she nods but says nothing else.

"I understand why people like talking with you," she says, and I frown, not understanding. "A lot of my patients have said how easy it is to talk with you, and I wasn't sure if that was just your position. It's not. It's you."

"Trust me, my pack may have nothing to fear, but not many actually enjoy talking with me."

She snorts. "A powerful woman is not the thorn that people think it is. You're strong and should never be ashamed of that."

"I'm not." Mostly. "I'm just... nervous, I guess."

"Nerves are understandable with the stakes on the line for this one, Luna. If you weren't nervous, you'd be cocky and overconfident and far more will go wrong."

I look at the half-eaten sandwich, and I can't finish it. Sadly, this type of nausea is not one that Theo can heal away from me; it's one born from the anxious pit filling me.

I feel a pull on the pack and sigh, pushing to my feet. Abel has arrived at our place, sadly.

"The bastard has arrived, I take it?"

"Don't let Alaric and Cassie hear you say that," I tease, and she groans. "But yes, he's here. I'll grab whoever has finished eating so we can greet him."

"I've got a meeting in... eighteen, I mean *eight* minutes," she says, seeming slightly flustered. "Thank you for your time, but I must be off."

I nod, and don't tease as we head into the house. Scottie makes her excuses to Elijah and then disappears before Abel can even say her name. Elijah tugs me into his arms.

"You okay, sunshine?"

"I have no idea. You?"

He smirks, and kisses my neck softly. "So much better since you're here."

"Sap," Caden taunts from across the room. "Baby, are you sure you're done with this?" He gestures to my food, and I nod. He takes a massive bite, and I roll my eyes.

"Where is he?" I whisper, and Elijah laughs.

"Kitchen with the others. But, before you go, may I please have a top-up?" Elijah asks, and I nod, moving my hair out of the way. "Caden?"

"What?" Caden asks, looking over at us before a slow grin appears on his face. "Oh, yes. I will definitely assist with this."

He's in front of me before I can blink and connects our lips together just as Elijah's teeth sink into my neck. I whimper into Caden's mouth, letting him swallow the sounds I'm making as Elijah's fingers brush across the seam of my shorts.

This could've been an innocent feeding.

But I love that it's not.

Elijah rubs me through my shorts as he drinks from my neck, and Caden's delicious mouth is putting in an equal amount of effort at making me feel good. The three of us are suspended in our own little bubble of lust.

"Charlotte," Theo calls, and based on the humour I can feel from him across the bond, I know he knows what we're doing in here. *Asshole.* "We've got guests."

"Ugh," Caden whispers against my lips. "Can you cum before he gets here and ruins our fun?"

"Not like this," I whisper back, grinding into Elijah more.

"Then I'll just have to up the ante," Elijah whispers.

"Nope," Theo says, standing in the doorway with an amused grin as he takes the three of us in. "Clean your neck, let's go greet Abel, and then it's time to head off."

"Ugh," Caden moans, throwing his head onto my chest with a huff. I laugh because the position he is in is so clearly not comfortable.

"Let's move it," Theo demands. I disentangle myself from the two men and head to the toilet to quickly wipe myself clean—my *neck and... other areas.*

"Luna," Abel says, dipping his head in respect as I enter the room. "Are you sure you're happy with me residing here?"

"Absolutely," Caden says. "Your room is set up, and you have keys and everything."

"You're good at maintaining the barriers around the pack?" Noah asks, and Abel nods. "I think it's just now hitting me that this is real."

"It's going to be fine," Rhett says, patting him on the shoulder as I send love across the bond.

It's all going to work out exactly as it should.

CHAPTER 32

"*I* swear to all that is holy—" I hiss, turning in my seat to glare at the morons behind me. Sure, we're bonded, and I love them and all that positive shit. But we're not even an hour out of the pack, and they're *already* fighting over the music, snacks, and directions.

The directions.

Theo is driving, and I'm in the front seat. Some may argue I used my pregnancy as an excuse to get this seat, and they would be correct. I claimed I'd get sicker sitting in the back than at the front, where I could see the road.

Theo has already healed me this morning so I could eat— ignoring that I didn't get to eat much due to my anxiety—and his influence has yet to wear off, but nobody argued against this arrangement.

I had no doubt they'd be this annoying for the drive, but I'm glad we did it this way. We've got a minivan for the trip, but I made the caveat that if we start to fight too much, we're breaking down into more cars to split up and give ourselves a break from each other.

Currently, we've got Caden and River right at the back of the vehicle. They're not the issue since they're talking quietly to each other, which does surprise me, but I'm not complaining. In the row in front of them, we have Dillon and Wyatt. The latter involves himself in the drama and is probably a big instigator of much of it, but Dillon is quietly reading on his Kindle with headphones in.

Unsurprisingly, Rhett is the biggest instigator amongst the others and can easily draw Noah into the fights.

The surprising one, to me, is Elijah. He's in the row behind us with Warren, and Elijah's constantly hammering on about how Theo's the wrong choice to drive and how he's missed certain turn-offs. The complaining about Theo isn't the surprise—it's the fact that he's cracked this soon.

"Sorry," Elijah says, sitting back in the seat when I glare at him. "I get to drive next, though, right?"

"At this point, you're last on the list to drive," I say, and he gasps. Theo's lips tilt up in a smirk, but he's smart enough to not say anything.

"Do you want some headphones, princess?" Warren asks, leaning forward with a surprisingly gentle look on his face. My bag is at Rhett's feet since he wanted the sandwiches Caden had packed for me. Sandwiches. A lunch item. At ten a.m., when we'd not even been on the road for an hour, they had a full English for breakfast.

If there were a zombie apocalypse, none of these fuckers would have the skills needed to survive.

I nod, and Warren smiles, pulling his out of his pockets. The car turns quiet as I connect them to my phone, and I pull out the file on the pack we're visiting. Lexie was the critical force in preparing these, and they are *everything*.

I feel the mischief from Warren now that I can no longer hear them, and I know he only offered his headphones out so he could join in on the antagonising behaviour without upsetting me, but it's something I'll accept.

We're going to see Alpha Moore of the Wildfire pack. He's a little further up North than us, and it's a four-ish hour drive. From all accounts, he's a nice enough guy with a small pack who has minimal turnover. When it came to taking people from their abusive packs, he had nobody reach out, and he's voted for Elder Green twice now as a councilman. All good things, as far as I'm concerned.

The downside, from what we can see, is that he fights with the local humans for quite a few issues regarding his pack.

The local humans think he's a cult leader who refuses to allow anyone to leave his lands. He, on the other hand—rightly so—is pissed at the implication he'd ever force his people into solitude and servitude.

I can see both sides of the dilemma. To the humans nearby, of course, it's weird that we have people living together, never leaving, never really interacting with anyone else.

We're lucky in Rose Moon that we're so isolated from humans and that all the nearest places are people we know. Rhett had Crescent Peak, my dad has Golden Eclipse, and Charles with Midnight Summit is a little bit further away. They don't have the separation.

But then, for the wolves, why would they want to leave? They have everything they need—resources, safety, *pack*.

Things seem to be escalating with more than one attempt from the humans to breach his pack lands, and I hope the Council will step in soon because he clearly needs help.

I've not done more than glance through the file in the past few weeks, so now I'm getting more acquainted with the other ranking members of his pack. Alpha Moore is mated to a lovely woman, and they have four children together. The pack has two Betas and no gammas. One of the Betas is the one he bonded with since they've been together for the last twenty-seven years, and the other Beta is his oldest son, Cameron.

It appears Cameron's learning the ropes in the Beta position until Alpha Moore is ready to hand the reins over.

They seem nice.

But the biggest monsters always hide their horrors under a pretty skin.

The songs blend into one another as we drive, and once I finish reading the file—twice—I let myself drift off for a short nap. Maybe the Guardian of All will steal me again, or maybe Conri will show his face once more. He promised he'd come back, and last night was a massive waste of time, so I pray that he'll be back before things go to shit.

Just once, I need the ancestors to give me the aid *before* it reaches the pinnacle stage.

"*G*randdaughter," Lena's voice says. My eyes fly open, and I'm surprised to see that I'm lying on the ground in a bed of flowers. I stretch out, unsure why I feel so achy in this realm since I never have before. I sit up and spot my grandmother a few metres away in her wolf form. "*We don't have long to talk.*"

I open my mouth, but she shakes her head, her beady eyes trying to convey something I'm missing. There's a weird feeling in the air, a sort of... uncomfortableness. It's as if the entire atmosphere of the realm is screaming, *pay attention* to me, but I don't know what I need to pay attention to. This realm has the ability to be so insightful, and yet it's far too mysterious.

I also get the feeling I'm not exactly welcome here. I've been brought here for a purpose, but there's unrest amongst the dead.

Fucking hell.

"*We must not disturb those who rest,*" she warns, and I nod. "*We must remain silent, less we will be disturbed.*"

"*We never have long,*" I reply silently. "*What is the message this time?*"

"*A forbidden one, with permission from the overseer,*" she says, advancing in her wolf form. "*Your choice is coming, granddaughter. The decision you fear... it'll be here soon.*"

I flinch, phantom pain racing through me. *"What can you tell me?"*

"That you need to choose correctly. Sacrifice one for the other. If you follow our advice and choose your mate... everything has the potential to play out as it should."

"I like the sound of that," I say, trying to take Theo's advice and play nicely with the ancestors—especially with this Guardian of All.

But honestly, the fact that I have to sacrifice something and only have the *potential* for things to play out as they *should* doesn't soothe me. Especially considering their *should,* and my *should* are probably two very different things.

"Can you advise me on anything else?" I ask when she doesn't say anything else.

"Your manners have improved, granddaughter."

"Politics seems like it will be a big part of my future in the coming weeks."

She nods. *"The overseer wants to speak with you. Remember those manners."* And then she's gone.

I don't have to wait long for the voice in the sky to appear. I see a butterfly, and I presume that's her way of having her presence here.

"We do not have enough time to cover all the questions you seek. But, yes, the author of that text was correct in the foundations," she says, and I nod once. *Be nice, Lottie, and get what you need.* It's harder to do than I thought. *"There is danger coming, and you need to be prepared. Sacrificing them will not be the end, and you cannot lose sight of things."*

"Sacrificing who?"

The butterfly flaps its wings in frustration, I think. *She can't answer.*

"It's okay," I reassure her, but my wolf and I are seething inside. We do not want to lose anyone else to this fight. *"What can you share with me?"*

"Not much, daughter mine. My sister played a cruel game with your fate, but you can rise to the challenge and become much more than just Luna to Rose Moon. You are already making big waves with your kind, and with the power of all wolf-kind now running through you, you can make so much more."

"*But what if I don't want to be* more?"

The butterfly stills and yet remains in the air. "*Then a different future entirely will play out. But I know you and know that you can't let any injustice lie when you have the power to help.*"

I sigh, and the butterfly comes to land on my hand.

"*You were chosen because your spirit is powerful and strong. You are kind and have a beautiful soul. You are worthy of the design my sister chose for you.*"

"Fate... she is your sister?"

"*She is. As flawed as she may be, she is never wrong.*"

I laugh bitterly, and as the butterfly disappears, I lay back down to sleep.

$$) \,) \, \bullet \, (\, ($$

"*T*ime to wake up, angel," River murmurs. My eyes fly open, and I'm hunched up in the seat of the car. My head is killing me, and my vision is a little blurry. I rub my eyes, easing the distorted vision, and take River's offered hand. I stretch out and then clamber out of the car. "We're here."

"I guessed," I tease, leaning into him a little. That nap didn't recharge me at all, but it has opened my eyes about what we have coming up. "Where is everyone?"

I move from River to grab my shoes from the footwell. River holds onto me as I awkwardly tug my feet into them and then dust myself off.

"Hey, baby," Noah says, grabbing my attention. I turn and see him approaching from another car. The rest of the group is behind him, all heading this way. "We're good to follow in now."

"Why did you all go over?" I ask, with a frown.

"They wanted to verify who we had with us," Noah says. "River stayed with you both to guard and wake you should be required, but they're fine with us."

"As they should be. They requested this visit," I mutter, and he laughs.

"Morning, sleeping beauty," Rhett says, leading the men back over. "We've got a ten-minute drive to their headquarters."

"What did they need from you all?" I ask, confused. River shrugs, opening the car door for me again, and I get back in, bucking myself up as the rest of them grumble but join me.

"Names to verify against what we provided," Theo says. "Proof that we were wolves, so they were a bit disgruntled with Warren and Elijah."

"I swear I nearly had to drink from someone to prove I was a vampire," Elijah mutters. "I have no idea why they were so strict."

"They've got issues with humans," I tell him. "It's probably to do with that."

"Maybe," Noah says, but part of him doesn't seem to agree—his wolf. His wolf is very unsettled and is waiting for the other shoe to drop, which, in turn, affects my wolf.

"It still rubs me the wrong way," Caden mutters, glaring out of the window.

"I was just excited to get out of the car," Warren says, and there's a lot of agreement from the group.

I've been asleep, so the cooped-up feeling hasn't affected me, but since shifting, I've not loved being in cars longer than necessary. My wolf prefers to be free.

By the end of this first week, we'll be lucky if we're all alive. I put bets on Rhett being the first one bodily harmed.

The other car beeps its horn, and we follow in behind it. It's a silver Toyota, but I don't know much more about it other than that.

There are two people driving, but I can feel a third wolf in the car. He's an adult for sure, but I can't see him. *That's curious.*

As we drive through the town, I'm not the only one paying close attention to the surroundings. There's lots of bright green grass, tall trees, wildflowers, and beautifully maintained gardens.

There's a big tennis court and a big lake.

It feels very luxurious here but also very relaxed.

I understand the cult vibes the humans are complaining about.

We come to a stop at a carpark, and after being buzzed in, we're directed around to park in a visitors' slot. There are three of them, which is peculiar in itself. Who visits here?

There are only three cars in the carpark, not including our minivan—two black and one very bright green one. A very bright green.

"What's that look of distaste for?" Warren asks, with a smirk.

I point to it. "It's a bit ugly, isn't it."

"I'm more interested in the flashiness of it, considering the issues they're having," Caden says. "It's a little suspicious."

"It is," Noah confirms. More of my men eye the car up, likely trying to identify anything about it that doesn't fit in.

The likelihood is someone bought it and is parking it here since he can't drive it out and about.

"Okay, before we go in," Noah says silently through our mind link. He's only opened this connection with me, and I'm not sure if that's because they already have their instructions or if I'm just a special case.

It better be the former.

"I need you to stick with River. He's your Gamma, which makes him your ally. But on the off chance anything goes wrong, we're lucky that he'll be with you. He's trained as a Beta, has the strength and security skills, and will be a valuable asset."

"Asset?"

Noah nods. *"I'll never be more grateful than I am now that River will be with you. If you and he get separated from the group, we're lucky he's with you, and of course, they can't sense a bond between River and you, which gives him another advantage."*

I nod, but if they can sense the lack of bond... what will happen once they reach the Council? How do we explain that?

Fuck, how do we explain this to anyone?

"Okay, I can do that," I reassure Noah.

"Depending on how much we split up, we will try to ensure we have at least one Alpha with you. But if that's not possible, you'll have Dillon, Elijah or whoever we can spare." I nod again, and he smiles. *"Theo and*

River are your shadows. For the entirety of this trip, you do nothing without one of them by your side."

"Just how I want it," I tease, as my car door is opened. River's there, offering me his hand, and he gently helps me out of the car.

We follow the group as a whole, and it's not surprising, after Noah's words, that Theo joins us. Dillon slits in on River's other side.

Warren is walking with Elijah, and the pair drop back to cover our backs, and the three Alphas are walking at the front with Wyatt.

We join up with the men from the other car, and as the back door is open, I'm unsurprised when a dark grey wolf jumps out.

He shifts into human form, and he's not familiar at all. With shaggy hair and a greying beard, he's older than me and my men. It's hard to gauge his actual age, though—eighty, maybe?

He nods at my Alphas, but there's no maliciousness from him. "It's nice to see you again, Alphas."

"You too, Chad," Noah replies. I'm not surprised that they knew each other, but it's weird none of my men mentioned it.

"He was part of our pack for forty years or so. Left us about ten years back," Caden says. *"His mate died, and he left for a change of scenery. He's a good wolf, and there's no hard feelings for him leaving."*

Fucking hell. I send Caden my thanks but don't say a word.

"We'll take you through to our Alpha now," the first man says. He was driving. "Thanks for your help, Chad; you can head off now."

Chad tips his head and disappears around the corner, humming a tune as he goes.

His appearance helps explain how they verified each of my men. The only real unknowns would've been Theo, Wyatt and Rhett.

We follow the two men into the building, and they greet the receptionist. We're left waiting again as the men disappear, and she calls for the Alpha.

My wolf bristles at the rude treatment, even though we'd likely do the same thing in the interest of safety. They've likely not heard great things about us—*about me*—and so logically, I understand this treatment.

"Don't be so accepting," Theo says.

"*We did the same thing,*" I remind him, and he scoffs.

"*They were arrogant, cocky, rude, and wanted to be there to cause trouble,*" he protests.

"The Alpha is ready for you now," the receptionist says, still not introducing herself to us. There's no name badge, likely by design. She leads us up the stairs, and River and Theo rush to escort me, which is amusing.

I can walk in heels without snapping my neck.

Well, I can right now. Give it a few months, and I'm sure I'll struggle.

The atmosphere is tense amongst my guys, and it aggravates my wolf.

No matter how nice they seem on paper, I just get the feeling that there's something deeper going on here. My uncomfortableness is likely fuelling my mates, who are, in turn, fuelling me.

But I've never ignored my wolf before—not intentionally, anyway—and I won't now. She's warning me to be careful, and I'm going to listen.

I'd be a fool not to, after the ancestor's warning this afternoon anyway.

CHAPTER 33

"*A*lpha Moore, Luna Moore, Beta Jones and Beta Moore," the receptionist says. "I bring you the Alphas from Rose Moon, their mate, and their entourage."

Holy fuck. That was rude.

"Not even an introduction," Theo says, with a slight frown. He takes a step closer to me, and I'm grateful for it. We're not welcome here, and it shows.

Alpha Moore is around my dad's age in looks, but I think he's at least a decade or two older. His hair is a light brown colour that is only a shade darker than that of his wolf. He's a few inches taller than I am but still shorter than all of my men, but he's as stocky as Rhett and River.

There's an air of dominance around him, and he is pretty

powerful. The bond between him and his wolf is strong and something to be proud of.

He's wearing a suit, but it's clear he's specifically chosen one that he wears often. It smells deeply like him but also shows off how not new it is.

He's not trying to make an impression on us.

"You may take your leave now," Alpha Moore says, and the receptionist nods before turning and leaving the room. The door slams behind her with a sharp thud.

The Luna at his side flinches, and I watch as Alpha Moore rubs soft circles into her back, offering touch and reassurance. The bond between the mates is strong.

She's played the same political game as her husband and is wearing a pale blue dress that clings to her figure, but she's not gone all out to impress us. Her dark brown hair is neatly tied in a bun, and the make-up on her face is tasteful and minimal.

Cameron Moore is a carbon copy of his father, except his eyes are the same pale green as his mum's. His wolf is also more powerful than his father, but he's content to learn the ropes underneath Beta Jones.

Speaking of the Beta, he's very unassuming. I'd have honestly placed him as a Gamma just based on his general demeanour. He's hovering close to the Luna.

Alpha Moore sidesteps around the table, approaching us with the two Betas flanking him. The Alpha reaches out to shake Noah's hand, and my mate looks at it and then looks at him. The Alpha frowns but doesn't let that faze him.

"It's nice to see you in person," Noah says.

"It's nice to see you too, son. Your dad was a good one, and he is missed, Alpha Moore says. I can sense the sincerity in his words, which once more just makes this entire situation weird.

"Thank you for the condolences," Caden says.

"What about my dad?" Rhett asks, almost tauntingly. It's only when I look deeper that I realise what Rhett really wants is acknowledgement of his dad.

Alpha Moore blinks up at Rhett, and it takes a moment before he realises who he is. He laughs joyfully. "Your dad was a very good man, Rhett. I almost didn't recognise you. Mating looks good on you."

"Thanks."

"Your dad is a great man too, Luna Mason," Alpha Moore says. "We've been friends for years."

Not that good of friends, but I don't say anything. The awkwardness returns briefly, but then Alpha Moore brings his mate to his side, and she melts into him. There's genuine love between the two, and it's another reassurance that this is a good pack to be in.

"This is my mate, Caroline, and of course, I'm Peter Moore," Alpha Moore says, pointing to each person as he says it—including himself. "My eldest son, Cameron and my Beta, Jason."

"We've heard a lot about you, Luna Montgomery," Luna Moore says, gently. Her voice is soft, with a musical lilt to it. "And it's really nice to put a face to the name. You're beautiful."

"Thank you," I say, quietly. I'm not sure why I'm feeling a little meek, but both the Beta wolf and the Alpha wolf dismiss me as not a threat. I can actually feel the relief pouring from Beta Jones, which is curious.

In this instance, the dumb blonde attitude may be needed just for a moment to let me step back and assess these people properly.

"I'm Noah Jameson," Noah starts, and I take the moment to step back into Theo, whose hand drops to the small of my back. As Noah introduces us, I let my wolf do what she does best and poke and prod our company.

If she can find any weak spots, that would be helpful. But even just how she analyses connections to figure out who they are to each other is beneficial.

Cameron, the Beta son, is quite angry right now, and all of that frustration is directed towards his dad. Neither my wolf nor I can tell why. His wolf won't admit it to us, and I think that's because he can't understand it himself.

There's some resentment, and I'm wondering if he's maybe ready to take over the role of Alpha, but his dad is holding onto the mantle. Or perhaps it's something deeper than that.

The other Beta, on the other hand, is quite impressed by my men and thinks he and his Alpha are a shoo-in at forming an alliance. His wolf is overly chatty with mine, determined to show that they're good people.

I can't fault that.

The Luna is quite meek and introverted but extremely devoted to her husband. She loves him, and they have a very, very strong mating bond. Their bond shows a lot about them—he's never abused her, or vice versa, they've never strayed from their bonds, and there's never been any real upset between them.

They're committed—a powerful, mated couple. I've never seen a bond this strong. Even my parents had some heavy tension in their bond from me being taken.

"And, of course, this is my mate, Charlotte Montgomery," Noah says, placing a heavy emphasis on my surname.

"It's so lovely to have us all meeting face-to-face," Alpha Moore says. "Can we sit?"

Noah nods, and Theo pulls a seat out for me by Noah's side. River darts to the open seat next to me, annoying Theo, who now needs to slide in there next to him. Elijah's next to Theo, with the other five of my mates on the other side of the table.

Caroline and Jason are on either side of Peter, and Cameron sits reluctantly beside his mum. He's frustrated with her, too, but not as much as he is mad at his dad.

Noah is taking the lead on this conversation, and I'm not sure how they've divvied them up between each other, but I'm grateful that they have. It, once again, shows that we can work well together without me micromanaging them due to a lack of trust.

I trust my mates, and this truly feels like we've overcome the issues that tried to break us apart. Our bonds might've been fractured, and we were all struggling with our mental health, but we're bouncing back so much stronger as a team.

"How would you like to proceed?" Noah asks, being nice enough to put the ball in their court.

"My mate wasn't lying when she said that we've heard quite a bit about your mate," Peter says, eyeing me up but still making sure Noah knows he's talking to him.

"I see. What's your biggest concern?"

And that's how the majority of this meeting goes. We're mostly just correcting the lies the Council has been telling and accepting the ones that are the truth. Theo, Dillon, and Warren are all jotting down some of the information being shared, which will be very helpful in remembering what has been said here and letting us know what needs to be clarified and corrected with the other packs we visit.

Peter and Caroline are very open, but we will definitely visit with some packs who aren't as forthcoming.

They've also been receptive to the issues with the Council and have been willing to hear us out on those. Peter is a big fan of Elder Green, and we also made that very clear.

It's been nice to be in the presence of genuinely nice people, and all of us have relaxed in their company. I'm not sure what set us on edge; maybe it's just the tension the pack is having with the humans, but I'm relaxed now.

"It's been nice chatting with you," I say, once we're all done with this part of the visit. Luna Moore surprises me by hugging me, and I return it as enthusiastically as possible.

"We're going to separate you into some smaller groups so you can do your walk around," Alpha Moore says. "And whilst you are free to chat with anyone you like, enter any of the businesses, the homes of our people are off limits."

"Of course," I rush to reassure him. "We'd never want to invade their privacy that way."

"Once you're finished, just find your way back here, and we'll have another chat," Peter says, his eyes twinkling. "We've not been to your pack since you boys took over, but I've been to both Lupine Valley and Crescent Peak many times."

"Nothing much has changed, has it?" Luna Moore asks. Her words are soft and interested, but her wolf feels a little judgemental.

"Nothing big," Noah says. "Our Luna hasn't been in her position long enough to make a big difference to the structures of our pack."

It's a very diplomatic answer, even if it rubs my wolf the wrong way.

"Then we'll discuss an alliance properly once you're back," Peter says. He summons a few pack members to escort us, and we break down into the smaller groups.

If the inner workings of the pack are as good as the Alpha has made it out to be, I think we're in for a true alliance.

)) ● ((

"*W*hat did you think of the walk around?" Theo asks. It's just me, him and River in the room right now. We're waiting for everyone else to return to the meeting space from their own visits. My group was escorted around the pack by Cameron Moore, and I was very interested in getting to know the prodigal son.

"*I think we should, at the very least, talk silently, even if we have nothing negative to say,*" I say, drawing River and Theo into the same shared mental connection. "*As nice as they seem, there's something going on here, and I want to be careful.*"

"*Do you think they're listening in on us?*" River asks. His eyes dart around the room as if he's looking for cameras or something.

I mean, sure, they might use cameras, but even easier would be for them just not to put us in a soundproofed room. They might have an open window or an air vent connected to another room.

We're supernatural creatures with heightened senses—I highly doubt River can catch them out.

I raise an eyebrow at him. "*Wouldn't we?*"

Theo snorts but nods his agreement. "*What do you mean something is going on here? Everything seemed to be going really well as far as I'm concerned. The pack are happy, if a little unsettled, about the humans, and they really do seem to like their Alpha and Luna. Not a single person had a negative thing to say—in fact, I'd argue they're nearly as devoted to their leaders as our pack is to you.*"

"*High praise,*" River says, and I nod. "*So, how are you feeling about things then, Luna? What's got your feathers all ruffled?*"

"*There's a bit of an issue between father and son,*" I say, and their eyes widen. "*Didn't you notice that I spent that entire visit clinging to him like glue instead of paying more attention to the pack?*" I laugh a little bit at their expressions because, no, they didn't notice.

To those who are listening in on us—if anyone is—this must sound so concerning. The occasional snort or laugh whilst we're discussing the fate of their pack through the mind link.

"*How is there discourse between them?*" River demands. Theo gives him a warning look, but that's all he does.

"*He's very unhappy with his dad. Angry even. His dad has done something wrong, is going to do something, or is in the middle of doing something... I don't know.*" I'm frustrated at myself for not having the answers when I see the uncertain look the two of them share.

They might not say it, but I can guess what they're thinking.

"*The wolf within Cameron is locked down tight, and he's not sharing anything of use with me. He won't betray his dad.*" I sigh. "*But I can feel the level of his anger, and it goes so deep within him. It's terrifying. At first, I thought it was typical resentment, maybe over the role of Alpha.*"

"*But it's more than that?*" Theo asks.

"*It has to be. It's just a hunch. My wolf isn't eating anything more than I am, but something... something is happening.*"

"*Understood.*" Theo squeezes my hand, and it's all the reassurance I need. "*We'll keep an eye out, Charlotte.*"

"*Thanks.*"

In a perfectly timed move, the door to the office opens, and I grin when I see my mates. My three Alphas come into the room, closely followed by Dillon, Wyatt and Warren, and they're all pretty upbeat. I frown, waiting for the familiar feeling of Elijah behind the giant wall of men, but I can't feel him near us at all.

"Where's Elijah?" My question is more of a demand as I frown at them.

"Just gone for a piss," Caden says, and I nod.

"How did you find things?" Theo asks.

"Good," Noah says, and the entire group nods. "We're pretty impressed."

"We found the same," I say. "They had a very impressive greenhouse."

"They do," Caden says. "It's something we should look into doing. We've got the land and the space."

He's excited about it and smiles at me.

"We can definitely look into it," I say, crossing my fingers that we can get to it once we're done with all of this. "How do we get fruit and veg?"

"Just importing it in," Noah says, with a shrug. "Some we get from local packs, and other stuff we get from human places."

"Ah," I murmur, not too interested in that. That's an Alpha's job. I much prefer the peopling side of my job.

"Here, I'm here," Elijah says, and I beam at him.

"Nobody cares," Warren replies, with a smirk. Elijah moves faster than I can see, and I hear a grunt from Warren.

"Aw, are you in pain?" Elijah taunts, and Warren rolls his eyes. Wyatt and Caden are snickering away as Elijah pulls out a seat and sits himself down.

"What's the next step then?" Warren asks, kicking over at River. "It's not fucking funny."

"Course it's not," River says, sounding very solemn. "And we're just waiting for the Alpha and Luna to return."

Another coincidental timing of a knock on the door, we all turn as one to see Miss No Name and No Badge. She nods at us all.

"Hi, I'm just coming to let you know that my Alpha and Luna have been held up but shall be with you in a few minutes. Can I get anyone some tea or coffee?"

Everyone responds in the negative, and she frowns but leaves us be.

"I'm tired and hungry," I moan, resting my head on Theo's shoulder.

"Hungry?" Caden asks, and I nod. Rhett pulls a breakfast biscuit from his pocket, one with chocolate chips in it, and I grin.

"I could blow you right now," I say, reaching over to take it from him. I'm grinning at the immediate protests and rip into my biscuit bar.

They all pull out various snacks, and sure, I'm interested in the small packet of brownie bites that Elijah has, but I'll get those from him once I'm done with this.

The fact that they can fit this many things in their pockets truly amazes me. It also equally pisses me off.

The great pocket patriarchy strikes again. The pregnant Luna has to starve since she only has fake pockets and can't carry around her own snacks.

And now I'm mad at them for flaunting their pockets.

I hate hormones.

"Yeah, me too," Theo mutters, and I laugh, before taking another bite. It soothes the achy hunger inside of me.

These tiny humans are already hungry babies, and we've barely even started this pregnancy yet. Soon enough, I'll be eating all day, every day, and I have no doubt my men will cater to that need.

They'll bring me all the cake, cookies, doughnuts, and brownies I want.

Theo whispers, "Not a chance," in my ear, causing me to laugh.

The door opens, and the Alpha, Luna and their two Betas enter the room. The lack of Gamma and the familiarity between the Luna and Beta leads me to believe that Jason does both roles.

He just doesn't seem to have very good people skills from the little we've interacted. There's a lack of safety regarding him.

"I agree," Theo says.

"So, how did you find the walk around my pack?" Alpha Moore asks, getting straight down to business.

"Very, very, well," Caden says.

"I fully agree," Noah says, backing his twin up. "It went really well. Everyone was singing your praises, and they were all proud of the community that you've all built here. We're impressed with the pack's response."

"You've got thriving businesses and a truly happy pack," Caden adds.

The pride is pouring from the four of them, and I'm not surprised. They've truly earned it.

"The only real grumblings came from the issues you're all having with the humans," Rhett says.

"We understand that. We are in a precarious position with them, but we're hoping that in the next few weeks, we'll come to a bit of a conclusion resolving that," Peter says, with a nod.

"Oh really?" I ask, sitting forward a little so I can see them better. I feel a very large annoyance from Cameron, the eldest Moore child, but his face remains passive.

Unaware of his son's anger, Alpha Moore nods eagerly. "Yeah, we've come to an agreement of sorts, and we're just now starting to finalise the ins and outs of the deal."

"That's great news," I say softly. His mate grins at me, but that just seems to piss Cameron off that much further.

The wolf inside his mind is snapping at the confines he's trapped in, desperate to take over and shift. *For what reason, I have no idea.*

Cameron Moore is very self-controlled and is able to stop the shift from overtaking him.

I gently reach out and soothe the bond between him and his wolf to try and help bond their energy as one. Cameron's eyes dart to me, and I can see a plea in them, but I don't know what he's pleading for.

I've tried to get information out of him, but he won't speak.

There are no signs of abuse or mistreatment.

Cameron and his father share a bond through their wolves, as parent and child, as Beta and Alpha, and as pack members, and if something were amiss, I'd be able to sense it.

You'd be able to see a strain between the two men, but there's not.

I'm not sure if I had these powers before Conri's energy transfer, but now, I can not only see the bonds between people, but I can analyse them so easily. I can tell whether they're friends, whether they're lovers, whether they're enemies or something in between.

The bond between Cameron and Peter is so strong. Cameron

respects his dad more than anything, and he's so glad to be related to Alpha Moore.

But something has changed over the past week—*I think*. Timelines are complicated, especially in a wolf as old as Peter, so it could be closer to a month.

Peter has made a decision that Cameron's not impressed with.

I just need to know what the decision is. But as I poke and prod at the wolf, he stays silent. It's not often I go up against a strong wolf this way, who doesn't share with me just because I'm asking.

I don't want to force him just for the sake of a disagreement between family. I could put pressure on and make him talk... but it would damage what is going to be a good relationship between our pack and theirs.

Cameron blinks and moves his head away, severing the connection we were sharing.

"Now we've still got to finish our visits," Noah says, surprising me since I wasn't fully listening. "But you can rest assured that once we're back on pack lands, we will go through, and we would like to formalise an alliance with you. If you are wanting to be a bit provocative, you can draft up your own agreement, and we can make changes to it. If not, we'll send you one out within a couple of weeks of us being home."

"How long will that be?" Luna Moore asks softly.

"At this stage, we're looking at being around twelve weeks," Noah says, looking at all of us. "Three months."

More like four by the time we've dealt with King Lobo and his followers, but it's probably best not to advertise that fully.

There are a few more little questions, but for the most part, we're all happy and can wrap this up.

I'm exhausted and hungry, and despite being productive, it's also been *long*. We've been vigilant on the roads—my mates more so than me—and it'll be nice to be able to relax at the hotel, even if we are going to be around the humans that oppose this pack.

I doubt we'll spend as long with other packs as we have here, but since this one turned out so good, it just made sense.

"Any food recommendations in the human town?" Rhett asks, and Wyatt elbows him.

"Apologies, Alpha, Luna, we didn't mean to make light of your troubles with the humans," Wyatt says, and Alpha Moore's booming laugh startles me.

"Nonsense. Be wary in town, but as long as you're not seen coming from here, you should be fine," he says. "There's a local pizza chain close to the hotel, which we've visited a few times. It's quite good."

"Thank you," Caden says, and I rub my stomach thinking about pizza.

"I'll escort them out of town," Cameron says, ignoring the shocked look from Jason. "It'll save you having to bring anyone in from training."

"Excellent initiative, son," Peter says.

After another round of handshakes, we're finally permitted to leave. We traipse down to the car, and I think all of my men can feel the sombre air surrounding Cameron, so not a single one of them outwardly complains about the car.

I can feel the distaste from Warren and the boredom from Rhett's wolf, but I ignore it.

He leads us through the town, coming the same way we came, and I thought he would pull over once we exited the pack lands so he could turn around.

But he doesn't.

Instead, Cameron comes to a harsh stop a couple of metres away from the barriers, cutting us off from advancing further. He gets out of the car and stands leaning against it.

"Stay in the car," Rhett says, seriously, and I nod. He gives Theo a silent instruction before jumping out.

Alone.

My heart races, and I'm torn between begging one of my other men to go with him and hopping out of the car and stopping Cameron from hurting Rhett myself.

But the two exchange words and the atmosphere is not too uncomfortable. Rhett frowns before beckoning for me.

"I'm not sure about this," I say, hesitantly.

"You'll be fine. Rhett will keep you safe," Theo says, gently. I look over at my Guardian, peering into his brown eyes, and he gives me a nod.

"I never doubted Rhett," I say, teasingly. "But I'm glad he got your stamp of approval."

Theo rolls his eyes, but I see how his lips quirk up in his slight smile.

I get out of the car, and I walk over to where Rhett and Cameron are standing. There is an underlying tension, but I don't sense anything malicious from Cameron.

Why is he being so weird?

I take Rhett's outstretched hand and let him pull me closer to him.

"Beta Moore would like to have a few words with you that he apparently can't share with me," Rhett says, lowly. My mate's wolf is close to the surface, his chest vibrating lowly with small growls.

"What can I do for you?" I ask.

Cameron sighs, shaking his head. He's agitated but not at me. At himself, at his dad, at everything. "Be careful. Please."

I frown, and Rhett's hold on me tightens. "What do you mean by that?"

"I know that things are happening," he says, and it's almost as if the words are struggling to come out of his mouth. They're gritted through his teeth, and his body shudders.

I take an unconscious step back, and Rhett wraps himself around me that much further, offering me both physical and emotional support through the bond. Being in his arms is the only thing that keeps me comforted because I'm terrified.

Cameron's clearly got some shit going on, but everything has been so... *good* here. Has it all been a lie?

"This is scary," I say along the bond to Rhett.

"I know, but we can take him. Easily. Do not hold back with your

power if you need to defend yourself," Rhett warns. I nod against his chest. I didn't need the reminder, but I am grateful for it.

Cameron sighs. "I can't tell you everything I want to tell you for the same reason I also can't tell you. Soon enough, it'll come to light, and I'll take the penance. But for now, please, please be careful."

Rhett lets out a low growl. "Are you threatening her?"

"No," Cameron gasps, shaking his head.

"Are you aware of a threat to her?" Rhett snarls, and Cameron stays silent. The man can't answer; his wolf is locked down from opening up.

Weird.

"What's your message?" I ask him. "Ignore Rhett. He's a big baby."

"Yeah, a big baby who could rip my head off," Cameron mutters under his breath. There's a small amount of amusement from Rhett's side of the bond, and my wolf is prancing around as if Rhett's dominance is her source of pride.

"Talk, Cameron."

"Be careful. Don't leave your mate's side. Not until you're far, far away from my pack," he says. I frown once more, opening my mouth to ask something else, but he shakes his head and steps back. "I've said all I can. It's nice to meet you, Luna Montgomery, Alpha Simmons."

Then he turns and heads into his car, driving away without a second look back.

"That was weird."

"Yes, it was," Rhett says, pensively. "I've not felt a single hostile thing from them this entire time. But this was a warning."

The two of us are sombre as we get into the car, and Rhett explains to the rest of the group what Cameron has said. But we're all convinced that Cameron has given us a warning that something is about to go down.

Add in the big warning I got earlier from the Guardian of All, and I'm fucking terrified.

Something big is going to happen.

And deep down, I know I'm not prepared for it.

CHAPTER 34

"*L*ottie!" a voice roars, and I freeze when I realise it's coming from Dillon. A month ago, we went through this exact same thing—him yelling for me, me panicking, and it ended in us being attacked.

"Deep breath, princess," Warren soothes, brushing his hand across my shoulder. I look over at him, and he smiles. We're in my bed, and he presses a soft kiss on my shoulder. "We're not under attack. Would I really be wearing this if we were?"

He's completely naked, displaying his beautiful body for my perusal. There's a very pretty cock ring around the base of his dick, and the vibrations are very arousing. He's leaking pre-cum, and I'm desperate to lower my head and taste him.

"No, we're not," Dillon says, stepping into the room with a breathy smile. His glasses are askew, and his hair is a little messy. I frown, not truly sure why. "Room for a third?"

As I lift the blankets, my eyes adjust to the new lighting, and I see the panic in Dillon's eyes.

"What's going on?" I croak.

"We're under attack," Dillon says, and my wolf howls. She instantly connects to our mates and identifies the areas where they're struggling. Caden and Wyatt have minor wounds, but the rest are mostly okay. They're furious but so fucking focused.

"We need... I fucking hate to admit it, but we need you," Dillon says. "We're going to have to fight our way out, protect the humans and contain the scene to try and protect the secret of our world."

"Fuck," I whisper, my brain immediately jumping into overdrive. I'm luckily wearing a pair of pyjamas—a pale pink vest top with shorts—and I get out of bed and grab my trainers and some socks.

My hair is down, but I throw it into a high ponytail as Dillon's impatience increases.

"Where is everyone?" I demand.

"Theo is at the door waiting for us and will remain by your side. I'm grabbing you and will join Elijah and River in handling the humans. We're doing our best to get everyone huddled in one place so that we can protect them the best we can. It's not going well." He shakes his head. "Everyone else is fighting back to stop them from getting to us."

"Who? What? How?" My mind starts to race, and my wolf howls in frustration.

Have I really been in here asleep whilst they're out there fighting for their fucking lives?

Why the fuck didn't they wake us up?

My wolf is completely confused. She doesn't understand how she was caught so unaware, either. Did Theo intervene? Did he adjust our bodies to protect us? That would surely lie in his realm of power, but if not... how the fuck did this go down?

How can we have all this power and miss the fact that we're in a fight *for our lives*?

Of course, my mates aren't going to wake me up if they can help it, because if I'm here, safe, and asleep, why would they disturb me?

Bloody idiots.

I love them so fucking much, but I wish they weren't this bloody idiotic when it comes to my safety.

"There's no time for this, baby," Dillon says. He grabs my hand, tugs me into him, and presses his lips against mine. His kiss sends tingles down my spine, reigniting the passion in my wolf that she needs to help me get through this fight today. The kiss is deep and passionate.

It's very amusing to me how we don't have time to discuss the ins and outs of the danger we're in, but we do have time to kiss.

"We're going to join Theo downstairs, and you will do whatever he says, so you make it out of this. Do you understand me? Don't fucking dare even *dream* of not coming back to me, Lottie. I refuse to live a life you are not in. Understood?"

"Understood."

He all but drags me down the stairs, not even pausing as we enter the lobby. I'm unsurprised that Theo is standing at the doorway, keeping an eye on what's going on outside.

He's wearing the same clothes as he was when we went for pizza this evening, and he's untouched. His hair might be a bit messier, likely from his hands running through it, but otherwise, he's unharmed and put together.

Perfect. That soothes a tiny part of my soul.

I can feel the intensity of my Guardian; there's a power emanating around him like a shield as he asses the area and keeps us safe.

The design of this building isn't very good, because I can't see anything happening outside. The door Theo's at has a large window, but the rest of the building is all closed off.

It's not very good.

Although, I suppose it is because it's also keeping us hidden from view.

What I can do, though, is feel the energy of my mates, and it is *not* good. Things have changed slightly in the few minutes it's taken me to come downstairs, and Rhett is hurt, too. I send some energy his way, healing his wound.

"Do not do that again if you can help it," Theo says, and I jump in surprise. His tone is cold and hard, and I know that's just because he's in focus mode, but it's not nice to hear. "We're all going to sustain injuries, but we need your power for other things if it can be helped. Our priority here, Charlotte, is keeping *you* alive."

"I—"

"Am pregnant and in need of surviving for our children," Theo continues, finishing my statement for me, and I give a slow nod.

"Thank you, love, but do not worry about me," Rhett says, along the bond. He doesn't wait for an answer, which upsets me more than it should. They're busy fighting for their lives—they don't have the time to talk.

Every single one of my men is focused on what they're doing. Their wolves, or vampires, are determined as they channel themselves in a formidable way. I do not envy the men they come across.

Even if they're a little scared underneath it all.

The worst part is that I can feel more than just my men. There are a few wolves in the area, bad ones, and they're riddled with anger. It hurts to even brush against their wolves.

King Lobo has adjusted what happened last time, it seems, and to compensate, he's brought in a shit tonne of vampires instead. It might've just been a guess on his behalf, but I can't connect with vampires the way I can the wolves, so there will be no mass subduing in that regard.

Or... *can I?*

"Do you want me to try and force everyone to submit?" I ask, but both Dillon and Theo shake their heads.

"As powerful as you are, this is a lot of people, and we can't risk you doing it and losing power, putting yourself and us at greater risks," Theo says, and I nod slowly. If there are that many people here to attack us... how the fuck are my men still alive? How are they barely even injured?

I don't want to voice that out loud, and Theo doesn't seem to be reading my thoughts. But if that's the case, if there are too many vampires here for me to hold them all under my power... how are we going to make it through this?

Vampires are faster than us wolves and could take us out faster than we can even track them.

What the fuck are we going to do?

"The plan is for you and me to work together in subduing as many wolves as possible," Theo says, and I nod. "They will be our in for information once this is over. For the vampires, we need to disarm them as fast as we can because you're right—they are faster than us."

"But you're stronger," Dillon says, and I nod.

"My plan is to stick to you like glue and keep you from getting hurt," Theo continues. "So, behave."

"Lovely. I do really like being alive," I say, nodding. Theo doesn't react to my quip, but Dillon flinches, turns and looks away. I tone down the sarcasm, knowing how scared we all are. "Can you feel the lack of enemy wolves in the area?"

"Yes." His jaw clenches. "Your thoughts are correct, little wolf. They didn't bring many wolves because they knew you'd be here tonight."

"And," I say, shaking my head. "That means we've got a mole somewhere in our camp." Dillon's nostrils flare as his wolf rages inside of him, but Theo just gives one solemn nod. "Somebody has grassed us up for being here. We made it very clear that we were leaving our pack, but we did not share where we were going with anyone until the day of, and no matter how powerful King Lobo is, this is an organised attack. We didn't feel that presence, or at least I didn't, and we are in the middle of a human town.

"He wouldn't just randomly send his wolves up here on the off chance, especially when the issues between Alpha Moore and the humans here are so clearly publicised. Which means it has to be someone from Alpha Moore's pack. We've not come across anyone else on our way. Why would they betray us? What is in it for them?

Alpha Moore is a good Alpha; his pack all seemed lovely and genuine. I sensed no maliciousness *at all*—"

"Breathe, baby," Dillon says, cutting me off. "We need to focus on the attack right now. We've already been standing here a few minutes longer than I'm comfortable with."

"Okay." I nod, roll my shoulders, and do my best to clear my mind. My wolf pushes forward, merging with me, making things much easier.

"So we're going to be tracking each wolf down," Theo says. "And I need you to promise me—"

"I might not be able to incapacitate a vampire like I can a wolf, but I am still more than powerful enough to put one down on its ass for you," I say, giving him a stern look.

"Why don't you just completely drain the life out of a vampire? Freya can do it," Dillon says. He seems to regret it for a moment because two sets of eyes are looking at him like he's stupid.

"Because Freya *is a vampire*," I hiss. Dillon's eyes widen, and he zips his lips.

I know it's just the high stakes of this situation that has him saying things this dumb.

Or at least, I pray it is.

"Okay, we need to shift," I say, and Theo nods. "But I want it put on the record that I am frustrated you've let me sleep whilst everyone else is out fighting for their lives."

"It wasn't about letting you sleep, Lottie. It was about assessing our plan of attack and ensuring we're prepared to handle this situation whilst keeping you safe. Waking you up immediately would've been the wrong thing to do." I narrow my eyes, but he's unrelenting. "Try and argue that point." He waits a second, and he nods when I don't say anything. "We had only dispersed fifteen minutes ago, and as soon as we organised ourselves, we woke you up."

"The longest delay has been this moment here," Dillon adds, gesturing to the three of us.

Well, that puts it into perspective.

"Understood," I say, losing some of the fight. "We can talk about it properly after all this shit."

I shift into my wolf, and seconds later, Theo's identical one is opposite me. Neither of our wolves engages the way they usually do, both of them understanding the severity of the situation that we're in.

We don't have time to flirt with the other part of our souls when we need to fight to protect the entire mating circle.

Dillon opens the door for us since we're in wolf forms and can't do it, and I freeze as I take in the sounds and the atmosphere. Inside the hotel, we were cut off from the true danger of it all, but now? This is terrifying.

The presence of fear, confusion, and despair is so thick in the air that it's almost tangible. This isn't just a simple battle between two groups—it's a war on life itself. The smell of blood and death, which permeates the atmosphere,—even though, by Theo's estimations, it's only been going on for about twenty-five minutes,—makes me feel queasy.

I'm not going to get out of this without partaking in the bloodshed, am I?

Screams and howls fill the air from every direction, and my heart hurts for all those entangled in this chaos. I think of the innocent humans who should never have been exposed to this supernatural world, the attacking vampires and wolves meeting their end, and my mates who should never have been in such danger.

My wolf growls low in her throat as she takes in the carnage around us. But even though I feel righteous anger at the sight before me, there's also an overwhelming sense of sadness at all that is going to be lost here tonight, all because a madman thinks he's entitled to power he'd just do more harm with.

Dillon follows behind us, closing the hotel door and doing his best to seal it. I have no idea why since there's nothing of true importance inside, but he shifts into his wolf, kisses my snout, and then charges off before I can even ask him.

"I'm going to guess that we're going to be the targets of these attacks," Theo says across the mind link.

I nod, sniffing the air. I can feel a vampire nearby, and it takes my wolf less than a second to locate it. I frown when I feel it slowly advancing towards us.

He has advanced speed, so why the fuck isn't he using it?

"Apparently, they haven't been doing that for the most part," Theo says. *"When around one of us, they're slow and patient. Around the humans, they're vicious as they attack them."*

"So, what? They're going to pick the humans off as we pick them off? What do the humans have to do with any of this?" I ask, but I don't get a response.

"Gary," a man roars, his voice both panicked and excited.

My wolf cocks her head, darting her eyes over to the direction of that sound. I squint, edging a little forward, and spot a male vampire a few metres away in the trees.

He's around forty in appearance, but his power level is very weak —*practically nothing*—and I can't determine his actual age correctly because of that. His look says one thing, but the drained power confines me.

I refuse to waste my own power on him, so when Theo tells me to do it, I charge forward and dive on top of him. I knock him to the ground, and he's so startled he doesn't even bother to fight back. I reach up and slash his throat, blood oozing out as the life fades from him.

I freeze as I see him dying, *dying at my paws.* He's gone. This wasn't even a long death or drawn out... he's just dead.

He didn't fight back; he didn't try and plead or beg... *I'm a murderer.*

"There's no time to freak out," Theo says, and I growl low in my throat. *"We're not alone, Lottie."*

And my wolf lifts her head, scenting the air. Two more vampires zoom over to us and come to a stop, maybe fifteen metres away from where I'm currently sitting on top of their dead... *colleague.*

They're marginally more powerful, but they're still as drained as he is. I don't understand. Where is their power? Why are they this weak?

"This doesn't feel right," Theo says, but I can't react to him.

The two vampires standing before us come into focus; the first is a tall, imposing figure with a balding head and a thick beard. He's wearing an old tracksuit that looks like it's seen better days, but his black eyes are steady and determined.

The other is much smaller in stature, with short dark hair and an olive complexion. His clothes are much cleaner than his companion's, but he still carries the same air of determination around him as he stares at us with unblinking eyes.

Determination for what, though?

They don't charge us. Instead, they stand there, letting their presence speak for itself. They cock their heads, crack their knuckles, and even bare their teeth.

But they don't attack.

My wolf seems to be pleading with me to trust her. So, I do. I retreat just that tiny bit more, pushing away my conscience and my feelings of guilt. My wolf is right. Theo is right.

This is the time to fight.

I can't cry over the lives ended.

I get off the man I killed at Theo's insistence and sit down on my ass, watching the men before me. My tail wags and my hackles are raised. The energy in the air electrifies, and I swear I can see the breath they just let out.

"On my bark, I want you to force them both to submit," Theo says, and I'm very careful not to react and let on that we're planning. I'm sure they're doing the same thing—Theo and I just need to be faster. *"Force them as much as you can so that they can't even speak without your permission."*

Theo's bark is sharp and commanding, and I act on instinct as the vampires charge us. My power flies out, forcing them from their mid-air launch to drop to the ground.

The bald one whimpers softly, but I don't let up. My wolf is howling inside me, urging me to go in for the kill—but I resist her demands. I keep my power steady and strong so neither can move a muscle without my permission, just like Theo demanded.

My Guardian trots forward and snarls as he sniffs them deeply. I'm not sure what he's getting from them, but it agitates his wolf, and even when I try to soothe him, it doesn't work.

It's unfair to put them under this much because it hurts when they're as weak as they are.

Then again, it's not fair of them to attack me, my men and a town full of humans. Both of them have indulged in the taste of human blood, their clothes covered in it, meaning they've taken lives.

They're murderers.

Killing those weaker than them just because they can.

Isn't that what I just did?

I advance towards them, falling in line with Theo, and keep a tight hold on them. They're not escaping from me.

I'm surprised when Theo shifts back into his human form, but my confusion only deepens when he pulls some... *zip ties out* of his pocket.

"*Zip ties?*" I ask. My voice isn't as sceptical as it should be across our mind link, but I am very confused.

"These are not just zip ties," he says. "They're reinforced specifically to hold a vampire in place. They can't break it with their strength."

Don't get me wrong, I absolutely don't believe this in the slightest. Supernatural zip ties? What next? Do we have supernatural fucking Sellotape?

Then again, Theo knows far more about this than I do, and I know he'll not endanger me in any way. As he ties them up, they don't even attempt to fight my hold to fight against Theo.

It makes things easier, but their lack of fight just feels *wrong*. He puts something over their mouths to stop them talking—duct tape, it seems, and not supernatural Sellotape—but that doesn't fix our issues, really.

Their vampires are unwilling to talk, and I can't force them, even with how hard I'm pressing. They're so weak it should be easy to make them speak, but *because* they're so weak, they don't have the energy to do anything but stay alive.

"*They're not going to talk,*" I say, and Theo frowns. I share my findings with him, and his frown deepens. I try to resist purring as he runs his fingers through my fur.

"*It seems like they're here for something other than us,*" Theo says, and I let out a yip of agreement. "*How do your bonds feel?*"

"*They're all fighting, Theo. None of the others seem to be having it as easy as we are,*" I reply, and he sighs. "*Should we join them, or...?*"

"We've got a plan. We're to stay on the edges and locate the wolves. I think we give it a bit longer, but if things don't change, we try and retreat."

"*Sounds good.*"

But I can't shake the feeling that something deeper is happening here.

"*We're going to have to move. Nothing is stopping them from using their mind-link.*"

"Good point." He shifts back into his wolf and gestures for us to go left. I follow after him, and we leave the two men laid out on the floor, tied up so they can't escape.

Apparently.

But when I turn around to check on them, just before they're out of view... I don't detect any signs of life.

They smell dead.

Their hearts have stopped.

And I definitely didn't do that.

CHAPTER 35

"What's wrong?" Theo asks, noticing I've stopped.

"They're... They're dead."

He trots back over and inhales the air before fear fills his side of the bond. *"Vampires!"* He growls deeply and shakes his head. *"We need to run, Charlotte. Don't look back."*

I take his warning to heart and let my wolf guide me through the town as we sprint away.

The atmosphere is heavy as we charge through the trees, and I hear the manic laughter of the men chasing us. Four of them, I think, herding us away from the two dead men. We don't stop running, being led further and further astray as I bark and snarl at them. Theo's steps don't falter as he sticks close to me.

Dead bodies—humans and vampires alike—litter the ground, the grass soaked with so much blood that my paws and even my legs are coated with it as we run, making me feel disgusting.

These are the horrors of our world—the world I've only just learnt about, and it's so much scarier than the human one.

At least in the human world, we know people are monsters, but for the most part, they hide it.

Here? The monsters are always out to play, and they don't try to excuse that.

Theo is determined to get us away from the vampires, but we both know that they're taunting us. They could easily overtake us.

This time—we won't be able to escape without a fight. While I'm ready to take them on with bared teeth and claws, my heart is pounding against my chest as we meet face-to-face with our enemy.

Their screams have become less frequent, but I can feel so much death in the air. So many souls leaving this plane, so many being harmed. My men's snarls and howls seem louder than anything else, or maybe I'm just tuned in to them. They're all a decent ways away from me, but they're mostly okay.

The greenery of the trees might be beautiful, but what lurks beneath them is nothing short of death and destruction. *I just hope Theo and I don't join the nameless masses.*

"They're circling us," Theo warns, and I nearly trip myself up. *"Keep running. There's a clearing ahead; I think they're taking us there. I can feel another eight men in the trees coming to us."*

"What... Theo, what do we do?" I ask. I hope my voice is calm inside his head, but inwardly, I'm screaming in panic. My wolf is continuing to charge forward, readying herself.

But I'm too scared. My legs are shaking, my mind whirring in indecision. Twelve vampires, two wolves.

Who the fuck is going to come out of this alive?

I'm scared, Theo, I'm so fucking scared.

"The moment we stop, you force them to submit, and you leave the rest to me," he says. I can do that. I can do it.

As we come to the clearing, we're surrounded just as Theo predicted. We huddle together, and he tries to cover me, but he can't

387

protect me like he wants to when we're surrounded from every angle.

I can't see their faces properly in the shadows, but their presence is unmistakable—twelve men in the forefront, another six in the background.

Eighteen men is not a hard amount to subdue. I let my power storm out, taking each of them under its thrall, and the way they drop to the ground, baring their throats, is entirely too thrilling.

I can understand why King Lobo wants this kind of power, but it is because of that understanding that I know *why* he can't. I have the ability to warp the mind and take any wolf under my thrall, taking away their freewill, as I make them *my* vessels.

But where he seeks to harm our kind, I strive to nurture them into being their true selves. We shouldn't fear power; we should encourage it to thrive. We should protect those who can't protect themselves and make our community all the stronger for it.

King Lobo is everything I never want to be.

"And you never will be. Killing these men is protecting the humans that reside here. You're protecting our secret and stopping our kind from being hunted and harmed. You are nothing *like him,"* Theo says, and his words are so compelling that I believe it. *"Now, close your eyes."*

I do as he says, staying silent as he ties the men up one by one.

But as soon as I catch the scent of his blood, my eyes snap open, and without my conscious control, a surge of my power releases, directed entirely at Theo. He absorbs the burst of energy, his eyes glowing bright gold for a moment before returning to their normal black colour.

He charges through the crowd, no longer just subduing the vampires. Theo's on a mission, and it's one that ends in the slaughter of our enemies.

Some might argue this is the coward's way out—one man did—but this is the easiest way to ensure we return home to our people.

Theo's rampage is a blur; his movements are so swift that I can hardly keep up with him. The sound of his victims' screams is like music to my ears, an affirmation that we are the superior beings in this world. King Lobo's followers didn't stand a chance against us, not with my power and Theo's brute strength.

Not when he did something to them to make them so weak.

The smell of the blood is nauseating, and seeing it clinging all over the pure whiteness of my mate's fur kills me. My body shifts without permission, and I stand on two legs instead of four.

The shift is too quick, and my head is spinning as I hunch over, vomiting up the contents of my stomach. It's fucking disgusting, and I'm glad they're all dead so they don't see me throw up.

I could imagine the headlines now.

Weak Luna can't even keep the contents of her stomach under control— how can she lead a pack?

Theo rushes to my side, not even pausing in steps as he shifts from wolf to human. The change was so gracefully achieved I'm in awe of him. His energy boosts me, healing the sickness and removing the headache and the blister forming on my ankle.

He's perfect. Or at least, he would be if he had a mint or a toothbrush in his pocket.

"Never satisfied, are you?" he teases. I laugh and shrug. "You did amazing there, Lottie. I am so proud of you, so in awe at your strength."

"Did you not just see me throwing up?" I whisper, trying to ignore the blood coating him *and* me. "Did you not—"

Theo places his lips to mine, his tongue forcing its way into my mouth as he presses our bodies together. I whimper, reaching up to run my hands through his hair, and he moans as I tug slightly too hard.

There's a loud howl in the distance coming from Wyatt, and I immediately jump back from Theo, shaking my head as he reaches for me again.

"We can't do this now. We do not have time," I say, and when he opens his mouth to protest, I give him a dirty look. "The rest of my mates are fighting for their lives in protection of us and the humans." My eyes widen. "Fuck, has anyone reached out to Alpha Moore? How could I not think of that until now?"

"Alpha Moore was unavailable. We don't have the people to spare to go and help them, so we just need to hope that he's keeping his own," Theo says, and I nod slowly.

It doesn't sit right with me, but we can do nothing right this second. The moment we're done with our lot, though, we'll help him.

There's another howl, this one close by, and I look at Theo, who nods. Without a word, we shift into our wolves and slowly and quietly advance.

The two of us race through the forest, weaving our bodies through the branches and leaping over long-forgotten corpses. The howl we heard was from a wolf, but there isn't one close to us now— neither one of my mates nor one of the wolves attacking us.

Vampires linger in the shadows, some sending us looks of amusement while others just stare. None of them move to come near us, though, and I'm not entirely sure why.

Theo and I don't stop and examine it and instead remain on our guard. My power is just under the surface, ready to be unleashed on anyone who even blinks wrong, but they're not acting like the earlier group who were herding us somewhere. These... these ones are running *away* from us.

Maybe they know what we did to their friends, or perhaps it's something deeper. Whatever it is, I'm thankful for it as we continue through the woods with nobody trying to hurt us.

But the howl sounds again, and I track the source much easier this time. My wolf locks in on the sound and identifies his inner wolf. I charge in that direction, and Theo instantly follows me.

"Over here," I whisper across the mind-link. Theo nods, and we move, hiding underneath the trees before darting into a nearby bush.

Obviously, they'll feel us, but it gives us a good vantage point to avoid hurting him. We watch the lone wolf slowly looking around the area before howling again.

Whilst watching him, I let my senses expand to see if I can locate someone, anyone, who can explain his behaviour.

"There's something more going on here than a simple attack," I say, as we continue watching the wolf before us. *"I don't understand it. They're*

not just here to attack and kill us. We've had at least four attempts since our attack earlier, and they could've hurt us at the very least."

Theo lets out a low growl, and I bare my teeth at him silently.

"*Do not give away our position,*" I say. His wolf gives a firm nod, and I can sense his frustration. I just don't know what he wants me to do about it. "*I don't understand why they're not dealing the killing blow. Why are they not using their speed or trying to, actually, hurt us?*"

"*I don't know, Charlotte,*" Theo says, and now I'm the one getting frustrated. He sounds like he's patronising me. I don't expect him to *know* the answer, but would it kill him to theorise with me?

A plot is underway, and if I know anything about King Lobo like I think I do, then I know that we're the targets here, and it won't be good.

But then realisation hits, and my wolf whines quietly. Theo's head snaps my way, and his wolf steps forward, giving me soft licks.

"*How sure are we that this is King Lobo?*" I demand.

"*I have no idea,*" Theo says, and I know if we were in human form, he'd be giving me some weird looks right now. "*That's what we presumed because who else has cause to attack us?*"

"What if they're not here attacking us?" I ask. His confusion increases, as does his impatience."*Alpha Moore said that in a few weeks time, the humans will be dealt with.*"

"*Yes, through negotiations,*" he argues, shaking his head.

"*Yeah, but he never said he was negotiating with them,*" I point out, and Theo pauses, cocking his head. *Yes!* "*Come on, Theo, you've seen these men. You know what they're like. Do you really think they care about how they go about their means as long as they still get what they want?*

"*This is a man who is desperate to protect his people—his pack, his family. Do you really think he's sitting here, seeing the damage they're doing, and think his main concern is, 'Oh, how do I do this legally'? Of course not!*

"*We know what the Council are like, and I highly doubt they've done anything to help these people. They need support, but the Council don't give a fuck about that. Sure, he's working with Councilman Green, but he's still limited by the rest of the Council and what they're willing to provide.*

"*I honestly think this is a set-up that Alpha Moore has arranged. Or, at the very least, he might've thought he was doing something above board, and this was their solution. I don't know the technicalities—*"

"You don't seem to know anything," Theo says, and it's like ice water is thrown down my back. "*These are some interesting theories, but they're just that, Charlotte—theories. This isn't the time.*"

I let out a snarl and check to see if the wolf in the clearing heard, but he's just laid out on the floor, miserable and in pain—not physical pain, as far as I can detect.

"*Trust me, Theo, please,*" I say, tugging on our bond, pleading with him deeper than just his logical mind. "*I've got a feeling that this is how it's gone down, and if that's the case, it explains so much.*"

"*It doesn't explain why they attacked us in the first place.*"

"*But did they?*" I counter, because I had been thinking of this too. "*They herded us to a clearing, and we have no idea what they were going to do. They only fought back after we made the first move.*"

He lets out a harrumph, and I roll my eyes.

Sure, there are lots of unanswered questions with my theory. I don't know who Alpha Moore has been negotiating with, but I do think that this attack is involved with him—even if they're not entirely acting on his orders.

What if Theo believes that we are so significant that we *must* be the primary target? In reality, it feels like we're just collateral damage, stuck in the crossfire.

"Do you really think that it is this coincidental? In your theory, do you really think that we're just here at the *wrong* time?" *Theo asks, and I shake my head.*

"*I don't know. I don't have it all worked out,*" I say, shaking my head. "*But we no longer have time to deliberate it because another wolf is coming.*"

Theo cocks his head, looking around the clearing for it, and I gesture towards it. As the light grey wolf enters our line of sight, I get a phantom pain in my chest, and I cringe. One of my mates—Wyatt—is hurt.

It's not painful enough that he's dying, but it still pisses me off that one of the people here thinks they're worthy enough to touch my mate.

My hackles rise as the grey wolf approaches the sad tan one that we're watching, and before I can even react, the grey one pounces. The wolf slashes the chest of our wolf, and my power flares out before I consciously do it.

"Do not *heal this wolf,"* Theo snarls as the two of us charge over to the scene. The tan wolf shifts into a dark-haired young man. He's pale, covered in old blood, and very thin.

Fuck.

"Who the fuck are you?" Theo roars, at the grey wolf.

I keep my hold on him but require him to shift back into human form. I don't allow him much freedom, but I do permit him to talk so Theo can learn what he needs to.

I crouch down next to the injured man.

"Take a deep breath," I soothe, placing my hand on his. "I can't heal you just yet—"

"Don't," the man chokes out. "Traitor."

"I'm not—"

"Me!" he hisses, through his teeth. "I'm the traitor."

"You're not a traitor towards me," I say.

"You need to be wary, Luna," he says, before moaning in pain. "Alpha—" He starts to cough up blood, and I panic, looking over at Theo. He shakes his head, warning me again to not heal him. "I can't. Get it from my wolf—I know you can."

I frown because I was already doing that exact thing. I look at Theo, who has just tied up the secondary wolf. His mouth has been sealed, and Theo's currently tying the zip ties around his legs—his hands have already been done.

The dying man's wolf is very eager to chat, and I find out the man is called Bobby and is the youngest child of four. *As if that latter part is helpful.*

"Okay, then, Bobby," I say, softly, trying my best to keep pressure on his stomach. "According to your wolf, you've betrayed yourself, your wolf and the values you once swore to uphold."

"I-I-I belong to no pa-a-ack," he stutters.

"No, that's very true." I motion to Theo to help, which he reluctantly does. Theo's emitting a very dark aura right now, his thoughts purely focusing on my protection. I know for a fact that if this man even blinks wrong, Theo isn't going to hesitate before tearing him apart.

"I need to know why you're here, Bobby," I say, and whilst the man can't answer, his overly eager wolf does. The wolf knows he's meeting his end and is desperate to try and right as many wrongs as he can—as many wrongs as his human *caused*.

I add a little bit more power to help the wolf. I just need to be careful not to overload him since he's dying, and I can't incapacitate him entirely because I need his wolf to be able to talk and tell me the truth.

That does the trick.

"They're not here for us," I say, shaking my head. Theo's snarl sends shivers down my spine. "Well, no, they are..." I trail off, not sure I've got the true story. My wolf keeps prodding, and then I gasp as panic fills me. Theo lets go of the man's wound, not bothering to press on it, as he races over to my side.

"What is it?"

"They're not here for us. They're here to slaughter the humans and frame us for it," I whisper. Bobby's eyes flutter closed, the blood loss too extreme. "That's why they're all so weak—they're not here to survive, they're all sacrifices. Fucking hell. We've fallen right into their trap."

"Fuck," Theo roars, jumping to his feet. "Fucking hell." He kicks out, releasing a wave of power that my wolf and I instantly absorb and take as our own. As he releases his rage, my wolf and I do our best to contain it. If this is true—and I genuinely think it is—we cannot let more damage be caused. If we're lucky, we've figured it out just in time.

I jump as Theo's hand slams into a tree, the sound echoing across the mostly silent area.

"There's good news here, Theo," I say, and he stops what he's doing. His shoulders are heaving with his breathlessness, and he's carrying a heavy weight upon him. "We know now, for certain, that this attack did come from King Lobo. I'm not going to lie, I was worried that it was the Council who did this or even another random enemy."

"That would be our luck," he drawls. He turns to face me, raising a bushy eyebrow. "And the bad news?"

"Are you sure that's what this is?" Theo asks, looking at me and the dying man on the floor.

"Yes," I say confidently. "His wolf can't lie to me. His wolf doesn't *want* to lie to me."

"Okay." He pinches the bridge of his nose, and I let him have this moment to compose himself. As he allows his brain to work out our plan of attack, I start tending to Bobby. It's too late, really; the man is practically dead.

It would be kinder to snap—I gasp when there's a loud snapping sound. Theo doesn't even seem remorseful.

"You're right, it was kinder. Now, going forward, we're going to have to incapacitate the men rather than killing any. We need to subdue them, and the ones that fight back still need to be kept alive. They're fighting for their lives—we're fighting for our future," he says, and I nod. "We're going to have to get the humans properly locked up and do some very fast damage control."

"Damage control?"

"Once we're all together, we'll get Alaric here," Theo says. "He's the only one we can truly trust for something of this scale. He knows the type of people we are—the type of person *you* are. He'll know the truth."

"And what if these vampires are his? What if they're still loyal to him?" Cain was, after all.

"I don't think they would be his much longer if that turns out to be the case," Theo says. He crouches next to the tied-up wolf and checks the bindings.

They honestly look quite fun, and I'm very intrigued. They're definitely something we can bring out to play with in the bedroom.

"Really?" Theo asks, giving me an amused grin.

I laugh. "You should just be grateful I'm thinking of the future. Normally, I'm too much of a realist to believe we will be around to have these sexy times in a few months."

"Try nine," Theo says, looking at my stomach pointedly before making eye contact.

"Only nine?" I ask, sceptically.

"Didn't you heal the dick piercings that your mates got, which would have taken humans months to heal?" he asks with a cheeky grin.

"Fair." I shrug. "Okay, let's brief the rest and find a rendezvous point. The sooner we get on the same page, the better."

Theo nods, kicking the tied-up man out of spite before standing by my side. I pull each of my mates into the mind-link, waiting until they're not directly fighting before doing so.

"New rules: we do not kill. We subdue and restrain."

"What do you mean we subdue and restrain?" Noah says. *"There's no way we can restrain them, baby. They're here for our blood."*

"No, they're not," Theo says. *"Trust me—trust Lottie. Do not kill any more of them."*

There's a lot of anger across our bonds, and they're directing it at Theo instead of me. My Alphas are the worst at being told what to do when they've already made up their minds.

So, I step back in and take control of the conversation. *"There's a deeper plot here. They're trying to frame us for this attack. They're trying to work with the terrorist label that we've been assigned—that I've been assigned—and are trying to make it seem like we've gone rogue. We need to keep as many as possible alive so that we can prove that we're not bad people—that we're not evil."* I shake Theo's arm off me, hating that he's trying to comfort me right now. *"We need to show that we haven't gone rogue to kill a bunch of humans."*

"There's a small problem with that," Elijah says.

"What's the problem?" I demand. Theo tenses next to me.

"We're about to be raided," he replies. *"There's a lot of people here, and I don't think they're just here to play games."*

"Who is we? Who is in danger?" I clutch Theo's hand as we wait for this answer, and he soothingly rubs his thumb back and forth over the back of my hand.

"The three of us," Warren pipes up. *"Dillon, Elijah and I are here protecting the humans."*

"The same humans who have caused us more injuries than the supernatural creatures attacking," Dillon says. *"They're not happy that we're protecting them."*

"So, what do we do?" Elijah asks. *"Do we fight to restrain them, or do we fight to stay alive?"*

"You fight to stay alive," I hiss at the same time that Theo speaks.

"Stay alive, but try not to kill anyone."

"Fuck that order," I say, giving Theo a warning look. He opens his mouth to argue, so I send a wave of dominance at him, subduing my Guardian.

He absolutely could fight against it if he wanted to, but he doesn't because he knows I'm right.

"I'd rather we were all labelled as fucking terrorists—actual ones, with proof this time— but were alive to fight the claim. I'd rather be blamed for all of this and go to fucking jail than lose one of you. Do not let yourself be captured. Do not let yourself be hurt. Do not let yourselves die," I command. *"If you need to fight to kill, you will slaughter everyone in your path with no remorse."*

"Remember the days when she hated the fact that we liked to fight?" Caden says, and I don't think he meant to share that across the group mind-link.

"Those were the days when you were fighting for fun—for no reason other than to soothe your ego. This is a fight for your life," I say. *"I've killed tonight, and sure, I'll probably have a breakdown over it tomorrow, but I do not regret it right now. So, stop with the immaturity and be safe. Please."*

"I'm sorry, baby," Caden says. *"I am being safe, I promise. Nobody dies tonight."*

"Well, I don't care if the enemies die..."

"Let's all head over to where Elijah, Warren and Dillon are," Rhett

says. *"Then we can assist and at least all be in the same place at the same time."*

"Sounds perfect to me, and exactly what Theo would've suggested if he wasn't submitting at my feet," I say, breaking away from the mind-link.

Theo shakes his head but doesn't comment as he shifts back into his wolf. I follow his lead, not even looking back at the dead man and the subdued one. We've got the information we needed from them, and that's all I care about right now.

We make our way quickly, racing through the dark forest, trying to reach the others. The scents of fear, blood and death are heavy in the air, and it only serves to amp up my adrenaline. My wolf and I are desperate to get to our mates to help protect them.

But then, I hear the rustling in the trees, and I just know that it's not going to be that easy. The vampires, who were hanging back, are now coming for Theo and me. But is it to kill or pick us off before we can get to the humans, or is it entirely for another reason? I have no idea.

Theo and I move as one, our bond strengthening as we fight together, the two of us in synchronisation as we move. He's a part of my soul, and we don't even need to think about it when relying on our instinctual nature to fight.

We dodge and weave around the vampires, biting and clawing with everything in us. They're strong, but we're faster right now and fuelled by the need to protect each other. I won't let him die, and he feels even more strongly about that than I do.

Blood splatters everywhere, and the vampires howl with rage and pain, most dying before they even hit the ground. But we don't stop... not until every vampire is no longer breathing.

Death isn't fun, but if the choice is me or them... I will always choose myself.

Breathless and our furs covered in blood, Theo and I stand together, our eyes locked on one another. We're both panting, our chests heaving up and down as our tails wag in sync. We're alive, and we're together. That's all I can ever ask for.

"We have to leave," I say. *"Before more of them come."*

Theo nods, and we sprint away, paws pounding on the ground. *"We don't stop until we're with the rest of our people."*

"Alive," I say, and his wolf howls in agreement. *"Fuck, Theo, we're going to—"*

I'm cut off when I fall to the ground in agony, my body unconsciously shifting from wolf to human. A scream leaves my throat as pain radiates through my very core. I'm sobbing as I clutch at my chest. There's so much pain. *So. Much. Pain.*

"What is going on?" Theo demands, shifting back into his human form as he charges over to me. He bends down next to me, lifting me into his arms. "Lottie, darling, what's going on?"

My body is on fire, and I can barely move, never mind react to what he says. I sob as I writhe around, trying to escape this never-ending pain. But there are some deafening howls echoing through the air that my wolf locks in on despite the torment we're enduring.

One comes from Wyatt, and another slightly quieter is coming from River.

"River is down!" Wyatt screams across the mind link, tugging on my bond as hard as he can.

"So is Elijah," Warren says, along a private bond. Neither of them seems to realise the other is hurt, both of them pleading with me to come and help the person they're with.

"We need you here, Lottie," Warren says. *"We need you to save Elijah."*

"We need you here, Lottie," Wyatt says. *"We need you to save River."*

My heart stalls and the pain briefly dulls as I look up at the sky. It's so beautiful tonight, with the moon so high in the sky and the stars glittering. It's *too* beautiful, really, for the amount of death that has occurred tonight.

The pain has mostly faded into the background as I sink deeper into my subconscious. It's safer here, and I don't need to make any hard decisions about which mate I go to first.

How am I meant to make this decision? How do I choose between them?

I can't.

I won't.

CHAPTER 36

"*L*ottie, you need to decide," Theo says, shaking me hard enough that I feel my brain rattle in my skull. It barely snaps me out of my panic, but it's enough. *It's enough.* "You can either save River or Elijah."

"That's not a decision I can make," I scream, batting away at his hands. "You cannot tell me that I have to choose between my mates, Theo. I can't do it."

"They're not both your mates," Theo says, quietly. My heart stops, and it feels like someone has dunked me in a bucket of ice. I look at him properly, and I can see the serious expression on his face, and I just *know*. "*Elijah* is your mate. River is a member of our pack."

Tears stream down my face, the salty liquid coating my cheeks and lips, as my wolf howls in my mind. She's not howling because of the indecision. No, she's howling because there is *no* decision.

Between my mate and River... she's made her choice.

My back is in agony, my chest in pain, my arms feeling dull aches because of how *Elijah* feels. I have no connection to River's injuries.

But I wish I did.

The words of the ancestors echo through my mind—there's a choice to be made, and I *must* choose my mate. Is this the choice they mean? Did they really expect me to choose between two of my men?

I can hear Fate laughing right now; deep down, I know it's the truth.

River or Elijah.

One can live, and the other must die.

Fuck.

"You don't have the time for this," Theo snarls, shaking me once more. His words penetrate me so deeply, and I nod. "You need to choose. *Now.*"

"Elijah," I whisper, following the pleas of my wolf and ignoring the shattering of my broken heart.

This is cruel.

It's disgusting.

I do not deserve the power to decide who lives or dies.

"Warren!" Theo roars, and I can feel a tugging on Warren's bond as the vampire appears in front of us.

His eyes are lit up bright purple, and his vampire is furious. The veins on his arms are pink, and there's a scary intensity surrounding him right now.

I'm upset I'm losing one of my mates.

Warren is losing a *brother.*

His fury is almost tangible, and I can feel his desire to get revenge. He wants to kill someone, to punish someone.

But not me. He doesn't blame me.

"What are you going to do?" Warren asks.

"I'm going to save Elijah," I say, my voice breaking with pain. My wolf doesn't care about River; she's too concerned with the pain my vampire mate is in.

He's suffering badly, and I hate that someone managed to do this to him.

Tears fill Warren's eyes, but he doesn't let them fall. He grabs me in his arms, lifting me close as we race through the lands.

It's been a matter of minutes since I heard that both Elijah and River were hurt, and I could only get to one of them.

Minutes.

I never got five minutes to make a fucking choice over who to save.

My soul is convincing me this is the right choice.

My wolf doesn't care about convincing—she's telling me Elijah is the only one who deserves it.

My subconscious agrees that Elijah is the right one.

So why can't I believe it?

As we race through the town, everything flies by us too fast for me to pay attention. It's a blur of colours as the wind stings my face. My cheeks are numb, and I'm shivering in Warren's arms.

But I can hear the other victims' snarls, fear, and cries. The humans are mostly dead, if not completely wiped out, and there's not a single one of the wolves who attacked who survived.

Sure, we fought to kill, but they weren't going to let us take them alive. Too many of them have killed themselves, which only adds to my mates' fury.

The atmosphere is horrible.

There's too much death in the air. It's got a bitter taste that turns my stomach and increases my anxiety.

I'm trying to calm myself down, but I can't. My body is shaking, the cold seeping past skin level and settling within my bones.

I won't ever be okay again. Not once this day is over.

Warren comes to a stop in front of Elijah's body, and I gasp. Warren gently lowers me to the ground but maintains his hold on me. If it weren't for him, I'd be on the floor.

My legs can't support me any longer.

Dillon and Wyatt are here, too, but I can't even lift my eyes from the figure to acknowledge them.

He looks lifeless. He looks like he's been beaten to death.

If it weren't for the low hum of his exhausted vampire, I'd genuinely believe he was dead.

Elijah's brown curly hair is soaked with blood—both wet and dried—and his clothes are just as bad. I can't tell through my hysterics whether the blood belongs to him, someone else, or just a combination of everything.

Warren gently lowers me to the floor, the wet mud coating my legs. It feels weirdly warm, which is nice. It's so cold here.

Elijah's so cold. I touch the back of his hand, and faint sparks shoot up my arm, but it's not enough.

His face is black and blue, his nose is definitely broken, and I dread to think what he looks like under his clothes.

My mate is dying.

There's a gaping wound on his thigh, and if I look properly, I'm sure I'd be able to see his femur.

Fuck, I'm going to be sick.

"I can't," I start, before gagging and turning away from him. I lose the contents of my stomach, not that there's much after already vomiting earlier, but there are no loving hands or reassuring touches this time.

"We don't have time for this," Theo snarls, his anger snapping me out of my meltdown. "Heal him."

I nod, tears dripping down my face, as does drool and bile, and I lean over Elijah and press my lips to Elijah's forehead. I sob all over my vampire mate as I fill him with more healing energy, doing my best to repair the life-threatening issues first so that he's not sent into shock.

I can hear howls in the air, the mournful cries of my Alpha mates, who are likely by River's side supporting him the way I can't. I want to plead with them, beg for their understanding, and tell them I didn't have a choice. I didn't do this on purpose. I would never...

Not one of my mate's lives is worth more than another.

I love them all equally.

But tonight, I showed otherwise.

I choke back another sob, but it's futile. I'm a fucking mess, and Elijah deserves better. I can't overwhelm his system with too much energy, or I risk killing the vampire within, and this will all have been for nothing.

Caden howls once more, and it hits me deep in the chest, my soul crying out in pain for River. My wolf is notably silent on the hybrid, which destroys me that much more. My heart is racing, but there's nothing I can do. Elijah's heart isn't beating correctly, and I can't leave his side.

If only they could be moved. If only... *I want to fucking scream.*

I guarantee there were ninety different ways this could've played out where it wouldn't end with one of my men dying for another. But in this version of Fate's twisted games, there wasn't time to save them both.

I had to let him die.

I had no choice.

We're supernatural creatures. I'm the most powerful wolf in the world. And yet, I couldn't be in two places at once. All of my mates couldn't be saved...couldn't be moved.

They couldn't be moved.

They couldn't be moved.

"I know they couldn't," Theo whispers, crouching beside me. He supports my weight, stopping me from sprawling over Elijah. My vampire mate needs such intensive healing that it's taking so much out of me.

Well, that or the fucking situation.

"We can try and get you to River too," Warren whispers, coming to my other side. "Is he—"

"Is Elijah well enough to survive if you leave him now?" Theo asks, finishing off where Warren can't. Here I am, sobbing over my mate when *both* of Warren's *brothers* are dying. If he can compose himself, why the fuck can't I?

"No," I whisper, shaking my head. The tears fill my eyes again, and I shake my head repeatedly. "No. I can't leave him. If I do, we'll likely lose them both. I can't. I need to be here."

And the only thing worse than one dead mate is two.

"Elijah's so depleted," I whisper, my breath catching.

"Then fucking save him," Wyatt snarls, snapping at me. I don't even let his words process in my brain. Tensions are high, and at the end of the day, they're both *mine* more than they're anyone else's—even fucking Karen, who birthed one of them—and I know what needs to be done.

The moment Elijah's vampire is well enough, I bite my wrist and shove it at the man's mouth. I continue to push healing energy into him, but my blood is the best thing for him right now. His vampire starts to slowly lap it up, and I can instantly feel the difference.

I don't know how long we sit here in this bubble, how long it takes to save him completely, as the sounds of the men with River, wash over me. Their pain, their anger, their frustration, I hear it all. I *feel* it all.

Whilst I save one, the other dies.

Fate thought she spared me by not making me feel River's death, but I think it's the only thing I'd deserve.

"Lottie," someone murmurs, shaking my shoulders. I don't look away from Elijah—*I can't.*

"Lottie," the voice says a little more harshly this time. I'm pulled away from Elijah, and my eyes rest on his brother. Warren's got identical dimples to Elijah when he smiles. They're noticeably missing right now.

"If you want to say goodbye to River, we need to go now." Warren's voice cracks, despite his face not changing from the forced calm. "You won't get this chance again, princess."

"I..." I shake my head as tears fall once more. I look at the brunette underneath me, knowing I can't leave him. There's a burning sensation in my throat as I try to contain my emotions. "I can't leave Elijah."

"Is he not..." Warren trails off when I shake my head. His anger hits me like a freight train before he closes his feelings off. "Okay."

"I can't leave him, Warren."

"We'll do what we can to give you that goodbye, but you need to work faster, Lottie," Warren commands, and then he's gone. I fall slightly, but Theo reaches over and stabilises me, providing me with the support I need to do what needs doing.

Theo and I are the only ones here, and I have no idea when Dillon and Wyatt left. Did they say goodbye to me before going to see River?

I don't deserve that.

"They did," Theo murmurs gently. "But your focus was exactly where it should be. You are doing so fucking amazing, little wolf."

Amazing? One brother gets to live whilst I condemn the other to death. I don't deserve to whine about missing goodbyes from the others.

I don't deserve to whine about being tired.

I don't deserve to whine about being sad.

I don't deserve anything but the feeling of this excruciating pain.

"You're okay," Theo soothes, running his hand up and down my back as Elijah's teeth sink in a little deeper. His vampire is perking up more, which gives me hope that this wasn't all for nothing.

"You made the right choice, little wolf."

"How can you say that?" I hiss, taking my anger out on him. "How do you know that?"

Theo doesn't move, willing to absorb my nasty words and harsh tones. He's here, steadily by my side. He hasn't left to see River; he's stayed here, giving me support and making sure I don't need to go through this alone.

Theo's not closed off my feelings. He's not blocked away my pain. He's enduring it with me.

The tears are back—I don't think they even fucking left—and I'm trying my best not to get distracted from Elijah. But what the fuck did I do right in my life to get Theodore Lykaois?

"River made the choice the day he chose to no longer be yours," Theo says, gently. "And I became yours, the day you were conceived because even then Fate knew your need of me. She knew the future you had laid out, and she was giving you her best shot."

I let out a huff of breath, and turn away from him. My emotions are high, and I know anything I say to him right now is not something I want to say. Those were not the nice words I needed from him, not even a little.

Fate knew, Theo because she fucking condemned me to this life.

Elijah is yet to wake up, but my blood is helping his vampire within, and the healing energy is working to restore him to full health. I can feel the bigger issues no longer affecting him, which helps reassure me.

But he's still so pale, and it reminds me how close to death he was.

If it weren't for me making this choice, Elijah would be dead by now.

"This isn't something I can do," I whisper, when more howls fill the air. The wolves of my men can't handle seeing one of their own die.

But I'm a coward hiding out here.

"You need to say goodbye," Elijah croaks. His voice is weak, but it's there. My wolf cries out in euphoria at seeing his eyes, and I give him a watery smile. Some of the weight has lifted from me at just seeing him conscious. My wolf can't contain her joy.

Joy. Because she only cares about Elijah.

"I heard snippets whilst fading in and out," Elijah continues. "I know River's dying. You need to go and see him, sunshine."

"Save your energy," I murmur, seeing his eyes fill with pain. Sure, he's probably feeling upset about River, but he's also not at his full capacity right now, and I'm not sure how well he's processing this.

He's in physical pain.

Pain that I need to heal.

"You chose me," Elijah whispers, the blood on his cheeks making him look even paler. "You chose me."

"I had no choice. It was always going to be you." I sniffle. "The choice was a mate... or a, or a member of our pack." I choke back my sob, unwilling to let him feel guilty about my choice. This burden rests with me.

He nods, the weakness he's feeling making the movement seem erratic. "I'll be okay. I can hold on until you're back. I will not die, Lottie."

"No," I protest, lifting my head to glare at him. "I refuse to lose you too. You can't promise me that."

"Yes, I can. You *won't* lose me, sunshine," he says, and there's so much determination in him and his vampire that I half believe him. "You won't, sunshine. I'll hold on. I won't make this the day you lose two of your men."

Theo looks at me, and nods, promising that this is the right choice.

"If not for you," Theo murmurs. "Do it for River. Let him die without knowing your love was still there. Let him die, having gotten the chance to say goodbye. Don't... don't blame yourself for your choice, and just soak up his last few moments, okay?"

"Promise me," Elijah says, quietly. "Promise me you'll let him have his goodbye."

I take the selfish option and nod. "I promise." Because I need this too, I don't think I can live without River... but I know I can't live without at least getting the chance to say goodbye.

I check with my wolf that Elijah will survive if we leave him, and she gives her very reluctant approval. It's not much, but it's enough.

Theo calls for Warren, and he's back in front of me seconds later. His relief at seeing Elijah awake is evident, but there's no time to dawdle, and he knows it. He gives his brother a nod, which is returned.

"He's still alive," Warren reassures me as he hoists me into his arms. Hope builds inside me for the short four-second run, but that disappears the moment we come to a stop where the rest of my men are.

The ground surrounding River is red. He's laid out on the grass, his blood pooling over the land, and I'm terrified to know how much is left inside of him.

I just know I will be left with only the scent of his blood to remember him by.

Why do I need a mate when I can cling to blood-soaked pyjamas?

I charge over to his side, collapsing onto my knees near him, and take his hand in mine. His skin is so fucking cold, and my eyes fill with tears. I gather up my energy, preparing to try and save him.

"You can't heal me," he chokes out. His breaths are laboured and wheezy, and I can practically hear his chest rattling.

"I can fucking try," I snarl.

"No," he says as firmly, as firmly as one possibly can possible when they're whispering in pain, anyway. "Get her away from me. *Get her away from me!*"

Warren instantly moves and grabs me in his arms, tugging me back so that I'm no longer touching River. My Gamma gives me a sad look as a lone tear drips down his cheek.

"No, no, no, no," I roar, scratching at Warren's arms, kicking at his legs, trying to get him to loosen his grip on me. "Please let me try. Please let me fix this. I can't, I can't just sit here. Please. Please let me try!"

Warren surrounds me in a barrier, the warmth of his power flirting with my wolf, but it only enrages me further. It's the bright pink and purple colouring directly from the ancestors, which I can't break from.

I'm sure I would drain myself to do so, but I *need* my power to heal River.

"Please, River," I sob, crawling as close to him as possible within the barrier. "Please let me save you. I can't live without you. Please don't, please." I break down into sobs when he shakes his head.

Why won't he let me help him? Why won't he trust me?

I can help him. I can.

"He-he-help me," River pleads, looking to the side where Warren is standing. "Help me si-i-i-it up."

I slowly fall to the ground and watch Caden and Wyatt take River's arms and pull him up into a seated position. I watch my strong mate struggle even to breathe, the sweat dripping down his forehead.

My wolf is upset that one of her pack is hurt, but she's too relieved that it's not Elijah.

I wipe away my tears, but they reappear faster than I can erase them. It's a futile attempt at dignity.

Who needs to protect their dignity when the man they love is dying?

Nobody.

"I can't apologise more for the mistakes I made with our relationship," River whispers. His eyes flutter shut, and I inch forward slightly. I can hear him just fine; I just can't escape. "I fucked up, and this is the penance I must pay."

My heart fucking shatters. He thinks he hurt me badly enough it warrants *death*? I told him I forgave him. I told him there was a place in my arms, my bed, my *life* for him as soon as he could forgive himself.

River's always been part of me, and always will be part of me—bond or not.

I shake my head. "You—"

"I've forgiven myself, Lottie. I know it doesn't sound like it, but I have," he says, opening his eyes again. I can see the exhaustion on his face, feel the tether between this world and the next strengthening. He doesn't have long, and he's trying to fucking reassure *me*. "I've forgiven myself, and I know what I did to you was part of Fate's design. I accept your love for what it is. Pure—"

His body wracks with coughs, and he hunches over, struggling to continue.

Why won't he let me heal him? I can try. I can really fucking try.

"I love you," I whisper, pouring as much emotion through the words as I can.

"I love you too," he says. His eyes don't reopen, and I'm terrified they're not going to. *"I don't blame you for saving Elijah, Lottie. You made the right call, and I am so proud of you for that. I'll always be watching, angel. Always."*

"Please let me try and save you," I beg. I burst into tears again, not even bothering to hide them when he shakes his head.

River's slumped over, and my men rush over to get him comfortable. They lay him back down in the pool of his blood as they try to make his final moments comfortable.

"It'll only hurt that much more when it won't work," he says. His breathing starts to slow, his eyes no longer moving underneath his eyelids. *"Please let our children know the man I was. Let them know my love, my hope, my—"*

And then he's gone. His heart stops beating, his soul leaves this plane, and I just know that I'm never going to see him again.

I howl louder than any of my men have, the devastation and pain being channelled through the act. But where their howls came directly from their wolf... mine is all me.

The most devastating thing is how my power unleashes, the pure strength of it knocking me back, as it shoots out of me in all directions. I don't know what it does, or who it touches. I don't know who I hurt or what damage I cause.

And most importantly, I do not care.

My eyes fall shut without my permission as my grief plays war around me.

But I know that as I fall into the darkness, I'll wake up.

Unlike River.

CHAPTER 37

"How are you feeling, baby?" Noah murmurs, running his finger down my face gently. My eyes flutter open, and I realise I'm exactly where I was during my epic breakdown. It's only Noah and I here, though. I can feel the others not too far away— I think Rhett, Theo and Wyatt are at the hotel, and the others are all together.

"I'm—" I cut myself off. I would say that I was fine, that everything was okay, but that would be a lie. I'm not sure I can ever be okay again. "There's not even a word strong enough to convey how much this hurts."

Noah kisses my forehead. "I'm sorry. I wish I could give you more time to process, but we need you."

"What's wrong?" I ask, looking at him seriously. My wolf pushes to the forefront, both of us prepared for an attack or something.

"How are you feeling physically?"

"Fine. Genuinely, too. More balanced than I was before..." I trail off, unable to say the words. "I'm more balanced."

"Elijah's in pain."

Fuck. In my selfish outburst, Elijah has been left to suffer. Sure, I healed him from death, but I didn't *fix* him.

Fuck.

"Take me to him," I demand, and Noah nods. He jumps up to his feet and takes my hand. As we walk, I heal his injuries—most of them minor, that his wolf isn't bothering to heal so that he can conserve energy—and take comfort from his wolf.

In a horrible, bitter way, it's good that River refused to let me heal him. With the severity of his injuries, he'd have drained me, and I wouldn't now be able to help Elijah.

How's that, huh? Not even an entire day before, I'm grateful he wouldn't let me try.

Noah and I don't speak as we walk; nothing more can be said. We walk back over to where Elijah was laid out before, and he's still on the floor, lying there. All my mates are here by the time Noah and I join them, and the scene is so fucking desolate.

Tears fill my eyes as I take in my mate. Elijah's hair is still coated in blood, his face deathly pale. His eyes are clenched in pain, and I *hate* myself for leaving him to suffer like I did.

I hate Fate even more for making *this* my destiny.

Why me? Why couldn't she target someone else? It's not like I'm the only person worthy enough.

I'm not. I can't be. Not after what I just did.

Why would she make it a choice where I have to pick between two of my mates?

Sure, we chose to eradicate our bond, but we still loved one another. River was still part of my soul, just as much as Elijah is.

I shake my head, trying to rid myself of these thoughts, and gently cup Elijah's cheeks. His eyes weakly open, and he tries to smile at me, but it just doesn't seem to work.

"I'm sorry," I whisper. He shrugs the best he can, and he's trying to emanate strong vibes. But he has sustained some brutal injuries, and I didn't get the chance to heal him properly.

But as I send my power into him, to correct what I didn't before, my power fails me.

It's telling me that his body is healed correctly.

But that's not true. He's in agony right now, the pain from the damaged nerves making even sitting something that's causing him true torment.

His body did its best to save him, his inner vampire doing what he could to prolong their life, but it hasn't healed him correctly.

I reach out and try to funnel more and more energy into him, but it's not doing what I need it to do. My power heals his headache and fixes the pain he had in his eye from a burst blood vessel.

But it won't target the spinal issues because to Elijah's body... there's no issue at all.

I frown, sitting back on my heels, getting increasingly pissed off.

"What's wrong?" Wyatt asks, reaching over to pat my shoulder.

"I don't know," I reply, but that's a lie. This isn't the first time I've seen something like this.

It's just the first time I'd be willing to sacrifice everything else to make Elijah whole again.

"Help him sit up," I command, and Warren frowns, but at Elijah's nod, he does as I ask.

I take Elijah's hands this time and give him a soft look. "Tell me when it's too much." He gives one pain-filled nod, and it breaks my heart.

I did this.

Yet again, I'm damaging my men in irreversible ways.

First River and his wolf.

Then Warren.

Than River and his life.

And now... Elijah and his quality of life.

I flood my vampire mate with power, and I can feel it racing through him, searching for something to heal. It's charging around his body, and we both know what we want it to heal, but his body just won't allow for it.

"You can't heal what has already been healed," Theo says, quietly. "You know this."

"But why?" I hiss, glaring at him. I know he's explained it, but I was willing to accept that answer back then. I was willing to let Benedict wait a few more months, until we had the time and the resources to help him.

But for Elijah? For part of my soul? Leaving him in this perpetual agony is not something I can do.

"What do you mean she can't fix him?" Warren demands.

"There's nothing to fix," Elijah says. His tone is laced with his pain and exhaustion, and he grasps Warren's arm as he pulls himself to his feet.

He stumbles a little when he tries to put weight on the wrong leg. His entire left side seems to be oversensitive to the pain, and it seems very weak.

The nerves, or the ligaments, or—*I don't fucking know*. Something is not lined up correctly, and it's sealed itself together in a way that causes him extreme pain.

"You might be able to take the edge off," Theo murmurs, stepping up behind me. I take his offered hand and stand, too, both desperate to see Elijah's eyes and too terrified to actually look into them.

I'm too scared of what I will find.

I nod slowly, and look up at him. "How?"

"Like this," he says, as his power rushes into me. "Mimic, exactly what I'm doing to you."

And as I follow Theo's directive, I slowly watch as the pain creases fade from Elijah's face. The stress lines are gone, and he even stands taller as he stops relying on Warren for support.

"Fuck," Elijah says. "I didn't realise how badly it hurt, until you took it away."

"I'm sorry." My words are nearly silent; I don't think anyone but me hears them.

"It doesn't hurt anymore," Elijah says, in awe. He gives me a grin that I genuinely don't deserve.

"Her influence *will* wear off," Theo says. "And the pain will come and go. But this is a solution for now."

"Thank you, sunshine," Elijah says, softly.

"Will it do more damage to him, though, to keep providing temporary relief?" Warren asks.

"Potentially," Theo replies, and I flinch. The honesty was necessary, but it's just digging that knife in even further. "Pain is the body's way of warning you that something is amiss."

"But if there's something amiss, why the fuck can't she heal it?" Warren hisses, and as much as I know, he does not mean that as something to hurt me; it does.

I thought I had moved past the trauma with River... but I haven't really. Not if I'm sitting here, terrified that it will happen all over again.

"I've explained that already," Theo says, and Wyatt squeezes my hand in an effort to provide me with some support.

"So why does it need to stop?" I whisper. "Why does my influence ever need to wear off?"

"Think about when I heal your headaches or sickness, little wolf," Theo says, still using a gentle tone of voice. "As soon as my power fades, the natural body inclinations come back."

"For fuck's sake," I whisper, shaking my head. Tears fill my eyes, and I look up at my vampire mate. Elijah wipes my cheeks, still giving me that soft smile.

"You leaving me, meant you got to say goodbye to my brother. You gave him comfort in his final minutes, and you had the chance to heal and move on from what happened whilst he was still alive," Elijah whispers. "This is a pain I will live with until the end of our days, knowing you won't have that burden on your soul, sunshine."

"Don't try and erase what I've done to you."

"Nothing," Warren says, glaring at me. I flinch at the intensity of the action. "You have not done *anything wrong*. We're done blaming ourselves for the actions of a madman. You said it yourself—he's a dead man walking. So let's figure out our next steps and stop placing blame where it shouldn't be, princess."

"Oh, trust me, I know *exactly* who to fucking blame," I say, remembering what one of the fallen wolves had said. "We're going to pay Alpha Moore a little visit."

"Baby?" Noah calls, and I turn to look at him. I forgot he and my other Alphas were even here, since they're guarding the area just in case. "Last time you faced off against an Alpha, I told you not to kill him. I'm going to make that same request again." I frown, the cries of my bloodthirsty wolf not liking that Alpha Moore might survive where River didn't. But Noah doesn't waste a second before tacking on, "Let Caden do it. Let Caden be the one to kill him."

I look at the other sandy-haired man, who cracks his knuckles, a look so intense it gives me shivers. "Please let me do it, baby."

"If he deserves death, he's yours," I say. Elijah squeezes my hand, and I give him a stern look. "The *moment* you feel an inch of pain, you will tell me. I do not want to spend the rest of my life spying on you through our bond, but I will. You mean everything to me."

"I promise," Elijah says, and I don't detect a single lie in his words.

"Believe me, I will *not* be letting this rest. The moment we are free of this shit, I will find a way to repair your body so you don't feel the pain of your selfless decision."

And if it benefits others, then so be it.

"Okay, this might sound crazy—" Warren starts, but he stops that train of thought at my dirty look. "What's wrong, princess?"

"If something sounds crazy, it likely is."

Elijah laughs, and gives Warren an indulgent look. "What's your idea, brother?"

"What if we like... snap your spine again?" he asks, with a shrug when I growl at him. "That way, it's *broken* broken, and you can fix it."

"And how do you plan on breaking it the same way it was the first time?" Dillon asks, tilting his head. "The likelihood is, if you broke it, it wouldn't actually fix the issue."

"But could make it a lot worse," Theo says.

"No. We're not doing that," I plead, looking up at Elijah.

"I wouldn't do that to you," Elijah promises, squeezing my hand. "I love you." He drops a kiss on my forehead, the lingering presence of his lips sharing more than his words do.

I bask in that feeling momentarily before letting my anger consume me again.

"Now, it's time to split up," I command, turning to Rhett for guidance.

"Lottie, Theo, Caden, Noah and Wyatt can head to Wildfire. The rest of us will remain here to handle the scene. Warren, you and Dillon will see if any humans are alive. I can't feel any—"

"Me neither," Theo and I say together. We exchange looks, and he gives me a small smile.

"But I want you to check anyway," Rhett continues as if we didn't interrupt. "I'm calling Alaric to inform him of what's gone down, and Elijah, I need you to call Abel. Whichever one of us finishes first will call Charles, an Everett, in that order."

"Shouldn't I—" I sigh and shake my head when I feel more than a couple of pointed looks in my direction. "We're splitting up. I've got my task."

"We're splitting up, and you have a critical task," Rhett repeats. "Go. Trust us. We've got this handled."

"What about..." Warren starts, eyeing me nervously, before trailing off with a nudging of his head.

"River's body." I stumble back, my knees giving in, and it's only due to the quick reflexes of Elijah and Warren that I don't fall to the ground entirely.

Everything is just fading out of view as I hone in on the words *River's body.*

Fuck.

What are we... his body. His funeral. His death. *Fuck.*

My vision blurs, my stomach rolls, and tingles dance down my spine. *He's dead.*

One of the loves of my life is dead.

"We're taking him home," Rhett says softly, as Dillon steps forward to be closer. I can feel so much love radiating from each of my men as they send it to me through the bond. They're shoving it my way, trying to drown my system with love and positivity.

But underneath it all, I can feel their pain and their despair. I can feel their grief.

They're trying.

But they can't erase the pain of losing him.

Not when they're still feeling the pain themselves.

"We're taking him home," Wyatt echoes, as Elijah squeezes my hand. I nod, but I feel numb.

Empty.

Fractured.

Where has the anger gone? Why is the need for vengeance no longer fuelling me?

I was coping when I was angry, but now that I'm just grieving, I don't know if I have the ability to keep going. I'm unsure I can push through and be the figurehead I need to be.

I lost my human life when I was opened to an entire world I've unknowingly belonged to since birth. I've lost pack members I may not have known, but were still mine to protect. I lost my mum without ever truly knowing her. I've now lost River.

Why is his death the one to break me?

Well, that's obvious why.

"Then don't sit here and mope," Theo says bluntly. "Get angry." He grips my chin, as Elijah and Warren huddle in closer.

It's ridiculous, them thinking that I need protection from my Guardian, but that's what they're doing.

"Yes, you need to grieve, and I will never advocate for you to skip that process," Theo says.

"Thanks for trying to steal my job," Elijah says. It was a weak protest, but it made me smile, which takes some of the tension out of my men.

"It's going to be okay. Yes, River's gone. We're never going to bring him back. He's dead."

I nod my head, again and again. Again and again. My head won't stop nodding.

River's dead.

Forever.

His soul has gone.

He's no longer mine.

"Stop," Theo commands, tightening his grip on my chin. "Get mad, Charlotte. We're going to confront Alpha Moore and his mate, who caused *all* of this. We are not going to let this lie. His death deserves to be avenged."

"Theo's right," Caden says, swapping places with Dillon as he comes to stand in front of me. Theo moves over ever so slightly to make room for him, and Caden gives me an intense look full of his fury. "We need to know what has happened, Lottie. We've got far too much resting on this to let it end now. Don't give up—we can't do this without you."

"I get it," I say. I look up at Warren and Elijah. "I'm sorry. I'm so sorry."

"If you apologise one more time, I'm going to bend you over my knee right now and spank the living daylights out of you," Warren says sternly. I laugh weakly, but it's something.

"I love you so much," Elijah says softly. "This was not you. This was fate, once again, playing her games and fucking us over in the process. So, let's go ahead and put on a very good show. Because River is up there now, able to see everything that happens down here, and he deserves to see us enact vengeance on his behalf."

"We'll honour him," Caden continues, sounding gruffer than both Warren and Elijah do. I give him a smile as tears drip down my face. "Our children will know him. They'll know that River was their dad, that he died loving them more than anything else. We won't let his death be in vain."

I cover my mouth to try and disguise my sob.

"It's a shame that he's not here, but maybe this doesn't need to be the last you see of him," Warren says softly.

And that ignites a little spark within me.

I stretch myself out and rotate my back a little because it's aching. Theo immediately reaches over and heals me a little more, soothing the aches and pain. I then get cuddles and reassurances from my men, who aren't coming with us, before the five of us get ready to leave.

I shift into my wolf, letting out a howl—one similar to the one my dad let out months ago when he lost my mum.

It's the call from someone who has lost their soulmate.

And everyone around us knows it.

I hope to fucking hell that Alpha Moore hears this and sits quaking in his boots, knowing what is coming his way.

Me.

Vengeance might not be pretty... but his blood splattered across nature really will be.

"I love you, River," I silently whisper, before turning and running off.

CHAPTER 38

*W*e're now outside the boundaries of Alpha Moore's pack, staying hidden yet close enough to observe the pack grounds. It's the dead of night, and the silence and tranquillity are both deafening and ear-piercingly loud because one thing is clear.

After all we have suffered, they're most definitely *not* under attack.

I fucking worried about them. I promised myself I'd come and help once our situation was handled because we should never leave our own to *die*.

But they're traitors.

Peter sat and shook our hands, excited about an alliance with us. *A fucking alliance.*

Whilst all along, he was likely plotting on how best to sell us out, how he was rubbing his hands together, laughing at us behind our backs.

You know how the saying goes—two birds, one stone? Well, he thought that was how it would go, but that's not the game I am playing.

Fool me once; shame on you.

Fool me twice? *Not fucking happening.*

I shift back into my human form, and the others follow suit, and we begin to walk along the perimeter, searching for a weak point.

My heart hammers in my chest, and I try to ignore the pang of guilt from leaving Rhett and the others to handle River's body. I'm here to get revenge; I need to let go of my guilt.

Deep down, I know this is *not* my fault.

It's Alpha Moore's. It's whoever he teamed up with.

It's Fate's fault.

"Their barriers are up, and I can't find a way in," Noah says, turning to me with a raised eyebrow. "Can you overpower them?"

I shrug, and my wolf howls viciously in my mind. We're both very clear on the plan for how this particular confrontation is going to go down. "There won't be any safety left for these people once I'm through with them."

My wolf and I work as one, pushing forward to shred the pack's barriers piece by piece. I have no shame about leaving them vulnerable. They did the same to us, after all.

I press my hand into the barrier, feeling the repelling nature, but I ignore it. I'm not here to play fucking games.

Alpha Moore knows why my mate was murdered—*he was part of the reason we're being framed for terrorism*—and now it's time for justice.

The barrier begins to crackle and spark as my power overwhelms the system that Alpha Moore has in place. I wear their protection down bit by bit, slowly siphoning the power into myself.

I'm not stupid enough to waste something of this extreme.

"You're doing it," Caden says, encouragingly. "Keep going."

"You could help, you know," I tease. He steps forward, and rather than touching the barrier, he touches me instead. There's a soft squeeze of my waist, as he opens up his power to me, letting me draw what I need from him. I don't need the top up, not really. Alpha Moore's pack is small, and his barriers aren't overly strong, but it's nice to connect with Caden this way.

There's a large crack, and my wolf howls. We've done it. There's nowhere that can keep me out.

Not anymore.

"And it's down," Noah says, with an approving nod. "Well done, baby."

"Hey," Caden protests, but Noah isn't listening. Instead, his head is cocked slightly as he listens for something. In response, my power expands, but I don't feel anyone near us for at least a mile—and even then, it's the people within the Wildfire pack.

"I can hear him panicking," Noah reveals. "He's losing his shit."

I frown. "Isn't his house sound-proofed?"

"No idea, but it probably should be," Noah replies, with a shrug. "Are we ready to go and confront him?"

"I am," I say, echoed by Theo, Caden and Wyatt. My wolf pushes forward, our shift about to overtake us, when Theo lets out a hiss.

"Wait," Theo says, holding his hand up. He shifts into his wolf and takes a few steps forward. I watch the wolf identical to mine walk around, sniffing the air occasionally as he assesses something. I clutch at Caden's hand, and Wyatt steps closer to me to provide cover if needed.

"He's trying to put up a new barrier. I can taste the power in the air," Theo says.

"Fucking bastard," Caden snarls, shaking his head. "Wyatt, shift and go find the other Beta. Drag him to wherever we end up." Wyatt shifts into his wolf, gives a yip, and darts through the night, effortlessly blending in with the shadows.

"Lottie, surround his pack with a barrier so that he can't keep us out," Caden commands. With a brief nod, I pull on my power, ready to do what my Alpha asked, but Noah shakes his head.

"No, Lottie, don't," Noah says. "I'll do it, using the resources of our pack if need be. I don't want her losing any power on this—it's your show, baby."

Caden nods, and I shrug, letting Noah take over. It only takes a few minutes before he nods, and then we join Theo in our wolf forms.

The four of us fly through the town, our scents and power-level making us stand out far more than Wyatt did and for more than just the colour of our fur. Theo and I are a bright white and the twins a sandy blonde, neither of blend like Wyatt did. We're emitting a lot of power, drawing eyes and whispers to us, despite the dead of the night.

We follow the snarls and anger and reach a street I think is his. Sure enough, his front door is wide open, and he stands on his driveway, giving instructions to his son and mate.

The four of us stop a few houses away, well within smelling distance. We're even in viewing distance.

Oh, how fucking *perfect*; the two of them together, on a proverbial platter.

Only before I feast on their cries, I *will* be getting all the answers I need.

The son who was furious at his father and the slimy coward who has fucked us over.

Luna Moore gasps, pointing us out silently, and Alpha Moore turns. The realisation hits him, his wolf cowering back without me even saying a word, and my stomach sours.

He knew.

I thought... deep down, I hoped...

But no. He knew.

It makes this easier, I suppose. I don't need to waste time explaining why his reckoning is coming. I shift into my human form, charging forward with fucking purpose, as the atmosphere crackles under the weight of my anger. I feel the shift in the air as Noah, Caden and Theo change.

We're a fucking formidable group, our wolves giving us an extra air of dominance as we approach. Fear tinges against Alpha Moore's face, although I know he's doing his best to hide it. But it's too late; I've seen his cowardice for what it is.

He was a good Alpha and man and protected his pack the way he thought was best.

It's a shame, really, because we were so impressed with the people we met.

Oh, well, all snakes reveal their true skins eventually.

Cameron steps out of the house, and Luna Moore clutches at her son desperately. I can feel the distaste from his wolf, and I'm truly curious about his part in it all. He closes his front door, and the night is mostly silent, just the whistling of wind.

That only makes this all the better.

"Luna Montgomery," he starts, taking a hesitant step forward. "Now isn't the right time—"

"How could you do this to us?" I snarl, my power raging in the air, preparing to strike. The unlucky fucker I want to attack is the Alpha, but honestly, I care very little about his mate standing there or his son. I give zero fucking shits.

My... *River* is dead.

And it's his fucking fault.

"I don't understand what you mean," he whimpers, shaking his head.

"Oh, don't fucking play me, Peter," I hiss, coming to a stop three meters or so away from him. "

My voice is shaking, my fists clenched tight together, as my wolf pleads for vengeance inside my mind. I'm trembling with the weight of my rage. My throat burns, and my eyes are stinging as I hold back tears.

I refuse to look weak by crying.

But fuck me do I hate this man.

"You're a terrible fucking Alpha, a terrible man. What did you get out of betraying us? *What did you get out of betraying* me?" I demand. I've not revealed that River's dead yet, that he cost me the love of my life.

As much as I dislike River's parents, they deserve to know their son is dead before anyone else. They need to know. Karen and I have never gotten along, but she's pulled her head out of her ass the last few months, and I hate that after all this time... she was right about me.

She told me I'd ruin her sons.

And I did.

As I prowl forward, I scent two wolves, one mine and one not, as they slowly advance towards us. I pause, and Peter scans the area, trying to locate his Beta.

The atmosphere is thick with tension as we all wait, and only a second later, Wyatt comes into view with an unhappy Beta behind him. The Beta is wearing a pair of joggers and a thin t-shirt, and he has no shoes on. Caden smirks, and Wyatt dips his head as he approaches.

"Alphas, Luna, I found the Beta," Wyatt says, shoving Jason towards his Alpha. Jason snarls at my mate, who immediately teaches out and backhands him.

My eyes widen ever so slightly, but my wolf nods in appreciation. She likes that Wyatt did that.

"I warned you," Wyatt hisses lowly. "Join the traitorous assholes, Jason, or join the humans. Take your damn fucking pick."

Jason shuffles towards Luna Moore, and as Alpha Moore's eyes dim, I know they're having a silent conversation, but I'm not allowing for that.

"What do you have to say for yourself, Alpha Moore?" I demand. "Tell us how you could do this."

"How dare you act as if I did this *to you*," he roars, finally finding his damn backbone. Is that because he's now putting on a show for his Beta, or because he thinks his Beta has changed the tides for him? *Newsflash, you annoying fuck, I'll take you both down without breaking a sweat.*

"What would you, Charlotte?" he demands. "Tell me what the wise fucking chosen one would do. The golden girl of the wolf world, so incapable of just letting things play out as they should."

He steps forward, seeming taller in his anger. It's embarrassing for him because I know any of my men could take him out before he reaches me—even without my assistance. Wyatt is growling by my side as Noah bares his teeth, and Alpha Moore is a fucking idiot for not backing down immediately.

My mates are powerful but in control.

Me? I'm holding my wolf back, stopping her from unleashing our power on him. She wants his blood, and I get it, I really fucking do.

"We're being targeted by the humans. We're in danger because of them—my people are in danger. The wolves, who have trusted me with their safety and lives, are terrified. They can't leave pack lands without being harassed because of the prejudice that we're facing. Mindless, idiotic humans who can't grasp what we are to each other, the life we've built, the bonds we rely on... they deserve whatever fate they are given. Our Council have turned a blind eye, refusing to aid us, leaving us to struggle on our own. I had no choice."

"There are more—" I begin, but the bastard cuts me off. My wolf is furious, and I can feel the pressure on my skin as she tries to force our change. I refuse to let her, knowing that this isn't the time. She doesn't appreciate the disrespect he's just given us.

To her, we're far superior to this cowardly wolf. *He is nothing.*

I give Peter a dirty look, hoping he understands that he speaks now because I *allow* it.

I want to know everything before I let Caden gut him.

"One of our people decided to leave in wolf form," Alpha Moore continues, his tone less aggressive now. "He needed to visit a dying family member, and there was no other way he could've left without being noticed, so we decided for him to go in his wolf form. He was spotted by the humans, and they never once suspected it was *us.*

"They were so excited about the wild beast they had seen. They never once suspected it was anything more than a phenomenon. But do you think that it was all left there? Do you believe that everything was fine for my pack member whose *family was dying*? No, of course not.

"The Council decided that they needed to intervene. Somehow, they managed to buy out the local newspaper and bury the story. But what about the wolf, you ask? What about the person responsible for nearly opening the human world to the secrets we hide? *He was murdered, Charlotte.* The Council took him, and we never even got to say goodbye before they wiped him out. My link was torn away because I did the one thing I could to help my people.

"We're hunted, targeted, bullied. So, what more could I have done? Tell me, oh, powerful one. Tell me exactly what you would've done if not the same thing?"

His speech was decent, and I completely feel for the man, but not enough to undo what he's done.

I will never sympathise.

"When the door is closed to you, Peter, you open it," I say, taking a step forward. "When the voices in charge won't listen, it is your job as Alpha to make them listen." I take another step forward, drawing my power to me. "You lost a life, and I know how that feels. As a leader, it is soul-destroying to lose someone who puts their trust in you. I've been there. But never once did I give up an ally—a potential ally even. I would *never* throw someone else under the bus to protect my people, not the way you did. It's cowardly and wrong."

Cameron nods, his wolf seeming to agree.

I think I've found the source of their discourse.

"What the fuck are you talking about?" he demands, raising an eyebrow. "We didn't throw you to the wolves. I negotiated a deal to rid my pack of the humans—you were never going to be harmed."

"And I'm not physically harmed," I say. "Who did you make a deal with?"

He shakes his head. "You don't get to come here and demand—"

"We are not equals," I roar, shaking my head at him. "You do not get to sit here and act like we're on the same page. You are *nothing* to me. Now answer me, or I'll let my Alphas tear you apart, and we'll get the answers from your mate."

Caroline gasps, and Cameron reassuringly pats her arm.

"You wouldn't," he says. There's a tiny bit of bravado in his tone but mostly fear. His wolf is terrified. *As it should be.*

"Oh, believe me, *Alpha*," Noah sneers. "We really fucking would."

"What were we meant to do? I've told you how the Council failed us, and I needed to protect my people." His tone has turned desperate, begging even as he tries to resist our call. He's trying to protect this other party, and I'm not leaving here without a name.

And likely a head.

"Times ticking," Theo says, just before he shifts into his wolf. My Guardian takes a few steps forward, coming to sit at my feet, and I stroke his head. Cameron and his mum watch the movement with two different reactions—one is weirdly amused, and the other is angry and scared.

"We were approached by a man with big promises," Peter says. "All he asked for in exchange was to know when you would visit. He promised he'd get rid of the humans, that they'd never know what hit them, and it wouldn't be linked back to us. He promised we'd be free of the fear we're hiding under, so we wouldn't need to live such a sheltered life." Peter's eyes are lit up. "We're wolves, Charlotte. We're the predators, and yet we're being treated like prey. My people can't live in this cage. It's not fair to them; it's not fair to me.

"We have such little turnover, as you've seen because they're desperate to be here where it's safe. This is no life to them. I am a good Alpha, and I have a good mate. We are good leaders to all of our people. And he recognised that within us, and he promised to help us —"

"And you sold me out to do it," I say, my tone devoid of emotion. "You chose to let me, and my people pay the price for something *you* should've solved."

He scoffs. "And yet you stand here whole."

"My mate is *dead* because of you," I roar, my body shaking with the effort to withhold my shift. "Whole? I've lost a part of my fucking soul due to your selfishness."

"And I am truly sorry he was caught in the crossfire," he says, giving me a solemn nod. "That was never my intention."

"You are sorry he was caught in the crossfire?" I snarl, charging forward. Theo moves at my feet, ready to back this play, but Noah holds onto me, not letting me do what my wolf is begging me for. The coward backs away, hunching in on himself as if that will make him a smaller target.

"You are a fucking weasel," I hiss, and he flinches. I turn away, taking a deep breath as I try to calm myself down.

It's hard when I'm vibrating with this much disgust.

"What is this man's name?" Noah asks, giving me my moment. "Who is this person that promised you all this goodness that you just blindly accepted *like a fucking fool*?"

"King Lobo. King of the Wolves, our new future," Alpha Moore says. "He's going to be good to us—nothing like the current Council. I did it for our people, all of them."

"Calm down," Caden says across the mind link. I can't. I genuinely fucking can't.

"My mate is dead," I argue. *"All because of that spineless fucking—"* I whirl around, jabbing a finger in his direction, and a pink spark shoots out. He darts out of the way, and it flies through the air, crashing into a tree instead.

But that doesn't soothe my irate wolf. It just aggravates us both that much more.

How fucking dare he? How dare they all?

He doesn't deserve to stand there *whole* and unaffected.

Not when River is dead.

"You had so many options," I say, with a quiet calm. "And now you've got none. Now you're going to live under the rule of a Council who hate you and a madman who will be dead as soon as I got my fucking hands on him." I glare at the trio of assholes behind me. "You could have done so much more to help your people. You could've made allies and strong fucking bonds between you and other packs.

"Hell, you could have asked us, and we'd have helped you without asking for anything in return. Do you think my offer to help people all those months ago was limited to one or two people per pack? You've seen what we've done for *our* people, my pack, and the wider community we're part of. You've seen what we've done for everybody that reached out and needed us, even knowing the enemy it made use seem to the Council.

"We did it. We saved people, and I'd do it again, even knowing the consequences. Every day, I reject the ways of the patriarchal Council, who only care about furthering their own power. I argue with them; I go to war, to fucking battle for our people. And yet you fucking idiotic fools—"

"Lottie," Theo soothes, shifting into his human form as he sends some soothing energy across the bond. *"Breathe, little wolf."* He's trying to calm me down and help take some of the edge of my anger, but it doesn't work.

None of his efforts will help me.

I'm furious, drowning in despair at losing a mate. He showed me on his deathbed that he loved me, that he had finally forgiven himself, and I lost him before we had the chance to evolve past what happened. We could've been everything, and now, I'll never get that chance again. I lost the father of my children because of some fucking coward.

Peter was so scared to reach out for help, tell me, or tell anyone he needed assistance. He couldn't rely on the strengths of others—*of genuinely* good *people*—that he went to the first person who promised him an easy way out.

Yes, we have different allies, packs, rules, and beliefs, but we have an entire system for situations like this.

He should have pushed harder; he should have tried harder.

In the face of adversity, you don't ever back down; you keep pushing, and you keep going until you get what you need. You do not settle for less than you deserve.

But that's what he did, not just for him but for his pack and all those lives that have been lost, for the level of fear that they're living under. Sure, the humans are idiotic, but now they are dead because of him.

Humans who have...*had...* families and dreams, and in their heads, they were doing the right thing.

So many things could have been put in place to not only protect the pact but the humans as well. We could've reached a settlement, an understanding. Instead, an entire town of humans are now dead.

I shake my head, taking a step back to face them. "If it was up to me, the four of you will be brought in on charges."

"The four of us?" Cameron asks, daring to take a step forward.

"Yes, the four of you," I say, glaring at him. "Because you knew exactly what he did. You knew what was coming, Cameron, and your warning was pathetic. I felt your resentment and anger all day, and I tried to work with you and find out why. You were so discontent with your place, yet you wouldn't tell me the truth. You could've saved my mate, and you didn't."

"I had no choice," he argues, glaring at me. "Do you think you're the only one who elicits vows from people they can't trust? I wanted to tell you I wanted your help. We were drowning, but I was overpowered." He's telling the truth. "I had no choice."

"Oh, so just your parents and the one Beta were in approval of this plan then?" Caden asks, taking my hand.

Cameron nods and gives his dad a scathing glare before returning to us. "I begged him to let me ask you and your pack for the support. I begged with everything I could because he was right about one thing —our pack didn't deserve to live this way. I knew you'd give me the support, and I knew it wouldn't even come with a cost. But nobody would believe me. His generation is so different to ours," Cameron says. "My dad has lived under a neglectful bureaucracy for so long that he doesn't know how to keep fighting. He's exhausted from the grind and did what he thought was best."

"That's no excuse," Caden says. "I'd never have followed my father into a decision like this."

"Yeah, well, yours is dead, so we can't say what decision he'd ever have made if the roles were reversed," Cameron says. "And if I were able, I would have fought back."

"Then do you want that now?" I ask, quietly.

"Yes! My dad is tired from fighting, but I am not. My dad made a mistake, but he felt like he was backed into a corner and tried to do what was best for his people. It wasn't the right decision, and that's clear to be seen now. It's damaged so much for you and tarnished our relationship with you."

He takes a step forward, and I hold my hand up, halting him in place

"On your knees," I command, sending a little wave of dominance towards him. However, he doesn't try to fight it and drops to one knee, bowing his head. His neck is on display, baring it to me, acknowledging me as more powerful.

"*What are you doing?*" Caden asks.

"*Trust her,*" Theo says, sticking by my side. "*She's following her instincts, and she'll make the right call.*"

"Swear your loyalty to me and mine," I say, and when he nods, I say the vow that ties him to me in the same way I've tied others. He doesn't hesitate to repeat the words, and I can feel the vow bonding us together. I push more power into him once he's done, severing his bond with his Alpha.

I don't take the child from the father. I take the position of Beta from Cameron, severing the tie he shares with his Alpha. There's a weight off of Cameron's shoulders, and his wolf is extremely grateful.

"You," I say, glaring at the Alpha. "On your knees." He hesitates, so I throw as much power at him as he can handle, removing the choice from him altogether.

He's no longer allowed to submit in a dignified manner like his son and is now bent over, his head pressed into the grass, as he bows.

I can feel the fear in the man, and the wolf within him is so unhappy.

But I don't care.

This is *his fault*, and it's not my job to soothe and reassure assholes who don't know how to behave.

"You are no longer fit to be alpha," I say, towering over him. I can feel Jason's anger and Caroline's panic, and I honestly don't care.

My wolf and I know this is the right call to make.

Whether his actions were a mistake or not, this man is a big part of the reason that hundreds of humans are dead, and that is not the kind of man who deserves to be a leader.

"You don't have the power to take that away," the Beta hisses, and I fling my hand in his direction. I shock myself when pink and purple sparks dance off my fingertips, targeting him.

I love that my men surround me, backing me for this. They support me—they *trust* me.

And I won't let them down.

"You never could," Theo murmurs.

The Beta drops to his knees, not even forced by me. He doesn't submit, though, which pisses me off.

It enrages my wolf like nothing else could. She hates to be disrespected, and this is the ultimate form of that.

She dismisses him, and I take her lead, turning back to the Alpha.

"You are no longer fit to be Alpha of this pack, Peter Moore," I say, crouching down to him. "And if it were up to me, you wouldn't have a wolf at all." I press my finger into his forehead, purely for the dramatics of it all, and let my power wash over him.

I rip his ties away from his pack entirely, leaving them destabilised without an Alpha. Peter's face pales, his wolf shrinking in on itself, but he doesn't try to fight against my dominance.

I turn to Cameron, raising one eyebrow, and he nods.

It takes me seconds to reinstate the pack links, this time tying each of the wolves in the Wildfire pack to Cameron instead of Peter.

Hopefully, the son was right, and he'll thrive in this role and be better than his father ever could.

"Your pack has a new Alpha," I say, glaring down at Peter and Jason. "I hope he's good to your people. I hope he's righteous, strong, and determined to be better than you ever were."

"I will be, Luna," Cameron says, keeping his head bowed low. I can feel the pride radiating from him, the joy from his wolf at finally earning his place.

But it goes deeper than that.

His wolf is proud *I* deemed him worthy of his place.

And that's nothing short of an ego boost in itself.

"And trust me, Peter," I say, crouching next to the asshole again. "Believe me, you want to hope that King Lobo manages to take me out because you *will* be on my list for restitution when we're victorious. Trust in that Alpha Moore, or should I say... *Alpha of Nothing.*"

I lift the dominance I've been holding over Cameron, and he rises to his feet, giving me an almost sceptical look.

"You *will* liaison with my pack, and you'll make yourself available the moment you're summoned," I say, and he nods his head once.

"Can we..." he trails off, raising his hand nervously.

"Yes?" I ask, sounding bored.

"What do we do about them?" His words are a near whisper, and I can feel his unease.

"That's my burden to handle," I say. *He shouldn't have to deal with his parents.* "Because when your fucking coward, father"—I raise my voice unnecessarily here, glaring at the man—"decided to betray me and mine and break the trust we had put in you and all of these people, he made it my duty. He made this my fight, and trust me, it's one I will *not* be backing down from."

"Okay, but that doesn't answer my question," he says quietly.

"Your parents and Beta Jason are going to be dealing with the vampire monarch, Primus Viotto, in answering for their crimes," Noah says, stepping forward. "You'll have a lot to handle in processing your pack and appraising them of the situation. Ordinarily, we'd stick around to help, but you don't deserve that from us."

"You don't," Wyatt snarls, when Cameron goes to protest. "We've lost an important person to us, and it was someone your family willingly handed over to save their own ass. You get *nothing* from us."

"I'd get your stories in order," Caden says. "Because Alaric Viotto will be calling, and there is no place you can hide."

"It should go without saying, but on the off chance it needs mentioning," I say, gathering a lot of my power and just holding it at the forefront. It's mainly an intimidation tactic, but I also have it ready if needed. "You better not say a fucking word to anyone about what has gone down last night. You do not contact the Council, law enforcement or a representative for either until *we* give you the say-so. Is that understood?"

"Yes," Cameron says. The three cowards all nod, but that's not enough for my wolf. She draws agreements from them, and I'm still not entirely convinced we can trust them.

Alas, we have no choice.

"Let's go, love," Wyatt says, taking my hand. We turn, walking away from the new Alpha of Wildfire and the traitorous criminals who don't deserve the boon Caden just granted them.

Even after hearing their stories, my wolf is so desperate for blood she'd have no qualms about letting Caden kill him.

And his mate.

And their Beta, just to round it off.

"It's a good thing you're so righteous," Theo murmurs, and I snort. "But I think you'll have to give Caden something else since he's just as desperate for blood."

"Trust me," Caden says, shaking his head. "Seeing King Lobo dead will be justice enough."

And that's all we want.

CHAPTER 39

"*How* is everything going over here?" I ask, slipping into the space next to Rhett. He's away from the rest of the group, standing outside the front of the hotel. I'm unsure if he is finishing a mind-link chat or just taking a few minutes, but he is quiet as I approach.

My Alpha wraps his arm around my shoulder, drawing me close, deeply inhaling my scent to soothe himself. He's exhausted, and his wolf is very antsy. I take the offered comfort, soothing our bond to settle him, but when he doesn't answer after a few moments, I pull away to look up at him.

He sighs, giving me a hesitant look as the uncertainty builds. "Not good. How's your side of things been?" I can feel his wolf pleading with mine for some good news, and luckily, I can deliver.

"My side of things has been handled," I say, and some tension fades out of him. "We sorted things out, and everything is as okay as it can be. Cameron is the new Alpha—"

"By choice?" Rhett asks, a hint of incredulity in his tone.

"Sort of. Cameron might have been aware of what his father was planning—" I start, but Rhett cuts me off with a deafening growl. I move closer to him, moving from underneath his arm so our bodies are flush against one another.

I press my back against his chest, wiggling ever so slightly until he gets the hint and wraps his arms around me again. The contact helps soothe his wolf, and honestly, I need it too. An onlooker would assume we're just being cute and romantic when, really, I'm just trying to calm the rage of an angry Alpha male.

"Cameron was held under a vow so that he couldn't speak up against his father," I say.

"Smart man," Rhett growls, causing his chest to vibrate.

"Smart, maybe. I think it's rude as fuck." I lean into Rhett's chest. "He's a fucking bastard."

"Who knew about it then?"

"The previous Alpha Moore, his mate, and their Beta," I say, with a frown. "The three of them were all willingly in on the deal they made."

"The deal? What did they get?" Rhett is furious, and I don't blame him.

"King Lobo reached out to Alpha Moore and offered to help him with their problems with the humans, and all he asked for in exchange—"

"Was to know when we'd be here," Rhett finishes, and I nod.

"Yep. And obviously, to Alpha Moore, that was easy to agree to. He offered us up on a platter, got rid of the humans, and his pack would live happily and unbothered the rest of their days. The fucking prick," I hiss. I clench my fists together, now relying on Rhett to calm *me* down—unfortunately, his growls of frustration only egg my wolf on that much more.

"He thought that he was doing the right thing. He thought he was protecting his pack, and in his eyes, working with King Lobo was the only way he could." I sigh and pull away from Rhett, turning to look at him properly. "But the difference is, we know the truth. We know how this game plays out, and we're never *ever* going to get drawn into it like he did."

"I love you," Rhett says.

"I love you too." We fall silent for a moment, but my brain is whirring, and I can't let this rest. "What I don't understand is how it's all gone down. To them—to Peter and Caroline—they did what they did to protect their people. They couldn't handle it themselves, so King Lobo kindly stepped in. That was the trade-off they made. Obviously, Cameron couldn't give us any actual warning, which is why what he did say was a very vague mention of safety. He did his best; I can admit that.

"But the vow prevented him from sharing more, or he honestly didn't know it. But then the wolf that Theo and I cornered was more than willing to tell us everything. His wolf was overly eager to share their plan, and he was trustworthy enough. I think that he had been beaten before he got here, or maybe during it, but not by one of us. The inner wolf was confident that the plan was to frame us for killing all the humans in town.

"He was *adamant*, and my wolf and I could tell he wasn't lying. That even sort of explains why there were so many vampires."

"It does?" Rhett asks, raising an eyebrow.

"Well, yeah. The vampires were coming to stop us because they weren't going to let us kill a bunch of humans and expose our world." Rhett's sceptical look makes me sigh. "Okay, fine, I don't have all the details—but that's my point. It all still feels a little too unsolved."

"No, this makes sense to me," Rhett says. "Their entire purpose was to kill."

"Unfortunately."

He nods. "Speaking of death." I narrow my eyes, panic building inside of me as he pauses. "Every single wolf and vampire we had found and subdued is dead. Suicide by wolfsbane."

My jaw drops, and I shake my head. "No, Rhett, that's impossible."

I raise my arms, shaking them off. "We tied every single one of ours up—every single one. We had zip ties, supernatural ones, according to Theo, that they couldn't have broken out of. We covered their faces with supernatural Sellotape so they couldn't break out. There's no way they could've moved to inject themselves."

"But what if they didn't need to inject themselves? What if they already had the wolfsbane pill in their mouths and just had to bite down?"

I scream in frustration, kicking my foot into the grasp. "Fucking typical."

"I'm sorry, love," Rhett says.

"It's not your fault," I say, squeezing his hand. "But that's once again putting us in the position of being the scapegoat. We're in the exact position King Lobo wants us to be in, and this isn't going to go down well with the Council."

"The good news is that Alaric is here working and helping with this situation. He's brought some of his people along, and they're working quickly to clean things up," Rhett says.

"And yet you said it wasn't going well," I say, giving him an apologetic look.

"Alaric is aware of the situation, and so far, most of the vampires haven't questioned our role in it.... but one of his vampires here recognised one of the dead ones. It was his brother."

"Shit."

"Shit indeed. Having a group of angry vampires here is problematic. As far as Alaric knows, some of these vampires have not rejected him or the monarchy."

I take an unconscious step back, my stomach churning. "Freya," I whisper.

"She's out of town," Rhett says.

"That means she's in hell," I say, nodding my head. At least my best friend didn't need to feel them die. That's a good thing, I suppose. I turn away from Rhett to compose myself, looking at the night sky.

It's rare that we've got such nice nights at this time of year, but of course the universe would just rub it in that I'm living through my worst night yet, by giving us such beauty tonight.

"Right, where is Alaric?" I ask.

"Here," Alaric says, appearing in front of me between blinks. There's a grim look on his face, and the usually pristine man is coated in blood. "I am so sorry for your loss, Luna."

Tears well up in my eyes, and I step into his arms, taking the offered comfort. "Thank you for coming."

"I wouldn't want to be anywhere else," Alaric replies, and as sarcastic as his words sound, his tone shows he genuinely meant it. "I'm going to be blunt—we're not in a good position right now. I had brought quite a few of my men with me, and unfortunately, one of them recognised a family member."

"Rhett said, and I am so sorry for the position we've put you in," I say, hanging my head in my hands. I rub my face, giving myself a second, before looking at him properly. "How do we handle this now?"

"Already done," Alaric tells me, but his soothing tone doesn't have the intended effect. "I've reassured him that we will be closing the scene down, and his brother will be returned home. But *I* know, and *you* know, that these men were not here because they were our friends. Not a single one of them came to stop this attack, and none of them were *my* vampires any longer."

"There was a wolf," I say, and Alaric frowns. "The man wasn't here willingly and told us all about the plan in motion." Alaric and Rhett exchange looks, and it pisses both my wolf and me off. "Ask Theo about it if you don't believe me. He told me everything—his wolf did."

"It's not about disbelieving you, Lottie," Alaric says. "You have more than proven yourself to me and everyone. My concern was about his people starting to defer. How is this *King Lobo* going to handle it? Does he have one traitor or multiple?"

I shake my head. "Everyone is dead. So, we won't get the answers to that question."

"Sadly," Alaric says with a sigh.

"But that brings the next problem. If everyone is dead, what do we do now, Alaric? He wanted us framed for this. How are we meant to handle all the dead vampires?" I frown. "How are we meant to handle all the dead *humans*?"

"That's something I will have to handle," Alaric says. "But for me to do that and to handle this how it needs, you and your mates need to leave."

"Well, yeah, I got that part," I say, trying not to get frustrated at his condescending tone. "But how are you going to handle this? What will you do about Wildfire—about the previous Alpha Moore and his mate? Their Beta, who knew about this, shouldn't be spared either."

"The local pack will come under my purview," Alaric says confidently. "It becomes a game of politics now, and I'll do my utmost to protect you and your mates the best I can. But legally, this matter is mine since the major party involved is vampires. The entirety of your Council is on lockdown, which only helps my cause since it means the local pack is mine to handle, too."

"And the Council are just going to accept this?" Rhett asks. He raises his eyebrow, folding his arms over his chest.

"No, but unless they want to lift their lockdown to handle it, they'll stay silent," Alaric says.

"That doesn't mean they won't blame me for it," I argue.

"No, but it gives you time to get things organised without being in handcuffs," Alaric says, simply. "There are three guilty parties, yes?"

I nod. "The new Alpha knew of it but was unable to stop it. He did his best to warn us of the situation without breaking his vow. My wolf and I scoured his soul and were happy to leave him in charge."

"I don't doubt your capabilities in leading your people," Alaric says. "Walk with me?"

I follow him and motion for Rhett to take my hand, but he shakes his head and gestures in another direction. I nod, and he disappears as Alaric and I move off together.

"Fill me in on what happened last night. I've heard it from your Alpha, but I think you may have some extra insight," Alaric says.

He's not wrong. I fill him in on everything that happened and then include the extra information from our meeting this morning whilst Rhett was here.

Alaric is a good listener and probes me in the right places when I don't give him all the information.

"These are not good optics for you, Luna," Alaric says.

"No, I can't imagine it is," I reply. "I'm glad you trust us, even without Roman here. But I'm worried about the relationship this will have between me and your Clan once everything is over."

"I trust you with more than just my life, Lottie, with more than my people's lives," he says. "I trust you with *Freya's* life. She's everything to me, and in her vulnerable state, you've done nothing but support her. No matter what the *optics* look like, I will always know the truth."

I choke back my emotional response and just nod.

"Abel is doing damage control with your pack and preparing them for whatever may come." He comes to a stop and gives me a hesitant look. "I hate to be so insensitive, but what of River? Have you discussed how you're going to handle this?"

"Well, so far, only the four assholes at Wildfire know," I say. "But nobody else."

"Good," Alaric says. "Keep it that way."

I frown, looking up at him. "Why?"

He opens his mouth and then closes it. "Just trust me on this. Fate has a plan, and whilst I don't know it all, just trust me for now. Don't say anything about his death until it's over."

"If that's what you think is smart." I don't argue, mainly because I'm not yet ready to process his death myself.

And I don't want to have this conversation with Karen over the phone.

"I've been alive for a very long time, Charlotte, and throughout my life, I've seen my share of death and far too many corpses to count." His words are chilling, but he's not done. "You need to play things smart. Trust me to handle the situation here and leave. Go onto the next stage of your journey and continue with the battle you've outlined. Rely on your allies, and leave."

"I've got no idea where we're going to go," I admit, with a sigh.

"Everything is now up in arms, and we need to regroup and replan before something else crops up."

My head snaps up when the name 'Lottie' rings out, laced with a tone of panic, sending a chill through my body.

Of course, coincidence strikes yet again.

Well, some may call it a coincidence, and some would call it an omen.

I go the route of neither.

This messy game has one person's hands on it—*Fate*.

I let out a low growl, shifting into my wolf and charging towards my mates. Alaric sticks to me despite being so much faster, and we follow the pull from Theo and Caden.

There's a wolf laid out on the floor, a dark grey one with lighting shades that I've never seen before. He's coated in blood, a wound on his neck from where Caden has ripped his throat out.

He's not entirely dead yet, but there's no chance I can heal him, even if I wanted to.

Which I don't.

Theo is in his wolf form, hovering by the body, likely in case it moves, and Caden is now in his human form, blood covering him from the mouth down to mid-chest.

I raise an eyebrow at the sandy blonde, and he winks in response.

"I got my blood after all," he says. "It wasn't the most satisfying, though. He was far too easy to take down."

"Who is it? How did he get here?" I ask, looking at the wolf. I don't recognise him, but my eyes widen as he dies and he shifts into his human form.

I crouch on the floor, recognising the man I saw only a few hours ago.

Jason.

CHAPTER 40

"Jason," I whisper, brushing his hair from his face. It feels weird to touch him this way since we're barely more than strangers, and the guilt I'm feeling shouldn't exist either.

This man sold me and my mates out, leading to one of them dying, and he showed *no* regrets for that action.

He looks so pale and lifeless, his chest covered in blood. *Come on, Lottie, be reasonable. Of course, he looks lifeless—he's dead.*

Caden steps back, his eyes wide and face pale as he looks at Theo. The guilt has hit him, too. We're no longer dealing with a random rogue wolf who wanted to harm us—there's a name to this one, and it's a bigger shock to the system.

But Caden was defending himself; he shouldn't feel guilty for that.

I check for a pulse, even though I know it's futile. There's definitely none. I knew that as soon as he shifted; the man was dead. There's nothing I can do here. I raise to my feet, turning, looking between the two men.

"What the fuck happened?"

"Clearly, they killed him," Alaric says, sounding amused. I roll my eyes, not bothering to dignify that with a response. I raise an eyebrow at Caden, my demeanour showing I expect answers.

"It was an accident," he says. "Well, no, I killed him on purpose." Caden's jaw is slack, the panic in his chest close to bubbling over, and I know he's in shock.

"Sit," I soothe, and Caden drops to his ass, resting his head on his knees.

Theo takes centre stage. "He came running at us from out of nowhere. We were aware, but we didn't realise someone was coming," Theo says. "We tried to get him to stop and subdue him without killing, but then he started to attack."

Caden nods. "I had no choice. It was him or me."

"We thought it was one of King Lobo's people," Theo adds. "I didn't expect him to come and attack us like he did." He rubs the back of his neck, giving me a sheepish look. "I thought he was just going to try to get to you and reacted."

"No, I was the same, although I didn't think he'd be a threat. I thought it would be like the night after the attack on our pack, where they brought us a message and killed themselves. I never dreamed it would be Jason," Caden says. "Don't get me wrong, I'm not upset that he's dead, but I might've tried harder if I knew it was him. Why was he here in the first place?"

"Yeah, no, that's not a good response. 'If I knew it was him, I'd have tried harder'." I shake my head, giving him a dirty look. "You either fought to protect yourself and Theo, or you were fighting to kill."

"Protect," Theo and Caden say at the same time. I give one nod and move on.

"Caden brings up an excellent point. Why is he here?" Alaric asks.

"We made it very clear before we left Wildfire that they were not to leave their pack, since we knew you needed to see them. We made it clear that they would be dealing with you directly for their crimes," I say, looking at Alaric. "I've got no idea why he'd disobey to come and attack us, but Cameron will have the answers."

I look over at Warren. "Can you take me?" He nods.

"Then let's go," Primus Viotto says.

It's weird how quickly he shifts from just being Alaric, the man who is my friend—a man who supports me, teaches me, and even protects me—has been since I found out about this world. He's offered me his trust. He's offered me his people. He's offered me his aid. And yet, right now, this is Primus Viotto, the King of all Vampires. I can feel the danger surrounding him, feel the powerful aura he's emitting.

Even though he's now significantly weaker than when I last saw him.

Warren takes my hand, squeezes our hands together, and then lifts me into his arms.

I barely manage to adjust myself in his arms so I'm comfortable before he takes off. We race through the woods, closing in on the town we're visiting.

Our run takes a minute or so, and despite the wind being freezing cold—and my ears and fingertips potentially never gaining feeling again—it feels good to be this secure and safe.

Of course, that's ruined the moment we come to a stop at the office building. I've been to this pack too many times in the past twenty-four hours, and I really hope this is my last visit here.

"How come the barriers didn't stop us?" Warren asks, looking at me with a raised eyebrow.

"They're not his barriers yet."

"I sense your pack's energy," Alaric says.

"Noah's still projecting them around the area," I reply. "The plan was for him to disable it once they were in your custody. I didn't want to risk them keeping you out."

"We'll address that once we're back. Your Alpha is strong, but he cannot afford that level of strain for very long."

Warren snorts, and I give him a weird look, but he doesn't elaborate. *Weirdo.*

"No, I fully agree," I say, ending the conversation there as I lead Warren and Alaric through to the reception area of the building.

The same receptionist that was here yesterday is still here, sitting at the desk, typing away. She doesn't look up as we enter, not until Warren coughs.

Then the woman jumps in surprise, her wolf curious but not as hostile as the human.

She's still not wearing a name badge, which pisses me off.

"Hello," she says, a little bit frantic. "Who may you all be?"

"We've already met," I say dryly. "Where is Cameron?"

"Alpha Moore is currently upstairs having a meeting," she says. "He's not to be disturbed."

"Is that so? I doubt he'll mind," I reply, pivoting on my heel. I sense his energy and head upstairs. It's easy to find his office—it's just a few doors down from the meeting room we used the other day.

His receptionist chases after us, just until the stairwell, before returning to her desk in a hurry, likely to call Cameron and complain.

Why wouldn't she just use the mind-link?

Cameron is on his feet, waiting for us when we enter his office. He's a little frazzled, clearly not expecting visitors in person, but there's also relief in his tone.

"You got his message, then?"

"Whose message?" I demand.

"Jason's."

I take a step back, unsure how to gently break the news to him. I lost my mate thanks to them, and I care very little about tactfully breaking this news.

Alaric steps forward for me. "I am Primus Viotto, and we have a lot of business to handle."

"And I completely understand that," Cameron says. I can feel the tension radiating from the new Alpha wolf, and I'm unsure why. "I'm here. I'm not trying to flee the responsibility left to me. My parents fucked up. I played a part in it. I could have tried harder to fight, I know. But we don't have the time for any of that right now."

"We don't?" Warren drawls in his most sarcastic tone.

"Can you explain why you think your message is more important than us handling the situation your family got us into with the humans?" My tone is chilling, but he doesn't protest.

"Because I got a message from him—from King Lobo." My heart drops, panic rising in my chest, but Cameron continues. "King Lobo has decided that I should be rewarded,' Cameron says, almost hesitantly. He sits down and shakes his head. "Didn't even seem to care that I wasn't the same Alpha he made the deal with."

Cameron's face is pale, and there are bags under his eyes. I can feel the unhappiness from his wolf, their combined exhaustion obvious.

He knows how badly his parents fucked up, and he's not trying to hide from that or his part in it.

He's trying.

Who am I to crucify a man for trying?

"Here," he says, all but throwing the letter at my face. I grab it from the air and smooth it out so that I can read it properly.

It's short, concise and offers him a reward for any additional information he may find. Once he's officially crowned as the next leader, he promises a boon to this pack.

How lovely.

What a generous master he is, offering *prizes for the death of my mate.*

I hand the letter to Warren, who reads it quickly before shoving it into Alaric's hands.

"Thank you for sharing that with us," I say. "But it's with regret I have to inform you that Jason is dead, and the reason I'm here is not because of your message but because we killed him."

I could've tried to sound more guilty about that.

"Fucking hell." Cameron's face drops.

"If it helps," I offer, giving him a small smile. "The day my friend was coronated as Alpha, King Lobo bombed his entire pack."

Cameron turns around, giving me a blank look. I can feel his surprise but also his disdain.

What are you thinking, Lottie?

"I know it's probably not very helpful," I say. "But it could be worse, right? They've spent the last couple of months filled with terror, panic, and distaste for the man who so easily gave you and your pack what you wanted." I take a small step forward. "You're not alone, Cameron. An Alpha without a mate can be a lonely role, but you don't have to *be* alone. If you make the right choice and choose to be on our side, the right side, you'll have allies for days."

"That's why I contacted you in the first place," Cameron says. "And now, my Beta is dead."

"Wasn't Jason your dad's Beta?" Warren drawls. I elbow my vampire mate, and he gives me an amused look.

"He is," I say, quietly. "And he's not the only one."

"But you know what this means, don't you?" Warren says, and Cameron looks at him in surprise.

"It means that you've got a clean start," I say, taking over from whatever sarcastic and mean thing Warren was about to say. The vampire within him is disappointed, so I know it was going to be entirely unsupportive. "Your parents are going to be going away with Alaric, at least for a little bit whilst they work everything out. You've got the chance to sort out your pack and give those who want it the freedom. Your people have been too scared to leave their lands, even for a quick trip to town, let alone to do anything else. You get to be the Alpha who delivers on those promises."

As Cameron begins to get excited, Alaric holds his hand up. "I understand how excited you are to handle that, and when the time comes, I'll do what I can to help. In the meantime, we need to keep a lid on the actual dead human part of the ordeal because that's a mess I am trying to clean up as quickly, efficiently, and politically as possible."

"How can I help with that?" Cameron asks.

"Do exactly as I, or my people, say. Work with us when it comes to it," Alaric says. "And I promise you, once it's all done, my people and I will work with you to sort out all of the problems you've been having —like it should've happened before all this erupted. Your Council had a duty to you that they failed, and I won't make that mistake."

Cameron nods his head. "So, Jason was killed by your mates?"

I nod. "He came to deliver your message, but I think he got something twisted from your delivery, or he saw his chance and took it. He came through the borders directly to us, and when stopped by two of my men, he decided to attack instead. They've never seen his wolf form, so they didn't recognise him, and well... he's dead, and they're alive."

"Of course, that's how it happened," he says, shaking his head in disbelief.

"How dare you," I roar, slamming my hands on the table as my wolf rushes to the forefront of our mind. I have no doubt my eyes are black as I stare him down. The two of us are ready to wipe him from this Earth.

Fuck, I really have become obsessed with bloodshed.

"How dare you doubt my truth after everything you and your people have put me through," I hiss. "My mate is dead thanks to *your* family, and you're sitting here thinking that what I count as revenge is killing your pathetic Beta just to have the platform once more to air my grievances? Do you really think that would be for you, Cameron? Is that what would soothe the anger and despair you'd feel at losing your soulmate? Would killing some random fucking Beta, you barely know, take away the hurt and pain of seeing your mate laid out on the floor, dying in front of your very eyes? Would your pound of flesh be killing a weak Beta who did nothing but follow instructions?"

His mouth is open, his wolf shaking in fear.

I scoff. "Trust me, when I come for a pound of flesh, it will not suffice for it to be something that pathetic. I tell you the truth. Jason came to us, and he would not stop fighting. My men did what they had to do so that they could survive. Considering we've already lost one person tonight, after they've spent the night battling vampires and werewolves that want to kill us *and* a bunch of humans that we had to protect because of, oh wait, *your family*. You know, the humans who were ungrateful and put up a decent fight as well, that they were being herded somewhere by random people. It was chaos.

"And yet you think we'd stoop so low as to kill your Beta just for the fun of it. Thanks, Cameron, seriously, thanks a fucking lot. We showed you mercy. Showed you the kind of people we are. We did everything by the book, unlike you and your father."

"I didn't mean to call into doubt your character," Cameron says quietly. "All I meant—"

"Well, you did, and there's no way you can just undo that," I say, shaking my head. "My character has already been so badly damaged that I doubt I can even blame you."

"I—"

"Can we keep this letter?" I demand. It's pretty useless as far as letters go, but I want out of here.

"Yes, of course."

"Any more contact with King Lobo or one of his followers should be reported to Alaric," I say, and he nods. "If anything goes wrong, or there's anything out of the ordinary, you *will* tell Alaric."

"Understood."

And with that, I turn and leave the room, giving the stupid receptionist a dirty look on my way out. My power is building up once again, ready to unleash, and I know that I can't keep going this way. I can't keep being so emotionally charged.

"You're an emotionally charged kind of girl," Warren says, and I whirl around, not having realised he had been scanning me. I look behind him for Alaric and raise an eyebrow when I can still feel his energy upstairs with Cameron.

"He's got a few things to say to Cameron," Warren replies.

"I see."

"Which is perfect since it gives us time to address your upset," Warren says, and I sigh. "You've always been emotional, princess. But the fact that you're pregnant and in the first trimester, makes it all the more understandable. Your hormones are all over the place. You've been powering through and working and doing so much that you're not giving yourself credit where it's due. You're growing a child—*four children*—and that's not something to be making light of."

I nod slowly before shaking my head. "I don't think I can just blame this on pregnancy."

"Maybe not all of it," Warren says, giving me a cheeky smirk. "I did say you've always been emotional. But think back to the days when you didn't even know you were a wolf. How many times did you sit and cry for no reason? How much panic were you constantly feeling? You were a hysterical mess in the early days, yet you survived it."

"Thanks," I mutter.

He laughs. "We can laugh about it now, but that's just the truth of how it is. We know that you're emotional, princess. You feel everything deeply, and it's one of the things I love most about you. But for pregnancy, it's heightened, and you just have to accept that. The babies are adding to it, and then your grief over losing my brother isn't something to be ignored either."

"No, it's not."

"So, stop beating yourself up. You are doing what needs to be done and doing it the right way—the Lottie way. Now, wipe that frown off your face, fix your crown, and let's go back to the others because we've still got enough to do."

"You're decent at pep talks," I say, taking a step towards him. "Five out of ten."

"I'll take it, considering you're an eleven out of five when it comes to being an emotional mess."

"I love you."

"And I love you," he replies, pressing a kiss to my temple as we wait for Alaric to finish up inside.

As he returns, the vampire monarch gives us a nod, silently promising that he's handled the situation with Cameron and Wildfire, but doesn't say a thing out loud. We're not sure who is listening or what their motives are.

We head back home, and I'm not sure if Warren and Alaric were deliberately keeping speed with each other or if the drain on Alaric's powers has made him this weak, but it concerns me.

I'll have to bring it up with Freya when she gets back.

Everyone is anxiously waiting for us, and someone has brought some garden chairs from who knows where. Caden's got a full-length deck chair and is actually sitting with his feet up, whilst the others all have the cheaper, normal ones.

"How did it go?" Noah asks, a little anxiously. He's wary about what has happened and likely worried about the repercussions.

"Not bad," I say, and there's a sigh of relief. "What's happening here?"

"We've received a text from Officer Jones," Rhett says, almost too calmly for me to relax. "They've got some information they can share —information they won't be putting on the books."

"And?" Warren asks when I don't.

"They've located where King Lobo is staying. They've found his hideout. They've found where he's holed up."

"How?" I demand, edging forward. Hope flares in my chest at how easy this has turned out to be, and it's quickly replaced by a bitter feeling. "How likely is it that this is true?"

"Here," Noah says, handing me my phone to see for myself. I read the messages and see the attached photos as my eyes widen.

It's good that Cain Viotto is dead—he's a very foolish man.

"Holy fuck," I say. My wolf is pacing around in my mind, desperate to go and track King Lobo down. She wants us to destroy him, to get the revenge River deserves—that we deserve.

I can't help but agree. This is a very good opportunity, and we can't let it pass us by—especially now that the original plan has been thrown out of the window.

We've gotten very lucky indeed.

CHAPTER 41

"What do we do now?" Warren whispers, probably to avoid waking me up. It's a futile attempt, though; I've been awake for a few minutes now. I'm not sure what time it is or how long I've been asleep, but it was a waste of time, as far as I'm convinced.

We left the human town, ditching our minivan once we were in the next town, and we replaced it with three cars, just on the off chance we were being tracked. We doubt it, but Theo's paranoia is worth paying attention to.

We drove for an hour, going into Morpeth's city centre, and booked into a hotel for the night, buying ourselves some time to figure out our next steps.

I passed out almost immediately after getting into the hotel, but sleeping was pointless. I didn't get to see River. I didn't get to see *anyone.* Neither Conri, my ancestors, nor the Guardian of All thought I was worth enough of a visit.

Fucking assholes.

I just slept the evening away, moving on from River's death as not even a single bad dream burdened me. *I didn't deserve that.*

My wolf disagrees. She thinks we were running on empty and were too weak to be taken to the realm, but I ignore her. She doesn't grieve River with me; she doesn't really care that he's dead.

I can feel all of my men in the room with me, each struggling with the depths of their grief, yet they're trying to be brave for me. I haven't even opened my eyes yet, and I'm already filled to the brim with their love and support. All eight of our bonds are thrumming with our proximity, and my wolf only slightly feels the absence of River's.

Bitch.

His death is now true, but to her... she grieved when we broke the bond between us. I can feel her relief that she won't be confused by the hybrid anymore, and it fucking kills me.

Because me? I'm drowning in the depths of my despair. River was everything to me. He was another part of me; we still loved each other, even without the bond. He had a life ahead of him, and that's all been taken away.

I've lost yet another loved one to a war that never should've been mine to fight in the first place.

I fucking wish my wolf had a voice, so I wouldn't need to try and differentiate her feelings from my own.

Maybe then, I could separate them and not feel guilty for feeling this pain, for feeling guilty over his death.

"We move on," I say, opening my eyes. The light blinds me briefly, but my eyes quickly adjust to it. I can see them, all of them, and there are plenty of red eyes around the room.

The worst goes to my curly-haired brunette, who gives me a weak smile when my eyes fall on him. I heal him, hating the pain he's been in whilst I've slept, and I immediately see the difference in him. It might not take the grief away, but it's provided him with one less thing to fight.

On the other hand, his brother is pale, but that's the only thing that's off about him. Warren's face is so determined I don't think he's even permitted his lips to quiver. Warren's brother is now dead, and he's still not yet allowed himself to grieve.

Caden, Noah and Rhett are all upset, but the latter two are not as destroyed as Caden and Elijah seem to be. Dillon's upset is clear, and Wyatt's trying to be strong despite how unhappy his wolf is at the loss of the hybrid.

My Guardian seems a little unbothered, but I know that's untrue. Theo is trying to hide his emotions from me again, placing a block between us, but I'm too powerful for that to work anymore. I can feel the love he has for me, and it's one of eight pillars of strength, helping boost me up.

But Theo's upset is buried under his strong demeanour, and I won't push him for more. I'll not push any of them for me.

Well, that's unless they start pulling away from me again. We survived it once; we'll not survive it a second time.

"Nobody is leaving you," Theo promises, and I'm grateful for his mind-reading abilities right now. *"I'll kill them myself if anyone even dares."*

"And you?"

"I'd sooner slash my own throat."

And that's that, then. Theo's feeling the loss probably as bad as I am, even if just as my echo. We're two halves of a whole, and my pain is his. But I know he's struggling with his guilt on top of that—Theo takes the blame for every single thing that goes wrong in our life.

No matter how untrue it is.

"We live, and we need to fight to make that the case," I say, looking at my men. "We've been playing it safe as we can; we're on the defensive even though we want to be on the offensive with the Council. So why are we playing it this way with King Lobo? We need to find a way to take back some of the power, or I fear that River won't be our only casualty."

"How the fuck do we do that, though?" Wyatt asks. "We barely even know what we're up against, and he's got something we don't."

"Which is?" Rhett asks.

"Decades against us," Dillon replies. "You're forgetting that this goes back to when Lottie was a baby. She was taken as an infant and hidden from this world. He's had years to build his power, to amass an army, and to prepare his plans for this day. We've had *months*, and even then, I'd argue we've only really had a month."

"And our focus has been split," Theo says, giving Dillon a nod. "So, you're right, Charlotte, but I don't think it will be easy."

"Nothing worth doing is ever easy," I say, with a shrug. "But this is not just worth it—it's our only option."

"They're right, though," Rhett says. "The theory is easy, but we don't have any power."

"But we do, though," Warren argues, hiding his hands out in front of himself, and shivers race down my spine as pink and purple flashes through the air. His veins are bright pink, his eyes a deep purple. "We've got a lot of power. We're just not utilising it."

"I think they targeted us for a reason," Dillon says, hesitantly. "it was more than just a ploy."

"What do you mean?" Theo asks eyes narrowed.

"I think they targeted," Dillon pauses, eyeing me warily. "River." They give me an apologetic look, but I just shrug.

I can handle his name being said, even if it hurts.

"I think they targeted River for a particular reason," Dillon continues.

"And that reason is?" Rhett asks, almost mockingly.

"I think they wanted him because he's a hybrid—a true hybrid."

"So what about me?" Elijah asks. "Was I targeted for a reason?

Dillon bites his bottom lip and shakes his head. "In this theory? No. You were just a convenient man there so that Lottie would have to choose between the two of you."

"Choose," I whisper. "How the fuck could King Lobo know about my choice? The one the ancestors told me about?"

"Choosing between saving Elijah, your mate, and River, the true hybrid, might not have been a choice that King Lobo set out," Dillon says slowly. "But I definitely think River was the target of the attack."

"But you're saying that like I made the wrong choice," I say slowly. My chest tightens, and I look down at my hands.

Does he really think that I chose wrong? How could that be the case? I chose Elijah, the man I have a soul tie. I chose my mate.

How could that be wrong?

"You're saying that like they knew she chose a life," Theo says, and Dillon shrugs. He doesn't have the answers. None of us do. None of those will get answers until we talk to King Lobo. And that's not going to be done until at least tomorrow."

"I think that they were targeting River because he was new, he was rare, and he was very fucking powerful. River was a true hybrid. He's an unknown." I notice that he keeps talking about River in the past tense.

I hate how badly it hurts.

"So, who else is on this mystery target list of his?" Rhett asks with a frown. "We're all powerful men."

"Warren," Dillon says, and the cheeky curly head smirks, saluting with two fingers.

"I'd also say that if we're going by that logic," Wyatt says. "Theo's there."

"Right on the money," Dillon says. "Removing the three powerhouses of the group, the three unknowns, will mess with Lottie's offence more than anything else. At least, it will in his eyes."

"Well, that's lovely," I say. Theo reaches over and tries to soothe the nausea, but since it's a product of my anxiety and not our tiny humans, it doesn't disappear. If only anxiety-induced nausea were an actual physical condition.

"It's going to be a big, long-drawn-out battle," Dillon says. "So we need to reassess our plans. We had the idea of going to see each pack one by one—"

"But I think that's stupid," Caden says. "Especially after this visit that went so perfectly. I don't want to go through that again. Peter was a fucking snake, yet everything looked perfect—his pack loved him, his family was strong, even their workspaces. The only rude part was their receptionist, and I think that's just her personality."

"She was rude when we went there again today," Warren says.

"But that's it. Everything went to plan," Caden says. "And see what happened? So, going into a pack where we *know* there will be problems?"

Caden shakes his head.

"I agree. Peter has been the biggest snake we've encountered this far," Noah says.

"I agree with you. But then, how do we proceed from here? What do we do?" Wyatt asks.

"Well, maybe we ditch the plan," Rhett offers.

I snuggle into the blankets, listening to them plan things out. I know what I want to do.

We've got the location of King Lobo, and we should go down there and ready ourselves for the fight that's coming.

"The best way to gain the allegiance of the people is to be the figurehead for the people, right?" Rhett says.

"We can't just elect ourselves as King," Wyatt protests.

"*You* can't, you weak little beta," Caden taunts, and Warren snorts.

I don't laugh, though. "We're not just able to take over the Council here, guys."

"Can you honestly say you don't have a plan to overthrow the entire Council?" Noah asks, raising an eyebrow at me.

"And don't deny it. Considering we've sat through more than one plan to do just that," Warren adds.

When I open my mouth, I wrinkle my nose and laugh. "Fine. My plan at some point was to get rid of the bad people, not just eradicate the Council as a whole. It's still an important structure of our society."

"Well, then clearly, we're not focusing hard enough on these goals," Caden says. "Let's just fuck the Council. We can go in and blow up—"

"Can we not talk about blowing things up in front of the suspected terrorist?" I ask, raising my hand in the air.

"River's the only one with true PTSD from that, and he's not complaining," Wyatt says. "Probably because he's dead."

He freezes, as do the rest of us. I don't even know how to speak. My heart stops, and even my wolf falls silent. His joke was not funny or appropriate.

"What the fuck?" Warren says before bursting out laughing.

"Fucking hell," Caden whispers, shaking his head.

"Too soon?" Wyatt asks with a grimace. He doesn't look at me, but I know the question's directed my way.

Rhett snorts. "Yes, way too soon."

"River probably would have found it funny," I say, biting back the urge to cry. "So let's just move on before I do cry. What do we want to do next?"

"Well, that was my original start to this type of conversation," Warren says, giving me a teasing grin. "And your response, princess, was to fight."

"Then it looks like we need to figure out how to plan an attack," I say.

"And fast," Wyatt says. "Because at this point, I think King Lobo will be upping his attacks to try and take out the rest of us if Dillon's correct."

"Especially once he gets wind of his terrorist plan not working out," Noah says.

"Well, we've got this location," I say. "So we can at least head down there and plan the attack properly."

"What about the ancestors' warning of handling the council first?" Theo says slowly. "I don't think it'd be wise to ignore that."

"But we've got King Lobo's location," I argue. "The Council isn't a threat to our lives, not really. They're currently on hold from executing me, whereas King Lobo is actively trying to kill me."

"I agree with Lottie," Rhett says.

"Unsurprising," Theo mutters.

"Then let's take a vote," Caden asks, "Hands up in the air. Who wants to do King Lobo first?"

Every hand bar Theo's raises, and he sighs before putting his up.

"Fine. Let's handle King Lobo first."

"It might give us an advantage," Dillon adds. "If he's got an in with the ancestors like we do, he might have been advised that we're going to the Council first. This will then give us the chance to change the game."

"Looks like we're going down south," Caden says. "We'll leave in the morning."

"And what do we do when we get there?"

"We take it bit by bit," Noah says, a little hesitantly.

Bit by bit. That I can do.

42

CHAPTER 42

"Try and get some sleep on the drive down," Dillon says, softly. "This level of exhaustion is *normal* in the first trimester, okay? We'd be more surprised if you weren't tired at all. And besides, you slept for a few hours last night and were tossing and turning with nightmares—you're exhausted, Lottie, and that's not good for you or the babies."

"I know," I say, with a sigh.

Theo's look of utter devastation makes me feel guilty, but he shakes his head when I open my mouth to apologise. "Why do you feel guilty, little wolf? It's me who can't heal you."

I shrug, not sure how to put it into words. "You take the sickness away, and that's the worst part. I can deal with being tired."

"Can you deal with the fighting from the rest of them, though?" Dillon whispers, a mischievous twinkle in his eyes.

"Fighting," I ask, raising an eyebrow. "We're splitting up. Why would there be fighting?"

"Yes, we are splitting up," Dillon says. "And do you really think there's not going to be a fight over who gets to be in your car?"

I groan and look over at Theo. "I'll feel better if you're driving."

He gives me one nod. "Already planning on it, little wolf."

"Then I shall take Dillon," I say, trying to think of who else in our group can fit in with us without causing fights. Rhett, Caden, Warren and Elijah are all out. Wyatt would probably be better with Warren and Elijah, leaving me with Noah.

I break the groups down. Caden, Warren and Wyatt in one car—the former is a little exhausted and processing from River's death, whereas the latter would likely really enjoy riling each other up as a distraction tool. Rhett and Elijah will also be together, which I think will work well.

Hopefully, this way, there won't be any big fights.

"Don't worry, Charlotte," Theo says, with a smirk. "The three of us will have such a lovely time while you're asleep."

"Please don't pick a fight," I say, looking at my Guardian this time.

"I won't," he says. "I just want to drive down there, and I promise you I'll be safe."

"So," I say, "what *is* the plan for going down there?"

"I think, at this point, the best idea is just to stay alive," Dillon says.

I groan. "How certain are we that this isn't a trap?"

"80%," Dillon says.

"60," Theo counters.

"Well, that's reassuring because I thought my 75% was a tad too optimistic."

It doesn't take much longer for us to get packed into the cars, and Dillon was correct. There was definite tension when it became clear that the others wouldn't be in my car, but I made my desire for a fight-free drive very clear.

Hopefully, this arrangement will allow for that.

"Are you comfy?" Noah asks, and I nod my head. My chair is reclined as far as it can go. I've got a blanket wrapped around me, and I'm attempting to get some sleep.

Lord knows I need it.

The drive will take a good few hours, and we've planned a stop approximately two and a half hours in for food and, more importantly, to stretch our legs and possibly rearrange the seating if necessary.

My eyes stubbornly refuse to stay closed as we drive, and it's pissing me off.

Whether it's because of Noah's heavy breathing, the clicking of Dylan's Kindle when he turns the pages or the rhythmic tapping of Theo's fingers on the steering wheel, I just can't quiet my mind enough to sleep.

It's driving me insane.

There are no files to review, no people to converse with, and nothing I can do to reassure myself that things will be alright. This is the moment we've been anticipating, the grand confrontation, the ultimate showdown, between us and King Lobo.

And yet, I can't shake the feeling that it's the wrong move, that we shouldn't be doing this.

Logically, that's not true. Now is the best time to attack, but it's just a heavy weight on my shoulders.

"I just hate it."

"Did you mean to say that out loud?" Noah asks, softly.

I turn to look at my Alpha wolf in the back seat and shake my head.

"It's hard not knowing if we're doing the right thing," Noah says. "But no matter which route we take, there are no guarantees."

"I trust that we're doing the right thing. But there's still that general feeling of anxiety," I say, with a shrug. "It's silly."

"It's not silly," Theo says, coming to a stop in front of the traffic lights. I watch them, waiting for the lights to turn red to green. "That's just your feelings, little wolf. It's *normal*."

"Maybe," I concede.

The traffic lights still don't change, and I furrow my brows as I look around. This isn't a busy road, and no towns or houses are nearby.

Why is there a traffic light here?

I look up and down the road, and in a blink, a good hundred or so vampires appear before us. My eyes widen, panic filling me.

"Shit," Noah whispers. He looks at Dillon. "You ready?"

My mate nods, and the two jump out of the car, preparing to fight all those vampires.

"No!" I scream, shaking my head. The vampires race towards our car, picking it up underneath them with Theo and I inside it. I scream as we're launched through the air, but instead of dying, the background changes, and I'm sitting on the grass.

In the Ancestral Realm.

What the fuck is going on?

"It was a nasty dream," Conri says, and my heart races as I whirl around to see him. He gives me a pain-filled smile. "I am so sorry about your mate, young one."

"Yeah, well, it's a bit too late for that now," I say, pushing up from the floor and rising to my feet. "How are you here?"

"It's been determined that you are ready to hear the truth. You have a decision to make—"

"Another fucking decision," I say, bitterly. "Of course I do."

"If there was any other way..."

"You'd still prefer I did it this way to follow your path?" I ask, with a sneer.

"And that's your choice, this time. You have two clear paths outlined as far as we can see. One, where you follow our guidance and play the fame, as you so aptly put it," Conri says. "The other is that you can charge forward with the plan you and your mates have and see where it takes you."

"So we can what? Attack King Lobo now, or we can... what is your plan?"

"You've been told to handle the Council *before* you handle King

Lobo," Conri says. "If you can handle the Council before him, everything else will likely fall in line."

"But if I do it my way?"

"There's a lot of uncertainty," he says. "And some consequences you might not be prepared to handle."

"So play by your rules, or I'm going to be fucked over," I say.

"I'm not sure that's the exact terminology I'd use."

I sigh, shaking my head. "What can you tell me now?"

"Let's start right back at the beginning. I told you I was the original wolf, and whilst I may not have lied... it wasn't the whole truth either."

I narrow my eyes, cocking my hip as I stare him down. "Then what is the entire truth."

"I have a twin brother."

"Of course you do," I say.

"He's not like me and wasn't awarded the same power perks I was. Sure, he's immortal and strong, but he's not... *King*. I was given that privilege, and it was something my brother was envious of," Conri says, not looking at me. "He was not impressed with that. We always had a strained relationship and a lot of jealousy between us. He ended up leaving the United Kingdom for a very long time. He travelled the world and made himself King at each location he visited before finally he came back here.

"By that point, I was done being King. I was bored with the life, and the responsibilities of it all, and I knew I couldn't keep up with it all and still be fair, which is when I created the Council. He was furious I didn't hand things over to him, and it didn't end well for us.

"He started researching everything he could, tracking down the other immortal beings, learning the rules and regulations they were upheld to, and he found out that the first female of my line would get my power.

"It warped him. It twisted his sense of morality, and that was already pretty skewered in the first place.

"It became a battle between us, as he started hunting down my heirs, anyone from my direct line, so he could track them and stop them.

"Sure, he flew in and out over the years, just like I did, but the moment you were born, my wolf knew. You were special, and I had to save you.

"So, I took you. I worked to keep you hidden, and I kept you far away from him and far away from wolves in general. The goal was not to shift until you were older and could handle the responsibility."

"Nice of you to identify that for me," I say, trying my best not to sneer the words at him. "So instead of getting a handle on your crazy brother who *hunted your family*, you just... left him to it?"

"Of course not. I..." He trails off. "Did not do enough because the man hunting you down is my brother. King Lobo is him."

"Fucking lovely," I snarl, shaking my head. "And you left me, knowing this. You weren't even going to admit it before your death. Do you understand the position you've put me in?"

"I do."

"I can't even be around you. This is... is wrong. What about Razor? Does he know about your brother, the sociopath who murders his family?"

"Not all of the ins and outs."

"Of course not. That would be far too easy," I say. "But what am I supposed to do now? I can't just sit here and wait for King Lobo to come after me. What's the plan? What would you have done?"

Conri takes a deep breath, his expression grave. "You need to kill him. It's the only way for this to end."

I nod. "Before I go—what is his name?"

I hear it whispered as I'm shoved out of the ancestral realm.

I don't know much more than I did, but at least what I do know will help.

It just seems to have cost me yet another betrayal, and I was just starting to like him.

CHAPTER 43

"Wake up, Lottie," Noah soothes, and my eyes fly open. He's standing in the doorway of my side of the car and gives me a smile. I look past him in confusion, not understanding where we are. "You slept the entire way here. Are you okay?"

"I'm okay," I murmur, although I'm not too sure if I believe it or not. "We're here?"

"Yes. Well, we're half an hour out. We're in a human town, and there are no supernaturals around. Not a vampire, wolf, or *anything* in between."

"And that's good, though, right?" I ask.

"It is," he says, with a nod. "We're safe enough here. On the way down, I rented a house, so we're heading over to that as soon as Theo and Dillon get the keys."

"Where are the others?" I ask.

"Gone shopping for food since we'll likely be here a few days. We're trying not to look too suspicious to the locals. We're not sure what they're like here, but humans and wolves... we don't get along. They can sense that we're different, and it makes this kind of thing hard."

"Huh," I murmur, thinking about Katie and her family. Sure, they had the pack, but Katie was very immersed in human life when she was younger.

Or was I immersed in wolf life?

"Once we get settled, we need to talk about Conri," I say, and his eyes widen. "Yep. I finally had a talk with him about all the things he was keeping from me."

"All of them?"

"The big one."

Noah lets out a slow breath. "Are you okay?"

"Not really. But I will be. We just need to figure out what to do next. He told me I need to kill his brother," I say.

"His brother?" Noah hisses, leaning into the car to talk to me more. But when I don't speak, realisation hits him, and he lets out a snarl.

"Shh," I soothe, squeezing his hands. "We'll discuss it at the house. I'm sorry."

Noah nods, as Theo and Dillon come out of the building holding some keys. Dillon probes about the atmosphere as we take off, but I'll share once we're at the house.

We don't have the luxury of having my men lose their temper in a town like this. But as we keep driving, we leave the town, going much further South. Maybe an extra 20-minute drive away from the human town.

We pull up in front of a large, sprawling house. It towers above us with three stories and at least five bedrooms. It's a far cry from the cosy cottage I was expecting.

"Wow," I say as we get out of the car. "This is amazing."

"Right?" Theo says. "We're only here for a few days, but it's isolated and gives us the time to plan what we need to do."

"And there's no humans who will be watching us come and go at odd hours," Dillon says. "Genius thinking, Noah."

"Absolutely *genius*," Theo adds.

I eye the three men, not sure what I've missed, but Noah's cheeks are red, and they're all smirking.

I wave it off, not bothering to press even further.

It only takes an hour for the others to arrive, and we unpack the food before sitting down to talk about my meeting with Conri.

"Fucking hell," Caden snarls. "Is he taking the piss out of us?"

"I think he is," I mutter, resting my head on my hands.

"Well, at least we've got a bit of an idea what we're going against," Wyatt says.

"Do we?" I ask, with a frown. "Because to me, it seems a little bit sketchy. A random man we've never heard of who is more powerful than most wolves but not me wants me dead."

"It does sound sketchy," Noah agrees. "But we can't ignore it. We need to come up with a plan."

"Agreed," Dillon says. "I think we need to plan our attack as soon as possible."

"Plan it or launch it?" I ask, raising an eyebrow.

"Plan it" is echoed around the room.

"Then why did we come down here so soon? Why did we risk being seen and being caught and blowing this all up... if we're not going to attack for *days*?"

"Because we need to be here to see his town to figure out the defences and how to handle it all," Rhett says.

"Come on, little wolf, you know how to plan a war, right?"

I shrug. "Sort of?"

"Then let's get planning."

"*I*t's been two days of intense preparation," Noah says. "But we're ready. Come tomorrow evening; this should all be over."

The exhaustion is evident in his tone, and we all feel it. We've been pushing ourselves, preparing, and doing everything possible to stay undetected. We're ready.

Our allies are prepped. Each pack has teamed up with the nearest clan; each prepared to be here for the fight tomorrow. We're not hesitating anymore.

Tomorrow... it all comes to an end.

"Where are the others?" I ask, quietly. It's getting late—well, if you count 8 p.m. as late. Noah fills me in on what they're all doing, and it's only Rhett's task that I'm worried about. He's double-checking that our entrance tomorrow has still not changed. I highly doubt it will since they still don't know we're here, but I'd much rather be over-prepared than under.

It took some strategising from everyone involved, especially since many of the more prominent players, like my dad and Charles, couldn't be here to see things from our perspective. They're putting so much trust in us, and I genuinely don't think it's warranted.

"Why don't you have a bath and relax whilst we wait for the others to get back?" he asks.

I sigh. "I feel like a..."

"The pregnant mother of my children who needs to relax so that she and they are healthy," Noah says, reaching over to squeeze my thigh. "I love you more than anything. Go relax."

I nod, heading through to the bathroom. I start to fill the tub and even go as far as using my bath bomb from River. It's cute and adds to the relaxed atmosphere I'm trying to create.

The water doesn't take long to heat up, and I undress as it does. Noah brings me a mug of tea, perching it on the side of the bath, and presses a gentle kiss to my head before leaving me be.

It's nice to have a little bit of time to myself—even if it feels selfish.

Everyone else is out working, and here I am, drinking decaf tea and relaxing in the bath.

Well, I will be in a minute.

Once it's ready, I get settled in the tub, and the water coats my skin so luxuriously. I never realised how nice it could feel. But then, it all goes to shit. The soft feeling becomes painful, and I scream so fucking loudly that Noah comes racing into the room, but it's too late for me. Agony rips through my body; my nerves are on fire, my muscles are aching, and my chest is ripped open. Elijah appears next to me, his eyes wide as he watches me writhe in the bath.

I can hear them shouting, pleading, trying to get my attention as I slosh around in the water, gripping my chest, trying not to die.

There's so much pain.

It hurts so badly.

I'm dying.

Bleeding.

Burning.

So much pain.

"Explain what the fuck is going on," someone roars, Caden, I think, but I can't tell.

I can't even explain what is happening when I don't understand it myself. My cries and sobs are so fucking loud, and it's all I can hear— well, that and the desperate howls of my wolf as she cries and begs for her mate.

"*I'm sorry,*" Warren whispers across the bond. I can hear his words so clearly, despite the absolute agony that I'm in—the agony that *he* is in.

"*I'm so fucking sorry, Lottie,*" he continues. "*I love you. I love you so fucking much, and I couldn't let them find you. I couldn't let them destroy our plans.*"

"What did you do?" I cry, shaking my head back and forth. "Why did you do it? How? How could you do this?"

My body is trembling, and someone is trying to get my attention, but I can feel anything except Warren's pain.

I'm drowning in it. Drowning in his torment.

What has happened to him? Who has hurt him this way? The only thing I can focus on is my connection to Warren.

More hands start touching me, and my body starts to shiver when I'm yanked out of the bathtub.

A hand grips my chin, and someone snarls, "Cut off the connection to Warren."

My eyes focus on him, on the bright green eyes of Elijah.

"Trust me, sunshine, *shut the bond off.*"

When I don't do it fast enough, I feel Theo reaching through our bond to do it himself. His presence is small at first before he overloads my system with him. The rest of my bonds are muted—practically gone—and I can only feel Theo.

His energy has taken over my conscious thought, and he blocks me from feeling anything Warren related.

"Warren is hurt," I whisper.

"How?" Elijah demands. There's panic in his words, and I know he's terrified.

We've already lost River.

We can't lose Warren, too.

"I don't know," I say, pulling my hands from Caden. I move to sit up properly, wrapping myself in the towel.

"*Why are you sorry?*" I demand.

"*They found me on the way back,*" Warren says. "*I had to adjust my route, so they didn't realise how close we are.*"

"*So, where are you?*"

"*Even with Eli's help, you'll not get to me in time. I think... I think this is my end, Lottie.*"

My heart stops, and my wolf howls in pain.

Our mate is giving up.

"*Fucking watch me,*" I snarl, disconnecting with him.

"We find him, and now," I demand, looking around the room. "He's playing the martyr, and I won't let him die."

I yank my suitcase out from under my bed and pull clothes out. I don't care what I wear, not when Warren is dying.

We've lost River. I refuse to lose another Ellis brother.

"I can't do this again," I whisper.

"We're handling it," Rhett says as gently as he can. "Just get yourself ready for when he gets back here."

I nod, moving into a trance as I pull my clothes on. I hear them moving and feel people leave the room, but I'm struggling so hard.

Warren is running to try and keep himself safe.

He's nearly been captured.

"Until he's somewhere safe, we can't intervene. It'll only cost us more lives," Rhett says firmly.

"No!" I'm not sure what's louder—my sob or my howl. Both my wolf and I are already mourning our loss, and he's not even dead yet.

"Warren, please," I beg across the mind-link.

He can't reply, not immediately.

And when he does, it's not to reassure me the way I need him to reassure me.

It's to say goodbye.

"My sacrifice means that you and the others will be victorious," Warren says, and my heart cracks.

I don't care about the greater good. Not when it means losing him. *"This is the best thing for us all."*

Fucking prick.

"I've got him," Rhett shouts, and Elijah grins and disappears.

I leave the room, going to the bedroom Warren and Elijah share. I manage to get the bed arranged as Warren is dragged in with Elijah.

"I've got him," I murmur, as Elijah flings him onto the bed. "Fuck."

"Fuck indeed," Elijah says. "He's not going to be able to accept any healing from you."

"I know." I can hear my wolf's howls for the two of us.

Another mate I must say goodbye to.

All thanks to King Lobo, the soon-to-be dead man.

CHAPTER 44

"*I*f I had known..." I trail off, shaking my head, my blonde hair flying around me. It's covered in some mud, probably blood as well, and I look an absolute mess. But, compared to my mate, I am pristine.

"What?" Warren whispers, blood dripping down his cheeks. The red colouring is a stark contrast to his super pale skin, and I'm reminded of earlier this week when Elijah *and* River were in this position. "What difference would it have made, princess?"

"I would've done things differently."

"I know," he whispers, before coughs wrack his body. He's shaking, his throat raspy as he nods. "I know you would have, princess."

I nod, blinking back my tears. I refuse to cry right now. He's

478

sacrificing himself for us and our children, and I won't take that for granted. I can't be weak when he's as strong as he is.

I can't.

Not when we've already lost River. Not when Elijah's barely functioning.

We told our pack we'd all make it out of this. Why the fuck hasn't that happened?

I was so confident, and, instead, I'm going to go back to them as a failure, with two less mates.

They're losing their Delta *and* their former Beta and current Gamma. They're losing two important men... and it's all because of their ties to me.

Their previous ties, I suppose.

"I love you," I whisper, dropping a kiss to his lips. He smiles against them, unable to do much more through his exhaustion. "I won't leave you. Not until the end."

"I appreciate that," he says, resting his head on my shoulders. "Want me to pass along a message?"

His question might sound innocent, but it fills my heart with warmth. I hold back the tidal wave of tears threatening to unleash and let my love for him shine across our bond.

Once again, the ancestors are interfering, but this time it's to prevent me from seeing River, my fucking soul mate.

I'm unsure if they're being difficult for a nefarious reason or because he's going through their *onboarding process*. I'll probably never know.

But they're blocking me from visiting him, and even with Warren's help, we've never managed to summon River. The theory is that we don't have the ability to call River. I don't have a tie to him beyond that of a pack bond, which isn't enough, and Warren... despite being raised as brothers, they do not share blood.

At least with my mum, I had a tie to her—through blood and connection via our wolves. But with River, he's just another soul, and it has to be *his* choice to come to us—to come to me.

I'm heartbroken that once more, the ancestors are denying me some closure I need. I've been sponsored as the fucking champion for whatever twisted game that King Lobo is playing, and yet, I don't get the rewards I deserve.

I want him. I need him.

And soon enough... I'll have lost two of my men.

"No," I say, quietly. "Your reunion is yours."

"Okay," he replies, closing his eyes. I press a kiss to the top of his head and support his weight the best way I can.

The silence hangs heavy in the air, and I try my best not to let it take me over. He slips away from me, his body slowly losing its warmth. A single tear escapes, but I refuse to draw attention to it. I will not cry. Not now.

I'm holding onto the hope that this isn't the end. That when this is all over, they'll let me visit him.

That every night, I can go and see him and continue our lives... even if one of us has to live beyond this realm.

I refuse to believe I'm never going to see Warren again. He's powerful and strong and has a connection to the ancestral realm that no living creature could.

"I need—" he starts, his voice weak and pleading. I don't need him to fill in the blanks. I know what he needs because I need it, too.

My voice is thick with emotion as I whisper to him. "I love you, Warren Ellis. I love you when you're being sweet. I love you when you're being your namesake—Mr. Grumpy. I love every single thing about you, and I'll never be able to thank you properly for the sacrifice you willingly made today. You saved me, our children, and the rest of my mating circle. I love you, and it's okay now. You can go, and we'll be okay. I promise."

And with that, he fades away from me completely, trusting that I didn't lie. *I hate that he trusted my lie.*

His soul transcends this world, and my heart shatters, the pain filling me so much deeper than it ever has before. I'm heartbroken and lonely and cold, all at the same time, because my wolf is mourning her mate.

He's gone.

And we're never going to be the same again.

I hold in my cries until I'm sure he's no longer here, and then I let myself lose it completely. I allow my grief to rage out as I cry, sob, and silently scream. I'm too scared to move, too scared to break the final connection that Warren and I share.

My heart breaks for him, for me, for our children. I'm broken into tiny little pieces and mourning the future that could have been—that *should* have been.

And only then do I let my grief all rage out. I cry, sob, scream, and do everything possible to restrain my power.

When there's nothing left to give, I gently lay him back down in the bed, press a soft kiss to his forehead and then close the door behind me.

It hurts to shut the door on a piece of my soul... even if he's not there to feel it.

I don't bother going to see my men where they're waiting for me. I don't try to hide where I'm going, either.

This is for me, and I won't argue against a witness or seven.

I need to release this power and do it now so I don't explode.

I yank open the back door, step outside, and then unleash it the safest way I can think of: through a scream.

But my scream isn't just a normal scream; it's supercharged by my grief. It's powered by the power of my wolf, of the power of me, of the power of every single wolf that has *ever* existed.

I make my displeasure known, and I'm making every single person with a tie to me aware.

I'm not fucking around anymore.

Conri was a King of these lands once, but he gave it up for democracy and stepped into the shadows, washing his hands of his obligations once bored.

King Lobo fancies himself the second reckoning, and I have no doubt he'll be an even worse King than Conri ever was.

But that's not a future I'm going to allow to happen.

This isn't the generation for men to take power that isn't theirs to have and do terrible things with it.

Fuck the Council.

Fuck democracy.

It's going to be my way... or there will be no way at all.

CHAPTER 45

"*L*ottie," Noah calls, rushing over to me. I shake my head, breaking down once again, as I scream and scream. "This is *enough*."

"They took him," I sob. "They took him. He's gone. Once again, we couldn't protect our people."

He nods, dropping to the floor to tug me into his arms. He tries to wipe away my eyes, but I move away.

"There's no point," I cry.

There's no point.

There is no point in doing this if we're going to continue losing the people who mean so much to us.

"There's no point," I silently scream, clutching his shirt.

This hurts so much more than when I lost River, and I resent myself for that.

I fucking hate that this is my truth.

Losing Warren feels like my soul has been ripped out of my body, danced over, and shoved back in all wrong and weird.

I thought I could cope. I made my vow, I promised myself.

And yet, that strength disappeared.

"Because you're mourning," Theo says, coming out to join us. Rhett, Wyatt, Elijah, Caden and Dillon are hot on his tails, each of them with red-rimmed eyes.

I think Warren's death has hit them harder, too.

"You're struggling to control your emotions, Lottie," Dillon says, his voice more gruff than usual. "This is just how it works when you lose your soulmate."

"Warren's not lost. He's *dead*," I hiss, shaking my head as the anger builds up inside me once more. "King Lobo's head will be mounted on a fucking spike for me to remember this by. He's taken far too much from me. My mother, my... River, and now my mate. *He is a dead man walking.*"

And then I break down into tears once more.

I'm pregnant with four children, and for all we know, one of them is Warren's. We've still not identified the biological father of our singleton, and they could be his.

He's never going to see his children grow up, not on this Earth, in this reality.

He's got no choice but to settle on watching them from the ancestral realm and never getting to partake in the moments he should have.

This never should've happened.

And it's all because fucking men with dicks don't understand that a woman can be powerful.

I would've been so content just living my life with none of this shit ever having happened.

But other people couldn't just leave me alone to be happy. They've made this my mission. They've made this my destiny.

Noah presses a kiss to the side of my head, and I curl up in his lap.

"I don't know how to do this," I whisper, shaking uncontrollably as power continues to leak out of me.

"First things first, you need to get rid of some of this power," Caden says, sitting on the floor and reaching for me. Noah is reluctant to let me go, but Caden is insistent.

I'm happy he won out when he presses a soft kiss onto my head.

"When this was me, you helped me through it," Caden says gently. "Even if it wasn't the same situation, and even if it took me far too long to accept the help." I look down at my lap, but he cups my cheek, lifting my head so our eyes meet. "You need to let some of this power go. Channel it into us, into your mate bonds. We can absorb it, and we'll be able to share the load between ourselves."

"Okay," I whisper, too exhausted to argue. I open myself up, crying in agony as I feel the empty spot inside me.

My wolf isn't any better off. She's drowning, crying, sobbing.

Why us? Why do we need to be the ones to suffer?

"Clever girl," Caden guides. "Open our bonds—properly." I listen to his soothing voice and let our bonds open properly. My wolf and I travel along each connection, soaking up the feelings of love and support they each offer me.

And then, I channel my power into them. I let the unstable energy leave me and go into them. Caden was right—they're all capable of absorbing it, and I see some of the darkness leave them.

I feel it leave me.

My power is uncontrollable at the best of times, but during this moment of grief, I was losing control of it *and* myself.

I can feel my mate's strengthening, our bonds powering up, as we work to soothe the gap filled by losing Warren.

He's never going to be forgotten.

I won't allow for it.

But we don't have the capabilities to grieve this heavily right now. We'll go through another stage of mourning as soon as we're done fighting for our survival.

I know we will.

But right now... we're adapting.

We're preparing for the fight that is coming.

Fate might be punishing me—*and Warren*—by letting him die because I disobeyed the future that had been written out for me... but they're not going to take anything else from me.

King Lobo will die tomorrow.

And then I'm coming for the Council.

I will not live in fear. Never again.

"I feel... stronger," Rhett murmurs.

"She's boosted our power levels," Caden says, keeping his voice as quiet as Rhett's. "You okay, baby?"

I nod slowly. "I think my power was making me so erratic."

"I think it was that *and* the combination of your grief," Caden soothes. "But you're doing better now?"

I nod and look around the circle. "How are you all feeling?"

"We're going to end it," I say, making my words solid and believable. If there was ever a time to sound overconfident—it's now. "Tomorrow. We'll call every fucking ally we have, and he is going down. We're not living this life anymore."

"Then let's get working on that," Caden says.

"No more deaths," Elijah says, and my heart sings with the silent promise.

"No more deaths," we all echo.

Sure, there might be more bodies... but not a single one of those will be one of my mates.

What stood as ten people connected via a bond more profound than friendship, more profound than love, deeper than recognition... it was a bond embedded and etched into our very souls.

There are now only eight of us. We've lost two of our connections, and our bond is damaged, but we can repair it.

We nourish ourselves, deepen our bonds, and fortify one another.

I've laid the groundwork, and I know my men will rise to the occasion and make sure we leave here tomorrow as a well-connected octet.

"Tomorrow is the day," Noah says.

"Go shower," Rhett says, softly. I look down at myself and realise I'm still coated in Warren's blood. *Fuck.*

"I'll take you," Caden says, gently.

"We'll all get ourselves ready and start making preparations," Noah says. "Meet back downstairs in an hour?"

"Make it 90 minutes," Theo says, giving me a hesitant smile.

I nod, and Caden rises to his feet, holding onto me. I gasp, but he's extremely steady. He adjusts me in his grip and grins. "You thought I was going to drop you."

"Maybe just a little," I say, with a laugh. My face falls as I remember what's inside the house. "What are we going to do with Warren's body?"

"I'm presuming you'll want to take it home with us, right? Do a send-off with him and River together?" Noah asks.

"Yes."

"Can you handle having him remain in the house until tomorrow?" Rhett asks, giving me a grim smile.

Elijah's lips tighten into a straight line, and he deliberately avoids eye contact with me.

"Yes," I whisper. "But will he... will he be okay?"

"He'll be okay for about 48 hours," Dillon says, gently. "After everything tomorrow, we'll get Roman or one of the angel twins to help us transport him home."

"Why don't we do that today?" Caden offers, and my heart lurches, and my wolf howls. I tighten my grip on him and shake my head. "Okay. Tomorrow then."

"Okay."

The mood turns sombre once more, but Caden doesn't hang around. He holds me close as he carries me through our rented house and up the stairs.

He's smart enough not to even walk past Warren's room as he leads me into his own. My room here has a bath, and Caden and Noah's shared room has a shower.

Caden doesn't stop in the bedroom and carries me through to the attached bathroom. Only then does he gently put me down on my feet.

He's methodical and gentle as he strips me off, all of his touches soft and loving before he shreds his own clothes with none of the finesse he did mine.

Once the shower is heated up, he leads me inside and waits until we're under the spray of the warm water before repeating the promises and reassurances I made to him that day when it was his turn to be this low.

"I love you," he says, wrapping his arms around me. "You are the strongest woman I have ever known."

I nod, my eyes fluttering closed as he grabs a loofah. I smell the coconut body wash we picked up yesterday, and he starts coating my skin in it.

I stand under the warmth of the water and accept all the love that Caden offers me. He washes my body, cleansing me of the blood and taint of death clinging to me, and then he does the same with my hair.

Every touch is methodical, deliberate and yet perfectly crafted to be gentle and soft, and it's everything my wolf and I need.

"*W*e're ready for tomorrow," Caden says before yawning loudly.

"Well, as ready as we can be," Theo modifies. "We need sleep."

"We definitely need sleep," Dillon adds, nudging the half-asleep Elijah. "Come on, get up. You can share my bed, Eli."

"That's kind of you," Elijah says.

"It really is," Rhett says.

Wyatt's smirking. "Is that because his brother died? I don't have a brother to die—"

"You're a fucking asshole," Caden says, kicking Wyatt, who laughs. "You get away with that one because it's a joke Warren would've made, but fuck me, go to bed."

"And fuck you?" Wyatt asks, scrunching his face up. "Not to be a dick, bro, but you're just not my type."

"None of you will be *my* type if you don't go to bed," I say, rolling my eyes. There's some laughter and far too many lewd comments, but eventually, we manage to pack up and head up to bed.

"Are you sure you don't want company tonight?" Theo asks.

"Not tonight," I whisper, and he nods slowly. "I just... I don't know how to explain it."

"Then don't," Wyatt says, nudging Theo forward. "We'll see you in the morning, love."

I nod and head into my room. It's nothing special, just a standard bedroom with a bed and a set of drawers. The furniture is old but well looked after, and the decor isn't anything special.

But it represents my own space, and being here alone gives me the time to get my head screwed on right.

Tomorrow is a very big day, and I need sleep for it.

I wind down, ignore the urge to go and check on Warren's body, and snuggle into the duvet instead. My eyes flutter shut, and I'm more than happy when I don't remain in a dreamless sleep.

No, I'm in the place I deserve to be, and I hope my visitor is one of my lost men.

The ancestral realm is a fucking pain in the ass at the best of times...

But tonight, it might just be the very thing that saves me.

CHAPTER 46

I look around and grin when I spot him leaning against a tree with no care in the world. He's not wearing the usual attire of this place—instead, he's wearing a faded t-shirt and a pair of jeans. He's got a pair of socks on, but no shoes and his hair is perfectly messy.

He's fucking gorgeous, and my wolf howls at seeing him, at feeling him, at being able to connect with him.

He died, but now he's here in the flesh.

"You fucking prick," I shout, charging over to him. My dress flaps in the air as I launch myself into his arms. He laughs, swinging me around whilst holding me close.

Tears drip down my face, soaking into his shirt, and I pretend I don't notice the tears soaking my hair as he holds me close.

"I missed you," I say, squeezing him tight. He laughs and kisses the top of my head. "I really fucking missed you."

"I missed you too," he murmurs, breathing in my scent. He hasn't released his grip yet, and I also find myself hesitant to pull away.

I never thought I'd get this again.

I deserve to relish the hug.

"I love you," I whisper, and he finally pulls away.

"I love you too, princess," Warren says gently.

"How are... how are things here?" I ask, with a slight frown. "Have you seen River?"

He shakes his head. "I can't see River this way, nor can you."

I nod, as tears fill my eyes. *One is good enough, Lottie, stop fucking whining.*

"But I do have some good news for you," Warren says, brushing his thumb across my cheek. "You can see me as much as you want."

"Well, that'll be every single night," I say, holding back my sob.

"I saw your display of power after I left." My eyes widen, but he sounds so smug—so *proud*. "You're so fucking powerful, princess, so powerful."

"I love you with my entire soul." I give him a hesitant smile. "I just wish I was powerful enough to bring you back to life. I'm sorry."

"So do that," he says, with a nod.

Tears still pour down my cheeks, and my jaw drops as I step back to look at him properly. "What?"

"Do that," he says. "Bring me back to life. Take me home with you, and let me return to Earth."

"I... are you telling me I've got the power to bring you back to life?" I ask, with a confused look. "I know I've got the power to take a wolf, but I don't have the power to give one."

"That's an entirely different conversation than we should have," Warren says, with a smirk. "But I don't need you to give me a wolf, princess. I just need you to bring me home."

"How can I do that?" I demand, getting frustrated at the lack of direction. Why does nobody ever tell me *how* to do things?

My wolf and I are powerful; we lean heavily into our instincts and let our power guide us, but this isn't *her* instinct. We're following the guidelines of a mystical power we know nothing about.

Nothing.

But before Warren can reply, there's a flash of light, and my grandfather appears. Alpha smiles at me, but I can do nothing more than stare at him.

"Hello, granddaughter," he says, "You've been making waves over here."

"Is that a good thing?" I ask, hesitantly. *Probably not.*

"It's a thing I'm not meant to tell you about," he mutters, rubbing at his chest.

"Are you okay?" I ask, reaching over to take his hand. I send healing energy through his chest. I'm unsure if it works in this realm, but he gives me an appreciative look, so it must've.

"We're now physically being punished when we break the vows we took," Alpha says, and I glare at the sky. I want to tell them all to go fuck themselves, but I don't want to piss even more people off right now. Not when I need them. Not when we *all* need them.

"So, what can you share with me?" I ask.

"Warren has a tie to this place that he should not have," Alpha says.

"I see," I say, before sighing. "No. No, you know what? I don't see. I don't understand. I truly don't." My breath catches, and I try and wipe away the tears in my eyes. "Look, I've gone through several ordeals lately. I'd already lost one mate to this fight. I had to choose between my mates, remember? Remember that lovely warning you all gave me about choosing my mates over everything else? Well, you never once said that the choice would be sacrificing one mate for another."

"One was not a mate," Alpha says quietly. "And he is right now undergoing his onboarding to the Ancestral Realm. You will see him again one day. Granddaughter, I promise you that."

"The promise of one more day does nothing to me. You all forced me into this life. You set out my future; you plan my destiny without me getting a say."

"You think you are that special?" Loukas asks, shaking his head.

"Do you genuinely think we decided immediately to pick you out of everybody? We had no say in it either. Everyone is a part of Fate's plan—of the destiny she's written out. We had no choice in any of it. The Guardian—" He groans, rubbing his chest. "I know, I know," he mutters.

"The Guardian? Hm, you weren't meant to mention that." I say. He frowns at me.

"It's hard work, being this involved in your life and not being able to fix everything I can, knowing what I know," Alpha says. "Life's hard, Charlotte, and yeah, it's harder for you. But enough with this pity game. You're in a very good position. You wanted to go tomorrow, and you wanted to show him that you are the queen, then do that."

"But don't do it alone," Loukas says. "Don't be foolish. You've got the vampires. You've got wolf allies. You might've made an enemy of the Council, but you still have some of the stronger members on your side. Be smart and plan this out properly."

I nod my head, looking at Warren.

"And take your secret weapon with you. They took Warren out deliberately. They took River out deliberately. And Elijah, well, he was a useless casualty, I suppose."

"Enough," I say, glaring at Alpha. My mate is not fucking useless —even if he doesn't have the extra perks that some of them do.

"I just mean that the vampire wasn't anything special. They just took him out because he was there, and they needed you to make the choice so River could die. River is one of your more powerful mates, even without the fact that he's now one of the last—well, actually, he's one of the only *true* hybrids in existence. You've got Theo, who never leaves your side long enough to be a target, which then leaves you with Warren—the vampire who's not a vampire, the one with wolf tendencies without a wolf. You lose your advantages Charlotte, and to him, you're that much easier to cripple."

I nod my head. "How can Warren come with me?"

"He has a tie to this realm. Just like he has a tie to you, and whilst both exist, he's technically immortal just like you." I grin before letting out a sigh.

Fuck me. Could it really be this easy?

I fall to my knees, struggling to hold myself up. My soul seems to return to me; the fracture when Warren died has bounced back.

I'm just scared to trust it. When has anything in my life ever been this easy? It *never* has.

But... maybe it could be.

"You need to take him home with you," Alpha says, answering the unwritten question on my face. "All you need to do is call on his soul and travel it back with you. Warren will know what to do, and once he's back, he'll be fine."

"And his body?" I ask. "Won't he just die again when he goes there and feels the pain?"

"Did you not heal it of the damages?" Alpha and Loukas ask, speaking over each other. I look at them like they are stupid and shake my head.

"No, obviously not. Why would I heal his *dead* body?"

"Well, you should have, you stupid girl!" Alpha snaps, running his hands through his hair.

"Do not talk to my mate like that," Warren demands, yanking on their souls. I see the pink and purple threads as he tugs them towards him and then shoves them away. They disappear out of existence, and Warren turns back to me. "Go home. Fix me, and then come back for me. Princess, please."

I nod and disappear more gently than I imagine Alpha and Loukas did.

I shoot up in bed, and both Caden and Noah are wrapped around me. I don't know when they came to bed, but I hate it. I wanted to be alone—I needed to be alone.

"Get off me," I scream, pushing them away as I try to scramble out of the bed.

They don't understand. They think I'm hysterical in my panic and grief, but they're wrong. I'm *excited.*

I can bring him back to us—back to me.

"What is wrong with you?" Noah demands.

"Noah!" Caden hisses. "She's gone through something traumatic

494

and is struggling."

"We all have!" Noah counters.

"Warren is alive! Warren is alive; he doesn't need to die." I can't listen to them fight when they're wrong.

"What do you mean he doesn't need to die? He's already fucking dead," Caden says, his jaw clenched.

"You don't understand! I just saw him in the ancestral realm, and I can bring him back," I say. "I can bring him back to life. I can bring him home to us." The tears begin, and I choke on my words.

"Sweetheart," Noah whispers, his tone broken as he takes me in. "That... that's not possible."

"It is. They told me. They told me this. And maybe..."

"Maybe it wasn't a physically ancestral dream," Caden says, tears in his voice as he talks to me. "Maybe this time it was just a dream." I shake my head.

"That's not the case. Just... just let me try. What harm could it cause?"

"I don't know," Noah says, eyeing his brother, but they both seem as out of their depths as I am. "I don't want you to get your hopes up over this. We need to process it when we've got a day like today."

"Speaking of, they told me to bring our allies in: the vampires, the wolves—everyone."

"We know this, remember?" Noah says softly. "Remember, we had this conversation before you went to sleep. We talked about all the different things that we would do. We made this plan together, Lottie. We're ready for tomorrow."

"No," I say, shaking my head, looking at them both. He's trying to say it was a dream because we've already discussed this. I know the truth. I saw Warren. He was alive. He was there. "No."

"Yes."

"I don't, I need. I don't... I need, yes, I need to talk to Theo, please," I say.

"Come on then," Caden says. He's talking to me like I'm hysterical —as if I'm not in my right mind. I'm not stupid, and sure, I've got tears dripping down my face, but that doesn't make me irrational.

Still, I don't protest when they each offer me a hand. I clasp them tight, clinging to them and stealing some of their strength.

We go through from our bedroom and knock on Theo's door. They're sharing a room: Theo, Elijah and Wyatt, and the three jump up.

"Are you okay?" Theo demands, racing to my side. I feel his energy race over me, healing some of my panic and pain.

But it's not enough. It will never be enough until Warren is back here standing in front of me, whole like I know he can be.

"What's wrong?" Theo asks.

"Lottie seems to think she went to the ancestral realm and can bring Warren back to life," Noah says.

Theo shakes his head, giving me a very sad smile. "You're not a necromancer, little wolf. And even if you were, Warren is not one of yours. He is a vampire, not a wolf. Even with the new powers he has... had," he corrects himself. "may have given him some extras, but it didn't make him a wolf."

I look at Dillon, who is standing in his doorway with a pleading expression. Surely, he will be on my side.

"I've never seen anything like that, Lottie, or heard of anything like that," Dillon says, regretfully. "But there's no way you could have seen Warren. It takes a little bit before you can see any of them, remember—even Conri told you that. There's the onboarding process, and you can't disturb it."

"None of this makes sense. None of you believe in me," I say, and they begin to protest, but we both know the truth. "Just, please, trust me."

"It's not about trust, sweetheart," Theo says, cupping my cheek. "You've gone through something so traumatic that, in this instance, it was a dream. It's your natural body response to something of this magnitude."

I sigh.

"Tell us anything that was different," Dillon asked softly, "About the realm this time."

"Everything was..." I trail off. "The trees," I say quietly. "They weren't the same. They were shorter."

"Shorter?" Theo asks, and I nod slowly.

"The lake. It was darker." But was it darker? Or was it only darker when Warren got annoyed on my behalf?

I try and think back, my head aching as I clutch at it. Is this how it works? Was it all just a dream?

"I need to heal Warren; that's the true test," I say, looking at each of them. "They told me that Warren could be our secret weapon when it comes to our upcoming battle."

"Will healing Warren give you the assurance you need to go back to sleep?" Dillon asks. I nod. "Then come with me."

He leads me to Warren's bedroom, the one which he was sharing with Elijah. I push the door open, seeing the way my pale vampire lays in the bed, so still, so dead.

I don't even flinch as I reach over and pour my energy into him. It doesn't do anything really. It fixes his skin, sure, and it sets his ribs, but it doesn't bring him back to life.

He's still dead.

"Was that what you needed to do?" Dillon asks. I just nod, and he gives me a kiss. His silence says it all.

I'm not impressed. They're all assholes.

"I want to sleep in here," I say, not looking any of them in the eyes. "Alone."

It's not fair. I'm not being fair. But I've lost two of my men, and my body tricked me.

I'm allowed to take a moment to be a little unfair.

They all look at me, but eventually, each one leaves with a solemn air surrounding them.

I throw up a barrier that is soundproof and can't be penetrated even by Theo.

And I break down again. That one tiny bit of hope that I had that I could bring Warren back and that he could be here with me—it's gone. It's all just been ruined.

Why the fuck would my body do this to me?

497

CHAPTER 47

My eyes fly open, and I eagerly dart around, looking for the familiar landscape, but disappointment fills me when I realise I'm most definitely not in the ancestral realm.

I'm in Elijah's bed in the house we're renting... and Warren is across the room from me, still as dead as he was when I went to sleep.

I sit up and creep over there, just to check he's not pretending.

There's no breathing, no rise and fall of a chest, not even a flicker of life.

He's still dead.

It was just a fucking dream.

My wolf is still in shock, but my heart shatters once again.

How many times can it break and put itself back together before it becomes irreparable?

There's a hesitant knock on the door, and I beckon them inside. It's Theo, one of the only ones who can handle being around Warren's body.

Elijah is out for obvious reasons, and the twins and Dillon are too close to it. They've lost River and Warren, who they've been friends with for *decades*.

Rhett, Wyatt, and Theo are understandably upset, but it's not as soul-destroying for them.

Although, that's probably not a fair assumption to make.

"It's nearly time," Theo says. "We'll be meeting the others in an hour. How are you feeling?"

I sigh. "I owe everyone an apology."

"You don't."

"I do," I say. "I want to have a bath, and then I'll be down if that's okay? Fifteen minutes, tops."

"Anything you need, little wolf," Theo murmurs, stepping forward to give me a soft kiss. "Anything. I'll prepare breakfast for you coming down, so give me a tug on the bond so that I can make sure it's hot for you."

I nod, and take his hand, letting him lead me out of the room.

Warren is dead, and there's no coming back from that.

No matter how realistic my dream was.

I go into the bedroom, grab my outfit for the day, and carry it to the bathroom. I bend down to put the plug in the bath, and I'm so grateful someone cleared it out last night—even if it meant my bath bomb from River was wasted.

As the bath fills, I move to the mirror so I can sort out my hair. I need it out of my face.

I do my hair in plaits and wrap them around my head, going as far as using granny clips to ensure it's tightly pinned down.

Once the bath is ready, I strip myself off and climb in. The combination of the warmth and the nice-smelling lavender bath oil I use is relaxing. Even knowing what's coming up, even knowing the fight that's going to be had, I'm able to close my eyes and let myself truly space out so that I can prepare myself mentally for the battle.

"Over here!"

My head snaps to the side, but there's nobody there, and I frown.

"Over here," they call again, and I look the other way. My eyes widen, and I shake my head.

My eyes fill with tears, and I step away from him, wrapping my arms around myself.

"No. This is a dream. A dream. Wake me up. Wake up," I repeat, pinching my arm, but nothing is happening.

"Lottie, what happens if you pinch your arm while dreaming? You wake up, right? If you pinch yourself and you're aware of it, the truth is you're awake," Warren says, taking a hesitant step forward. I can see the uncertainty on his face, and my wolf whines at me for hurting him this way. "Why are you upset, princess?"

"Because you are dead," I snap, turning to look away from him. "This ancestral realm is messing with my thoughts. It's trying to confuse me, trying to punish me for not listening."

"This isn't a punishment."

I look at Warren now, turning to him so he can feel the full weight of my anger. "You're dead. And this is not real. I'm not here. Not like I normally am. I'm just dreaming."

"You're not dreaming now, Lottie. You're never dreaming when you're here. It's always real."

"Of course, you'd say that," I hiss. "How can you prove that this is real to me? Go on, I'll give you a chance. Because last night, while we were together, you lied to me. Fake you told me to go back to Earth and heal your body. I did that. I made myself the fool, causing the rest of my mates to doubt me."

"That was real."

"It was not real. Just go away. Go away, go away, go away." I shake my head, and I'm tempted to stamp my feet too. If they want a pity party, I can throw one. "This isn't how it works. You can't just keep pulling me out of my sleep and messing with my brain for fun."

"Am I pulling you here and messing with your mind, princess, or are you dreaming?" Warren asks, taking another step forward.

I give him a dirty look, not liking that he's trying to use logic against me.

"Try me, Princess." He opens his arms wide with a cocky, arrogant look. And I lash power his way. But then he's gone. I flip my head to the other side and see him standing there. And he grins. "We could play this game all day, princess, but the one thing I have that you don't is that in this realm, *I* am the more powerful one."

"How?"

"I have a tie to this place. It may not want me here, and it may not even respect me as a vampire, but this place is *mine*. It's home to me, just like the Earth is, so you *need* to bring me back."

"Why would you want to leave your home?"

"Because you're my true home—being with you is all I could ever want," he says. "I love you so much."

"Fake or not," I whisper, "I love you too."

"Then take my hand and bring me home."

I scrunch my nose up. "I'm not doing this," I say, tears welling. My voice breaks. "I can't do this again. We went through this last night. I tried, I woke up, I healed you, and I waited, pleaded, and tried to return to the realm to bring you home. You lied to me—all of you."

"Yet you were exhausted, and you needed to sleep. I can't—*I won't* —let harm befall you. Especially not at my hand."

"I can't trust you." He raises his hand, and I shake my head.

"Trust me, princess, take my hand." I take a step back, dropping my hands to my side.

He counters that by walking forward. Every step backwards from me becomes a step forward that he takes.

I can't escape him.

Instead, I hide my hands behind my back so he can't steal a touch.

"Please, princess," he begs.

"I can't," I say, broken. I can't get my hopes up, not with what I've got to do today."

"Trust me," he says. "Take my hand."

Do I do it? Should I try one more time?

I sob, lifting my hand and offering it to him. I close my eyes just as he takes my hand. I can feel the change in atmosphere, the cold air in the bathroom freezing my body from where it's been under the water and now no longer warm.

I open my eyes, still clinging to Warren's hands, and I sob when I see him sitting there, just as he was the day before.

I try not to think about his blood-soaked clothes because it makes me ill.

It's horrible.

But this time, he's so *lively.* His skin is full of colour, his cheeks a gorgeous rosy red. The brightness in his eyes makes me smile because I know he's okay.

He's alive.

"Hi," Warren says with a smile. I've got tears in my eyes, tears of joy this time. He brings my hand to his lips and presses a soft kiss to my knuckles.

My wolf howls in excitement, and I'm not far behind her. I launch myself out of the bath, and Warren cares very little that I'm soaking him right now.

I curl into his lap, let the tears fall, and hold onto him as tightly as possible.

I send so much love, reassurance, apologies, and gratitude through our mating bond.

He grins at me. "Do you really think they'd let me die for real?" he asks.

"It was a punishment," I whisper.

"I think you are thoroughly punished," Warren replies. I laugh, but it just doesn't feel right.

"You're really here. I can't believe it."

"I am," he says, "but we need to play this smart." I frown. "I can't come right now and destroy the plan you have with the others. You are all ready, and I will be there the moment you need me."

"What? We need you now!"

"No, you don't. I'll just be a distraction," Warren says. "I will be there, but don't tell any of the others I'm alive, okay? You need that advantage."

"But, Warren—" I say.

"Trust me, princess, please," Warren says, and I nod.

"Lottie!" Theo shouts, and I gasp as I'm placed on my feet faster than I blink. Warren winks at me, and as Theo opens the door, he disappears.

But, of course, Theo doesn't miss that. His head snaps the way Warren disappeared, and he raises an eyebrow.

"What's wrong?" I ask, hoping the panic at him seeing Warren covers the panic I'm meant to feel in this situation.

"Something's just not right," he says, looking up and down the hallway.

"What's not right?" I ask, reaching over to grab my towel. Theo distractedly watches the movement.

I grab my things when he suggests moving to the bedroom to escape the draft. *The draft.*

I hold in my amusement.

But... how can I keep this secret from Theo when he can *read my mind*? They're all going to be so mad at me—they miss him too.

"What's going on in your thoughts?" Theo says, raising an eyebrow.

"Um, nothing?"

My Guardian and I fall to silence, and our wolves push forward to do their part of keeping this ruse. My wolf does not relent, which surprises Theo's wolf. My Guardian is so used to me giving in, in giving up the secrets he so desires. But when it comes to Warren, to a promise my soulmate elicited from me, I won't give it up.

But eventually, we come to an understanding.

Theo finally nods, no questions, no extra prodding. "Are you happy?" I smile and nod once, a warm feeling in my chest. "Then let's go get ourselves ready because we've got a lot that needs doing today."

"We do," I say, not dropping my grin. "It is the final showdown, after all."

We head to my bedroom, and I pull on a tight-fitting, long-sleeve t-shirt and some tight-fitting leggings.

I pull out a pair of trainers which are a bit muddy so can afford to be used for this purpose.

"Are you ready?" Theo asks, raising an eyebrow.

"I'm so fucking ready."

Watch out, Conall, because we're coming for you.

CHAPTER 48

"The moment I bring these barriers down, we are going to be *swarmed*," I say, looking at my men. "We've got *seconds* to get everyone here and launch this attack the right way, or we're going to be the ones who are overwhelmed."

"We don't know what resources he has, and honestly, that's a bit terrifying," Noah says, and I nod. "But we're here for River, for Warren, for every single person we've lost, and we're not giving in. Stay safe, stay together if possible, and let's end this."

"Any sighting of King Lobo, let me know," Theo says.

"Keep her safe," Elijah adds, giving Theo a stern look.

"No need to remind me," Theo says, with a grin. I hate how carefree he seems right now, even if deep down, I can feel how prepared he is. He and his wolf are determined—he will protect me and our children until his last breath.

"Everyone is ready, awaiting our command," Rhett says, looking at me. "Are you ready?"

"I'm ready." I press my hands against the invisible barrier and shove it with as much power as possible, and I don't just bring these barriers down; I shatter them. I don't know who called our reinforcements here, but they're standing behind me in seconds, ready to attack.

I know exactly where I'm going and exactly who I'm targeting. It's the same thing that happened when I met Conri and even when I met Freya since having these powers. I can feel our connection; this man is related to me, and that's not a good thing. But he's powerful, he's old, and I can't wait to bring him down a notch.

I shift into my wolf and let out a howl, and as two armies, we charge. The air is filled with tension, and I can feel his anger. I can hear his howl; so much weaker and more pathetic than mine is.

I turn to my Guardian, and, with a single nod between us, we propel ourselves through the air. Our barrier repels anyone attempting to approach us. Though Theo and I do our best to stay protected, the attackers aren't focused on us. Instead, they're targeting those behind us. I have to trust that the rest of my men will keep themselves safe and that everything will unfold as it should.

I can't think about them dying—not after River. But I smile thinking about Warren; he's going to be here. I tug on his bond, and he grins through it.

"I'm here," Warren reassures me. *"I'll be there the moment you need me."*

"Am I going to need you?"

"Oh, trust me, princess, you'll need everyone. Get to the centre, get to King Lobo, and end this. The sooner you do, the more lives we can save."

I nod, and Theo and I continue to charge forward. We duck under and dive over as we race through the town. It's overwhelming: so many howls, snarling, and fear tinge in the air. The smell of death is rife, and I can feel souls leaving this Earth. I can feel the pain, and honestly, I can only imagine how badly Freya will struggle. Feeling her people go. She hasn't arrived yet, but she's on her way, fucking pesky inter-dimension problems that she's got to deal with.

"He's inside," Theo says, giving me a look, but then we stop and he cocks his head. "We've got a decision to make," Theo says, looking at me. "We can go for King Lobo or down to the dungeons and free Razor fist."

"Razors here?" I hiss, and he nods.

"No." Warren cuts in, "Get to him; I'll get Razor."

"King Lobo," I say, giving Theo a look. He cocks his brow, but I shake my head, and we both head through. We shift back into ourselves as we come to the clearing that King Lobo was in. I could see him sitting on a throne, and honestly, he's exactly like I imagined. A carbon copy of Conri, except where Conri was only slightly crazy, this man is full-blown. You can see when you look into his eyes it's as if he's not even mentally there.

"What happened to you, uncle?" I say, dropping my barrier as I look at him.

"Do not address me, you..." But he falls silent when I let out a loud growl.

"Well, this was easy," I say, looking at him. "Everyone else doing your dirty work whilst you and I hash it out here."

"Oh, trust me, filth," he says, spitting that at me. "*This* is the dirty work, being in your presence. Your seething presence." He shakes his head, letting out a scoff. "Answer me this," he says, "how did you do it? How did you convince my brother to give you his power?"

"Convince him? He *begged* me to take it," I taunt him. "You know that attack you launched on my pack, where you sent your worthless little follower? What was his name?" I murmur, tapping my chin as I look around. "Oh, Cain! That was it, the vampire who *was* our mutual friend. Yeah. Well, the day you sent him, Conri came, and he was like, 'Oh hey, Lottie. You clearly need more power. Have it.'"

"No." King Lobo says, shaking his head—I need to stop addressing him as that—Conall says, shaking his head. I give the man a dirty grin.

"Oh yes. You see, you might have known him for hundreds of years. You might have grown up together. You may be so closely related. And yet he still chose me, a woman. Descended so many times through the generations over you."

"You've tricked him!" He roars.

"Your brother hated you just as much as I do; don't try and convince yourself otherwise." I hiss, and he glares at me.

"Well, it seems that Conri," he snarls his brother's name, "is a fucking liar," Conall says. "He used to love me."

"Maybe he did. Until you became this," I say, looking him up and down. He launches himself to his feet and throws out as much power as possible. I don't even bother batting it away. I just laugh in his face as I stand tall.

"I killed your mate," Conall says. "Me. I got my people to destroy you."

"Do I look destroyed?" I ask, raising an eyebrow. "Or do I look like a woman who can bring her mate back from the dead?" I ask. He falters, just ever so slightly, his eyes widening.

"That's impossible even for you."

"Oh, trust me," I say. "It's not. Who was the one that you just killed? Was it Warren, the vampire?"

"The other-worldly vampire," he whispers.

"I was called?" Warren says, appearing in front of me. He gives me a wink, and my heart races, seeing him alive again. I knew it. I could feel it. I've seen him. But there was still a tiny part of me who doubted that this was actually real.

"You see, I decided I *really* didn't want him to be dead," I say, looking at Conall. "So I went to the ancestral realm and brought him back with me."

"What about your other mate? The dead hybrid?"

"Well, you'll have to live in perpetual wonder, won't you," I say, giving him a smirk. "Is River dead? Is he hiding? Is he going to come and pop up in an hour? Is he just waiting for the perfect moment? Or did you succeed that one time?" I ask. "I guess you'll never know."

"I took your mother," he says.

"And I took your brother," I counter. "Now, this isn't a back-and-forth situation," I say. "You are crazy. You're broken. There's something wrong with you. I'm not here to reconnect and to embrace you into the family. I'm most definitely not here to give you the power that you think you deserve. The relationship between you and I is that I am here to put a stop to your miserable life." His eyes widen, and he lets out a booming laugh.

"You would do that?" He clicks his fingers, and five vampires appear beside him. I don't recognise any of them, and I'm not sure if they recognise me more than from through Conall, but they are quite powerful. "Fetch the prisoners, and fetch my descendant." Conall commands, and the five disappear as quickly as they came.

"I couldn't get to Razor," Warren says.

"That's okay," I reply, still keeping my eyes on Conall. I can feel the area, and there's nobody immediately around us. Obviously, he can call them very quickly, but I can surround us at least in a barrier and give us a minute to protect ourselves. The barriers are only a temporary solution; they will only protect us until there's a direct hit. I could sustain mine for at least a few, but none of the others could.

"Are you really going to make us wait this long?" I ask, looking at Conall. He sneers as the vampires reappear. Razor is gagged and beaten at one of their feet, and my heart lurches seeing the man that we saved. He meets my eyes and gives me one tiny nod, and it's probably all the movement he can make. I can feel my power itching to unleash, my wolf desperate to heal the man who risked his life for us, but I know we can't spare the power just yet. I can feel my power amping up, the full weight of my mate bond behind me, channelled into determination. The energy in this simple location is insane.

"We are gathered here today," Conall says, looking around the clearing, and my eyes widen as more vampires reappear. Amy and Alec are standing before me, and my wolf howls in anger, my mates echoing her fury along our bonds. Theo's betrayal flashes again, but I don't even pay him attention.

I wanted nothing to do with them before and less now. I knew, from the very beginning, that they were worthless.

"Hey," Warren says across the mind link. *"At least this explains the threads you two have tying you together."*

"I told you those threads were nothing but trouble."

He snorts.

"You find my offerings funny?" Conall demands.

"I find your choice of heir quite funny," I reply, waving at Alec. "Hi."

"Hey," he says, sounding arrogant and smug as he waves his hand. Amy is smart enough to stay silent because her face would receive a punch to it so fucking fast.

"Nice to see you again," I reply. "Didn't really know if we were going to make a new acquaintance since, you know, traitor and all."

"Traitor to you?" he says. "Or traitor to our family?"

"We are not family," I say, laughing. "And trust me, when we're done here, your father will be the next one on my list. I'll be taking everything he holds dear to him, too. Hmm, I might spare that mother of yours," I say, tilting my head, "then again, she is quite vicious." He snarls, and I shrug.

Warren and Theo flank me, and I take a step forward. "Lay the groundwork, Lobo; tell us what you wanted us to hear."

"On this eve..."

"It's not Eve," I say, giving him a dirty look.

"You are not funny," he hisses.

"I'm not funny?" I demand. "Your brother kidnapped me from my parents when I was an infant to stop his crazy twin brother—*you*—from murdering me. A baby, Conall. You desired to murder a fucking infant just because of the assumed threat I posed to you for being the first woman born," I say. "From the moment I was born, not only did I need to fight for my place in the world for that, I had to be hidden away to *survive* because you're that deranged. Believe me, you're the funny one here, thinking you have any claim to being the noble one. You're an idiot, and this whole charade? It's embarrassing how easily we've subdued you."

"I've got Razor, the man you're so hellbent on protecting."

"It is your time to show off," I say to Warren. I barely feel the air

ruffle past me as he zooms over to the other side of the clearing. Conall can probably track him as I do, and I smile as Warren secures Razor on our side of the clearing. "You said?"

Warren rips the duct tape off Razor's mouth and helps him stand. Razor is weak from beating and malnourishment, and I hate how long we left him.

Especially since his captors involved his son-by-mating and the horrible cow that is his daughter.

I thought my family relations were terrible.

"You're nothing, Conall," I say. "The Guardian of All, the woman who gave you these powers, recognised your greed and refused to make you an equal to your brother. She didn't give them to you specifically because she knew what kind of person you were. Your brother was the one that was worthy of them, and for the longest time, he did his part. But when people are given too much power, they grow lax and don't continue with what they're meant to do. Conri recognised that and diversified the power, offering it to a Council he didn't monitor.

"But you? You could've been his second. The two of you would've been an amazing duo who could have done so much for our people. You know, I've just dealt with people you promised to help, and instead, you sent your people to slaughter an entire town of humans and caused more issues for them. You are selfish, and you are a liar. Worse than nothing, worthless. Now get on your knees."

"You do not command me," he snarls, turning to his people. "Grab her."

I roll my eyes as the five vampires launch towards us. Warren and Theo immediately launch themselves forward, battling the two. Warren snaps one of their necks as Theo slashes the second's throat. A third sneaks up to me, pressing me into his sweaty body. He smells weird—like blood, cigarettes, and death.

Ew.

My two men end up pinning the remaining two vampires to them, and Conall laughs.

"They mean nothing to me," he says, with a shrug. "Kill her."

"And that's your issue," I say, with a sigh. My power floods the area, dropping everyone except my mates onto their knees.

I can't do much about the vampires without killing or keeping them under my submission. I wish I had the power that Freya does with them, but she's still not arrived here yet.

But the wolves? They're easy to handle.

I walk through the clearing, my movements echoing through the silent air, and come to a stop in front of Alec. I'm not sure if my face shows the disgust that my tone does, but the man doesn't seem to care.

"You were given a guardian for a reason, Alec. You're meant to do great things. Our power is vast, the bond we share with a Guardian special, but you've thrown it all away for nothing. We're meant to be good people—light people—and what do you do? Act the heir for a selfish prick who seeks to harm our people."

"Could you ignore what Conri wanted you to do?" he asks me.

"Yes," I say, with a laugh. "Yes, I could. And so can you—you're just choosing to do otherwise."

I shake my head, dismissing him as I turn to his Guardian. "And you. You're a traitor to your kind. Your people work hard; they train their entire lives in the hope that they're still worthy to breed the next generation of Guardians into this world. What do you do? You deny the vows you took and put greed above all else. Alec could've been your mate *and* your charge—two special bonds. And yet, you just take and poison."

Her wolf is defiant, and the woman spits at my feet.

I don't know why I thought it would be any different.

I turn my head to where Conall sits and advance towards the man. He's on his knees, his throat bared, but there is so much hostility in his eyes. He's not happy about this—not happy about any of it.

This isn't even a worthy fight. That's the worst part about it all. When he was hiding in the shadows, he was able to cause so much destruction. He had me fearing for my life, living in perpetual terror. It was easy for him.

He could have kept that up for so long, destroying me in my life bit by bit.

But then he got greedy and launched his plans way too soon. After all these years, he rushed it, ruining what might've eventually worked.

"I hope this shows you," I say, looking down at him. "How weak you truly are. Do you understand how mortifying this should be for you, that I'm here so easily? I have everything you've ever wanted and been working towards for decades. It's embarrassing that I have this here."

"It's embarrassing that you're part of my lineage," he spits.

"I thought I'd want revenge. I thought killing you would satisfy everything in me if I just made it painful and bloody. But that's not what I need. I've got enough satisfaction here, seeing this. I hate how much you don't care about your people, how much you're willing to let them suffer. It's disgusting. They were only ever a means of power to you."

I feel the familiar power of Freya, and I notice when he does, too. I hold in my smirk.

"It's the generation of women taking the next mantle, *Uncle*," I say. "You didn't expect that, did you?"

"I thought..." he trails off and changes his tune. "The two of you are bitches and deserve to die. You deserve to rot for stealing from us. She's killing her father to take that power. That's what you want to be?"

"I killed your brother to take mine," I say, innocently. "But this is enough. I've come to my end."

"Then kill me," he hisses. "Kill me, niece. Let the world see the monster you've become. Let the world see the monster you claim I am whilst you act so much better."

"I *am* better than you. Because where you want to destroy your people, where you want them to sacrifice their lives to prove themselves to you... A false king who does nothing in return. Your entire goal has been to amass enough people to steal my power—not to protect or offer them a better life. I've never needed to do that. You lost your edge the moment you came out of the shadows. You lost your hand the moment you showed how weak you truly are."

"Then kill me," he roars.

"You don't understand," I say, my wolf writhing inside of me, determined to let me unleash her on the man in front of us.

"This won't be a simple death or the type of punishment where you're given a smack on the hand by the pathetic Council members who look the other way because you've got a dick." I look him up and down and smirk. "Luckily, for your relationship with them, they don't care about the size or the skill of said dick."

He sputters, tugging at his ropes, trying to escape, but he won't ever escape from me. Not when his wolf and mine share ties, not after everything he has done to me.

Freya has many vampires who have renounced the monarchy, and as such, she's not emotionally entangled with them with her empath abilities.

Me? I won't be releasing any of my wolves from the bond we share. It's a checks and balances system that works in situations just like this.

I won't have any of my people being abused. Not now, not tomorrow, and certainly not for the rest of their lives.

"You're pathetic, Conall," I say with a sneer. "Just like Cain, just like everyone who has ever underestimated you. You weren't given my powers in the first place because of your *disgusting* nature."

He can't fight back. He can't argue with me. He can't protest.

"I'm not going to kill you," I say. "I have something so much easier and more impactful to do to you instead."

He starts to shiver as I pull up my hands and see sparks dancing from my fingertips.

"You say I don't deserve this power, well... I don't think you deserve a wolf," I say, with a shrug. "I'm here to fix the mistake that was made with you."

His eyes flash with fear, and his wolf howls in his mind as he tries to fight my dominance. He's not going to be able to flee.

My power explodes out of us, and my wolf and I work as one to guide it. I understand exactly how to sever the bond between him and his wolf. It hurts him, though.

I can feel his agony as he screams, feel the pain from his wolf, and I hate it.

This kind of mangling is something that I should never, *ever, ever* do lightly.

I close my eyes, hoping nobody else sees the tears dripping down my face as I rip the bond from him.

When it's over and done with, I release the wolf spirit into the atmosphere. I'm not sure if he'll go to the Ancestral Realm or stay here, but I think he felt happy in the end.

Conall, on the other hand, starts to fade, just like Conri. He's no longer the young man he was and is instead growing old rapidly. I release my dominance over him, not wanting to be cruel to an old man.

At least not physically.

I raise an eyebrow at him. "I think this is a fate worse than death. Don't you agree?"

"You—" he starts, likely going to spit something hurtful at me, but then he realises how it sounds. He just glares instead.

I don't have a connection to him anymore. This man is purely human, but that doesn't mean I don't scent death in the air.

He doesn't have long left.

As he collapses forward, I don't move. I leave him to fall to the ground. But I do release my hold on Alec, who jumps up and darts over to his great-grandfather, however many times removed.

Alec watches him die, and I'm somewhat in disbelief at how easily this all played out.

Everything up to this point has been hard, but this final moment, this goodbye, it wasn't a big fight.

It wasn't the disaster I thought it would be.

"That's because, in the end, he was nothing more than a man who fancied himself King," Theo says, stepping forward. "He was nothing, Charlotte, and you rose above and beyond what was expected of you to end it all."

"It's time for me to finish it then," Alec roars, jumping to his feet. I can see genuine tears in his eyes just as he launches himself at me.

My head falls back, hitting the grass as power blows out of me. I don't know how much I unleash, but it feels like everything.

My wolf is protecting me and our pups.

And like every other time I use too much power, my vision goes black, and I lose myself to the darkness.

CHAPTER 49

I can feel Theo's energy racing through my body, and my eyes fly open. My guardians face is a picture of true fear, but I'm not worried. Not anymore. My wolf is quiet, content even, and I can feel the eight bonds inside of me rearing with life. No matter what happens now we're all alive and that's all I care about. We lost river but I had already lost him. Now, we're ready to thrive. We're ready to move on to the next stage of our lives. You know, once we handle the council. Theo gently helps me into a sitting position and I see all of my people around me. My dad and Malcolm, stood together, watching and waiting for me to wake. My dad gives me a smile as I meet his eyes across the clearing, and I can see the relief on his face.

Everybody that we hold true and dear is standing around, waiting for me to wake up.

Freya is the first to break the silence, flouncing over to me, in her overly energetic way

"Well, that was a true ending," she says, and I give her a small smile. "You're gonna have to fill me in," I say. "The last I remember was being attacked by Alec."

"Oh well," she says rolling her eyes. "You had a very epic power explosion." She says, "Alec is gone."

"Gone?" I asked, sitting back ever so slightly. She gives one nod of her head.

"You had pretty much destroyed his wolf," She says, "between him and Amy, they're dead."

"Well, fuck..." I whisper, turning and spotting Razor. He looks sad as he talks to Alaric, but he's not heartbroken. Caden's standing by him, but my mates eyes are just on me.

"Yeah," she says "so what do we do now, Luna?" she says with a teasing grin. I'm at a loss as I take the hands up and rise my feet. It genuinely looks like a battleground. I don't know what's going on, but clearly in the time that I've been unconscious, they're all okay. Every person of importance, the people that I hold true and deeply dear to me are alive and healthy. Sophie is even here which is a very big surprise, and I can guarantee that both Katie and Lex are going to be terrified back home. She gives me a grin as she leans into Theo, and the two of them murmur quietly in what sounds like Greek. Once my guardian knew I was okay, he was more than happy to move to his sister's side.

"The battle may be over" I say raising my voice slightly as I addressed the crowd, "but things are not dealt with. What happened to those attacking us?"

"The Vampires are all under my command," Freya says, "and as for the wolves, well, they're under yours." She says. "Can you not feel their ties to you?" I nod my head. "Well yeah and you're keeping them in submission." she says. I looked down at my stomach, is this a power my children have? Are my children doing this for me? Because surely I would feel, my wolf raises one lazy eyebrow cutting me off, and I can almost feel her indigence. Okay. Fair enough. My Wolf is doing this.

"If you would so kindly allow it, Luna," Alaric says taking a step forward, "we can begin to handle that here, as you go to your wolf council and get the aid from them. I will deal with my own people as it's my right, and I'm more than willing to take control over these wolves too if your counsel saw wished it."

"Understandable," I say giving Alaric a smirk.

"We're more than willing to aid in that," Freya says, giving me a wink. I look at her deeply and sense in her exhaustion and she shakes her head.

"Being with you was fun," she says silently, "and this was very great, but we've had our own little battle."

"I know you were off land," I say. "I would have brought you here sooner."

"You would have brought me here?" She says, "I wish I was here sooner." She snarls jumping in my arms and we hug tightly. "I am so sorry about River," she whispers.

"Yeah, me too," I reply, "but I can't let that drown me just yet. I need to get through this last part." She nods her head.

"You killed his son. The only way forward is to kill him too."

"To kill the Elder Patriarch?" I demand leaning back from her. It's a good thing we're talking through our mind link here, because I have no idea what would happen if everybody heard her terrorist words.

"Yes," she says, "Hudson, Hunter, Roman and I will help get you all get over there." She says, "because it's time to go storm your council."

"Fucking hell," I mutter. My mates come over to my side at my insistence and then we disappear from thin air. We reappear back at the council breaching their wards and I hear alarms immediately go off.

"We'll round up the council," Noah says looking at me. "We'll get our allies—"

"Elder Green and Elder Linus," I say and Noah nods his head. "I'm heading towards the big guy."

"I'll come with," Theo says. I turn and look at him and shake my head pressing my hand upon his chest.

"I still don't truly understand what went down, but my wolf and I, we've got this. You need to get everybody else into the hall, because as soon as he's down," I trailed off giving him a shrug. "At the end of the day, Mallon knew everything that was going on. I got my blood shed with the others. But Mallon, he's been mine for a long time."

"You're really going to kill him?" Caden asks, and there's a lot of scepticism from all of my mates.

"I've got no choice." I reply. "Elder Patriarch Mallon has lived his last breath on this earth as far as I'm concerned."

"Then let me take that burden from you," Caden says. "It's very different having to kill somebody in true light." Theo steps forward "Please let me do it, I allowed Alec and Amy into our lives. I let them fool me." I tilt my head before slowly nod in.

"Okay." I look around the rest of my mates but none of them seem upset.

"We'll get everybody here," Dylan reassures me, pressing a quick kiss to my cheek. "Go." I take Theo's hand and we stormed down the corridor and I let my power rage rampant. Anyone and everyone can feel me as I approach Mallon's office and my wolf bursts forward, merging with me ready for this.

"It's about fucking time," I say, shoving Mallon's door open and giving him a big smile. I walk into his office and I see him sitting in his seat, the office adorned with all his awards, medals and trophies. What a crock of fucking shit. There's a photo of the dead Alec and Amy on his desk along with a family photo of him, his mate and their daughter. They're the only personal elements of his that I can see in here, and it's weirdly symbolically that he'll die with their eyes on him. A man who would apparently do anything for his family no matter the cost is now going to lose everything in the office he will no longer hold. The man has created them, his family a shrine in here desperate to hide the true nature of his life and I'm about to take it all from him.

"You," he hisses, "You should not be here right now."

"Oh Mallon," I say, bursting out laughing. "Surely you felt the bond sever between you and your son." His face pales and his wolf howls both of them now knowing exactly what I did. "You know?" I say, raising an eyebrow, and he nods slowly.

"My son is dead."

"Your son is dead. Conall is dead. Amy is dead. They lost Mallon." I grin at the bastard. "All this time you are trying to frame me for their terrorism, trying to put it on me getting me here to give him my power. Was that was that your goal?" Mallon slowly shakes his head.

"I thought you would be good for this world," He says.

"A figurehead. A pretty little political pawn right by your side?" I ask, holding my smile in place.

"We've all got our parts to play in this society, Charlotte. That could have been yours."

"I'm sure it could have," I say, "but unfortunately, I'm never going to step into the mould that anybody else designs for me. Fate tried to screw me over," I say and his eyes widen. "Didn't hear about that, did you? I've been having so many fun visits with the ancestors. Each one of them trying to tell me to play things their way. Well, I said fuck them and I did it my way and guess what? I came out victorious. Following their way lost me one mate. Following my way made me regain another." His eyes widen,

"You brought someone back from the dead?" he asks.

"Is it really bringing them back from the dead if he's already connected to that realm?" I ask. "The ancestors didn't seem to think so."

"You're... you're crazy!" he says.

"Maybe," I reply. "But honestly Mallon, I think we all need to be a little bit crazy to survive in a world like this."

"So what now?" he asks, "Are you going to kill me? Kill my wife leave my daughter an orphan?" I pause, the fury raging through me but honestly do we even have proof that Elder Patriarch Mallon did anything?

"No." Theo says, silently, taking a step forward. *"Deep down we know he did. But no—there's no proof."*

"So, what can I do?" I ask along the bond. *"Because Caden's right. If I was alone, I don't know what I'd do. I can't just kill him. Sure, my wolf is demanding his blood, but morally, Alec and Amy were an accident that I'm sure will haunt me in the days to come. Right now, I can just feel relief. Everyone I love is okay, and the people that hurt me are gone. But right now, killing him in cold blood, even if it is justified, it's not a defensive move. It's not a consequence of something. It's just taking justice into my own hands."*

"You do what you do best," Theo says. *"You handle it* your *way."*

"I sentence you to a trial," I say, giving Mallon a look. "This will not be one of the trials you're used to, Elder Patriarch. This is not going to be one of the ones where you just get a slap on the wrist because you're a man, where you're stripped of your title but still regain all your power and riches and everything that you hold dear. I'm taking your position from you and sentencing you to a trial of the people, with Alaric Viotto or a stand-in from his court as the judge and jury for an impartial vote." I lean back into Theo, who wraps his arms around me. "Unlike the Shadow King trial that you dragged out to punish me, this will not be. It will be handled swiftly, and your punishment will be served."

He bursts out laughing. "That's not how it works in this world, girl."

"Watch me," I say. "I stormed in here. I've knocked you on your ass. I've taken the power back, Elder Patriarch, and trust me, I will be going through and dealing with every single member on this Council. All of them will have a choice. They can swear fealty to me and my wolf as the original of our kind, or they forfeit their position."

His eyes widen, and he shakes his head. "That will never go down that way. They will never allow it."

"I have been underestimated time and time again," I say. "Trust me when I say I've got a pretty good record of coming out victorious."

I shrug when he splitters away, and turn to Theo. "As much as I don't want to hurt him, it would be a lot easier if he was unconscious so we didn't need to worry about him."

"I can handle that," Theo says, charging over to Elder Patriarch Mallon. The man gasps, as Theo launches his fist into his face. I'm pretty impressed that all it took was the one punch to knock him out.

"I hope that's enough to keep him out for a little while," I say, and Theo grins.

"I'm more than happy to do it again even if it's not." Theo says.

I sigh. "Bring him with us. We'll need to find somewhere secure for him."

I don't bother taking him through the hallways; Theo manages to find the dungeons or some kind of holding cell for him and promises he'll join me once Mallon's secured.

I don't feel nervous as I walk through the corridors, and join the rest of my mates in the room where I have no good memories. Sure, I was appointed Luna here, but this is also the room where they accused me of being a terrorist and they kicked all of this into motion. I stormed through into the room, letting my power go wild. Everyone can feel the dominance that I'm emitting, and there are some uneasy looks and some smiles, and there's some downright hostility.

"You have a choice," I say, looking around the room. "You can take a vow like Elder Green and Elder Linus did when swearing fealty to me. If my Wolf and I accept, your position as a councilman is safe. *For now.*"

"And if your wolf doesn't accept?" a brave man calls out.

"Then you forfeit your position."

"And if we don't attempt this vow?" a different person asks, only this one's a coward.

"You're gone," I say, turning to face the crowd properly. All the old white men face me with fear in their eyes. It just disgusts me. "It's time for change, gentlemen, and I don't think many of you fit into the new future."

"So, who gave you this power?" Somebody else shouts from the crowd. I can't even see who that one came from.

"Fate herself," I say with a smile. "Sort of. Now, are you with us or..." Two men shift predictably, but I hold them from moving forward. There's loud murmurs, a lot of panic, and some deep-seated anger. "I told you I'm not playing games," I say. "Your choice is to be made now. You repeat after me, you say exactly what I do or you're gone."

I let my power broach across every single one of them, taking them under my energy. Elder Linus and Elder Green are the only ones saved, and that's just because we've already done this before. As my power draws each of their wolves forward, I start the vow. A lot of them, surprisingly, actually do take it. There's a lot more good men here than I expected, and obviously, that's a good thing. Quite a few do it but fail, and I keep those held down; everyone who completes it is let go and given their free will once more.

In the end, I'm holding 14 people, along with the two who could not complete the vow.

"Sixteen of you," I say, "have failed the test. Not only do you forfeit your position, you will be held to the same standards as an island where you will be held to a public court or opinion." There's outrage, but honestly, I don't have the energy to hear it. I hold my hand to keep them locked in other areas and just move them out of the way. This shuffling along, moving to the door where I look at my mates restaurant and then get them down to with us.

I address everybody else. "You're held under a vow and you cannot betray me."

"Who are you?" somebody shouts.

"Nice of you to ask. My name is Charlotte Montgomery Mason. A year ago today, I didn't know anything about my future, and I had no clue who I really was. I didn't even know that wolf shifters were real. But now, I stand before you as Luna to Rose Moon, and I am the new original wolf."

There's a bit of silence, and then there's a few claps.

I smile. "I understand that you've heard a lot about me, and obviously, a lot of it's not true. I understand some of your hands have been tied politically. Well, now I'm releasing you from that. There should be an upheaval of this court. I don't know how you do it. I honestly don't care. This is no longer my fight. King Lobo is dead. His followers are all restrained and alive. Alaric Viotto is currently handling that. I would like somebody here to lace on that with him."

I look at all Elder Green. "Can you deal with all this?"

"I can deal with it Luna," he says. "But be warned, this is likely a temporary solution."

I narrow my eyes and shake my head. We can handle this another day.

"Luna," a man shouts as I turn to leave. I turn back around, raising an eyebrow. "Congratulations on the pregnancy." I look down at my stomach, and my eyes widen. He taps his ears. "We can hear the heartbeats, now."

A rush of pride fills me even if, deep down, I don't think it's a good thing that this vulnerability has been announced.

I don't think that it's a good thing that they can eat smell the scent change.

But I leave the crowd, and rejoin my mates. It's weird, to not have this big bad hanging over my head, and it feels weird.

Where do I go from here?

CHAPTER 50

Over the last few days we've settled into a bit of a routine, and started to learn how to live without River. Bringing Warren back was nothing short of a miracle, but the thing about miracles, is that they can't be performed twice.

Karen wasn't the best pleased to hear about our adventures, but she surprised me by not blaming me for it. She's struggling with losing a son, but she's also glad he has his parents to watch out for him in the ancestral realm.

I think it helps her knowing that he won't be alone up there, and weirdly, it didn't occur to me until she pointed it out.

Since then, that thought has really helped me too.

Our pregnancy is coming along well, my tiny humans are developing exactly as they should. Being able to hear their heartbeats has been one of the greatest gifts, and on quiet mornings, I love sitting and just hearing the sign that they're alive.

Until they start to kick, this is going to be my lifeline that they're okay. That they're surviving. That everything is going as it should.

Katie is adamant we're having girls—she claims her godparent powers make her have a connection with them, that can't be denied. While that's true I *don't* think it gives my best friend the insight she claims it does.

Most of my men have claimed we're having boys.

Me? I'm trusting their crazy Auntie Freya who has an incubus mate with the gift of foresight. Where Katie doesn't have mystical powers that give her the secrets my children keep... Roman does.

In seven more months we're going to be welcoming a little girl and her three brothers into the world, and they're going to be everything to me—to us.

Next week, we're holding the funerals, and as much as I'm dreading them, I think it's something we all need. It's time to start our grieving process, and we can only do that by saying goodbye properly.

For some reason, for a sendoff this big, it's appropriate to do it on the full moon. I'm not sure if that's a superstition wolves cling to because of the human stories, but apparently at times like this, they use the strong energies to make the day that much more impactful.

I'm not sure I agree.

But next month—November 1st—my mates and I will be taking over Golden Eclipse, merging my father's pack with my own. As rude as Rhett was that day, my dad has decided it's time to hand over the reigns.

Mainly because he wanted to wait until after Christmas, but Noah put his foot down and said six months to give us time to adapt before the babies come, or there will be no taking over until they're five.

My dad is just excited to be able to spend time with his grandpups.

And honestly, I'm just ready to settle into the life I thought would've been mine. I've fought for my destiny now, I've done what was expected of me, and it's my time to rest and enjoy my life.

It's over.

The fight is done—or at least, my portion of it is.

And I can rest on my laurels as I live my life.

"You okay?" Dillon asks, giving me a smile over the top of his book. I grin and nod, and he raises an eyebrow. "You seem very contemplative over there."

I shrug. "Things have been wild for the last few months. I thought once it all died down, I'd bask in my grief, and struggle."

"But you're not?" I can't detect what emotion just passed over Dillon's face just there, but it only increases my anxiety about bringing this up.

"No." I purse my lips, waiting for the surge of guilt to rise, but it doesn't. "Does that make me a bad person? After everything we've been through, everything we've done... I'm just ready to be happy, I think."

"Nobody, least of all River, would begrudge you your happiness," Dillon says, putting his book mark in place. "You deserve it more than anyone else I know, baby. Don't feel bad for not feeling pain."

"We haven't even said our goodbyes yet."

Dillon shakes his head. "Not only have you said your goodbye, you got the needed revenge. You can't continue to hold on... when your soul is ready to move forward."

"When did you get so wise?"

He smirks. "I've always been this way, baby."

I roll my eyes, but a small smile tugs at my lips. I thought when Dillon stepped away as my Gamma, that everything would go to shit. I thought we'd lose our connection, we'd lose the friendship we had outside of our mating.

But no. Dillon adjusted his role to fit what I needed, and it was without being the Gamma. He's been my rock throughout all of this, and I can't imagine going through everything without him.

He leans over and presses a gentle kiss to my forehead. "But seriously, River would want you to be happy. He loved you, and he wouldn't want you to suffer forever."

"I know," I say, nodding against his chest. "I can believe that now."

"Good."

"I still wish he was here."

"And somewhere above us, he's thinking the same exact thing," Dillon murmurs, squeezing my hand. "But I have it on good authority that we're going on a date, so get your ass up, and get changed."

"Where are we going?"

"We're going back to the beginning, baby," Dillon says. "Italian, where you can fight with us all about paying the bill."

"Oh, no," I say, leaning forward to kiss him before getting up properly. "I'm pregnant with quadruplets. There's not a chance I'm paying for another one of my meals for at least the next... eight months."

He snorts, a grin filling his face. "That's a cheque I can promise you we're willing to cash."

I wink, and head up to my bedroom to get changed. I see the large photo frame River got for me on the side table, and the last photo has been filled in.

Not of one with

Dillon's right.

I'm ready to move on without River.

"Rest in peace, babe," I say, quietly.

Surely, I'm imagining the whispered reply of *"Not for much longer, angel."*

I shrug the weird feeling off, grab my bag, and leave the room, ready to spend the evening with my mates. Hopefully I can convince at least one of them to come to bed with me and we can celebrate our freedom over and over and over again.

CHAPTER 51

"You've got a journey ahead of you, Luna Queen," a voice whispers, and I dart around trying to find it. I fucking hate the games that are played here. And what the fuck is this *Luna Queen* bullshit?

"A big journey," another echoes. I look around again not spotting anything amiss.

"You get one aid," the first voice offers. "One reward from us for stopping this foe."

"What reward?" I ask, a little hesitantly. "I didn't really do much to stop him."

"Oh, but you did," the second voice says. There's a whooshing sound, as winds are thrown my way, and I'm knocked onto my back. My hands dart to my stomach to shield it, an unconscious action, even without my children existing inside of me in this realm.

My vision goes pink, before I see what would've happened had I picked other options. There were so many crossroads where if I made just one different decision, we'd not have survived this the way we did. We'd have lost more than River—we'd have lost everything.

My life would be gone, but so would that have most of the wolves. Humans would be alerted to our presence in the world, and we'd all be hunted. Alaric, and the other immortals, wouldn't be able to save their people. It outlined twenty years or so of mayhem and destruction, where nobody wins.

My eyes are wide as the vision fades, and I realise just how much I saved. We talked about how the fate of our pack, of my life, of even wolf kind as a whole was on the line... but it truly was the entirety of the UK.

And that's without them showing me the international effects.

"You deserve a reward," the first voice says again. I nod, my throat burning with the tears I'm trying to hold back.

"We'll return a lost one back to you," the second voice says, and my eyes widen, my jaw dropping. My wolf howls in my mind, as my veins turn to ice. Surely, they're not cruel enough that this would be a joke, right? "One lost life, brought back to the Earth realm. You'll need it."

"We'll all need it," a third voice hisses, far quieter than the other two. I flinch, not having realised there was a third presence with them.

"You may choose anyone," the first voice says. "They'll be granted powers of this realm, and foresight, to help you navigate the new life you'll be living."

"They'll teach you how to utilise the powers you were given," the second voice continues. "Teach you how to use them properly for the new fight that you have on your hands."

A new fight?

"You could bring back a mother," the first voice whispers, and my wolf howls silently. My dad... my mum. She never should've been lost. She could help me, build me up, teach me in the way that she should've all those years ago.

She'll get a second chance.

And so will I.

"You can bring back a wise one who have seen so much and can teach you so much," the second voice offers. "Alpha or Loukas, or Lena."

The knowledge they'd have is indispensable. Even without the extra boon offered by the realm, both sets of grandparents would be amazing to me, and even to Theo.

"Or you can bring back the mate who is no longer a mate," the third voice teases, and my breath catches, thinking about River. My heart beats rapidly, my wolf tense but she's not pushing for a certain person. "You could bring him back from the dead, giving him the second chance at life that was stolen from him."

"A second chance to mate," the first voice adds.

"Would bringing him back bring back our mate bond?" The words are a whisper, a tentative hope.

"No," the second voice says. "But just because a mate bond was lost... doesn't mean a new bond can't be found with someone."

"Do you mean a real bond, or a metaphorical bond?" But then I flinch. "His soul is part of mine and I will *not* relinquish that to anyone else."

"Aren't all bonds real?" the third voice asks and I grind my teeth to not say something that'll get them to change their minds.

"We're not supposed to offer this," the first voice says, with a sigh. "But we can show you something that'll help you choose."

"It's a lot of power to be gifted to one so young," the second voice says, with some kind of understanding tone. It just riles me up.

"It's not as if she's not seen it before," the third voice replies. "Step into the lake, Luna Queen."

"And your destiny shall be revealed to you," voice one commands.

I take the eight steps forward, letting my toes dip into the water, before propelling myself forward even more. But the moment my legs are in the pink lake, my knees give way, and I fall to them. Something shoves me forward, and my entire body gets submerged into the water.

But instead of drowning, I'm absorbed into a vision. It's different to that of the wind vision they've just shown, because this one is the future instead of a reality that's no longer going to pass.

Things fly past too quickly for me to truly take them in, but I see flashes of my children growing up, my mates constantly by my side, I see the wolves we've sworn to protect howling in joy, the changes that we've brung paramount.

Everything turns out as it should.

And when the vision stops, I see the face of the man who helped me through it all. There was never any real doubt.

I see my *custos spiritus* and I smile, reaching out to touch him. River smiles back at me, and I know that it's the right choice.

"River. Bring River back to life."

There's a flash, and somehow, I'm standing in the Ancestral Realm, in the forest, and I see my mum standing in a white dress. Her hair is braided around her scalp with pink and purple flowers tied through. She looks beautiful—ethereal.

"I'm sorry." The words tumble out of my mouth without my permission, as I reach for her.

"Don't apologise. Bringing me back would be something you did for your dad and I," she says, walking towards me. Tears drip down my face, and I'm struggling to breathe. "It wouldn't satisfy your soul, sweetheart." She kisses my forehead, and I smile, hugging her tight. "Your father will understand."

"I'm not really sure how we're meant to explain River coming back."

"I think you'll find the fates have a plan," she says, squeezing my hand. "Congratulations on the pregnancy, my love. I'm excited to see you grow."

I laugh, tears still dripping down my cheeks, but this time it's in happiness. "Four was a shock."

"Yes, four really was a shock," she says, grinning at me. "You're going to live a good life, Lottie. It'll just take a little bit more pushing to get that happy ever after you all deserve."

I nod, cuddling her tight because I can hear the goodbye in her words. "This won't be our last time, will it?"

"No," she reassures me. "But it will be for a little while. These visits are straining on your body, and with the pregnancy, we can't risk bringing you here."

"You can't, or don't want to?" I ask, the fear of this secondary fight starting to weigh on me.

"We can't," she answers with a knowing look. "But you're not going to be alone for it. I am in awe of what you have achieved, *Luna Queen*."

"What is that?"

"The Earth you return to is going to be a little different from what you left," she says. "But trust me, trust your *custos spiritus* and live. There's still time before the danger will arrive."

"How long?"

She glances up at the sky, debating on whether it's something she's actually allowed to share with me. "Two—"

And then she's gone, her words cut off and lost to the void that is this fucking Guardian of All who still wants to keep secrets from me. *Fucking hell.*

But I don't have much time to ponder it because I feel a familiar pop in the atmosphere, and I know I'm not alone.

"Lottie." One word. That's all it takes.

The hair on the back of my neck tingles, and I turn around, spotting the man who I've been missing for the longest time. That final missing piece of my soul settles at just seeing him again.

He looks the exact same as that day—the day I lost him.

I blink away the tears and take a hesitant step forward. He doesn't move from where he's lounging against the tree. And it's such a Warren position that it makes me cry out once again, thinking of the time he was here, when he shouldn't have been.

My Ellis boys have suffered far too much.

River smiles, and then there's the one difference that I see in him now than when he was... on Earth. His eyes. They're no longer dark —they're green, just like his brothers. I mean, sure they're a shade lighter, but still.

I take another hesitant step forward, and he holds his hand out.

"You chose me," he says. I nod, blinking away more tears. "Stop," he says softly, and I freeze. His tone is gentle, though. "Stop trying to hide those tears from me, angel."

"You're alive," I say.

"Well, not yet," River replies, and my hackles raise.

"Take my hand," He commands.

"Why?" I ask.

"Take my hand angel."

I charge forward, taking his hand and he lifts me up into his arms and I give him the tightest hug. My wolf howls in my mind as tears properly dripped from my face. It feels weird to cry in this realm because they don't seem to absorb into his shirt, they kind of just disappear, it's the weirdest feeling.

River presses a kiss to the top of my head before gently lowering me to my feet.

"To take me back with you, we need to complete a vow," River says softly.

"How is this going to work?" I ask "What about everybody who knows you're dead? How do I explain that? It's not like with Warren. He was dead for one night."

"Your mum already told you, the fates have a plan," River says. "The question is, are you willing to trust them once more?"

"Well, the last time they shared a plan, you died. They've shared so much with me, just to then take it all away," I say. "How can I trust them, when I nearly lost everything?"

"Because they had a plan, and it's all working out as it should."

I sigh. "Lay it on me, big guy."

"We're going to return to a bit of a different future," he says. "The earth you left will still be the same, but things will have changed to merge with our new reality. Everyone will have forgotten that I died. The details of the war and the past will be a little bit murky, likely even to us." He says softly, and I frown in confusion. "We'll know we won, and the biggest difference is you are not just the leader of the new council, Charlotte."

"What do you mean? I was never the new leader of the Council," I say.

He laughs. "Oh. They must not have got around to telling you then. Sorry, cats out of the bag." I frown. "You will no longer be the leader of the council. You will be the Luna Queen." My eyes widen and he smiles at me. "You will have kings, plenty of them, but you will be the one and only Luna Queen."

"How do they have the power to do that?" I whisper, my voice shanks as I consider the repercussions of their actions.

Luna Queen?

"They do not," says a voice, and I blink in surprise when instead of just the familiar voice of the guardian, a butterfly flies down and shifts into a gorgeous woman.

She smiles at us both, and despite her peaceful aura, I know how much damage she can cause.

"I made it happen, Charlotte. You're not going to like me very much in the near future," she says, and at least that's a constant. I already don't like her now. "So let's not focus on the future. You're going to have a fight on your hands. There's going to be a battle to be won, and you will be victorious. But to do so—you have to master your powers. We cannot afford for you to lose."

I nod my head slowly, glancing up at River who gives me a firm smile.

"We have awarded you a spirit guardian—a *custos spiritus*. You and he will know the truth, but before you leave here you must consummate this vow."

I think about how that would have worked if I have chose my mom or Alpha like I was offered, but she doesn't seem to want to answer that question for me. *Thank fuck.*

"You will consummate the bond, and... if you both desire, the option for you to both reconnect your mating bond, may be there," she says, and my heart begins to race.

"You mean we can have our bond back?" River asks, his eyes widening.

"You can have your bond back," she says, looking between us both with a somewhat proud smile. "You will have the additional spirit Guardian bond just like you share with Theo, Charlotte, but it will be different in nature."

"You said you're going to change things back on Earth. Will my mates still remember what happened, or is this a lie I must keep from them too?"

"Yes," she says. "You will *all* know the truth. But my time here is limited, and that's an understanding that is far easier to understand when you return to Earth."

I nod slowly.

"Now, repeat after me," she commands. She talks to us in words that are not a language we know, and yet intrinsically both of our wolves are able to not just understand it—but speak it too.

River repeats after her first, and after I take my turn, I feel the changes start to form between us. I can feel a pressure in my chest that expands to encompass my whole body, before settling into the spot River's bond used to be.

The bond is there, waiting, ready for us to reconnect. I feel a connection to him just like I did the day we met when he takes my hand that sparks shoots across our skin, and I burst into tears.

The Guardian of All presses one soft kiss into the top of my head, which is weird, but then she's gone. I turn to River, who lifts me into his arms, soothing me through physical contact.

"Are you ready?" I ask, and I start crying before he can even say yes.

"Ready for what?" he asks, with a smile.

"To accept the love I so freely offer you."

He grins. "The day I died, I told you that I had forgiven myself, and was ready. That hasn't changed. I was in a dark place, but now, I'm ready to love you as purely and unequivocally as you love me."

"I know," I say.

"And being here... well, I'm not sure how much I'll remember when we get back to our reality, so I'd rather share now if that's okay."

"Anything you need, River."

"They showed me a vision, and I saw so much of myself, so much of my life and how everything had to play out the way I did. This was always the plan Lottie. This was always the design Fate had written out for me. Everything was set out ready for me to become your spirit guardian. It was all foretold. I hate that I hurt you to do it, but I know I had no choice in the matter."

I sigh, hating on Fate even more, and he presses a soft kiss to my forehead.

"I love you," he murmurs. "Please, give me the be my mate once more."

"I love you too," I said. I reached up to the dress I'm wearing and slowly unbutton the first top. River shakes his head,

"Let me do it," and I nod, but instead of doing it softly and gently like I did, he rips it open and shrugs it down my shoulders. Weirdly enough, I'm not wearing underwear underneath this, which is not something I've ever considered whilst being in this realm. He lets me reach up and do the same to his shirt, but I undo the buttons one by one, pressing soft kisses where I undo them. I gently tug his trousers down and just like me, there's no underwear on him. "I definitely had underwear on," River says, rolling his eyes. I burst out laughing and he smiles at me.

"Here?" I ask looking around.

"I'm sure your mother's not watching."

"We're in the ancestral realm," I say giving him a dirty look. "I want nobody to be watching." He burst out laughing.

"I'm sure we've got some voyeurs," he says with a shrug. "So let's put on one hell of a show." I laugh, and he spreads me out onto the ground as a bunch of flowers appear around us. "Never fucked in a field of flowers before," River says. "Glad I get to do that with you." "Let's not talk about past lovers right now," I say giving him a dirty look, and he laughs.

"I've missed your possessiveness," and kisses just above my breast.

"I've missed your laughter, your smiles. The way you love wholeheartedly. The way you fight for what you believe in." He lays kisses down by body, holding me tight. His hands are so much bigger than mine. So thick, so warm, so full of life.

"I can't wait," I say.

"Oh you're going to," River replies. "We didn't have the chance to have the best mating the first time around," he says. "Considering everything that came straight after it. So this second chance is everything to me."

"And to me, too," I reassure him.

My mate grins. "Let me make love to you the way you deserve, angel. Let me show you how I ravish my queen."

I nod and spread my legs, as he circles my clit with his tongue. I pant and whimper, griping the fields of grass as I thrust up to meet his tongue. His fingers glide inside of me—one first, as he stretches me out. But then one becomes two as he thrusts in and out, stretching me more and more in preparation. I reach with my other hand for his cock, and he adjusts so that I can reach it without him stopping what he's doing. I smile feeling the piercing still in place.

"You excited?" he whispers against me.

"I was weirdly scared that this would disappear," I say and he bursts out laughing. The vibrations make everything feel amazing, even if he's not in the best spot.

"I want him inside me, please," I say motioning to his cock.

River nods and now he's the one laying down in the field of flowers as I gracefully lower myself down on top of him. As he fucks me into oblivion, I feel our bonds connect in place, pleasure soaring through us both. I cry, as he orgasms into me, and I cum around him knowing that this is everything we needed.

"We are one now," I say. "I thought I lost you for good, button you can't go anywhere." I cup his cheek, brushing my lips against his gently.

He's still inside of me, a lot softer than he was but still not fully. We are sharing each others embrace, too scared to actually go to sleep and wake up just in case this was a dream… or maybe that's just me.

"I love you so fucking much," I say, pressing a kiss to his lips, this time adding some pressure to it.

"I love you more than life," he says. "Now close your eyes It'll be okay."

"I don't want to." I can't close my eyes, not knowing if it's going to be real when I open them again.

"Trust me angel, close your eyes."

So I do. I don't do anything, I just keep them closed. Even when I feel the grass disappear and I smell my own bed. I still don't open them, too scared to know if the arms around me are truly still there, or if it's just part of the dream I've had.

"Open your eyes my queen," River whispers and when I open them, I see him sitting there in front of me.

"Holy shit," I gasp. "What the fuck!" I scoot away, looking up at him. "What, what?" He says, sounding just as panicked as me. The bedroom door flies open, and I see Warren storming in, his eyes wide, before a grin appears on his face.

"Fuck me!" he exclaims.

"What? Did you know about this?" I ask looking at Warren.

"Did his hair colour change?" he asks, instead of answering me.

"What hair colour change?" River demands, storming over to my mirror. I burst out laughing as tears dripped down my face.

The pure happiness radiates through me, through Warren, through River through my wolf. I tug on every single one of my bonds, not even bothering to be delicate about this.

I can feel my mates waking up, each of them confused and even a little panicked, but as soon as they sense my happiness, they relax a tad. In their confusion, they rush to my bedroom, wanting to see what is making me so happy for themselves.

"Holy shit," River whispers "My hair, it's white."

"It is," I say, a little amused.

"No, but it's like *white* white," he repeats.

"We can see that," I say, my voice husky with tears.

I'm so fucking happy. I could never have imagined this when I lost him and got Warren back, I knew that was it. There was no coming back for River. Yet somehow fate rewarded me. I don't think I deserve this. In fact, I know I don't but I got it anyway. I watch as River has his reunion with each of my guys, every single one of them feeling the same way I am.

Well, maybe not. They don't have the new mate and bonds to show it. They don't have the new mating bond in their chest.

"You're just like me," Theo says, giving River a sceptical look. "I wonder if your wolf will be identical to hers, even if you are a hybrid."

"No," River replies, shaking his head and we all pause at his serious tone. "Sorry Theo, but I'm better." Theo reaches out, his wolf prodding at River's hybrid and there's a brief moment of silence as Theo investigates. It's kind of cute, not that I'd say that out loud.

"So fucking freaky," Theo whispers, in awe.

"What the fuck happened?" Elijah asks.

"I have no idea," I say. "I don't know what's happening out here, but apparently it's different than when I went to sleep."

"Well, we remember you dying," Caden says. "But how are you back to life, brother?"

"Well, *that* I can explain," I say. "We know River died, but I got a present for saving the world, apparently."

"I mean, it wasn't really the world that you saved," Warren says. "You did good, don't get me wrong, and also it was a group effort." Wyatt rolls his eyes, nudging Warren.

"Shut up, and let her believe that she saved the world."

"I did," I protest. "They showed me. If it wasn't for us, me, humans would have found out about the supernatural."

"Uh-huh, Im sure they would," Elijah says winking at me to show he's joking.

"Anyways, they granted me a reward because apparently there's another fight we have coming. So have fun with that one. I'm becoming a stay at home mum, and leaving everything else to you lot."

"How long?" Caden asks with a sigh.

"And what kind of fight do we have coming?" Noah asks, "I think we've done enough for our lifetime."

"I have no idea, but my mum said it would be coming in two..." I trail off, unable to fill in the blank.

"Two what?" Rhett demands. "Two weeks, two days, two months, two years, two *decades*?"

"I get the feeling that it's sooner rather than later," I say, "But I think we can erase the idea of it being the very near future."

"Two years more than likely," River says. "I've learned a lot in my time over there, and a lot of it has faded. But I know enough that I can start preparing you and teaching you as is intended."

"So what kind of guardian are you?" Theo asks.

"I am a *custos spiritus*."

"A spirit guardian," Theo whispers, sounding excited.

"Oh shit," Dylan says. "Those are like a *myth*, myth. Remember the book that you read with Freya?" He says, and we all nod. "I'm positive it was outlined in that."

"It was," Theo says. "Spirit guardians are typically guardians who are dead," he says, eyeing up River. "You've been given a great opportunity. Congrats mate, I suppose."

"There's no supposing," River says. "I'm alive. I get to see our children grow up and my mate bond has been restored. That's the biggest gift I could ever be given."

"Well fuck, this really does lead to the celebration." Rhett says.

"I think we need to find Katie or Charles or somebody who will not have been aware of what's been going on, and see what they know, so we can piece together this new reality," Theo says.

"Can it wait until morning?" Noah asks, eyeing the clock and I see that it's 3:37am.

"I'm probably not getting back to sleep," I say bouncing on the heels of my feet in bed. "But, I suppose so. It would be rude to wake them up."

"Well, if you're not going to sleep," River says with a smirk. "Maybe we can reenact that night."

"Which night?" I ask, knowing exactly which night he means.

And if I didn't, my body certainly does based on the way my pussy quivers.

"I call dibs on the double penetration!" Rhett says, raising his hand, and I burst out laughing.

"I want to fuck you with Rhett!"

"Wait.. what?" everyone asks, looking at Warren.

"What?" Warren says with a shrug. "Feeling his very fun dick piercing? Yes, please."

I burst out laughing, knowing that no matter what, we're all sorted. We've got a fight coming ahead. But it's not today, and it's not tomorrow. So I'm gonna just take this time to learn about my new powers, to grow to figure out what's been changed with my new world, and adapt to life with quadruplets, before handling any more end of the world drama.

Because it seems not only am I adding the title of mother to my repertoire, I'm now adding the title of Luna Queen.

EPILOGUE

SIX AND A HALF MONTHS LATER...

"*A*nd here's your baby girl," Katie murmurs, handing me a small bundle that smells of nothing but me. My wolf lets out a howl, surprising me, as the room finally clears of people. Well, my mates and children don't count, but the staff are gone. Even Katie leaves, after squeezing my thigh, and giving me a smile.

My best friend is bursting with happiness that not only does she have god children but that she delivered them. It's very sweet, but she's not my focus right now. There will be plenty of time for my friends and family to snuggle with my tiny bundles, but for now, this is a time just for my mates and I to connect with our children.

I cuddle our daughter in close, pressing a gentle kiss to her forehead, before looking around the room. My heart is so full of love, that it could literally burst.

Theo is standing to the left of the bed and is holding our oldest son, and quadruplet, Xander, as Elijah fawns over him. They're both wearing big smiles, and it makes me happy to see them together. Rhett and River are sharing custody of Ajax, who's fast asleep. Despite only being an hour old, I can tell he's going to be our calm baby. After he's had his boob, all he's done is sleep.

And our final boy, Calax, is being cooed over by the twins from where they're hovering at the bottom of the bed. Caden and Noah are obsessed with him, and Cal seems equally as entranced, despite me knowing he can't truly see properly. He's the only one who is awake, and I get the feeling that my youngest triplet is going to be a tiny terror.

"She's gorgeous," Wyatt says, pressing a kiss to my shoulder as he looks at our daughter. I rest my head on his chest, a strong feeling of contentment filling me. "I'm so fuc—shit." He sighs, shaking his head, as I laugh out a breath through my nose.

Wyatt moves, and grabs me the cup of water from the side table. I take a few sips, as Dillon lectures Wyatt.

"You're not meant to correct your swear with another swear." Dillon's amused tone causes me to smile. I lean back against my pillow, holding Aria in closer. I'm exhausted, sore and desperate for a nap but I can't take my eyes off my babies. My eyes flit from child to child, despite knowing—and feeling—that they're safe and cared for with their fathers.

"She's perfect," I whisper, my eyes looking back down at my daughter as tears well up in my eyes. Does every mother feel this instant overwhelming urge to burn the world alight if they even look at your baby wrong? It seems smart to do it as a pre-emptive measure. "They all are."

"We know," Warren says, squeezing my ankle. He's sitting on the right side of me, near the middle, and his fingers are itching to steal one of the babies. I think we're all feeling possessive. "But you're looking very pale, princess. Why don't you hand Aria over to Wyatt, and we can snuggle so you can recover a little?"

Oh, maybe he's itching to get his hands on me.

"I can't sleep," I gasp, panic filling me at the thought, and he rolls his green eyes. His hand traces my ankle, as soothing waves of power roll over me.

Little cheat.

"Hey," Caden says, and we all turn to him at the surprise in his tone. Me in pure panic, and the others just interested. "Calax has a birth mark."

"He does?" I ask, and Caden nods as he comes over to my side to show me. Noah pouts at not only not getting to see the birth mark, but at also losing sight of our baby. "Whoa." My eyes spot the golden trident on his neck, and I gently reach out to touch it. "That wasn't there when I held him."

"No," Theo says, quietly. His dismayed tone annoys me a little, but I don't say anything knowing his attitude is worry for my son than anything malicious. His eyes are filled with an intensity that I can't link to an emotion. "It wouldn't have been."

"What the hell does it mean?" Rhett asks, his eyes narrowing at the adorable baby foot in his hand. "Ajax has one too. Although his is on his ankle, not on his neck."

"They've been marked," Theo says, handing Xander over to Elijah who completely lights up when his son settles in his arms. "I told you it was a possibility that they'd be Guardians, Charlotte."

If I weren't sore, bleeding heavily, and super exhausted, I'd attempt to wipe that annoying look off his face.

Alas, I can't.

"A possibility?" Rhett snarls, glaring at Theo as he passes Ajax to River. The hybrid beams, and kisses our son's forehead. I wipe away the tear that leaked out without my permission, watching the two of them in a future I never thought would've been possible. "Who the fuck marked our children?"

"Xander doesn't have one," Elijah says, frowning at our beautiful little boy.

"He will," Theo says, fingering his son's curls. Elijah doesn't seem to believe him, but everyone else does. "They're not just Guardians, though. There's more."

"Wait, look," I whisper, and nine eyes look to where I'm pointing at our daughter's bare chest. She's swaddled in her blanket to protect against the cold, but with her being smaller than the boys, and her temperature being a little lower, I've been doing some skin to skin with her. "Aria has a mark too."

"Holy fucking shit," Theo gasps, inching forward with a hesitant look on his face. "This... This is so... What on Earth?"

"Did you really expect anything less from the chosen one's children?" Dillon says, teasingly. "The ones prophesied to do great things?"

"I don't understand," I whisper. I can sense the panic radiating from Dillon, Theo *and* Warren and it has me extremely unsettled. "Tell me what's going on with my children, right now."

My power rolls out, forcing them all to bear their necks in submission—wisely skipping my children. The only one capable of staying strong is Theo, as always, which is annoying since he's the one I was directing my words to.

"There's a lore about a female with that mark," Theo whispers, and I think that's intrigue I can feel across our bond. "It's... concerning that she's been born from a Guardian pregnancy, but we know that Fate will have a plan for her."

"That's not helping," I shriek. I know half of their fucking plan for me and it was *horrible*. I won't have her playing twisted games with my baby.

Not when I've still got a full fucking journey ahead of me just to satisfy their fucking entertainment for the next decade.

"Aria has a journey ahead of her that you're not going to be very fond of," Dillon says, softly. He moves some sweat-drenched hair from my shoulder, and trails his finger down my cheek in what is meant to be a soothing gesture. "One none of us are going to be very fond of."

"I thought the concern was over the triplets," Rhett says, frowning as he gives me a look of commiseration. "Now our princess is under worry too?"

"The triplets marks mean that they've been marked as being part of the elite," Theo says, and my eyes glaze over. "Elite guardians who are going to be protecting one person."

"Three guardians for one person?" I murmur.

"Yes," Theo replies, with a nod. "Some little boy or girl has just been born with a matching mark, and I have a feeling we'll be seeing them soon."

"Of course you do," Warren mutters. "We can place bets another time. Tell her the rest."

"Aria is a different case," Theo says, quietly. "Can I take her?"

"Try it, and you'll lose your hands," I say, firmly. He gives a dry chuckle, but settles for coming as close to the bed as possible so that he can be close to us both. "Aria's been marked not by fate like our boys, but by something even more dangerous."

"Someone's touched our daughter?" Caden hisses, and that settles the tension some. Not by a lot, but marginally.

"By a God," Theo replies, quietly. "I don't know who. I don't recognise the symbol. But.. our sons aren't the only ones with a journey ahead of them."

Tingles appear across my skin, the fucking words of that fucking wolf, the Guardian of All.

She's marked my daughter.

I fucking know it.

"Our daughter is going to be dangerous," Dillon murmurs.

I don't understand this. My sleeping daughter, with her fluffy black curly hair and peaceful face is going to be... dangerous? She's perfect. Sweet. Tiny. Precious.

She's mine.

And I'll tear every fucking God, limb from limb, if they try to take my daughter from me.

A soft coo sounds from one of the triplets, and a smirk appears on my face. They might not be *her* Elite Guardians, but I know that Aria's got more than one protector in her life.

Three older brothers.

Nine protective fathers.

A giant pack, and more than one slightly insane family member.

My children are never going to experience the hurt I did.

Because if anyone dares to try... I'll show them *exactly* why I'm the Luna Queen.

. . .

*T*he End

*I*f you're desperate for more Lottie, that's okay, I am too. We missed seeing Lottie's pregnancy in this book, and with her men, there are bound to be a barrel of laughs. If you want to read the novella book, *Legacy*, you can pre-order your copy here!

*T*he Luna Queen Series will be a 6 book series that launches on the 7th August 2025, and will focus on the next stage of Lottie's life. We've seen her grow into a Luna... now it's time to see her take her place as *The Luna Queen.*

ABOUT THE AUTHOR

Letty Frame is a romance author who writes in the reverse harem genre. #whychoose, right? Letty lives in ever-rainy England with her fiancé and newborn daughter. Between baby playdates and boring household tasks, Letty gives the voices in her head the freedom to tell their stories. Whether that's in the form of a wolf-shifter on a quest to defeat her stalker or a witch trying to find her place in the world, Letty loves every story they bring her!

SOCIAL MEDIA LINKS

If you want to join my ARC team, you can sign-up here!

**ARC Team
(Type https://geni.us/LettyARCApplication into a URL and you can fill out the form there)**

Subscribe to her newsletter to receive monthly updates about new releases, and for exclusive teasers and POV scenes from the guys.

Newsletter: www.lettyframe.com/subscribe

Join her reader's group on Discord to hear about release information first!

Discord Group: https://discord.gg/gPthmJFZae

Feel free to follow her on any of the following platforms too (click on the icon for the relevant platforms):

ALSO BY LETTY FRAME

The Luna Series

Luna

Mated

Allies

Healer

Stalker

Destiny

Bonus Novella: Legacy

The Primordial Queen

Secret Witch

Oracle Witch

The First Shift

Baby's First Howl

Second Chances

Death is Easy

Survival is Hard

Happiness is Earned

Second Chances: The Complete Trilogy (including bonus novella: Family is Found)

Not All Men

Don't Touch

Eff Destiny

Rejected by the Phoenix

Printed in Great Britain
by Amazon